MARTHA GRIMES OMNIBUS

I Am the Only Running Footman

The Deer Leap

Help the Poor Struggler

MICHAEL O'MARA BOOKS LIMITED

Martha Grimes Omnibus
First published in Great Britain in 1993 by
Michael O'Mara Books Ltd,
9 Lion Yard, Tremadoc Road, London SW4 7NQ

A CIP catalogue record for this book is available from the British Library

ISBN 1-85479-906-1

Printed and bound in Finland

I Am the Only Running Footman

To Harry Wallace
and the cat, Stripey,
the only running footmen

*My special thanks to John Hayward of
The Old Penny Palace, Brighton.*

The author is grateful to the following for permission to
reprint excerpts from previously copyrighted material:

From "Stardust", Music by Hoagy Carmichael,
Lyrics by Mitchell Parrish, © 1929 Mills Music, Inc. and
Hoagy Publishing Company. All rights reserved.

From "Isn't It Romantic?" by Richard Rodgers and Lorenz Hart.
Copyright © 1932 by Famous Music Corporation.
Copyright © renewed 1959 by Famous Music Corporation.

Sometimes I wonder why I spend
The lonely night, dreaming of a song
The melody haunts my reverie
And I am once again with you.

HOAGY CARMICHAEL, MITCHELL PARRISH
Stardust

The rain set early in to-night,
  The sullen wind was soon awake,
It tore the elm-tops down for spite,
  and did its worst to vex the lake:
I listened with heart fit to break;
  When glided in Porphyria . . .

      . . . and all her hair
  In one long yellow string I wound
Three times her little throat around,
  And strangled her.

ROBERT BROWNING
Porphyria's Lover

PART I

Lonely Night

I

THE headlamps of the car picked her out through the fog and the rain; she was standing on the shoulder about a hundred yards from the cafe, her backpack on the ground beside her.

At one point, when the lorry that had been her last ride left the A30, he was afraid he might have lost her. Another one had come rattling onto a roundabout, cutting off his view. But he was fairly sure the Sainsbury lorry was heading for the motorway, on its way to Bristol or Birmingham. So he had taken the A303 exit and picked them up again.

He thought his chance had come when the driver turned into the car park of a Little Chef. But the driver and the girl both went in, so he slotted his blue Ford saloon into the short line of fog-shrouded cars and went in the cafe. Sliding into a booth in the rear, he had been able to watch her. She and the driver exchanged a few words, and then a few words with a waitress, and after that conversation stopped between them. No friendship had been struck up during all of the miles he had followed them.

She was young, twenty-five or -six, but she had a hard

6

face made harder by the sour light of the cafe, an artificial light that seemed to glance off the red tabletops and white paper napkins and starched blouses of the uniforms. The girl did not look at her companion. Her chin rested on her fisted hand and with the other she absently curled a long strand of blond hair. The waitress set down plates of beans and eggs and chips and then came back to him. He ordered tea.

They said nothing throughout their meal, finally took their separate bills and paid the expressionless cashier.

Their leaving together told him the driver was taking her farther, so he paid his bill and went out to his car, starting the engine as the lorry pulled out.

When he saw her through the fog not far from the cafe, he assumed she must have changed her mind about the driver or the destination or both. He leaned over to open the door on the passenger's side and asked her if he could give her a lift. The Ford idled on the shoulder as she slid in, tossing her rucksack on the rear seat and returning his offer with a grunt and a nod.

She was headed for Bristol, she said, as she rooted in the shoulder bag and brought out cigarette papers and a small folded paper. No, grass. The sickish-sweet odor began to fill the car. He rolled down the window.

She asked if he minded, but with no hint of apology for lighting up or intention of putting it out. The question seemed to suffice, as far as she was concerned. When he said he wasn't used to the smell, she only shrugged and turned back to stare at the windscreen, the cigarette tight in a little clip. Then, again without asking, she switched on the car radio. Voices, music swelled, died as she ran the dial back and forth, finally settling on a station where the plummy voice of a disc jockey was bringing up an old Glenn Miller recording.

That surprised him; he would have expected her to listen to rock.

For three days he had been in Exeter, watching her, following her. He had watched the house from several points across the street — news agent's, launderette, a tiny restaurant called Mr. Wong and Son. He had been careful to leave the blue Ford in a public car park; he had been less careful of himself. Once he had gone into the restaurant, a dark, boxlike place with tablecloths stained by soy sauce bottles, and ordered a meal. There wouldn't be any reason to connect him with her. And the waiter — Mr. Wong's son, perhaps — had stood staring out of the window the whole time, looking from the pallor of the unpapered walls to the pallor of the pavement. His face was a mask of indifference; he would hardly remember.

It had been careless also, going into the Little Chef, rather than just waiting in his car. The car itself he had bought, together with its plates, rather than using his own. Now, as the car swam in and out of misty pools of light thrown by headlamps coming from the other direction, he reminded himself again that there was no reason for anyone to connect him with the girl.

They drove on and she neither spoke nor dropped her eyes from the windscreen. He said to her that he'd never smoked grass and she snorted and said he must live at the bottom of the sea, then. Maybe she'd fix him one, he suggested. He'd be glad to pay her for it, just for the experience. She shrugged and said okay, that it made no odds with her just as long as he paid. It was good stuff, the best. No, she didn't bloody mind if he drove off and stopped the car to smoke. Like the Chinese waiter, she was too bored to question anything. Even too bored to be suspicious.

He pulled off the road into a thicket of trees. There would be tire tracks. He knew that casts could be made of tire

8

tracks, which is one reason he'd bought the old Ford. As he smoked the cigarette she'd handed him, he thought, There it is again — extreme care, extreme carelessness — the rational part of his mind being overridden by some other force. The chance that anyone in the cafe would recognize him after a lapse of time was slim; that there'd be a reason to recognize him, even slimmer. Still, he wondered. Had there been a compulsion to link himself to her? To sit in the same room, eat the same food, walk the same streets? He didn't know.

She didn't even ask him why he was getting out of the car, just sat there smoking, listening to the radio. With the car door open, he could hear the scratchy recording of the old song:

> *Isn't it romantic*
> *Merely to be young, on such a night as this?*

He moved a little farther off from the car. The rain had stopped, the sky had cleared. Through the black fretwork of branches he could see a few stars, far apart. Close by was a little stream, iced over, its banks hemmed with snow.

When he heard the car door on her side opening, he wasn't surprised. Too indifferent to be suspicious of his stopping or of his leaving the car, it wasn't odd that she'd leave it too. Not that it would have made any difference whether she got out or not. Her boots squelched along the wet ground as she came up beside him. "Isn't It Romantic?" kept on playing, its question insistent in the night. She asked him if he liked the grass and he said, Yes, except he was feeling whoozy. He handed her some money, which she took without a word and shoved in the top pocket of her anorak. She wore a woollen hat and her throat was wrapped in a plaid scarf, the ends falling down her back. She was pretty in a cheap, hard way; and her manner cold as the little crusted stream.

When he looked up at the sky, he felt light-headed; there was a star, he said, falling there in the west. She said he was

9

bloody high on grass and they argued about the star. It had really fallen, he insisted.

The distant constellations, the dead stars, the bored girl.

Isn't it romantic,
Music in the night . . . ?

When he reached for her scarf, she probably thought he meant to draw her to him and kiss her. He pulled quickly, forcefully. Almost soundlessly, her body slumped and fell, hitting and cracking the thin crust of ice. It was as close to a lover's tryst as they would ever come, he thought, the ends of the scarf fluttering away from his hands.

Wasn't it romantic?

In this desolate pocket of silence, a dozen members of the Devon-Cornwall constabulary stood near the body like mourners. It was nearly dawn but the stars had not faded from the sky. They had been waiting for over ten minutes for Brian Macalvie to say something.

He didn't; he stood, hands in pockets and shoving back his raincoat, looking down at the ground, at the body, at the glazed coat of the stream and then up at the stars.

A twig snapped; a bird called. No one moved. Not even the Scene of Crimes expert — in this case a woman — had ventured yet to disturb Macalvie's concentration. The assumption was that a camera's flash would disturb the aura of that part of the universe here in Devon that was the particular domain of Divisional Commander Macalvie.

They were all cold and impatient, which was safe if no one decided to act on it. Unfortunately, Sergeant Gilly Thwaite, with her wide blue eyes and rotten temper, had never responded to the Macalvie magic. She nearly stomped on the corpse in her impatience to set up her tripod. "We've been standing here for fifteen minutes. Will it disturb your *mise-*

en-scène, your atmosphere, your evidence if I use my brownie?" She held up her camera.

Macalvie just kept chewing his gum. "Sure, go ahead. You've screwed it up now, anyway."

The doctor, heartened by Gilly Thwaite's approach, tried dipping his own question in acid. "Do you mind if *I* go ahead with my examination?"

Someone coughed.

The difference between Sergeant Thwaite and the doctor was that Macalvie gave his sergeant credit for knowing her job. His expression didn't change; he just chewed his gum more deliberately. "I'm holding you up?"

Someone sighed.

The doctor was kneeling beside the girl, unclasping his bag. "I'm not your police pathologist, just a country doctor. And a busy man."

A constable dropped his head in his hand.

"I see," said Macalvie. "And what exactly do you think you're going to look for?" Macalvie turned his head again to look up at the night sky.

The doctor looked up at him. "Look for? I assume you'd like to know how she was murdered, whether she was beaten or raped." His hands moved toward the scarf.

"Uh-huh. Don't touch that yet, okay?" Macalvie asked pleasantly.

The doctor sighed hugely. "Are we going to stay out here —?"

"— the rest of the day if I say so. She was garroted, she wasn't beaten, she wasn't raped. What else you got to tell me?"

"Not even you have X-ray vision, Mr. Macalvie." He laughed briefly. "Not even you can see through a heavy anorak and blue jeans."

Macalvie might have been debating the X-ray vision comment. "At least I can *see.* Look at her jeans."

11

"Rapists have been known to redress their victims, Mr. Macalvie. Some are surprisingly fastidious."

Macalvie stared at the sky. "You'd have to be a fastidious damned paperhanger to yank those jeans off, much less put them back on. They're like flypaper; the legs have zippers. She probably had to lie down and use a crowbar." He turned and nodded to the rest of the team from headquarters.

Quickly, they fell about their business — literally fell, going down on hands and knees, searching every inch of ground for prints, tracks, fibers, anything.

"Name's Sheila Broome," said a uniformed constable, who'd searched the backpack. "Lived in Exeter —"

Macalvie bent down to pick up a tiny clip, a bit of white paper adhering to the end. "Roach clip. So she was standing here, smoking grass. Or they were. Killers don't usually stand around toking with their victims. Maybe it's close to home; a boyfriend, maybe."

The constable almost pitied the boyfriend as he looked at his chief.

"Get an incidents room out here," said Macalvie, walking away from the angry white glare of the camera flash.

2

RICHARD Jury had to reach across Susan Bredon-Hunt, at the same time trying to disengage himself from the long arms that always grew more tangled and vinelike when telephones rang.

She was definitely a phone-clinger. She marched her fingers up and down his chest, drew circles round his ear, dusted his face with her lashes as if she were taking prints, and generally made clever-telephone repartee impossible.

Fortunately, no clever repartee was needed. Chief Superintendent Racer, having been routed out of his bed, was determined to bounce Jury from his. "Four rings, Jury! What the hell were you doing?"

It was just as well the question was rhetorical, since Susan Bredon-Hunt's lips were brushing across his face. He raised his hand, but it was like trying to push cobwebs away. Bits and pieces of her clung everywhere.

"— hate to disturb you," said Racer, whose sarcasm poked at him like Susan Bredon-Hunt's finger. "Could you crawl out of bed and get yourself over to Mayfair?"

Crawl out was what he had to do in order to get past Susan

Bredon-Hunt. Finally, sitting on the edge of the bed, he said, "Where in Mayfair?"

"Charles Street. Berkeley Square. Hays Mews." Racer barked the names out like a BritRail conductor. "Woman's been murdered." The receiver on the other end crashed down.

Jury apologized to Susan and was into his clothes in fifteen seconds.

"Just like *that!*" She snapped her fingers. "You leave just like that!"

He was tired. "That's how people get killed, love. Just like that."

When he bent to kiss her, she turned her face away.

Jury collected his coat and car keys and left.

Police cars had converged, angling toward the curb in Charles Street and up on the pavement outside of the pub. Beneath the lamplit sign of I Am the Only Running Footman, Detective Sergeant Alfred Wiggins was writing in his notebook, asking questions of the short, plump woman who had found the body.

The whirring domed lights of the last two cars to careen up in front of the pub cast blue ribbons on the wet pavement, blue shadows across the faces of Wiggins and the woman. She had been walking her dog in the square late that night, and she and it were extremely upset, she said. The Alsatian sniffed Wiggins's feet and yawned.

Jury assured her that when she was taken to the police station she would be kept no longer than absolutely necessary, that any call she wished to make could be made, that they greatly appreciated her help, that she had done something not everyone would by calling for police. This calmed her and she was answering Wiggins's questions now. Up and down the short street and around the corner, uniformed policemen were asking their own questions of the residents of Hays Mews who had come out from their trendy little houses to stand in the drizzle. Screens had been placed at the end of the mews to keep the curious from satisfying much of their curiosity.

While the medical examiner was dictating findings to a tape recorder, Jury stood and looked at the young woman's body lying face down on the street, light hair fanned out, legs jackknifed. Wiggins had come up beside him.

"Through with that?" Jury asked of the fingerprint man and pointing to the small black purse whose strap was still hitched over her shoulder, tangling with her long scarf. The man nodded to Jury and Jury nodded to Wiggins. The M.E. looked over at Jury with annoyance. She didn't like questions crossing the comments she was tossing like a knife-thrower over her shoulder at her assistant. Jury looked at her sharp gray eyes and smiled brightly. She grunted.

"Ivy Childess," said Wiggins, holding up the identification he had taken from the dead woman's purse and which he held with a handkerchief. "Address is ninety-two Church Street, Bayswater. That's about all, sir, besides checkbook, bank card, some change. With that little bit of money, she might just have been having a drink in the pub, wouldn't you say?" He returned the license to the purse and snapped it shut.

"Might have been," said Jury, as he waited for the M.E. to finish. He knew she hated any interference.

Having brought his handkerchief into play with the purse, Wiggins used it to blow his nose. "It's this damned wet. Know I'm coming down with something. Flat on my back I'll be." His tone was pensive.

"Ivy Childess certainly is." The rain fell, steadily and tenaciously, but the medical examiner seemed not to notice it at all. Crisis-as-usual had worn her pretty face as smooth as stone under water.

"No marks I can see except for the neck. Strangled with her own scarf. Some women never learn."

Jury smiled slightly. Dr. Phyllis Nancy had a way of examining things for sexual bias, even dead bodies. Jury wanted to tell her that such bias in police work had pretty much gone the way of all flesh, male or female. But Dr. Nancy seemed as committed to her defensiveness as she was to her job.

"When can you do the autopsy, Phyllis?"

No one called her Phyllis. That's why Jury did.

"You wait your turn, Superintendent. I've got a schedule, too."

"I know. I'd just appreciate it if maybe you'd move this nearer the top. We know how she was killed and it looks pretty routine —"

Routine was not a word Phyllis Nancy liked. And his comment was, as Jury knew it would be, an opportunity for her to give a little lecture, something she seldom got a chance to do, especially around police superintendents. "The woman's still got skin, hair, fingertips, liver, pancreas, bones, tissue. Even a heart."

"So do you, Phyllis." He smiled at her. Jury had come upon Dr. Nancy once, window-shopping on New Bond Street, standing outside Dickins and Jones, ogling the elaborate display of bridal and bridesmaids' gowns. He had waited until she'd walked on to catch her up and invite her for a drink. Phyllis Nancy would hate to have been caught mooning over the Dickins and Jones window-wedding: bride, groom, lace, flowers. He turned from her to give directions to a police inspector. The street would have to be covered inch by inch. Then he turned back to Dr. Nancy. "Whenever you can, Phyllis. Thanks."

She turned away to hide a smile. The whole thing was a little ritual. If he patronized her, man to woman, he knew she got a kick out of it. Under all of that expertise and armor was a very nice person who liked to have lunches out, go to movies, buy nice clothes. She collected her bag and her assistant, said she'd get round to the autopsy as soon as she could, got in a car, streaked away through the rain.

3

I T was a well-tended terraced house on a residential street
dotted with estate agents' signs and a depressing similarity
of facades that was not at its best in the early morning
light. Next door was one of the houses for sale, unlived in
from the condition of the garden, where a small climbing rose
struggled for position between clumps of weeds and rusted
bicycle wheels. The porches and doorframes of several of the
houses had been painted in strong, riotous colors, but the dull
light returned them to anonymity again, reds and blues
barely distinguishable, looking caked and dried to the color
of old blood.

The Childess house had kept to a bottle-brown for the
small fence and the door, which looked the color originally
chosen, one more in keeping with what the street was originally intended for — a sensible lower-middle-class bastion of
British sobriety.

The woman who opened the door at Jury's knock wore a
flannel bathrobe the color of the trim and a piece of toweling

round her head either to hide the curlers there or to ease the strain when she slept. Her look at him was as taut as the door-chain.

"Mrs. Childess?" He brought his warrant card near the inch of open space. "Could we speak to you, please?"

He had seen that look many times, confusion outstripped by fear. It astonished him sometimes, the way in which otherwise imperceptive and even dull minds could in some circumstances make a leap of certainty to the worst possible conclusion. The woman knew that he had come about the girl, but had immediately buried that knowledge.

Behind her a voice full of sleep said, "Who is it, Irene?"

Into that uncertain silence between the question put by the thin-faced husband and her reply to it, Jury dropped his request to come in. The door closed and the latch scraped back.

As they entered, Wiggins touched his fingers to his hat. That part of Jury's mind that permitted escape into minutiae reminded him to buy a hat; he hated hats. He introduced himself and his sergeant to the couple, and the man, whom she had addressed as Trevor, blinked and started apologizing for the lapsed road tax sticker.

"It's not about that, Mr. Childess. I'm afraid that something's happened to your daughter. She was found in Berkeley Square. She was dead." There was no way to prepare anyone for this, no way to soften the blow; Jury had always felt stretching it out with words like "accident" only added to the agony. If you saw the crash was inevitable, if the lorry was bearing down on you, you shouldn't have to stare at the headlamps too long. "I'm terribly sorry."

Neither the mother nor the father said, *That's impossible,* or *That couldn't have happened,* or otherwise tried to hold the knowledge at bay. Maybe it was the heavy note of finality in his voice; maybe it was the empathy. Mrs. Childess's veined hands flew to her mouth, and she shook her head, tears spattering like rain. Her husband stared; his arm came up automatically to fall across her shoulders.

When finally they had sat down in a small parlor too full of Ivy Childess for much comfort, Jury waited for a few moments while she tried to combat another rush of tears. Wiggins, who always had a fresh supply of handkerchiefs somewhere about him, pushed one into her hands. Jury asked a few routine questions about Ivy in as dry a tone as possible without being curt. Too much sympathy was often worse than none at all. When the father finally asked what had happened and where, Jury put it as briefly and kindly as possible. "There didn't seem to have been much of a struggle and she must have died very quickly."

"But who could possibly have wanted to — do that to our Ivy?" Mrs. Childess said, addressing her husband as if he might have some secret store of knowledge about Ivy. "I don't understand. I just don't understand." She leaned her face against her husband's thin chest.

"That's why we're here, Mrs. Childess; that's what we want to find out. If you could bear with us a bit . . ." He nodded to Wiggins, who sat back and opened his notebook. "Could you tell us anything about her friends? Men, especially."

Trevor Childess looked startled. "Well, yes. There was one named Marr. Ivy said as how she was kind of engaged to him. Marr. Yes, I'm sure that's the name, wasn't it, Irene? David Marr, she said. Bit of a catch that was —" And he smiled briefly before he realized that the catch would never be landed.

"How long had your daughter known him?"

The question seemed to make Childess uncomfortable; he shifted in his chair and studied his hands when he answered. "Well, we didn't really know him, I suppose." That apparently sounded very odd even to his own ears, and he looked at the drawn face of his wife for direction.

Jury didn't think she'd heard her husband. The flow of tears had stopped, but the handkerchief was still wadded against her mouth and her arm was across her stomach, holding herself like something broken.

"Never did get round to coming here," said the father, "though Ivy kept saying she'd bring him to tea one day."

The father glanced quickly around the room and Jury saw what he saw: a parlor, well tended like the yard, neat and orderly, but plain if not actually shabby. The suite of furniture, probably purchased on hire-purchase, armchairs and a sofa covered with an afghan probably crocheted by his wife or a relative in colors that should brighten the place but only increased its anonymity.

To avoid heaping even more distress on the man's platter — inconsequential but still humiliating — Jury offered him a cigarette, lit one himself, and got up to walk about the parlor. He nodded to Wiggins to continue the questioning.

Several of his colleagues at headquarters had asked Jury why, given his position, he did not avail himself of a detective inspector for an assistant. Jury asked them why he should, told them the sergeant had saved his life at least twice. That was the truth, but it wasn't the reason. Jury respected Wiggins, for Wiggins felt a strong bond with those who were often labeled as underdogs. Sergeant Wiggins's presence was soothing; he gave witnesses the impression somehow that he was one of them, had come amongst them with his notebook and pen; his economical, even parsimonious gestures; his long silences and sympathetic stares (often not related to the problem at hand); not to mention his roster of maledictions that nudged awake the sleeping hypochondria in everyone; his ability to scale the Metropolitan Police down to the pleasant bobby on the corner. In an old morality play, Wiggins would have been the shepherd come to bear witness. And he always had a spare handkerchief.

21

Which he was using now, blowing his nose in the cold, dawn-lit parlor, along with Mrs. Childess, whose most recent bout with tears appeared to be, at least temporarily, under control. She held the handkerchief wadded in her lap; Wiggins stuffed his back in his pocket and went on with his routine questions in his nice, monotonous voice.

Given the photographs on the mantel, it seemed that Ivy had been the only child. Several snapshots were set round two studio portraits; one of the portraits was probably taken when she was eighteen or nineteen, a full-length photo in which she was holding a few drooping roses. The end of school term, perhaps, or of childhood. Her expression was rather smug and knowing, as if she'd passed through a bothersome phase of her life. The second might have been taken yesterday. Her hair spread like clear water over the shoulders of a jumper that he recognized as the one she'd been wearing when she was murdered, blue, scoop-necked, full-sleeved. He returned the photo to its place on the mantel and picked up its mate — a small one, unframed, also recent. Jury went back to the others and sat down a short distance away so that Wiggins could continue.

The mother looked completely spent; she rested her head, eyes closed, against the button-tufted back of the chair. The father had been talking about his daughter's job at Boots. "Makeup consultant, she was."

For this, Jury read sales assistant.

"Did you know any of her other friends, aside from what you'd heard of the fiancé?"

Again, Trevor Childess looked a little shamefaced as he shook his head. "Ivy never did go out much when she lived with us. She wasn't one for pubs and the like. She was more a homebody, like her mother."

There was a silence, during which Mrs. Childess roused herself and left the room. Then Jury rose and Wiggins pocketed his notebook. He told Childess he would have to be called on to identify his daughter's body. The man's face was blank and ashen.

"I'm sorry, Mr. Childess. It has to be you or your wife and I wanted to wait until she was safely tucked in before even bringing it up." Jury knew that the appeal to a greater strength than his wife could call on would help to give the man some purpose. "It can wait, at least until later today. We'll send a car round."

Childess murmured something that might have been unfelt thanks and then said to Wiggins, "You won't be coming yourself, then?"

"Sorry, sir. We'll be getting on immediately to whoever might have been with Ivy." From his coat pocket he pulled the packet of lozenges. "You don't want to let that cough go. Take these."

Whatever it was — amulet or anodyne — Trevor Childess took the packet gratefully.

"Terrible thing," said Wiggins, slamming the door shut on the driver's side. "And Ivy being the only one." Wiggins always got on a first-name basis with the victims quickly. It was part of his charm.

"Yes. Only, I wonder. If there were five or six or ten, would it be much comfort? If you lose one, don't you suppose it's like losing them all?"

The engine turned over, coughed asthmatically, and went dead. Wiggins tried again, mumbling. Death and weather had a way of knitting themselves together in his mind. "You'd think they'd give us something better than this ten-year-old Cortina," he said darkly as he tried to nurse the engine and hit the heater into action.

"What about Marr?"

"David L. Ex-directory and I thought for a moment I was going to have to call headquarters to get the address. Bloody operator gave it to me finally." The engine turned over and he pulled away from the curb. "It's Mayfair, all right. I didn't call him; didn't think you'd want to alert him."

"Good. Where in Mayfair?"

"Shepherd Market." He took his hands from the steering wheel and blew on them. "Not far from the Running Footman, is it?"

"No. Walking, how long?"

Wiggins thought for a moment. "Ten minutes, maybe. But I don't suppose he'd be walking in all this muck."

Despite the errand and the cold, Jury smiled. The new snow furred the rusted car parts and rimmed the garishly painted porches and woodwork, blanketed the shabbiness of the street ahead. It lay blue and untrammeled in the morning light. Undisturbed, it seemed to bond the houses and fences together.

4

AVID Marr fit his surroundings. He looked elegant and neglected. The knap of his dressing gown was as badly rubbed as the Axminster carpet, and the cord as frayed as the tasseled one that held back the Chinese silk curtain. The one on the robe hung at approximately the same angle as Marr's head. At six A.M. he was probably in the grip of a whale of a hangover.

Hangover or not, the man was handsome. Jury thought there was something vaguely familiar about the high cheekbones and dark hair, or perhaps it was the sort of face that might have belonged to some dissolute peer, one often served up by the seamier tabloids along with sex, drugs and girls.

Right now David Marr was sprawled in a worn-leather wing chair. His first reaction to the murder of Ivy Childess had been bafflement more than grief. His second, third, and fourth, Jury had been unable to see, since a cold flannel completely covered Marr's face, and had done during Jury's questions so far. Probably he could have used one or the other of Sergeant Wiggins's remedies, but Jury had sent Wiggins to the Bayswater flat.

"Go on, then." The muffled voice came from under the cloth.

"Mr. Marr, do you think perhaps we can talk face-to-face? It would be a help."

Sighing, he said, "So you can see the subtle change of expression that will testify to my guilt?" His breath sucked in and puffed out the cloth that he now withdrew reluctantly. "It's not that I drank so much, it's that I stupidly drank the Dogbolter at the Ferret and Firkin. Bruce's Brewery, my friend. I was doing a bit of a pub-crawl before I met Ivy." He dropped the flannel on a small table, and took the last cigarette from a black enamel case. "I'm being an insensitive boor, right?"

Jury smiled. "If you say so. You think I'm presuming you're guilty?" Jury lit up one of his own cigarettes.

Marr looked at Jury with a grim smile. "Your questions suggest that you've ruled out the most obvious answer: that poor Ivy was set upon by some mugger." He looked away, toward the window where the pre-dawn darkness was as black as the enamel on the lighter he fingered. "Was she raped?"

"I don't know yet." Jury pictured the body, a pale blue heap in the middle of the wet street. "I don't think so. Would you mind telling me what happened at the pub?"

Marr scrubbed at his hair with the cloth, then studied the end of his cigarette with an indifference that Jury suspected was feigned.

"We had an argument. She was angry and refused to let me take her home to Bayswater." He looked at Jury. "I don't usually leave women standing in pub doorways." He shrugged. "Ivy can be extremely stubborn. Doesn't look it, really, all that soft blue look and gorgeous hair. Well, I don't really care for confrontations with women. Not worth it."

"What was the argument about, Mr. Marr?"

"Money, marriage, you know. For some reason Ivy wanted to marry me, poor girl."

"I'd think one reason might be pretty obvious — you move in a much headier social circle, I imagine."

David Marr opened one eye. "How can you tell that?"

The question was rather innocent. Jury smiled. "I've been to the Childess house."

"Bayswater?"

"Mile End. The parents' house. They were the ones who gave me your name."

He frowned. "She hardly ever spoke of them. Hadn't much family feeling, had Ivy."

"But you *were* engaged."

Marr paused, his eyes shielded by his hand, in lookout fashion, as if he were tracking the progress of the morning light at the window. "That what the parents told you?"

"That's what the daughter told *them.*"

The hand now pressed to his head, as if he were holding it on, Marr pushed himself out of the wing chair and moved toward a rosewood table. He held a bottle of Remy to his ear like a huge shell, shook it and put it down, frowning. Then he studied the remaining inch or two in a Glenfiddich bottle, looked over at Jury, and held it up by way of not very enthusiastic invitation.

"Too early for me, thanks, or too late, depending how you look at it."

Marr poured the inch and a half into a tumbler. "I try not to look at it at all. If you're going to swallow a frog, better not stare at it too long, as they say. My head is killing me." He drank it down and retied the robe. "A boor I may be — desolute, depraved, whatever. But engaged I was not. Whether that particular bit of information is important to your investigations, I don't know; you've only my word for it. Whatever

27

she told friends, family, co-workers, I didn't mean to marry Ivy." He fell into the chair again and relit his cigarette.

"What was your relationship with her?"

"Um. Intimate, or at least sexual. There's probably a difference."

Jury was mildly surprised he'd make the distinction. Marr looked quite human with some of the cool hauteur missing from his voice and eyes. "Then the 'engagement' was a fiction invented by her?" Marr nodded. "Then she was simply trying to convince herself?"

"Trying to convince *me* is more like it." He closed his eyes and shook his head slightly. "On several occasions she definitely talked of marriage. Such as last night."

"What did you say?"

"I didn't answer. Have another fag on you, Superintendent?"

Jury handed him the packet and leaned back. "Are you sure you did nothing to encourage her?"

Marr eased himself down in the chair, crossed his long legs, and shook his head in wonder. "For heaven's sakes. A few nights in bed over a period of several months would hardly give anyone but the most naïve of women *that* sort of encouragement, would it? I did not absolutely say, No, we are not going to be married, but I do think I showed a certain amount of hesitancy over it. . . ."

"You left the pub around closing time?"

"About ten-forty-five or -fifty. When last drinks were called."

"Did Ivy stay on or did she leave?"

"The last I saw of her she was standing in the doorway, hand on hip, coat collar pulled up, looking extremely determined." He sighed and rubbed his head again. "Shouldn't have had the last of the Remy, I expect. She told me to more or less bugger off and I did. That's the last I saw of her, Superintendent."

"The Running Footman would have closed shortly after that. She'd have taken a cab to her flat in Bayswater, wouldn't she?"

Marr smiled ruefully. "Knowing Ivy, she might have taken the underground. Cheaper."

"You came directly home?"

Marr sighed. "Yes, of course. It's only a few minutes' walk. When I got here I called my sister, Marion. Talked for some time, but to no avail. I needed money."

"You said money was one of the things you quarreled with Ivy Childess about."

"That's right. I tried to borrow some."

"But surely Ivy Childess wouldn't have had the sort you might need."

Marr laughed. "If it has Her Majesty's face on it, I need it. The odd tailor here and there. A few gambling debts. Ivy would not dip into the money from her uncle's annuity; told me I should be gainfully employed. Yes, that's the way she put it: gainfully employed. I have *never* been employed. Much less gainfully. Work, good Lord."

"Yes, that does seem a dim future."

"That sort of irony exactly matches my sister's. She tells me I'm running through my share of our father's money with a speed that would have earned me a rowing Blue. Our solicitors do not like to advance me more than a sum which would hardly pay for the liquor." This reminder of drink sent him back to the table laden with bottles, where he found a measure or two of whiskey and poured it out.

Jury made another note in a worn pigskin notebook that Racer had in one of his rare moments of largess given him several Christmases ago. Or perhaps it wasn't largess, just a hint to get to work. "You said you called your sister. Could you give me her number?"

"You're not going to bother old Marion with this, are you? Oh, very well." He raked his fingers through his hair, sighed,

and gave Jury the number. "It's ex-directory, so don't lose it."
His smile came and vanished in a second. "She's not going to
be happy about corroborating my alibi, if that's what you call
it."

"You said 'after you got home'? Exactly when after?"

"After the rest of this, I suppose." He held up the glass and
turned it so that the whiskey ran round it in a little wave.

"Could you be more exact?" Jury asked mildly, quite sure
that the man's offensive carelessness over the girl's death was
pretty much facade. Underneath it, he was frightened, but
how much, Jury couldn't guess.

He closed his eyes. "A little after eleven, perhaps. Don't
hold it to me, Superintendent. Marion would know. She was
sober. Always is, worse luck. Her name is Winslow and they
have a place in Sussex, in Somers Abbas. Look, Superintendent. Couldn't you just leave old Marion out of this?"

"You want me to be discreet, that it?"

The clear, wide-eyed look on his handsome face made
Marr look as if he'd just come wandering in from larking with
a bag of kittens down at the lake. Wonderfully innocent and
sly. "Oh, would you? I'd cooperate all over the place. You
can question me for hours —"

"I would do, anyway."

"You're not going to cooperate, I can tell. I have reserva-
tions for Tuesday next for Cannes, but I expect I shan't be
permitted to leave the country now. Cigarette?" He looked
at Jury's.

Jury tossed him the pack. "My guess is you called Mrs.
Winslow because you were anxious to pay your tailor and she
couldn't see eye-to-eye, that right?"

"Clever of you. Well, I was dead drunk, wasn't I?"

"Oh?"

Marr looked at him through the small spiral of smoke.
" 'Oh?' What's that supposed to mean? You're worse than
Marion."

"Nothing."

"I'll bet. Well, there's plenty of money. Although I curse the arrangement at least once a day, I suppose our father was smarter than I like to give him credit for, not putting it up for grabs. The bulk of my own inheritance is contingent upon my marrying." He sounded rueful, then added, "Am I giving myself a motive for murder?"

"The opposite, I'd say."

"Good; let's keep it that way. As it is, I can only dip into the family treasure chest four times a year. This quarter's not up until December thirty-first, worse luck." He looked at a calendar attached to a bulletin board above a handsome lacquered desk. Jury could see that it held photos, cards, other bits and pieces of memorabilia. "Mind if I have a look?"

"Hm? Oh, no, of course not. I'll just have a lie-down." His head fell back on the chair and he rolled his whiskey glass across his brow.

The bulletin board was, Jury saw with a smile, more like the carefully chosen junk of an undergraduate, or the sort of lot one might expect to find in a youngster's shoebox of treasures: photos, of course; colorful and witless postcards such as people loved to send from their holiday spots in the West Country, or the Riviera, Monte Carlo, Las Vegas, Cannes.

"Been to the States?"

David looked round to the bulletin board. "No."

"You have friends there, then?" He nodded toward the card of a Vegas casino.

"No. An acquaintance or two. My *friends* go to Monte or Cannes, Superintendent."

Jury smiled. "Sorry. Didn't know there was much to choose amongst them." He continued scanning the board. A menu from Rules, a silver garter, telephone numbers on scraps of paper tacked about. Jury was more interested in the snapshots. "Is this your sister?"

31

With a wince, David turned his head. "Yes, and the rest of the family. That's my nephew and my sister's husband, Hugh."

It had been taken in a garden; they all looked very pleased with themselves, as if they were delighted to have met and had their picture taken. Another snap showed David Marr with the same young man, both of them laughing, holding what looked like tennis racquets. There were no photos of Marr by himself, none with Ivy Childess.

"Would you mind if I just borrowed these two?"

David was about to cadge another cigarette from Jury's pack. "What? No, I don't mind, I suppose. Just make sure I get them back, that's all."

"I will."

"What do you want them —? Oh, never mind. To show round, I expect. You're probably convinced I dragged Ivy into a dark street and — what *did* happen, Superintendent?"

"That's what we're trying to find out. Was there anyone else in the pub you knew?"

He started to shake his head, but then said, "Yes, there was Paul. Paul Swann. He lives down the street. If he hadn't been in the Running Footman, I'd have stopped in to talk to him, worse luck."

"Perhaps I'll stop in to talk to him."

"Can't. He's not there. Said he was leaving for Brighton at dawn."

"Where in Brighton?"

David scratched his head. "Don't know. Maybe it's Rottingdean. That's more artistic; he's a painter."

Jury made a note, and said, "Then as far as you know, Miss Childess simply left when the pub closed. Did you have any friends in common? Acquaintances?"

He frowned and slid down in the chair. "No."

"You knew of no one she considered an enemy?"

David Marr shook his head and picked up the flannel. He dipped it in what remained of his drink and slapped it on his forehead.

"You know, you seem more irritated by Ivy Childess's death than unhappy." Jury rose to leave.

The flannel moved as David Marr said, "Good God, Superintendent, I'm not irritated. I'm dying." He pulled the cloth from his face, gave Jury a weak smile and asked, "Got another fag?"

5

FIONA Clingmore sat at her desk with a mirror propped up against a dictionary, applying her eyeliner with the solemnity of one taking the veil. The hand that held the thin wand of lipstick was steadied by the other, and the prayerful pose further enhanced the similarity. That prayerful pose and the black scarf holding back her heavy yellow curls were about as close as Fiona would ever get to a nunnery.

Watching over her small arsenal of beauty products was the cat Cyril, who never seemed to tire of tracking the daily metamorphosis, as if expecting a butterfly to emerge from this black cocoon.

Cyril took his cue from Jury's entrance and slid from the desk. The cat knew by now that this foreshadowed admittance to Racer's office — hallowed ground, strictly off cat-limits.

"Hullo, Fiona," said Jury.

Realizing that Jury was standing there smiling, she deposited the tissue on which she had blotted her lips in the dustbin. Then she quickly pulled the black square from her head and a neat set of yellow curls sprang forth. Just as deftly, she swept the makeup into the black well of her purse. Permed and polished, she turned to Jury.

"You're early. Want some tea?"

"Thanks. Did you get that file from forensics?"

"Mmm." With the hot water pot in one hand and a chipped cup in the other, she nodded toward her desk. She swirled the teabag and handed Jury the cup.

"What's he on about, then?" asked Jury, long used to conferences with his superior that left him feeling older but none the wiser.

"I don't know, do I?" It was less a shrugging off of Jury's question than an indication that their superior was seldom on about anything that either wanted to know. Having inspected a fingernail, she got her manicure scissors. Fiona went at any imperfection quickly and summarily; she reminded Jury of a water-colorist alert to sudden shifts in shade and lighting who had to move in before the paint dried.

"I'll wait inside." Jury took his tea and the file and, accompanied by the cat Cyril, went into his chief's office, which Fiona apparently was "airing out" again, for the window behind the desk was open a few inches. Between his hand-rolled cigars and his hand-grown lectures, Racer managed to use up all the excess oxygen. Cyril leapt to the sill and flattened himself so that he could make swipes at the falling snowflakes.

Jury looked without interest round the office. Nothing had changed except that a small mountain of Christmas gifts was piled up on the fake-leather couch. Jury took out a fresh pack of Players. Cyril, who had managed to squeeze all the way out to the outside sill, tired of his daredevil acrobatics, pulled himself back, and made a perfect high-dive for the floor. His flirtation with death grew bolder every year; when the outside door opened, he pricked up his ears, snaked across the carpet, and settled down with a rustle behind the pyramid of gifts on the couch.

Chief Superintendent A. E. Racer made his usual abrasive comments to Fiona Clingmore before he came in to look suspiciously at the pile of gifts, as if Jury might have nicked one in his absence.

"Happy Christmas," said Jury pleasantly, as Racer deposited several folders on his desk and sat down.

"Not for me it isn't," he said, waving his arm across the active files he was carrying. Action, Jury knew, would be taken elsewhere. "What progress have you made on this Childess case?" Without stopping for an answer, Racer said, "Couldn't you shut up the press, at least?"

"Can anyone? I made no comment."

"With this rag you don't have to." He waved a tabloid in Jury's face and then read: " 'Garroted with her own scarf.' Hell. Every villain in London — rapists, muggers — will have a nice, neat way to go about his business."

"Well, it might warn women not to toss their scarves down their backs."

"A bit late in the day for that, isn't it?"

As if Jury had failed to issue the warning, had alerted the papers.

Racer crossed his arms, encased in what looked like cashmere from his bespoke tailor, and leaned toward Jury. "As for you, Jury —"

It was ritual, like Cyril's storming of the battlements. *As for you —*

"— do you think *this* time you could depend on police for your backup? Rather than deputizing your friends?" For Racer, Melrose Plant's role in that Hampshire business was a brand-new drum to bang. "Do you realize I'm still catching flack from the commissioner about *that?*"

"He did save my life."

Finding nothing here that merited a response, Racer went

on to test the waters of Jury's career, keeping as much as he could to the shallows. The career had probably come up in Racer's meeting with the assistant commissioner and would be bobbing up again, as it was now. "Understand Hodges is retiring. Picked a fine time for it, I must say."

There would be for Racer, of course, some personal affront to the lawkeeping forces of Greater London in what he seemed to think was Divisional Commander Hodges's capricious decision. That it left a district minus one of its divisional commanders was a point that Racer would sooner skirt around. For Racer it would be a real quandary if Jury were promoted. Having Jury around was like having a mirror in which a face formed out of smoke reminding Racer that someone fairer still lived; on the other hand, the removal of Jury was the removal of Jury's expertise, which now reflected happily upon Racer.

He was still talking about N Division. "Wouldn't have it on a bet, myself, not with its spilling over into Brixton. Riots, that's what anyone can expect with that thankless job." He went on. . . .

Jury tuned him out, turning his attention to the pyramid of gifts that had shifted slightly, and wondered, with a momentary pang of envy, at Cyril's determination to outwit the forces leveled against him. Racer was descending the ladder of Jury's career and would soon move from the CID to the uniform branch and have Jury back walking a beat. Jury, though, was way ahead of, or way behind him, in that sense. He wondered, with a feeling of guilt, at his own lack of ambition. He had nearly had to be shoved into a superintendency as it was. Perhaps it was the season; Christmas had never been any reason for rejoicing, except for one or two that might have started well, but ended miserably. Or perhaps it was the sky. Jury watched the snow drift down in big, feathery flakes that wouldn't stick, that would turn to gray slush by nightfall and drain away. He remembered the two boys, fourteen or fifteen they'd been, that he'd nicked twenty years ago for shoplifting in a sweet shop. They'd looked very pale and uncertain and reminded him of himself a dozen years earlier, younger even than they, when the owner of a similar shop had caught him leaving the store with a small box of Black Magic chocolates making a bulge in his anorak. He'd been easier on the teenagers than the shopkeeper had been on him, the way he'd called in police. *Set an example.* The aunt who'd just taken Richard in had been mortified.

The girl's name had been Ivy, he suddenly recalled. It was Ivy he'd wanted to give the sweets to as a Christmas present. But this sentiment hadn't softened the set of his aunt's mouth. His uncle had been a gentle man, one who made allowances, especially for a nephew whose own parents had been killed in the war. But his uncle's disappointment, the woeful look he cast upon the boy Richard, had been more difficult to bear than a physical blow.

Well, it wasn't nicking sweets anymore, he thought with an almost overwhelming remorse, as the pale face of the pretty girl lying in the street came back to him. Ivy. The name was probably the reason that memory had floated to mind.

". . . Jury! Can you stop woolgathering long enough to answer the question?"

"Sorry."

"I asked you if Phyllis Nancy had done the autopsy."

"No, not yet. Tomorrow morning."

"What the hell's she waiting for, her medical degree?" Racer slapped open the top folder once again. "So all we know about this Childess woman is that she lived in Bayswater, had a row with her boyfriend in this pub off Berkeley Square, and that he left her there." He shut the folder and leaned back. "You knew all that last night, Jury."

"Then perhaps I'd better be getting on with it? Anything else?" He unfolded himself from the chair and got up, casting his eye toward the couch.

"Well, when you *do* turn up something, lad, would you kindly let me know?"

"Be happy to." Jury eyed the small tower of gifts and turned to go. When he reached the door he heard it — them: the collapse of the boxes like a house of cards, the spillage, the voice of Racer shouting at the cat Cyril, the intercom and the voice of Racer shouting at Fiona.

Calmly, Jury opened the door and Cyril streaked through before him, another game-plan successfully executed.

"He's in a right temper now," said Fiona, filing her nails, undisturbed by the squawking intercom. Cyril had leapt to the windowsill behind her to have a wash as the telephone rang.

Fiona picked it up, spoke, then held it toward Jury. The black receiver looked like an extension of her darkly varnished nails. It fairly dripped from her hand. "It's Al."

Jury took the receiver, wondering if anyone else at headquarters besides Fiona called Detective Sergeant Wiggins by his first name. "Wiggins?"

The voice of Wiggins was adenoidal, but precise. "I've come up with something, sir. I was just checking in the computer room —" The pause then was not for dramatic effect but to allow the sergeant to rustle a bit of cellophane from a box. He apparently had completed his delicate maneuver, for now the voice was clotted. " 'N du-v'n'n, s'r —"

"Shove the cough drop under your tongue, Wiggins," said Jury patiently.

"Oh. Sorry, sir. It was this case about ten months ago, end of February. Young woman by the name of Sheila Broome. Well, I would have passed straight over it except for the description of the body *in situ*. Police made sure there was no

39

publicity because they were afraid of copy-cat murders. For good reason. She was found in a wooded area off the A303, just near the turn-off to Taunton. She'd been strangled, apparently with her own scarf. Well, it could be a coincidence —"

Jury stared blindly at Cyril, who was pressing one paw and then the other against the big snowflakes drifting against the windowpane. A serial killer. The worst kind. "Let's hope so. Get on to headquarters in Somerset."

"Police in Somerset wouldn't be handling it, sir. It's right over the border." Pause. "In Devon."

"Well, call Exeter, then."

There was another pause and a tiny rattle of paper. This seemed to be a two-cough-drop problem. Said Wiggins, wanly: "You don't suppose it's Macalvie's case, do you, sir?"

Jury half-smiled. "Every case in Devon is Macalvie's case."

6

THE snow outside the Jack and Hammer was tracked only by a narrow set of marks made by the Jack Russell belonging to Miss Crisp, which had left its mistress's rag-and-bone shop across the street to make its afternoon rounds of the village.

Through the dreamy motley of palette-tinted shops and cottages the sonorous drone of the bell in the church tower washed over the High Street and past the pub where the mechanical smith up on a high beam picked it up and made a simulated bong on his forge. Above him the clock struck five.

It was a call-to-arms for a few of Long Piddleton's residents. There was a half-hour yet until opening, but Scroggs often turned a blind eye to the licensing laws when it came to his family of regulars. One of these had biked the half-mile from Ardry End and was sitting at a table in the large bay window. His legs were outstretched and his trousers still pinched by bicycle clips. He had passed the halfway mark in the book he was reading.

No devotee of the thriller-novel, he would have ordinarily

skipped from the first chapter to the last, filling in whatever extraneous details were necessary for the resolution. But his longstanding affection for the author of this particular book had obligated him to read every page. Well, almost, thought Melrose Plant. Love me, love my books. His friendship with its author had not extended to a friendship with this book bearing the irrelevant title of *The Plum-Pudding Group*. It was meant, he imagined, to sell to the Christmas trade and had found its way onto the shelves of Long Piddleton's new book shop, called the Wrenn's Nest, a silly pun on its proprietor's name.

He wondered if he couldn't just take a peek at the end. The murderer's motive was the old kill-him-before-he-changes-his-will cliché, and the characters seemed at a loss to know what to do with themselves, like people looking vague on a railway platform after the train pulls away.

Melrose Plant checked his watch, not to see if the two others who usually joined him in the Jack and Hammer were late, but because he knew another body should be turning up — ah, yes, there it was. Colonel Montague. Too bad, he thought. He had rather liked old Montague despite that gin-beneath-the-palms manner that the author had saddled him with. Yes, there were bodies aplenty. If Raymond Chandler's prescription for a cure for midbook boredom was to bring in a man with a gun, Polly Praed's was to drag another corpse into every other chapter. This latest book must have been written in extreme agitation, for there was a jittery, hectic quality to the sudden discovery of body after body. Her mind, he thought, must be an abattoir.

All this murder and mayhem was interrupted by the arrival of two other regulars whom he was happy to see since they would relieve him of further delving into the death of Montague.

"Hello, Melrose," said Vivian Rivington, the prettier of the two, although Melrose wondered idly if Marshall Trueblood would insist upon a reevaluation of that assessment.

"Hullo, old bean," said Marshall Trueblood, looking this afternoon like a fairly ordinary rather than an eccentric millionaire. He wore a dark woolen jacket so beautifully tailored that it might have been the last best dream of a Hebredean weaver. But the weaver would have wakened wide-eyed at sight of the bold blue cashmere sweater and sea green ascot tucked in the neck of a turquoise crepe de chine shirt. For Trueblood, this was a costume downplayed. "Thank God, another day in the stews and sweats is finished."

Marshall Trueblood could afford anything but sweat. He was fond of slandering his own antiques business located in the small Tudor building next door, a thriving shop despite Long Piddleton's slender population. It prospered because it drew on a London clientele, among them some very knowledgeable dealers. Business was also helped along by the patronage of the two — even richer than Trueblood — who shared the table.

"It's only just gone five," said Vivian Rivington with a melancholy air. Winter's dregs left the trio with little to do but comment on one another's departure from the norm. "You don't close until six," she said, shaking her watch.

"There's no custom. I left a sign on the door to check over here if someone wants a distressed bureau. What're you reading, Melrose?" he asked as Scroggs set drinks before them.

Melrose Plant turned it cover-out so that his friends could see.

"*The Plum-Pudding Group.* Strange title. Cheers." He raised his glass.

Vivian was squinting at the name of the author. "It's another one of that Polly's, isn't it?"

"I'm afraid it's not very good. But don't tell her."

"She's not *around* to tell," said Vivian with just a touch of fractiousness. "I don't understand what your relationship is."

"Careful, careful, Vivian. You're not one to talk of *engagé* involvements."

"You're so right, Melrose," said Trueblood. "Is this another Christmas you'll not be spending with the ill-starred Franco of Florence?"

"Venice," she said, a little waspishly.

"Did you get bad news in your letter?" Trueblood dashed a bit of ash from the end of his black Sobranie and smiled roguishly.

Vivian's eyes narrowed. "What do you mean, in my letter?"

"Why, the one you must have got this morning. The one in your pocket."

The hand that had strayed to the pocket of her cardigan was brought back quickly to make a fist on the table.

"Postmarked Venezio."

"Just how do *you* know?"

"If Miss Quarrels *must* sort the post by spreading it out on the counter like a cardsharp, is it my fault?"

"And you went to the trouble of reading it upside-down!"

He had brought out his little gold nail-clipper. "No, I turned it right-side up."

"Snoop!"

Hearing her cue, Lady Agatha Ardry appeared in the Jack and Hammer's doorway, making her snowy entrance with a shake-out of her cape and a stamp of her shoes. "I looked in your windows, Mr. Trueblood," she said to Marshall Trueblood even before she called to Dick Scroggs for her double shooting sherry. "It's not six, Mr. Trueblood. Your shop should be open. But then if custom means so little . . . my dear Plant, I was just bucketing along to Ardry End —"

Doing her rounds like Miss Crisp's terrier, thought Melrose, turning a page and finding Lady Dasher dead in the hydrangeas. . . .

"— and I passed a car —"

Lucky for the driver. Usually she just drove into them. Agatha had acquired an old Morris Minor that looked like her: rounded dome and dumpy body.

"— just coming down the drive as I drove in. Woman driver, thirtyish, brown hair, black Porsche —"

"Number plate?"

"What?"

"Surely, you got the number so we can run it through Scotland Yard's computer system. They do wonders finding hot cars these days —"

"Don't be daft, Plant. Well, she got straight away before I could stop her. Who is she, then? She's *not* terribly attractive."

This was said with some relief, as if removing the lady in the Porsche from the running of marriageable females. These Agatha appeared to see as so many lovelies hastening toward the family vaults of Ardry End, its chinoiserie, crystal, Queen Anne furniture, and the titles that Melrose had dropped like petals in the dust — earldom, viscountcy, baronetcy — that could still be gathered up (she seemed to think) and glued back on the bud.

"You don't have visitors this time of year, Melrose." She sighed and called again for her sherry. Scroggs went on turning the pages of his newspaper. "It's not like the old days. Remember your dear mother, Lady Marjorie —"

Here she would go again, poking along the paths of his family memories like a pig rooting through rosebushes. "The Countess of Caverness, yes. And my father, and my uncle Robert. I have always had a very good memory for detail. But what were you doing up at Ardry End?"

45

"To see Martha about the Christmas dinner. She said it hadn't been decided yet."

"It has. Poor Man's Goose and Idiot Biscuits."

"My favorite!" said Marshall Trueblood. "I hope we're invited."

"Of course. You always are."

"You're making it up," said Agatha, stomping her cane on the floor in an attempt to unglue Scroggs from his paper. "There's no such thing."

"There certainly is. It's actually ox-liver. And for your sweet you may have raspberry flummery. Or would you prefer the gooseberry fool? Martha's quite good with a fool." Melrose yawned and watched the Jack Russell through the leaded window that spelled out Hardy's Crown in amber lettering. It was sniffing round the feet of a woman in a brown hat standing on the pavement looking speculatively at Trueblood's window. Melrose thought she looked familiar.

"There she is!" cried Agatha, craning her neck to peer through the leaded glass.

"I didn't mean to barge in," said the young woman in the brown hat.

It was, thought Melrose, looking at the dreamy, gawky girl, exactly the sort of comment that Lucinda St. Clair would make. She was the sort of woman who people would still refer to as a "girl" even in her late twenties or early thirties.

"You're not barging!" said Vivian with the first display of brightness she had shown since she'd walked in.

For Melrose, Vivian Rivington had always embodied in near-equal measure beauty, grace, and kindliness. She could wear as she now did the old wool skirt and twinset or doll herself up in what Trueblood designated as "the Italian period," but she still never seemed to know what to do with herself or whether the one or the other persona fit. Thus it wasn't surprising that she should take the measure of Lucinda St. Clair, probably thinking that here was a female in even worse shape than she, Vivian; one who was dressed in an even drabber twinset.

"Thank you very much," said Lucinda with a look of gratitude hardly occasioned by the simple act of Trueblood's pulling out a chair for her. He himself knew Sybil St. Clair, her mother, who was an occasional customer of his. This made it that much worse for Agatha — that even Trueblood had indirect knowledge of their visitor and she none.

Lucinda's eyes were large and chestnut brown. When they met the beady black ones of Agatha, she quickly looked away. Agatha had been silently scouring Lucinda St. Clair for signs of marriageability, signs which Agatha always seemed to think such ladies sported in neon-bright arrows. Then Agatha squinted and demanded to know if they had met.

Melrose sighed and hoped neither would track the memory down. They had indeed met, albeit very briefly, at one of those dreadful parties at Lady Jane Hay-Hurt's. But he didn't think Agatha could put a name to this memory, for she had been busy talking to Lady Jane, who was in absolutely no danger of joining the Ardry-Plant line and raiding the inheritance. Lady Jane was literally long in the tooth, resembling as she did an Alsatian, and Agatha liked to push Melrose in her path, realizing that the Ardry-Plant fortune was perfectly safe. But in Lucinda, Agatha would see a possible adversary relationship; here was an eligible woman who had crossed Agatha's field of vision and had the temerity not to withdraw from the field. She was youngish and nice and merely plain. Melrose hoped that nothing would jog his aunt's memory because then she would recall having met Lucinda's mother, Sybil, with whom his aunt had had a wonderful time sitting on Lady Jane's settee, demolishing teacakes and characters.

"No, you haven't," said Melrose, putting a dead stop to speculation. "Miss St. Clair somewhat resembles Amelia Sheerswater." It was a name plucked from air. But it would make Agatha wonder about this *new* addition to the ranks of Melrose's women. "We're just having a drink; what would you like?"

Lucinda St. Clair drew her brown hair away from her face and appeared to be in deep colloquy with herself over the drink selection.

"How about sherry?" offered Vivian helpfully. "The Tio Pepe's very good."

As if Tio Pepe were a drink so rare, refined, and quixotic that it changed from bottle to bottle and pub to pub, thought Melrose. But might as well let Vivian do her thing. Lucinda nodded and Trueblood called to Dick Scroggs for the sherry before he settled back to plug a blue Sobranie into his holder.

Everyone smiled at Lucinda except Agatha, who still was scanning the St. Clair face for telling signs of the Sheerswater one.

It occurred to Melrose when Dick brought her Tio Pepe and stood there looking at the newcomer with his bar towel draped over his shoulder that perhaps the girl was uncomfortable amidst all of this attention. Indeed Lucinda looked from her glass to him and smiled weakly as if she thought she were expected to perform at this little pre-Christmas gathering, to jump up and recite something or tell a clever anecdote. What she did not realize was that they had all been saying pretty much the same thing to one another for years now and it was refreshing to see an unfamiliar face joining their ranks.

Melrose saw Lucinda sliding down a bit in her chair and decided to extricate her before the group all burst into carol-singing or something. He picked up his drink and hers, smiled, and excused both himself and her. "I really think Miss St. Clair has come to Long Piddleton for a bit of a talk with me."

When they were seated at a table near the fireplace, she began with another apology for presuming upon their brief acquaintance, and told him she was just on her way back from Northampton where she'd gone to pick up some materials and things. "For Mother. She's doing up a house in Kensington. You remember Mother?"

Didn't he just. Sybil had once been plain wife and mother before she'd taken up the artsy ways of the world of interior design. Typical of her, too, that she'd send the daughter to do the dog's work, running about with swatches of material, matching and measuring. As he remembered her, she seemed to prefer frocks without waists, all folds that hung aimlessly here and there. There was all the shine and glint in her complexion that Clinique could give her.

Melrose had met her again on one of his infrequent trips to London. He had befriended Lucinda, feeling something of the agony of a young woman with no social graces and the thin-legged, long-nosed look of a crane. She wore white and shouldn't have, as it only increased the image. Poor Lucinda managed to turn a deer park into a rain forest with her large, damp brown eyes. They had been staying at the hotel he liked. Tea at Brown's had escalated into dinner, where he told them about his visit at that very hotel with an American tour group. The story of those murders had enthralled them.

"What I remembered was that you seemed to have some experience with police —"

"Well, I do know one or two, yes. But I'm not really a dab hand at the business. Why?"

She took a long breath. "There's a friend of mine, see, who seems to have got himself in trouble. I just thought perhaps that you might be able to sort things out — Oh, I don't know. It's dreadful."

"What's happened? Who's the friend?" He was a little sorry he'd asked when she colored and looked away. The "friend" was undoubtedly more than a friend, or she hoped so.

"No one special, really," she said looking everywhere but at him. "A friend of the family. We've known him for ages. . . ." The whispery voice trailed off. "Did you read about that woman murdered in Mayfair? It was in the paper today."

The one Scroggs had talked about so juicily. "You don't mean your friend is mixed up in that? That *is* dreadful."

All in a rush and with a great deal of intensity she said, "I'm afraid that he might just be arrested or something. He was the last one to see the girl alive. Or at least that's what they're saying." From her large bag she drew out a copy of the same paper Scroggs had read them.

"Scotland Yard CID," he said after reading the account. "Is this your friend? The one who's 'helping police with their inquiries,' as they say?"

Lucinda St. Clair nodded. "I just thought that since you're so clever about these things —"

"If that's the impression I gave, I didn't mean to." He carefully folded the paper. He certainly had been decidedly unclever when he had helped Richard Jury on that last case. The memory still sent chills down his spine. "There's really nothing I can do. Civilians can't go messing about in police business, Lucinda." How many times had he been told *that* by Jury's superior?

It was a crestfallen look he got. "There's really no one else I can think of."

"Surely he has a solicitor —"

She nodded and looked desolate.

"I take it this gentleman is a very good friend."

50

The look of desolation only increased. "Yes."

Melrose thought for a moment. It wouldn't hurt, he supposed, to call Jury. "You've got to understand, though, that I can't do anything by way of interfering —"

"Oh, no one's thinking of your *interfering*. I just thought you might be able somehow to look at it from another perspective." She lost that rain-forest look for a moment. "Then you *will* come?"

"You mean to Sussex?"

"Somers Abbas. We could drive down together; I have my car —"

Melrose held up his hand. "No; I'll really have to think about this."

Lucinda sat back, looking more desolate than she had when she came in. "Will you call, then?"

"Of course." Melrose looked over to the table where Vivian, Trueblood, and his aunt still sat, the two women pretending not to be interested in the goings-on before the fireplace. Agatha was making a far poorer job of the pretense than was Vivian. Melrose smiled at the familiar trio in the bay window. Vivian smiled back and even wiggled her fingers in a friendly little wave. Perhaps her difficulty in crossing the Channel lay in some deep-rooted need to keep the little party intact. Benevolently she beamed at Lucinda.

He studied the girl. He felt a tacit agreement with Vivian that Lucinda St. Clair would probably never break up a party.

On this rare December morning Melrose sat at the rosewood dining table, the *Times* folded beside his plate of eggs. He penned in two down and one across. But he was only giving part of his mind to the crossword; the rest was on the call he had made to Richard Jury, who had told him certainly, absolutely to go to Somers Abbas. That he was acquainted with someone who knew the Winslow family could be extremely helpful. And for all of the past help, well, Jury thought he deserved a knighthood. A bit redundant, perhaps, but anyway . . .

"I doubt very much that Chief Superintendent Racer would oblige with a knighthood. I doubt very much that Racer has been pleased. . . ."

Melrose looked down the length of the table and out the French windows that on this unseasonable day had been opened. Their creamy curtains billowed slightly in the breeze. Beyond the window he caught a glimpse of the serpentine path that wound through the grounds and down which he loved to stroll. All of those grounds out there — the wide expanse of gardens, the silver wintercrust of the lake, the yew hedges and willows — reminded him of the walk he had taken with Lucinda St. Clair at Lady Jane's party. Melrose could imagine, all the while, Sybil St. Clair watching with the patience of a puma straddled on a branch, waiting for the least flicker of movement from the quarry below. It was maddening to feel sorry for Lucinda, and impossible not to. She had, of course, been delighted that he was coming. And in face of all her mother's objections, Melrose had insisted at a room at the local inn.

He sighed and looked up, his eye moving round the walls and the portraits there that hung in such stately procession that the whole crowd of them might have been on its way to Westminster Abbey. Viscount Nitherwold, Ross and Cromarty, Marquess of Ayreshire and Blythedale, Earl of Caverness . . . one could hardly name them without pausing for a stiff drink in between. His eye came to rest on the portrait of his mother, one of the most beautiful women he had ever seen, and one on whom that coronet must have weighed awfully heavily at the end. Filtered sunlight fell in dancing sequins on her pale gold hair, and humor was written all over her face.

52

He smiled. His mother, if not the Queen, he was sure had been pleased. . . .

"More coffee, m'lord?" asked Ruthven, Plant's paradigm of a gentlemen's gentleman, who had been in the family practically as long as the portraits on the walls. He held the silver pot aloft.

Melrose shook his head and put down his pen. "No thanks, Ruthven. I'd better be on my way." He pocketed his gold-rimmed spectacles and shoved back his chair.

"Will you be requiring the Flying Spur or the Rolls, sir?"

Melrose looked again at the portrait of Lady Marjorie. Was she smiling? "You know, Ruthven, I think anyone who's asked a question like that should be shot."

7

THE last time Jury saw him, Brian Macalvie put his foot through a jukebox. Today, at least, he was only playing it. For a man whose sentiments ran toward moving through his men like Birnam Wood and shouting at suspects, the divisional commander showed a remarkable affinity for old songs and soft voices. It was probably Macalvie's choice now that filled the Running Footman with its whispery *tristesse*.

He barely raised his eyes from the menu of songs when he spoke. "Hi, Jury. Took you long enough." Macalvie slotted another ten-p piece into the jukebox and hit the side when it didn't respond.

Jury could have run all the way from headquarters like the footman in the huge picture that gave the pub its name. However fast he was, it couldn't be fast enough. Time did a peculiar dance around Macalvie; he picked up exactly where he left off. Two years ago, ten minutes, it made no difference. Just as last year's murder was still today's news for Macalvie. He never gave up.

Jury smiled. "The world wags by three times, Macalvie: God's, yours, and Greenwich Mean."

Macalvie might have been checking his watch against the other two because he shook it before he nodded. "Yeah. Have a beer. Just be careful of the Gopher; it'd take the scales off a brontosaurus." He picked his pint from the top of the jukebox and walked to a table beneath the painting.

When Jury came back with his own pint, Macalvie was standing and drinking and studying the painting. "That's what we are, Jury, messengers. Good news, bad news — people'd complain no matter what we brought." He sat down. "Where's Wiggins?"

For a divisional commander who was his own one-man police force because he couldn't put up with the slightest show of foot-dragging or malingering, it was surprising that he got on so well with Wiggins. As good a man as Wiggins was, he could be sluggish. Sickness wouldn't slow Macalvie down any more than a flea on a cheetah.

Macalvie brought out a cigar. The cellophane crackled like Macalvie's eyes. A walking conflagration with its roots in his Scotch-Irish ancestry spiked by a strong predilection for American cop films.

"Why aren't you chief constable yet, Macalvie?"

"Beats me," he said, with no trace of irony. "I would've got here sooner, only that train from Dorchester stops for chickens."

"You got here fast enough, considering we found the girl early this morning. I take it you think there's a connection —"

"Of course. Sheila Broome, found on a stretch of road beyond Taunton. For ten months I've been waiting for the other shoe to drop."

"You were sure it would? And Ivy Childess is the shoe?"

Macalvie shot him a look. "Yes."

"I don't want to tread on your theory, Macalvie —"

As if you could, the look said.

"— but murderers aren't all serial killers, and women get mugged every day. I don't much believe in startling coincidences."

"Oh, *come* on. You don't believe this started out as a mugging any more than I do."

True, he didn't. "I'm just more conservative, Macalvie."

"No wonder you got to be superintendent, Jury."

Jury ignored that. "So tell me about this Sheila Broome."

"She set out on the night of twenty-nine February to go to Bristol. That's according to her mum, only she told Mum she'd got a ride. To Bristol, that is. Since none of her friends knew anything about her leaving town and no one gave her a ride from around here, we figured she was getting lifts from along the road. She was *not* prissy Priscilla. There was nothing unusual about her — she snorted coke and slept around, her friends said. Age, twenty-six, hardly a schoolkid, never married. Pretty in a sulky way; not very likeable; did two O levels and then quit, so not ambitious, either. Worked at a pub in the new part of Exeter and didn't tell the landlord she was quitting. She put me in mind of an old newspaper; you could have blown her to Bristol, and no one would notice."

"What is it about the murder that makes you think it was more than Sheila Broome being in the wrong place at the wrong time?"

"Because she wasn't robbed and she wasn't raped. And they were out of the car, both of them, smoking grass in the woods. Now, if you were tooling along looking over the hitcher situation, what'd you be looking for? Sex or money or both. But with Sheila it's neither. I think it was someone who knew her; could have been a man, could have been a woman. I think it was someone *looking* for her —"

"That's a chancy way to get your victim, waiting until she hitches a ride."

"If you're not in a hurry, it's a swell way. Removes both of you from home ground."

"But the scarf; that doesn't sound premeditated, Macalvie. He just used the available means."

Macalvie got up and collected their glasses. "Oh, I imagine he had something else, a stocking, a gun." He went off to fill the glasses and, while he was waiting, to play the jukebox.

The Running Footman wasn't crowded; a few couples, a half-dozen singles that looked pleasant and not hurting for money. Jury supposed you weren't if you lived in Mayfair.

Macalvie walked back to the table, where they sat for a moment drinking and listening to the honey-voice of Elvis Presley. Elvis was Macalvie's favorite.

"Like I said, she wasn't robbed. She was carrying about seventy quid in a rucksack, another ten or eleven in her jacket. There was a gold watch, strap broken, in the pack and a couple of rings on her fingers."

"What about cars, drivers? Did you find anyone?"

"There was a lorry driver. I wouldn't have found him except for a waitress in a Little Chef who thought she remembered Sheila Broome's face, not so much because of the face itself, but because she was wearing a vest the waitress fancied and asked her where she got it. Electric blue, it was. And she remembered the artic because it was so big it took up nearly half the car park. Lucky for the driver that the waitress watched when they left; she said he must have started off with Sheila, but when Mary-the-waitress looked out the window, Sheila was stepping down from the cab. She could hardly see through the fog; it was that neon-blue vest. Then Sheila was trying to hitch another ride in front of the petrol station next to the cafe."

"And she didn't see anything else? No car stopping?"

Macalvie shook his head. "Next time she looked, she didn't see Sheila. Now, tell me about Ivy."

Jury told Macalvie the little they knew. Nodding his head

57

in the direction of the side street, he said, "You've had a look, I suppose."

"Of course."

"It was two or three hours later that she was found."

" 'Hours'? You ought to be on my forensics team."

"Thanks."

"No problem. Patience on a monument, Jury, that's me. Go on." Before his patience could be pressed into service, Macalvie turned to the table beside them and told the occupants to hold it down. They just stared.

"Princess and the pea is more like it. How many mattresses do you sleep on, Macalvie? The last her boyfriend saw of her she was standing in that doorway over there"— Jury nodded toward the entrance—"doing a slow burn." Jury told him about the interview with David Marr.

"Cab-driver said she flagged him down and then changed her mind?"

Jury nodded.

"Cab-drivers can't see. All you have to do is grab a taxi to know that."

"Let's assume this one could," said Jury dryly. "It's not much of an alibi, anyway."

"How true. So this makes two."

"But muggings happen every day, a murder here and a murder in Devon —"

"Come on. We've just been *over* that. No rape, no robbery."

"Those are *un*knowns, Macalvie. The only *known* here is the way they were garroted."

"What more do you want? A bootprint on her forehead? It's like I said."

Like he said, thought Jury. Case open. Theory closed.

PART II

Reverie

8

S HE spent the morning and part of the afternoon in the
shops, not buying, only looking, and after a while not
seeing much of what she looked at. In an antiques
shop in the Lanes, she picked up a miniature, one of several
on a black walnut table, and opened the heart-painted top to
read the legend inside: *Love Always.* Kate disliked these little, porcelain boxes that had no purpose but to sit on dressing
tables or in escritoires gathering dust. Her mother had collected them, tops painted with ribbons, flowers, hearts, in
that rather vague if feverish excitement her mother affected
in nearly everything she did.

So Kate was surprised to find herself in another part of the
shop looking at the old books, still holding the miniature in
her hand. She must have been carrying it long enough to
draw the riveted gaze of the shopkeeper to her. He had appeared again in the opening above the half-door to the room
beyond, his hands clasped behind him, staring at her like a
guard from a castle keep. Kate imagined that he thought she
meant to nick it and she was embarrassed enough that she
turned it over to see the price. Twenty pounds. It was not

even a good example of its kind: the heart was threaded with scratches, the gilt round the oval top was flaked. Indeed, it might not even have been an original, but under the censorious stare of the owner, she felt compelled to tell him she'd have it. Of course his manner altered accordingly, the gaze shifted, the tone when he spoke was as cottony as the small square placed into an overlarge box to act as a cushion.

It was easy enough to explain to herself when she was outside on the pavement once more. Another little gift to appease the gods. What a conscience she must have, she thought, standing there outside the shop with its partly shuttered windows. If she had ever tried to do anything criminal, it would have caught her out immediately. How had her parents, both shallow, feckless dilettantes, managed between them to fashion it? Far more artistry had tone into this paste momento she held. She smiled grimly, pulled up the high collar of her lamb's wool coat, and started down the narrow street toward the ocean. Her conscience put her in mind of some medieval chalice of the sort she remembered seeing at the Victoria and Albert. An elaborate, supposedly splendid (but Kate thought vulgar) liturgical icon, heavily chased with gold beading, studded about with jewels. Her conscience, she thought ruefully, was as impractical and flashy as her sister, Dolly.

Kate maneuvered the narrow space between a Ford Granada with its bonnet up and the drab window of a boutique. The snow had had time to turn to slush, and the shoppers sluggish. None of the faces that she passed looked pleased with their errands or with their glittery surroundings. It was old glitter anyway, not new. The Royal Pavilion was banked in by scaffolding, and a wide, blue hoarding covered part of its front while it underwent repair. How many hundreds of pounds must be going into keeping these impractical, flashy minarets and turrets up. Kate thought again of Dolly.

No one except herself had forced Kate into those years of nursing their father, so she shouldn't blame Dolly for getting off scot-free. A flat in London, a score of lovers, and enviable looks were the rewards of self-indulgence — not to mention the money itself. Kate did not feel any bitterness with regard to her sister; Dolly had done nothing by way of manipulating the old man into leaving her the lion's share of the inheritance. It had long been clear that he would favor the child who, short of being the son, most resembled himself.

Kate had watched the progress of her father's illness over the years uncoil and make its slow way through tissue and bone. Still to the end the society of others had been his vocation; he drank champagne at breakfast and Glenfiddich at tea. Illness and dissipation had turned him into a hollow-cheeked, wasted man who looked twenty years older than he was, one whose mind had clouded over at the end: he had "visions," he said. The visions were usually uncomplimentary to his elder daughter, thought Kate wryly, and undoubtedly helped along by the Glenfiddich.

What had surprised Kate and what now all but overwhelmed her was the knowledge that it hadn't made any difference and that if her years of servitude had been intended as some sort of sacrificial offering, she had to face now the fact that there had been no gods to appease. Brighton beach in the winter dusk and the hard, dark shell of the sea was not the place to mitigate against her terrible disappointment at the lack of freedom she felt. That was something she had been sure she could have counted on, a sense of freedom and release. Now she was able to go anywhere and to live as she liked. She had made all sorts of plans before her father's death that she meant to put into motion when he was dead. Now she watched them idle there at the ocean's edge as if trying to grab hold or gain purchase on the shingle, breaking and pulling back, and breaking again. The romantic fancies became as repetitive as the collapsing waves and as dull and cold, too. A heavy drapery of fog covered the Palace Pier, hiding the flaking white paint, the rust. It had grown dimmer and dustier with the years, like the Pavilion back there. The West Pier farther away had been closed to visitors; it was dangerously in need of repairs. Away in the distance, floating like a shadow on the water, it looked delicate and fragile, made of matchsticks.

Kate went down the stair to the long seawalk, past the Arches beneath the King's Road, where most of the amusements were closed up now. She nodded to a young man who was painting the facade of the Penny Palace, painting bright marine blue pillars on its front. It was one of Kate's favorites, with its old machines that evoked so much of a Victorian Brighton. When her sister was small, she had loved to walk along the seafront with their father, past the Arches, licking ice cream or a stick of Brighton rock. But why her sister, who came down from London rarely, had appeared in Brighton now, Kate couldn't understand. On an impulse, Dolly had said.

Kate walked on to the next set of steps leading up, the carryall holding some chops and the wrapped-up box hitched on her wrist and her hands stuffed deep in her coat pockets. She could feel a frayed seam. Whenever Dolly came down from London Kate grew more sensitive to things like her seven-year-old coat or an outmoded frock. Dolly stopped short of actual wardrobe trunks, but the several cases she would bring for her short stays bulged with outfits that spent their time in the cupboard, since there was nowhere they could go festive enough for turquoise silk or a fox-fur collar. Kate wondered sometimes if Dolly were still caught back in days of dress-up and blind-man's-buff.

Why had Dolly come? A man, perhaps. Dolly had never

had good luck with men, beautiful as she was. Well, that might have been part of it. Too beautiful. Perhaps because of the difference in their ages the two had never been close, and Kate supposed she had resented the baby sister and little girl that Dolly had been. She must have, but Kate couldn't really remember, though she would have been twelve when Dolly was born. A very awkward twelve that had replaced an ungainly eight and in turn a square-jawed, dubious-seeming child of five. In the photographs Kate saw herself always as hesitant, standing on the edge of the occasions that prompted the photographs, as if she'd strayed into the family circle grouped against the dark backdrop, Dolly centered there and always dressed in something soft with tucks of organdy or spills of ribbon.

Dolly spent her visits trailing what could have been a trousseauful of negligees and velvet wrappers through the dark, high-ceilinged rooms of the house in Madeira Drive, sometimes sitting long enough to leaf through a magazine and always with a cigarette and a cup of tea. Dolly was so much like their mother that Kate had once or twice felt a surge of panic, seeing her in the shadowed hall or in the dark of the stairwell. It was no wonder that their father had doted on her, had exaggerated notions about Dolly's career, and fantasized about her life in rough approximation to those fantasies he had had about his own. They were fantasies that Dolly fed, not for any gain other than that she fed her own ego in the telling.

For professional reasons, she said, she had changed the spelling of their name to "Sands." It was easier to remember, looked simpler when the name flickered on the television screen at the end of the news report. Dolly had done well, very well. She had popularized something pretty dull.

Kate switched the carryall to her other hand, finding it a tiresome burden. The rashers and chops were best quality and probably half again as much as the price she would collect for the room. Dolly had been extremely put out to find that the house, old and dark but still elegant, was being turned by Kate into a bed-and-breakfast. They didn't need the money, she had complained, and taking in roomers seemed terribly lower class.

Privacy. Kate had always heard her sister complain before of too much privacy — not even a servant to bring Dolly her early morning tea. Since Dolly never rose in the morning before nine, Kate didn't know to what use the morning would have been put.

Kate made for the promenade and the news agent she patronized, where she bought a *Times* and a piece of Brighton rock. It was a sweet she had loved as a child before they had moved here permanently, when they had come (as her father liked to say) for the season — as though those were the Edwardian days of parasols and tea at the Royal Pavilion.

She walked toward Madeira Drive. Round and round in her mouth she turned the rock candy, its cloying sweetness like the aftertaste of childhood.

Dolly sat at the kitchen table, smoking and drinking tea and occasionally reading a tidbit from a review of a new American film as Kate cut up some potatoes and swede. They might have presented a picture of conviviality, even intimacy, to a stranger. Kate knew they were neither. She had said almost as much, asking Dolly why she bothered with this Brighton trip now their father was dead. The answer had been a stock one, that she didn't want Kate to be "on her own" for the holidays. It was all dead dialogue out of one of Dolly's own television programs.

Leaning her chin on her cupped hand, Dolly said, "I don't know how you stand it, Kate. You should sell up and come to London and get a flat."

"And do what?" Uninformed advice always irritated Kate. Dolly's was always that sort, suggesting that changing her life was of no more moment than handing over a claim ticket at the lost luggage counter.

"Oh, you'd find something," Dolly said vaguely, her eye returning to the social page. "You've got the education and you're really good-looking when you fix yourself up."

Kate turned up the flame on the cooker and positioned the pot with the basin over it. She laughed briefly. "Thanks for *that*. But when anyone says, 'Fix yourself up a bit,' that generally means a thorough turnout, like spring cleaning. The face will of course have to go. And the results of my A-levels dusted off and displayed —" She was getting angry. It was what she felt to be Dolly's total indifference to her masked by this spurious interest that made her situation stand out in sharp relief. "You haven't really thought about it. There's something a little mean about dragging out my dubious qualifications for this hypothetical something." Loneliness washed over her in waves. She felt she was back looking out over the sea again, not here in a warm kitchen.

Dolly's silence in face of this little outburst made Kate turn to look at her. She was looking out of the window with much the same intensity of Kate looking out over the sea.

"Dolly?"

Her sister turned. In the clear skin Kate saw little lines etched, worrisome little lines.

"Is something wrong?"

"No, nothing." Dolly shook herself and went back to reading her paper. Then she said, "I don't like the idea of turning this into a bed-and-breakfast. It's so —"

"Lower class?" Kate felt the anger dissipate. She turned back to the cooker. "It gives me something to do."

"And what do you know about the people you take in?"

"Not much. But I don't take many, you know."

Her sister arranged the lime-green nightdress in folds over her good legs, and the shift in posture accentuated the play of light across her breasts. It was all unconscious, Kate knew.

68

The way she now held a match straight up to the tip of a fresh cigarette, the way she lowered her lashes, smoothed her hand over her pale gold hair. Then she rose and stretched, saying she thought she'd go up and have a bath and wash her hair.

As the slippers tapped down the hall, Kate sat down with her coffee and pulled the newspaper around, looking it over. Another drop in the economy, a shocking rise in rape cases, a child abused, a minister disrupting a cabinet meeting, a murder in Mayfair. Nothing ever changed much.

9

THE sign of the Mortal Man made the dusk hideous with its creak and clangor, swinging precariously above the road that wound about the village green. The gentleman pictured on the trembling sign was appropriately depicted, his gouged eyes seeming to reflect not so much on his own mortality as that of the sign. It was an old gallows sign, the sort that was made illegal over a century ago because of the traffic hazard. Probably no traffic hazarded the narrow lane crossed by the beam on which it swung.

From the outside, the Mortal Man wore much of the look of the country inn — black-and-white Tudor timbering and thatched roof. Inside, one of these beams was in the process of being hammered to splinters by a spindly young man up on a ladder. As Melrose looked left to the lounge and right to the saloon bar, he thought the inn had been caught in the middle of being taken apart or put back together again. Wood paneling leaned against the bar, a gold-framed mirror sprightly with cupids was in sore need of resilvering, a stained-glass window looked recently boarded up.

The hall was appropriately dark, with its thread of turkey carpet running along to a gloomy staircase. A porcelain leopard appeared to be guarding the dining room to his left. To his right a half-moon-shaped desk was attended by a burly man who was arguing with an unseen opponent, and through the archway to Melrose's left, the inn's personnel came and went — a maid with saucy curls demanding her wages of the gentleman behind the counter, who turned her back with vituperative rhetoric; a woman with a saucepan; a boy with a notebook followed by a muddy, hybrid hound; a thin girl with a mop and a slack look both in face and dress.

The dog welcomed the new guest by grabbing his trouser cuff and hanging on for dear life until the owner rousted him with a kick. Nathan Warboys (for so he had introduced himself) then stood with his arms splayed over the counter under a sign reading *Reception*, with the intention of giving Melrose a hearty one by letting him in on the family secrets.

"And my Sally. It's a treat, it really is, and 'er comin' in night after night lookin' like the leavin's of a dogfight. Thought that'un 'ud stay on the shelf, I did, but no, she's got t'be gettin' up t'mischief just like the other. 'Ang about, 'ang about, now. Got to sign this, it's the law, mate." Whereupon he thwacked a card down for Melrose to fill in, and hit the bell with such force it sprang from the counter. This was by way of summoning the young lad with the terrier panting with the expectation of another go at the ankle. During their trudge up the narrow staircase, whose creaks and crepitations echoed the sign outside, the boy introduced himself as William Warboys. The dog's name was Osmond. Midway in this tortured ascent of a staircase only fit for one, Osmond had hitched his steel jaw to the toe of Melrose's shoe and no manner of shaking could dislodge him; to lift the shoe was to lift Osmond, who hung as tenaciously as a high-wire artist without a net. When William swung the bag at the dog, it

71

slid from his hands and slapped Melrose on the shin on its dive down the dark tunnel of stairs.

Looking out from under the dripping thatch of the Mortal Man, Melrose was still rubbing his shin, and wondering if the tibia was in one piece. There was an unfamiliar rasping sound coming from his knee joint, an echo of the gallows sign.

He saw that the dull rain hadn't stopped, nor the fog lifted. The pavements were unpeopled, the green across the way uninhabited except for some geese and swans gliding on the pond, their white feathers threading in and out of the fog like graveclothes. The Norman church at the green's center looked buckled up and riveted shut. He made out the dimly lit windows of a cafe and a cluster of cottages with the same thatched roofs of the inn, all so close they looked stitched together.

Lucinda St. Clair had told him he would be collected for drinks at seven. He was glad it was drinks and not tea, for he was drinking that right now. He had not ordered it, but it had been brought nonetheless by the shapeless Sally Warboys, crockery dancing on the tray in her uncertain hands, tea slopping out from the pot and wetting the napkin. Even after she had set it down, tea dripped and china jangled, as if moved by a tremor of fear that Sally would take it up again. Melrose felt that the Warboyses, unable to direct their energy or even contain it, had unleashed it into the air, where it had then been absorbed by chairs, tables, glass, and cutlery. And now all of them were emitting it in nervous little jibs and jerks. Probably, he thought, it would all lead up to some Poe-esque denouement, where the Mortal Man, like the house of Usher, would be rent and fall apart, shuddering into dust. Every whack of the hammer on the floor below, every bellow of a Warboysian voice, told him this fancy must be so.

Hard on the heels of Sally came Mrs. Warboys, a stubby woman who moved like an eggbeater in fits and starts of stirring the log in the little fireplace, sending a burning particle onto the threadbare rug, which flamed up. They managed between them to stomp out the fire, but in the excitement Mrs. Warboys dropped the poker on Melrose's arch. She apologized and went about whipping a dresser set into place, sending the two glasses there crashing to the floor. Assuring him that Bobby would clean that up, she jerked together the muslin curtains and tore out one end of the rod so that the whole thing drooped pitifully. Her work done, she would now send up Bobby to undo it.

Up came Bobby with the hammer in his hand and a determined look on his face. He would certainly beat that curtain rod back into place, he said, until Melrose convinced him that he had a migraine headache and didn't care who looked in the window, anyway. Thwarted in his dedication to his hammer, Bobby shot Melrose a dark look and left.

Bobby's place was taken by William, who came with notebook and pencil like a plumber to give an estimate on fixing the toilet. From the bathroom came a tearing sound and a thump: William had slipped in the water from the overflowing toilet and fallen in the bathtub, taking the shower curtain with him in an attempt to keep his balance.

Melrose was beginning to wonder if a stay at the Mortal Man was so short-lived that each member of the family had to see the guest at least once before he died.

When the door had slammed behind William, Melrose thought that must be all of them, until he heard the scratching at the bottom of the door.

His welfare, he saw, depended upon his getting out.

There was little to see in the dark beyond the saloon bar's window, but Melrose thought it a safe place to stand, for if he suddenly toppled perhaps some passerby would see him and go for help. Fog drifted in threads round the street lamp, and lay like a canopy over the pavement, giving an oddly truncated look to the person wading through it, a tall man in a muffler and deerstalker. His face was long and sad and the pouches under the eyes reminded Melrose of Osmond. He shook Melrose's hand and introduced himself unhappily as St. John St. Clair, Lucinda's father. Perhaps it was having to trip over that name that made St. John St. Clair look so sad and grave.

They walked across the road to the large old car and once in it, St. John St. Clair began as if no time were to be lost in filling in the gaps in Melrose's store of knowledge about pickles. He was, apparently, a pickle baron, and was quite trenchant in his observations of the hopelessness of such a suzerainty. Not a good year for gherkins, seemed to be the top and bottom of it. He said this while grinding the very stuffing out of the gearbox of his ancient Morris.

St. Clair slapped the gearshift with the heel of his hand and the car lurched forward and they darted away from the curb. A patch of ice spun them sideways and slapped Melrose against the dashboard. St. Clair nearly strangled the wheel getting the Morris back on course without missing a beat in his pickle-talk.

Melrose sighed and mumbled and rubbed his shoulder. As he wondered if he'd leave Somers Abbas alive, he tried to be sympathetic. To have three unmarried daughters (so St. Clair had gravely informed him) all living under one's roof and to have devoted one's time and talents to pickles were perhaps not cheering thoughts for a winter's night.

10

B Y the time the Morris slid to a stop in front of the
Steeples, had Melrose had any stock in Shrewsbury
Pickles and Fine Relishes he would have called his
broker immediately, so grim were St. John St. Clair's prog-
nostications for the fate of his company. Perhaps the dark
months ahead (for so his host painted them) goaded him into
several flirtations with danger on the roads: they had only just
missed a collision with a wagon, an overhanging willow, and
a stone wall; and now the car had shaken the snow from the
privet hedge and nearly toppled an urnful of frozen stalks
that sat at the edge of the broad steps.

Definitely a Warboysian ride, he thought, as he swept a bit
of boxwood from his coat and a twig from his shoe and followed St. John St. Clair up wide iced-over steps inviting
death.

Sybil St. Clair rose to greet him, hands outstretched
and — given her dress — flags flying. The frock seemed to
consist largely of loose ends and scarves that looked about to
flutter off through the long drawing room. Melrose could see
that it had been a very handsome room with rosewood pan-

eling and an Adam ceiling. "Had been" because Sybil, who fancied herself a decorator, had refurbished it in the Art Deco style: there was entirely too much of blue glass and green marble. He remembered now that she had quite an extensive clientele eager for her services. He couldn't truly imagine anyone with any taste going to Sybil, who managed to put together rooms that reminded him of old cinemas. Indeed, she herself put him in mind of an old cinema star, with her frock of scarves and winged hairdo totally wrong for her plump face.

He could do nothing but take her two ringed hands in his own and accept their affectionate little squeeze as if he were an old and very dear friend. With her whispery sort of speech, Sybil St. Clair had a way of fashioning intimacy out of the briefest acquaintance.

Fortunately the St. Clair daughters did not share their mother's tendency to rush and gush, Lucinda being too well bred and shy, and the others too haughty and holy in turn. The middle girl was named Divinity, and she sat pale and righteous by the fireplace on a hard chair; the youngest was Pearl, who kept herself on display on a giltwood fauteuil. Melrose wondered if the mother had meant to put a price on one head and a wimpel on the other. Pearl fingered a very long and very costly strand of them, and Divinity offered a limp hand and a lopsided smile probably meant to suggest that this little gathering was beneath her heavenly office.

It was unfortunate that Lucinda, a good-natured and honest girl, had got her father's long face and mournful eyes. And her dress was hardly flattering to her, though it might have been to her father's business; it was an ugly shade of gherkin green that, in the firelight, reflected up and deepened her sallow complexion.

Said Sybil to Melrose, "We did so want our neighbors, the Winslows, to come. But they couldn't make it. We try to do what we can to help." Sybil sighed and took an intricately decorated canapé from an Art Nouveau tray.

Before Melrose could ask why their neighbor was in need of help, St. John St. Clair said, "It would be nice if she were nearer." He passed a critical eye over the canapés and selected two, which he put on his small plate. "— or if someone were nearer. I don't know why we need all of this land." He sighed.

"Good heavens, Sinjin, *you're* the one who wanted to buy here. *You're* the one who wanted land, you said."

"*Good* land, yes," said St. Clair.

"What do you mean? It's perfectly good land." Sybil offered Melrose a grating little laugh as if assuring him their land was as good as anybody's.

"We can't grow anything properly. Peters is always telling me that nothing will grow in this soil."

"Don't be ridiculous. We've a perfectly *beautiful* garden. Marion was remarking on it just the other day —"

"It is the Winslow garden that is perfectly beautiful, my dear. Not ours. And of course poor Marion would say that, she is the soul of kindness. Her floribunda would win ribbons. All we can grow is creepers because they seem to withstand mildew and black spot very well, of which we have an ample supply." He said this with a sort of resignation that bespoke long acquaintance with the vicissitudes of blight and black spot. Then he bit into his cucumber sandwich, frowned at it, and with a sad headshake returned it to his plate.

"Oh, Lord! Both of you," said Pearl, adjusting a little pillow behind her back. "I doubt Mr. Plant wants to hear about our garden and land!" Which sounded more sensible than he expected Pearl to be until she added, "I'm sure Mr. Plant has gardens of his own."

"I'm sure he has, too, and better," said St. John, rather sadly. "Can't I freshen your drink, Mr. Plant —?"

"Thank you."

"— although I doubt very much you care for more gin. It's really not up to standard. The whiskey might be better. A little." He raised the whiskey decanter.

"The gin seems fine, thanks."

St. Clair raised a curious eyebrow. "Really? Well . . ." With some doubt he went about refilling the glasses as he continued talking about gardens here and there. "Of course your gardens in Northants would be considerably finer than ours —"

Melrose laughed. "Now there you are absolutely wrong, Mr. St. Clair. Sussex is the place for gardens. Always has been."

Handing Melrose his glass and reseating himself he said, "Oh, yes indeed. Certain parts of Sussex. But here in Somers Abbas the wet just drowns everything in its path." He tasted his fresh drink and frowned.

"That's ridiculous, Sinjin. And let's stop all this talk about *gardens* —"

"Heavens, yes," said Divinity, as if the word had come down from there.

"We did want the Winslows to come this evening —"

In the midst of studying over the label on the bottle of malt whiskey, St. John said, "I can understand why poor Marion would not want to socialize —"

"Poor Marion?" said Lucinda. "I should think it would be poor *David.*"

Sybil leaned forward and said to Melrose eagerly, "You heard what happened?"

"Really, Mother," said Divinity. "We shouldn't be talking common gossip."

Replacing the bottle with a frown, St. John said, "I've nothing against gossip, nor rumor, just so long as there's no truth in it and, therefore, cannot damage a reputation through repetition." He sighed. "But in this case, one does wonder. David Marr has always been unlucky — well, but haven't they all? The unluckiest family I believe I know, even more so than my own. Edward had a bad marriage, didn't he, my dear? Wasn't her name Rose? And didn't she leave him flat? Yes, I believe she did. And there was the little girl, poor little Phoebe, who was killed in that accident. And we mustn't forget Hugh. Hugh is Marion's husband, but we seldom see him. Hugh keeps to himself in that house in Knightsbridge and does not come down." St. John sat there, sinking deeper into gloom and finally stopping, like a man in a cave striking match after match, only to watch each one, and finally the last one, gutter out.

"Hugh does not keep *precisely* to himself," said Sybil. "I don't think Marion will *have* him down —"

"Oh, but we shouldn't go talking about that, my dear. We do not absolutely *know* that Hugh has other women. Not more than one, surely. And now here's poor David, with his fiancée murdered."

"He wasn't *engaged* to her, Daddy," said Lucinda.

"How do you know that?" asked her mother.

"Marion told me. She met her the one time. At the London house. David and some others were there for drinks."

"You mean the girl was at the house?"

"Well, what's so odd about that?" asked Lucinda, incensed. "He was going round with her."

St. John was closely inspecting the plate of canapés. "It is too bad about those boys; they both should settle down. I don't care for this fish paste; it's not the brand we usually buy."

Pearl had left her seat to arrange herself before the fire, catching whatever she could of the leftover light spilling from Divinity's person. "Edward was supposed to have come this evening. He was to bring me his new book."

"But I've got it, my dear," said her father. "I believe it's in the car."

She pouted. Apparently, since Edward Winslow had not

79

come with it, better it had not come at all. Now she would have no excuse for running to the Winslow house and collecting it herself. "Mr. Winslow is a writer?"

"A poet, yes," said St. John. "Unfortunately, poetry doesn't sell."

Sybil laughed. "It hardly needs to, with all of their money. Now, Mr. Plant, I'm sure you'll reconsider and stay with us."

This so caught Melrose by surprise he hadn't time to muster his forces before she continued.

"There's simply no reason why you should stay at the Mortal Man when we've a half-*dozen* perfectly lovely rooms."

"He wants to stay there, Mother," said Lucinda. She looked unhappily at Melrose as her mother continued, obviously deaf to any attempt to scotch her plan.

"Oh, Lucinda, don't be ridiculous. You think you're putting us out," she said to Melrose, "but you aren't at all and I can't imagine why Lucinda didn't insist you stay here —"

"Mother, he doesn't *want* —"

"Lucinda, please. I've had the maid fix up a room with a perfectly marvelous fireplace —"

"It smokes," said St. Clair, putting his whiskey aside.

Melrose was actually becoming alarmed when he saw Sybil St. Clair ring for their servant. "The inn is fine, Mrs. St. Clair, please don't —"

"It does *not* smoke, Sinjin. The fireplace was seen to by Parkins just this summer —"

"Parkins doesn't do a good job, my dear."

"Mother —"

"The Mortal Man is an architectural gem," said Melrose quickly, as the servant Peters came through the double doors. "And as I told Lucinda —"

"We can just have Peters get your things for you. He can take the car."

"I told Lucinda" — Melrose was practically strangling his whiskey glass — "I've a special interest in inns, and the Mortal Man is a remarkable example of the old coaching inn —"

"I shouldn't think so," said St. Clair, who was staring up at the ceiling. "I shouldn't think the Mortal Man was much of an example of anything."

"It's no trouble at all Mr. Plant. And it won't take more than a moment. Peters —"

Melrose's paean to the English inn rushed ahead (he hoped) of Peters's leaving for it. "You see I *always* stay at an inn whenever there's the chance. As a matter of fact, I'm doing a sort of study of the English inn. Why, only the church has a richer history —"

"Oh-ho!" said St. Clair, with a crimped little smile. "Not *our* St. Mary's I assure you —"

"— to sit before an open fire and see the copper catching the light; to drive through the coaching archway into the cobbled yard and imagine the strolling players of Elizabethan times —"

"Not the Mortal Man's, I shouldn't think. The milk-float lost a wing and got its sill torn off there; and as for strolling players, well . . . unless one thinks of the Warboyses in that way. They do tell me he sings. . . ."

Melrose hoped not. "The timbered frontage, the fittings, the cellars, the carved woodwork, the rafters and beams —"

"Dry rot and rising damp," said St. Clair, pleasantly.

Into this overlapping conversation came the ringing of a telephone from deep in the house, and Peters, duty calling him elsewhere, nodded and begged to answer the sound.

Melrose leaned back, as breathless as if he'd run the mile, and feeling between the Warboyses and the St. Clairs like an object to be sent here and there, bag and baggage, dropped and collected, dumped and thumped on, and generally traded for a mess of pottage.

II

BREAKFAST was an occasion involving the usual hazards. He should have known that the juice would spill, the porridge tilt, and the mackerel slide and taken the precaution of wearing a bib.

As Melrose ate the mackerel he had rescued from his lap, he listened to the keening sound coming from the kitchen. It increased and diminished each time Sally Warboys slapped open the door to bring him another dish. It might have been the screech of a kettle forgotten on the hob or the youngest Warboys (there was a baby, too) with some intractable demand. There had already come from the kitchen the clatter of breaking crockery and the usual assortment of angry voices as the Warboyses took their battle stations.

Sally Warboys, in washboard gray, came out of the kitchen in her half-run, half-walk, to deposit Melrose's pot of tea, which struck the table edge and sent hot water splashing down the cloth, just missing his hand by an inch. To call the Warboyses accident-prone would have been to do them an injustice, he thought; there was something here that smacked of deeply rooted tribal behavior.

As he blotted a bit of grease from his cuff, he noticed that the lad who had done porter duty and dropped his bag had come into the dining room. This room was undergoing a Warboysian transformation, with Bobby up on his ladder swinging his hammer.

William sat at the table across the room. In another this might have been called a "respectful distance," but in a Warboys it looked like the first step in a campaign from which Melrose doubted he would emerge the victor. The boy sat stiff and staring, with a gaze so intent it pried Melrose's eyes up like a lever. He was assisted in this scrutiny by Osmond, who lay on the floor with his head on his paws, eyes unflinching. Melrose assumed this was tactical necessity on the dog's part, like a falling back of troops readying for a surprise attack. He wondered if there had ever been guests at the Mortal Man before he happened along, for none of them seemed to know what to make of one — whether to hold him hostage or kill him outright.

"Good morning," said Melrose cheerily. "It's William, isn't it?"

The boy responded swiftly and came over to the table. He sat down and placed a small notebook and pencil, or the stub of a pencil, beside the plate of buttered crumpet that Melrose had not ordered. When Melrose invited him to have one, he pulled the plate and marmalade pot over with an alacrity that would have made one think he'd been on prison rations up to now.

Melrose pointed toward his notebook. "Are you writing something?"

Mouth full of marmaladed crumpet, William nodded energetically. The Warboyses had trained themselves never to waste a gesture, apparently.

"What?"

83

"A story." He mounded some currant jelly on another crumpet. "I wrote one once and it won a prize."

"It did?"

"Ten pound. Mum bought a new frock."

"That's very generous of you, to give her your prize money."

"I didn't. She took it."

Since there was no rancor in the boy's tone, Melrose assumed that this was the usual Warboys transaction. "What's this story about?"

"Chillington's has this contest going and there's fifty pound prize money —"

Melrose frowned. "The only Chillington I know is a brewer."

William nodded. "They're the ones that have all of them pubs with squirrels in them —"

As William paused to put another dollop of jam on his crumpet, Melrose tried to imagine a pub filled with squirrels.

The boy continued. "You know, the Squirrel and Pickle, the Squirrel and Mouse . . . everyone has a squirrel. So they want a story about a squirrel they can put a little bit of on their beermats each month. Here —"

He reached in his pocket and brought out a square of cardboard, somewhat stained. There was a picture of a squirrel sitting snugly inside its tree cave, wrapped in a checkered bathrobe, reading.

"It's fifty pound prize money. Mum wants to put heat in the toilet. I hate it when I'm still sleepy and have to go down to the toilet. This morning there was ice on the chain."

"That *is* pretty rum."

"Can I have some tea?"

"What? Oh, yes. It still seems hot." Melrose took the precaution of pouring. "What have you got so far?" He nodded toward William's notebook.

William stopped slurping his tea and opened the notebook.

84

" 'Sidney reared back. There was blood on his anorak. The strange shape disappeared into the bushes.' Sidney's the squirrel."

"An exciting story. Where did the blood come from?"

"I don't know."

"Is he dead? Or dying?"

"I don't know."

Melrose wondered if this was the way Polly Praed wrote her mysteries.

"Maybe his friend Weldon is dead," said William, licking marmalade from his knife.

"Who's Weldon?"

"A weasel."

It was beginning to sound like an X-rated version of *The Wind in the Willows.* "Did somebody kill Weldon?"

"I don't know. Probably. It could have been with a knife," he said, using his own for demonstration purposes.

Melrose moved his chair back. "Well, what's the body doing in the bushes?"

"I don't know."

Better that a Warboys work off the inherited tendency toward destruction even if his narrative did have a few holes in it. "I must say you've not much to be going on with. Anyway, you might be quite rich some day if you keep to your story-writing."

William said he cared nothing for riches; just that he would like some heat in the toilet.

"That seems reasonable. I wish you'd stop playing with that knife."

"I had a weasel once. It's out back. With the others."

" 'The others'?" Melrose was beginning to wonder if this was not an inn but a Hitchcock motel.

"That's right. In the graveyard. They die and I bury them." William dusted his hands of death and crumbs and

85

rousted Osmond. "There's a lady and man wants to see you."
He nodded backwards. "Out there in the hall."

"You mean they've been out there all of this *time?*"

"Told me to give you a message." William had got up,
clearly bored and with an eye on the headier environs of the
kitchen.

Melrose was on his feet. "What message?"

William studied his notes. "Don't remember. But you can
just as well ask them." And he was off, followed by Osmond,
who took a swipe at Melrose's ankle before his paws click-
clicked off.

The man was Edward Winslow, and Melrose had come in
on the tail end of a conversation he was having with Nathan
Warboys, who left for the bangings and hammerings of the
saloon bar.

They had come, said Lucinda, to collect Melrose for morning coffee. David was down from London.

Her expression when she spoke the name David reaffirmed
Melrose's belief that love must surely be blind. He did not
have to meet David Marr to wonder how any young woman
could prefer another man to Edward Winslow.

He was extremely handsome — hair the color of tawny
port, eyes like burning brandy. Perhaps it was their proximity
to the bar and Nathan's fixation on his happy family of ales
and liquors that put Melrose in mind of these spiritous meta-
phors. But the coloring was Winslow's, nonetheless. And the
rest of him lived up to that richness. He was the type who'd
be any man's mirror: you couldn't help looking at him without wanting to straighten your tie and curse your tailor.
There was nothing fashionable about Winslow, and certainly
nothing trendy. In his dark gold cashmere jacket and plain
brown silk tie, he was the paradigm of unself-conscious ele-

gance. He would wear a trench coat over evening clothes and think nothing of it.

And that the man could find conversational possibilities in a Warboys monologue was a mark of extraordinary inventiveness, even for a published poet.

As Edward Winslow smiled and shook his hand, Melrose could understand why Pearl nearly strangled on her necklace when Edward had failed to present his book personally.

Though thoughts of strangling were perhaps not in the best of taste, Melrose thought, as they walked out into the cold and the wet to Edward's car — a black BMW, of course, the Savile Row of cars. Not ostentatious, just well made and made to stick it. Melrose slid down in the back seat as the doors clunked shut, thinking of his Flying Spur, his Silver Ghost. Well, perhaps they could talk about poetry.

12

DAVID Marr was in the library getting himself drunk at ten o'clock. He was standing by a commode of lacquer and gilt bronze that looked as if it should have been in a museum instead of doing service as a drinks table.

Indeed, the entire Winslow library looked like a place in which Marshall Trueblood could have happily expired. If the house had seemed depressingly stark from the outside — rock-faced granite with all the weight of medievalism upon it overlooking a choked and tangled woods — this severity was not repeated here in the library. An Italian marble fireplace was flanked by panels of bas-relief; the upholstery was Italian cut-velvet; the wallpaper and draperies, William Morris; around the walls were family portraits, oils, watercolors, Belgian tapestries. Melrose would have liked to spend several hours with these bound volumes in arched recesses, and a few more hours studying the paintings and portraits. Beside a Belgian tapestry was what looked like a Pissaro, beside that a Millet. It was a warm and peaceful scene of a thatched-roofed inn, quite lovely, he thought, in spite of his present doubts that thatched-roofed inns could contribute to the general happiness of the world.

David Marr held up a bottle of vodka. "Care for a saltwater?" he said, as soon as they were introduced.

Melrose smiled. "Never heard of it."

"Two goes of vodka, same of ginger, splash of grenadine." He poured more than two measures of vodka into his glass. "It's romantic, makes me think of the sea. Of course"— he set down the bottle —"I leave out the grenadine. Actually, I leave out the ginger, too. Sure you won't join me? Ned? Lucinda?"

"No, thanks," said Edward Winslow. "I see you switched from brandy."

David Marr sank down on one of a pair of Queen Anne sofas, sliding down on his spine. He was a handsome man, and he looked like his nephew despite the difference in coloring. Edward was fair; he was dark, eyes glitter-black, chips of the night sky, intense. Too intense to make the drunken-playboy manner believable, the slouching position on the sofa anything but self-conscious.

As he measured out his drink with a frown of concentration, David said, "Lucinda says you're staying at the Mortal Man. And here you are, alive to tell about it." He put down the bottle, turned, and smiled at Melrose.

"Here I am, yes. Aren't people always swearing out complaints or suing them, or something? So far I've had three narrow escapes — my carpet very nearly caught fire, my suitcase fell on me, and my breakfast landed in my lap. The place is a minefield. But the Warboyses take it all in stride and soldier on."

"No one's sued them yet that we know of," said Lucinda. "But I don't think they get many overnight guests. How about that coffee, then?"

"Yes, I'd love some coffee. As for the guests: you might have seen them go in; but did you see them come out?"

David laughed, then asked Edward, "Where the devil are the servants?"

"Bunburying," said Ned Winslow, smiling.

"What, again?"

"What's bunburying?" asked Lucinda.

"Bunbury was Algie's mythical old friend; don't you remember? Anytime he wanted to leave London, he'd say old Bunbury was ill. Well, I shouldn't complain, I suppose I'm doing it myself. Anything to get out of London. I expect Lucinda's told you about what happened." He looked at Melrose, got up again, and headed for the vodka. "I'm glad to help police with their inquiries —" He smiled. "— but it's getting tiresome. If not actually dangerous."

"There's not a bit of evidence, David," said Lucinda. "They haven't found anything yet."

David stopped the brandy decanter in midair and said to her, "I like that 'yet.' It's not particularly reassuring to think tomorrow they'll find my fingerprints smeared all over Hays Mews."

"They won't," said Ned shortly, as he went to poke up the fireplace. He turned and rested his arm along the green marble, much in the manner in which he was posed in the portrait above. It was a portrait of the three of them — the woman there looked enough like David Marr to be his twin. Melrose could not put his finger on what was so compelling about the painting: it was perhaps what it said of the relationship between the three. Melrose wondered where the husband was. Perhaps St. Clair was right. "They won't because you had nothing to do with it," said Ned.

"If only the *police* would see it that way."

"They will."

David rolled his head, resting against the back of the sofa, back and forth, sighing. "Well, not to worry. It's just a damned nuisance being told not to leave the country. Why does one always want to leave the country when one is told not to? Why does one always have the urge to visit Monte Carlo or the Himalayas when someone insists one stay at home? Why —?"

"The Himalayas might do you good. The last time you were in Monte, Mother had to send money."

There was great good humor in Ned Winslow's tone. Melrose had the impression they all indulged one another's weaknesses.

David shrugged. "Maybe I shall do a Bunbury. Incidentally, Marion is having a lie-down; she's not feeling well. I hope it's not because of me. Where's the coffee, Lucinda?"

Lucinda went as she was bid, Edward to help her. Melrose wondered how she could think she had a chance with this man, who watched her departing back without a flicker of interest. It was too bad; Edward and Lucinda seemed a suitable couple, though he wondered why "suitability" had anything to do with it; love was not a well-cut suit of clothes.

"Lucinda says you're quite an authority on the French Romantics." He smiled. "About which I know sod-all. But did you know Edward is a poet." David rose with his glass; this time, however, he headed for the bookshelves rather than the commode. He drew out the volume Melrose recognized as Edward Winslow's. "You should read it."

"I have; Lucinda gave me the copy intended, I fear, for Pearl St. Clair."

David laughed. "I'm sure Pearl didn't mind; that relieves her temporarily of having to pretend she can read." He leafed through the book, and said, "It's so simple, Ned's poetry. I guess I mean old-fashioned or something. " *'Where have you gone to, Elizabeth Vere* —?' " David snapped the book shut, replaced it, moved to the lacquer commode. "Ned isn't very happy. He should get married again."

"I'm a little surprised you'd think *that* an antidote for happiness." Melrose smiled. "In their refusal to gossip, the St.

91

Clairs did manage to let slip that your nephew was once married . . . to a woman who was, well—"

"Not terribly reliable. No, Rose was not reliable at all." His smile this time was decidedly chilly, a crack in ice. "He's very deep, Ned. Not at all like me. I'm about this deep." He held up the bottle with the remaining measure of vodka.

"Oh, I'd say you're a great deal alike." Melrose looked up at the portrait above the marble mantel. "The artist who painted that seems to think so, too."

"Paul Swann. Well, he's known us for a long time, but I don't see that in the painting, really."

"He's a friend of yours?"

"Yes; he lives near me in Shepherd Market. Paul was in the Running Footman that night. Only he'd left, I think. If my memory of events weren't so clouded by this" — he held up the glass — "it would be easier. Fortunately, there's that telephone call to my sister."

Fortunately, thought Melrose.

After coffee, they stood in the entry hall, a vast expanse of walnut paneling and sweeping staircase. Ned Winslow was to return Melrose to the Mortal Man; Lucinda was to stay behind to keep David company. The only company that David seemed interested in was the fresh bottle of vodka he'd found.

It was down that staircase that the woman in the portrait came. She was tall and dark like her brother, her hair a shimmery mahogany, swept up on her head in a carelessly done knot, dressed in a velvet morning robe of deep sable brown.

If this was poor Marion, there was something to be said for the ennobling effects of misfortune.

Inclining her head toward Melrose, she apologized for not coming down earlier. "I have a fierce headache, Mr. Plant. I hope you'll pardon me." That she remained standing on the stairs testified to her intention of going up them again as quickly as possible. Still, she struck Melrose more as a withdrawn, distant woman than a cold one. And very well bred. After all, she hadn't needed to come down at all; she could merely have conveyed her regrets, or indeed said nothing. He thought she gave Lucinda a chilly look, probably for having gotten her son to invite this stranger here in the first place.

Melrose wished she would stay; he would have liked to get more of an impression of her, which was why she was leaving, probably. In the circumstances, he supposed she thought the briefer the acquaintance, the better.

"Good Lord, Marion," said David, "why do you give that layabout couple leave to go when you're not feeling well?"

She smiled, but the smile did little toward warming the high, cold brow. "Too tired to pour your own brandy, David?" There was no real recrimination in the tone. "Don't worry, they said they'd be back today or tomorrow."

"I don't think you should be here alone and fending for yourself, that's all."

"Well, now I have you to fend for me." The humor in her voice was mixed with concern.

The expression on David Marr's face was strange, looking up the staircase. A strained, almost rapt expression, as if he were looking but not hearing.

Indeed, Melrose thought, all of them in this moment of silence and studied attention might have been grouped here, sitting for the portrait in the library.

A telephone rang in the distance, and Edward made a move toward a door across the wide hallway.

"Oh, hell!" said David. "That's the police, I'd bet my last drink on it." As Edward disappeared through the door, David called, "Don't answer it, Ned, let the damned answering machine do it. That's what it's there —"

He must have realized what he'd said the moment the

93

words were out, for he broke off abruptly and polished off the rest of his drink.

There goes the alibi, thought Melrose.

"Is this the garden that Mr. St. Clair seems to feel is the happiest in Sussex?" asked Melrose. They had come to the end of a path that led through beeches to an informal garden at one side of which ran a long, serpentine wall overgrown with moss, covered in wisteria, and under the shelter of over-hanging laburnum whose branches dripped rain.

Edward Winslow laughed. "Yes, this is it. It might be larger than his, but it's hardly impressive. Still, try to tell Sinjin that. If he owns it, it's dreadful. Modesty run amok. He's a nice man, though. Actually, I'm surprised that John manages to keep things in such good shape." Ned waved to the gardener, who seemed to be hacking away at a monkey-puzzle vine in the distance. "Crusty old beggar thinks he's Gertrude Jekyll; still, he does a good job out here. You see the garden wall there?" Ned nodded toward the laburnum grove. "It's our family plot. Several great-aunts and my grandpar-ents are buried there. And Phoebe."

"That must have been pretty dreadful."

Ned was silent for a moment, staring at the little grave-yard. "We all loved Phoebe so much."

"I'm sure. I've never had children."

"Nor I. My wife didn't want any. Rose didn't much care for the country here. Actually, she didn't much care for me, I think, and the proximity to Mother. Mother can be, as you might guess, a formidable person. But she never interfered, never. It's just her presence. She can move us about, you know."

There was no resentment in his tone. Melrose could well imagine Marion Winslow "moving them about."

"One day I woke up," continued Ned, "and she was gone. I don't know where; she had talked about the States, about Canada. But she didn't bother leaving a note. So I don't know where, do I?"

"*Where have you gone to . . .?*" Melrose could not help but think of the poem.

Ned looked from the graves to the wall to the sky. "There was another man, I'm sure. Didn't even know she'd been seeing him. Didn't even know *him.* That's how blind a poet can be."

"Or how blind a wife can be." Ned Winslow gave him the impression of a man who'd accepted the past as nothing but a missed train on a wasted journey; he would stand on the platform or travel through life with his cases empty.

Melrose had been carrying the small book of poems in his pocket and drew it out. He thumbed through the pages until he came to the poem David had mentioned.

"It's very old-fashioned, as David says. Rhyme, meter, quatrains."

"There is something to be said for what you call 'old-fashioned.' Here it is." Melrose read:

> "*Where have you gone to, Elizabeth Vere,*
> *Far from the garden, the blossom, the bole?*
> *Rain glazes the stream —* "

Melrose looked off toward a small stream partly shrouded in ice that meandered close to the garden wall. "It sounds like this place. Was it meant for someone in particular?" He returned the book to his pocket.

Ned stood looking off toward the grove of beeches, frowning. "A writer never really knows who he means, does he? Perhaps that really is blindness, not to know." He changed the subject. "If you knew David, you'd know it's impossible for him to have strangled that girl. Anyway, there's no reason, no motive. Ivy must've been killed by a mugger, some-

95

one like that. Wouldn't you think that the obvious answer?"

Ned Winslow looked at him as if Melrose were a magician who just might pull the right rabbit out of the hat. "If that were the case, the killer certainly didn't want much. There appears to be no motive."

"There's none with David, either. He had no motive."

Melrose thought of what Jury had told him of the women, Sheila Broome and Ivy Childess. " 'Then glided in Porphyria — ' "

Ned reached out to pull a weed from between the stones of the wall. "That's an odd allusion. If you're thinking of David as a Porphyria's lover type —" Ned laughed. "Believe me, he hadn't any passionate attachment to Ivy Childess." He turned those molten umber eyes on Melrose. "And what about Porphyria herself?"

"Porphyria? She struck me as being rather pathetic."

"She struck me as being a bit of a tramp," said Ned, with a smile.

13

"WHAT *is* the matter with you, Dolly? You've been in a sulk — well, not that perhaps — on edge, more, ever since you came here." And as Kate set the cup of tea and a toasted tea cake before her sister, she wondered once again why Dolly *had* come. Her visits up to now had been in the spring or summer, especially summer, the clement weather and quieter ocean allowing her to show off her near-perfect figure. "Job? Man? What?"

Dolly looked up at her sister. "Nothing's wrong. I'm just a bit under the weather is all." She set about cutting up her tea cake.

"And speaking of being here . . . you know you're always welcome, of course . . . but why now?"

Dolly sighed. "I should think that would be obvious. It's the Christmas holiday, isn't it?"

Kate watched her lick the butter off her fingers, slowly, like a cat. Dolly moved with a languor that was also catlike and totally at odds with her temperament. The edginess of which Kate had just spoken was not unusual, except in its intensity.

"It's a man, isn't it?" With Dolly it usually was.

"No." She said nothing else as she pulled up the glove-leather high-heeled boots. She fitted a magnificent white fur Cossack hat to her head and shoved the ends of her hair up under it. She reminded Kate of a photo of a Russian spring, cold light shining on ice and snow.

"Where're you going?" Kate was clearing away her tea things.

"Only to Pia's."

That was another thing, thought Kate. Dolly was forever waiting for Fate to step in, always counting on the planets to tilt in her favor. Two years ago it had been the medium, and following her fall from grace, the astrologer and the reader of tarot. Pia, to whom Dolly was currently entrusting her future, was a clairvoyant with a reputation in Brighton for honesty. The astrologer had been safe. With all of the open doors in one's horoscope through which one's fate could exit, astrology generally *was* safe. Unfortunately, Pia Negra wasn't. She told her clients what she knew, good or bad. And in Dolly's case, Kate supposed it must be rather bad, for she often came back more nervous and anxious than when she'd left.

It must be a man, thought Kate once again. The wrong man, of course. Why was it Dolly, who could have probably any man she fancied, always chose the wrong one? Married, sometimes; too old, sometimes; sometimes both. Whenever she told Kate about one who sounded (at least to Kate) eminently suitable, Dolly sounded bored.

It occurred to Kate just then that it was Dolly, not she, who had been the loser, had been the unfortunate object of their father's obsessive love. He had left her a legacy of his two broken marriages, disastrous love affairs, frustrations. And then he had left her the means to get all of these things for herself. Dolly needed only to sit and be adored, like their mother, beautiful and, now, rich. Perhaps that was really the reason that Kate did not resent his leaving everything but the house to Dolly. Kate had always thought of herself as the prisoner of this house; but wasn't Dolly a prisoner of the wider world? Had her freedom been bought with a fence around it?

At least she had her television work to steady her, although perhaps it offered Dolly too much celebrity for her own good.

In that little role of hers, Dolly had probably entered into the fantasies of most of the men in London.

PART III

Garden Wall

14

THE parlor of Stella Broome's terraced house had a view across the street of a launderette and a Chinese restaurant and take-away called Mr. Wong and Son.

Jury sat on one of a pair of armchairs slipcovered in a design of fading chrysanthemums; the rug was garlanded in the center and the corners with roses; the wallpaper was an endless repetition of pagodas, Roman columns, and hanging gardens down whose walls trailed roses and wisteria. The apron that Stella Broome wore was patterned with camellias, and the ashtray she held in her lap gave off a woodsy odor.

She had, he suspected, the beginnings of emphysema, given the way she hacked when she inhaled. He was glad Wiggins wasn't here to see her light one cigarette from the stub of another. She was a woman in her fifties, overweight and careless of her looks. Her face was round and the skin tight and slightly waxy, reflecting the camellia pattern of the apron.

It was depressing, this dead garden of a room, and as if to emphasize the fact that nothing moved or breathed, there were vases spotted here and there on tables and mantel filled with either plastic or paper or dried flowers.

Stella Broome had been talking about the death of her daughter: "I told her, didn't I? I told her she'd get into trouble, hitching rides like she did. But she wouldn't listen, not her." She shook her head and reclaimed her glass of sherry.

That she talked about the death as if it were an infraction of parental discipline suggested to Jury an attempt to bury the fact, to draw her daughter back — late perhaps, drunk perhaps, but back.

"No, I can't help. All I know is Sheila left here in the morning for work and said she'd got a ride to Bristol."

"From all we've found, she didn't seem to know anyone there," said Jury.

"Oh, that'd make no odds to Sheila. She just wanted to get away. She was always wanting to get away." Stella Broome poured another glass of sherry, pulled a tissue from the box beside a silver-framed photograph of Sheila.

"What about her friends, Mrs. Broome? The fellow she was going about with, for instance."

"I've told all this to police before. That commander or whatever he calls himself —"

"Divisional commander." Jury had to smile. From the way she spoke, Macalvie might have been pulling ranks out of a hat.

"Whatever. Harassment, that's what I call it." She lit another cigarette.

"Divisional Commander Macalvie is very thorough. And sometimes that might seem like harassment —" And sometimes is, he thought. "— but witnesses have been known to forget details that can come out if questions are asked over again." Especially if they're lying first time around. Though Jury didn't think the mother was lying, necessarily.

"Maybe," she said. She sounded doubtful. "Well, there's Gerald, Gerald Fox. That was her young man, such as he is."

She sniffed. "Though I will say he was cut up over her —"
Stella Broome pressed the wadded tissue to her mouth to
forestall a bout of tears.

It could have been that glassful of sherry, he thought, but
perhaps that merely helped release bottled-up feelings. He
wondered if the flowery sentiments of the room were not
some unconscious desire to express emotions she otherwise
repressed. He thought Stella Broome probably prided herself
on toughness. Her life must have been lonely; perhaps she
had to marshal all of her forces in order to defend herself
against this new onslaught. Hence the carping criticism.

"I wonder if I could have a little of that sherry?" asked
Jury. It might afford her a bit of companionship. He filled her
glass and went to the kitchen for another one. It gave her a
few minutes to weep without being stared at by Scotland
Yard.

"Thank you." She blew her nose. "Don't know what came
over me."

"You should let go more, Mrs. Broome." Inwardly, he
smiled. He sounded like Wiggins. He asked again about
Gerald Fox, feeling it was merely repetitive; Macalvie would
have covered that ground thoroughly.

"Yes, well, he was devoted to Sheila and she treated him
like he wasn't worth nothing. Felt sorry for him sometimes, I
did. That's the only reason she went up to London — to make
him jealous. Oh, I knew it was probably all lies, the men she
said she went out with. An old man with plenty of money,
used to call him her Sugar Daddy — that was one. She said
he'd come round to the flat to pick her up in his fancy car. If
that ain't something! Then there was a dancer in some West
End musical, fairy I'd bet; and —"

Jury interrupted. "Did she ever mention any names?"

"Guy-somebody. That was the dancer. Had a fancy car,
some foreign make. Anyone had a flash car Sheila'd just
swoon over. Flash cars and flash men, that was Sheila's style.

Well, she didn't have a license herself; I mean, they took it away from her for drink-driving. Far as I'm concerned, they should. Too much drinking these days, anyway." Mournfully, she looked at her glass. Perhaps she was thinking she hadn't set the best example; that she might have nudged Sheila off the straight and narrow herself. "If I'd of got married again, maybe Sheila wouldn't have been so wild. It needs a man to straighten out a girl like that. All those men she said courted her —"

Stella Broome pressed her fingertips to her forehead as if remembering gave her a headache. Finally, she shook her head. "All I know is Sheila'd talk and talk about these fellas, probably to Gerald, too, to make him jealous. I don't even know she was telling the truth. Why'd any rich man dance attendance on Sheila?"

Jury looked at the photograph sitting next to the sherry bottle. "She was very pretty." Pretty, in a tartish way, he thought. Too much makeup, bleached hair. What had Macalvie said — "bottled-in-blond"? Jury frowned. "You said something about an older man. What about him?"

"Him? Well, I don't know, exactly. When she'd start in like that, I'd just stop listening, sometimes. All those men she claimed she'd got on a string." Her forehead creased with the effort of thinking and she stopped rocking suddenly. "That lorry driver that picked her up. They let him go." Stella Broome wadded the handkerchief under her nose again and shivered.

"A waitress at the Little Chef saw her get out of the cab, and the artic pull away. Commander Macalvie was satisfied he had nothing to do with it."

"Well, it's past now. I don't know why police are raking it over again. It was some psycho picked her up. Some psycho."

"Yes, that's perfectly possible. But I'll tell you why we're raking it up, Mrs. Broome. There was a woman killed in

London, killed the same way your daughter was, with her own scarf."

She stopped rocking suddenly. "Oh, dear. Oh, that's terrible. You think it was the same person?"

"Because of the — method, it's just possible."

"But then it must be like I said. Some crazy."

"Did your daughter ever mention a David?"

"Not that I remember." She had taken another plunge or two into the sherry bottle; by now she was on her fourth or fifth. The words slurred slightly as she said, "Don't think she ever said that name." Stella seemed to be studying the wallpaper over Jury's shoulder; taking an imaginary walk through her botanical gardens, perhaps.

He waited for a moment to see if anything would occur to her. But she appeared to be rocking — and drinking — herself to sleep. Her head nodded like a flower on its stem. He got up and said, "Well, I'll be leaving now, Mrs. Broome. If you remember anything, anything at all, you'll get in touch, won't you?"

Her head snapped up and she shook herself. "Yes." She got up with considerable effort, steadying herself on the arm of the sofa. "But I ain't calling *him*, that commander or whoever he is." On their way to the door, she plucked the dried flowers from the table and ran her fingers over them, dusting them. "Where'll you be?"

Jury handed her a card. "New Scotland Yard. Just call this number, Mrs. Broome."

Now she seemed as reluctant to let him go as she had first been to have him stay. She kept looking and looking at the card as if it might be a lucky souvenir.

He did not like leaving her alone, but he couldn't stop here all day. And anyway there would always be another day to be faced. Jury looked round the room, at the dried bouquets, the walled gardens. A fragment of a poem came to him ... *Be still, the hanging gardens are a dream . . . that over Persian roses blew to kiss. . . .* What had "kiss" rhymed with? He could not remember where the lines came from or for whom the kiss was meant. A queen, he thought. What Sheila Broome had wanted to be, perhaps.

"I like your wallpaper. It's very . . . pretty," he added lamely, unable to find a proper word. "Good-bye, Mrs. Broome. Don't forget to call. You've been very helpful."

On the pavement, he looked back. She was still there, clutching the fake bouquet. He wondered if the younger Stella had clutched her bridal bouquet that way. Probably she had forgotten the happiness of such a day. And Sheila would never experience it.

Sergeant Wiggins was sitting in Macalvie's office drinking a cup of tea when Jury walked in.

"Where is he?" Jury nodded at the desk as big as a lake and afloat beneath a pile of papers, pens, and files.

"Forensics lab," said Wiggins. "To see someone named Thwaite." He sniffed and drew out his snowdrift of a handkerchief. "Only glad I'm not Thwaite."

"That makes two of us." Jury smiled and nodded toward the door. "Come on, let's go look for him."

A uniformed police constable directed them to the lab, which lay at the end of a confusion of corridors.

Once through the swinging doors to the last corridor, the directions became superfluous. Jury simply followed the sound of a voice, which finally gave way to an onslaught of invectives as they came nearer.

It wasn't a *him*, Jury saw, as he looked through the glass square set in the door. The woman barely came up to Macalvie's shoulder, but she was reaching for somewhere around the temples, given the way she was handling the microscope.

Macalvie, although not inordinately large, managed to gain six inches in height and girth by arranging himself like a cliffside in front of this object of his displeasure, whom Jury assumed to be Sergeant Thwaite. Given the tension in the room, any knock would probably have ricocheted off the door, so Jury simply pulled it open to hear the divisional commander going on about the ax.

Or Exe, as Jury now deciphered it.

". . . stand there and tell me all day, Gilly. We pulled him outta the Exe, but he wasn't *in* the effing Exe when he died —" Macalvie turned a fraction, caught sight of Jury, nodded by way of indifferent greeting, and returned to his argument.

"If I could just have that back now," said Gilly Thwaite, reaching for the microscope that Macalvie had wrested from her. "Do you think that specimen is going to stand up and salute?"

"You're not forensics, Gilly."

"Neither are you," she snapped.

Jury gave Thwaite a gold star for courage. She had brown curls as tight as springs and smoky gray eyes, the smoke no doubt funneling up from the fires within. One arm leaned on the black marble of the lab table, the hand fisted as if she could hardly wait to slug him. When she opened her mouth, Macalvie looked at it like a dentist with a drill.

He turned to Jury. "Let's get out of here; I need a drink," he said, pulling Wiggins along with him less by the hand on his shoulder than by the air sucked into any vacuum the D.C. left in his wake. He turned back to Sergeant Thwaite. "Would you just let Waliman do his job? Such as he is," Macalvie added sotto voce.

Gilly Thwaite, back to her microscope, looked up. "You'll just have to carry on without me."

108

"What a mouth. If she parked her tongue, it'd be on a yellow line," said Macalvie.

The pub was in the old part of Exeter in one of the Tudor buildings surrounding the cathedral green. The short trip in the police Cortina, with Macalvie cannoning from curb to curb around old Exeter's confines, was filled with various complaints and imprecations — he hadn't eaten in two days (Jury could believe it); he was going to quit and take off for America (Jury didn't believe it) and get a private license (ditto). "You've seen *The Maltese Falcon* once too often, Macalvie," said Jury as they pushed open the door of the Black Swan.

Macalvie peered through the glass-surround of the steam table and asked the girl to serve up a plate of cottage pie, sausages, peas, and bread. He inspected the plate to see if there was any more room, then said, "You guys want anything? They do good bar meals."

Jury shook his head; Wiggins asked the girl for a cheese toastie. Then, looking at Macalvie's piled-up plate, Wiggins shook his head. "Roughage, you need. Lettuce. You're probably like him." Wiggins nodded toward Jury. "Don't eat right for days and try to make up for it all in one go, and stuff yourself with the wrong things."

"You call a cheese toastie a *right* thing?" Still, he looked doubtfully at his plate and handed it back for some salad. Jury went to the other end of the bar for the drinks, thinking they must have some common ancestor. Macalvie, who took advice from no one but the archangel Gabriel, often took Wiggins's dissertations on health with more than a grain of salt.

It was salt they were arguing over when Jury sat down at the table. "Hypertension, hell." He snowed his cottage pie under with a half-dozen shakes. "So what happened with Stella Broome?" Macalvie made a little pool in the center of his potatoes.

"Nothing that you don't already know, I imagine. She talked about Sheila's boyfriends, a Gerald Fox, Guy somebody, others nameless. Unfortunately, Stella often tuned her out. What about this older man, the one Sheila called her Sugar Daddy?"

"That's a nil, Jury. Oh, there apparently *was* some old guy — old meaning twice her age. I chatted up Vera, the one she used to visit, about him. Too bad Vera didn't much care for Sheila, said she was a freeloader, and didn't pay a hell of a lot of attention to what she said either. But she did catch a glimpse of him standing beside his car. One of those Jag XJ6s. You know, the kind with the fourteen interchangeable roofs they issue cops like us. But we couldn't trace the guy."

Macalvie shook his head, poured on more salt. "It's all in the files. We talked to two, three hundred people. Relatives, relatives of relatives. Friends, friends of friends. Nothing."

Wiggins was depositing two or three drops of a neon-yellow fluid in his lager. "Couldn't this lorry driver, Riley, have picked her up later —?"

Macalvie was fascinated, watching the descent of the drops as he said, "It wasn't the driver. There wasn't the sign of any lorry parked in that woods. . . . Wiggins, what is that stuff?"

The lager had taken on an alien color. "Got something in my chest." He coughed and hit his chest with his fisted hand.

"Probably a Martian," said Macalvie, as he went back to his sausages. "The waitress said he set Sheila down at the edge of the road just after they left the Little Chef. The Higgins dame certainly wasn't lying and she seemed to be very observant. Though she couldn't identify the picture of David Marr we showed her. I mean, couldn't say yes or no, definitely. Just that he looked 'familiar.' That's something to go on. Only the constable I had go in there and grab a coffee, he's tall and dark like Marr — he looked 'familiar' too. I think she was trying too hard to be helpful."

Wiggins was following up the yellow drops with a small white envelope filled with pink crystals that he tapped into the lager. "It's just that you seem determined it was someone who knew Sheila. That silence inside the cafe sounds like maybe they'd been fighting and it flared up again when she got in the cab." He drank the lager, which had turned a turgid shade of pinkish yellow.

"What condition have you got, Wiggins, the Black Death? Yes, they knew each other, I still say they knew each other."

"The scarf doesn't suggest premeditation to me, Macalvie. It sounds spur of the moment."

Macalvie shrugged. "Not if he knew she always wore one. Most women do. Anyway, you think he couldn't have been carrying something else? Knife? Gun?"

Jury shook his head. "As I said, it could have been that Sheila just walked into the wrong place at the wrong time."

"You make it sound like Fate, Jury. I don't believe in star-crossed paths."

"It happens."

"Not in Devon." Macalvie smiled.

15

❧❧

THE house itself had no name. Through the twilit snow, Jury's lights picked out only a small bronze plaque bearing the single word *Winslow*, set in a stone pillar at the end of the curving drive. For a few moments he sat in the car, smoking and looking through the small wood where fallen branches and rotting logs showed the groundskeeper — if there was one — was anywhere but in the grounds. He slammed the door of the Ford, sending a small landslide of snow from the bonnet of the car to the ground.

Jury pulled at the bell and looked up at the straight gray face of the house. He would not have chosen it as a sanctuary from London, although it was certainly quiet enough. "Desolate" would be a better word, he thought. Perhaps it was that, really, that added to its baronial splendor.

A rustic-looking man, his face fretted with the tiny lines of the excessive drinker, opened the door and stuck his head around it, scanning Jury's person with suspicion that only increased when Jury showed him his warrant card and said he was here to see Mrs. Winslow.

The man opened the door farther and beckoned with his hand as if he were trying to pull the malingerer on the step inside. "Coom on in; I'll tell 'em." No proper butler, certainly; probably the absentee groundsman or gardener.

The hall was large and cold and added to the impression of baronial splendor, with the array of armaments on one wall, the niches on the other into which plaster busts of saints or gods had been set. A central staircase of highly polished mahogany climbed up to a galleried first floor. He walked to the newel post and looked up; the picture Plant had mentioned on the telephone showed a blond young woman and a little girl of perhaps seven or eight.

On each side of the front door, an arched window gave a narrow view of the woodland. Snow drifted slowly down, masking the black beeches and yews. They looked more like shadows of trees. It turned his mind toward the Bristol road, the wood in which Sheila Broome had been found. He frowned slightly; something bothered him, something he had heard about Sheila Broome, a tiny print left on his mind much like the dark and delicate tracks of the birds. A missal thrush landed and rocked a thin branch of the nearest beechwood; small clumps of snow sifted down.

"Sorry, Superintendent, for keeping you waiting."

It was David Marr. Jury had not heard him coming and was momentarily disoriented from staring out at the hypnotic scene.

Marr smiled slightly. "We've met."

"I know." Jury also smiled. "I think I was a little mesmerized by your wood. I like the snow."

Marr raised his eyebrows in mock surprise. "You go out in it, do you?"

"Occasionally. I'm a little late because of the roads."

They were walking toward a double door to the right of the hall. "Don't apologize. We're the ones who kept *you*

113

waiting. John isn't really much of a butler. Not much of a groundskeeper, either, come to think of it. We're in the drawing room here, all properly arranged for your questions."

Properly arranged was what the Winslows were. It was masterly, in a way; they stood or sat rather like actors who had just been blocked and who had now left off wrestling with their scripts. Marion Winslow, wearing a black velvet lounge-robe, sat in a high-backed mahogany armchair pulled out several feet from a huge marble fireplace. A Christmas tree, undecorated except for strings of unlit lights and a tiny, spun-glass angel on top, stood rather gloomily to the right of the mantel. Edward Winslow stood in front of the fireplace, smoking. David Marr lent the casual touch, just the right touch to make it all convincing, impromptu, as he fixed Jury and himself a whiskey and water. In the positions of Marion Winslow and her son, there was almost an imitation of the pose in the portrait directly above the overmantel, yet it did not seem at all to be a self-conscious posing. After handing Jury his drink, David sat down on a fine Queene Anne sofa, his legs stretched out before him.

Jury intended to talk with each of them separately, but not right now. He did not want to break up this family gathering; it was interesting.

They talked for a few moments politely about the condition of the roads and the unexpected snowfall, while Jury lit a cigarette and let his eye stray to the circular claw-footed table near him that held a collection of photographs, some small, some large; simply or elaborately framed. When the talk had died down like the slowly drifting snow, Jury reached for a small picture in a chased silver frame of the child in the painting on the landing. She was very pretty,

114

with large liquid eyes and pale hair. His little sister looked, Jury thought, as Edward Winslow might have looked at that age.

Jury noticed that Marion Winslow was watching, tracking the movement of frame from table to chair and back again. "That was my daughter, Phoebe." Her voice was pleasantly low, but as flat and calm and cold as the wintry landscape he had passed through on the road from Exeter.

"I heard about the accident. I'm sorry."

She gave a slight nod; her brother had risen to replenish his glass and now stood, hand in pocket of jacket, looking down abstractedly at the fire. Then he turned, as if to say something, but it was Edward who spoke: "I was very fond of Phoebe." He sighed. "Well, we all were." He moved closer to his mother's chair and laid a hand on her shoulder. She seemed to be looking off at blankness.

Jury wondered about the black dress. The child had died over two years ago, not, certainly, a long time. Like yesterday as far as grieving was concerned; but for the clothes of mourning, a little long. Though Jury doubted that Marion Winslow meant anything like this by the simple, elegantly cut black gown.

"Look, the family album is fascinating," said David, reclaiming his seat on the sofa, "but have you turned up anything that'll let me off the hook?"

Jury felt rather sorry for Marr despite the callous comment about the family album. Put aside the circumstantial and there was no evidence to say he had killed Ivy Childess. But there was the circumstantial, nonetheless. "I'm afraid nothing conclusive, Mr. Marr."

"Hell, let's settle for something *in*conclusive."

Jury smiled, but shook his head. He was glad that the subject had been introduced by one of them. "It would be helpful if I could talk with you alone, Mr. Marr. As a matter of fact —"

This was interrupted by Marr's saying, "You've already talked with me alone, Superintendent."

"I was just saying, I'd really like to talk with each of you alone. If that wouldn't be too inconvenient."

He was a little surprised when Marion Winslow laughed. "Somehow I think we'll find the time, Mr. Jury." She rose from her chair and with Edward, left the room.

"This is getting to be the highlight of my day," said David, splashing more whiskey into his glass, then holding up the decanter and looking at Jury.

Jury shook his head. "I'm glad we're not boring you."

"Not at all, not at all. How many ways are there to inquire into a telephone call. At least now, you can ask my sister in person."

"I was wondering, Mr. Marr, if you've ever been in Exeter?"

David Marr looked up from his drink, surprised. "Well! Here's a new approach." He leaned his head against the back of the sofa. "Exeter, Exeter, Exeter. Yes, a long time ago. Took a turn round the cathedral. Then round the pubs."

"How long a time ago?"

David shrugged. "Ten years, perhaps." He looked at Jury. "I can see a whole new line of questioning's opened up. What happened in Exeter?"

"Sheila Broome. You didn't happen to know —?"

"Never heard of her." His answer was quick, tangling with the end of Jury's question. "And that 'didn't' suggests something's happened to her." He turned his gaze ceilingward again. "Good God." He sighed. "I *do* hope the next question isn't going to be 'Where were you on the night of —?'"

Jury smiled. "Twenty-nine February."

Marr turned quickly to look at him. "That's ten *months* ago, Superintendent."

"I know."

"Although the dates of my tumultuous affairs with young ladies are seared into my brain, I honestly cannot remember that particular one. Sheila, you say?"

"Broome. That's too bad. When you've a bit of spare time, try."

David groaned. "Are you going to tell me, Superintendent, that *another* woman has had her life snuffed out? Snuffed, you apparently think, by me?" He slipped farther down into the sofa and rolled the cool glass across his forehead.

"No, I wasn't going to tell you that." Jury sat forward. "David, for someone in your position, don't you think you're being a little glib?"

"Thank you. But my position happens to be that I hadn't one damned thing to do with the death of Ivy. Or anyone else." He drank off his whiskey and stared morosely at the fire.

"Okay. I'd like to talk with Edward."

David turned, surprised. "You mean that's *all*, Superintendent? I was certain you were going to grind me to powder. Well, I'd be gleeful about this, but it bodes ill: you haven't even come up with something or someone more interesting than I. And I doubt I'm much fun anymore."

"I'll keep trying."

No painting or photograph could really do Edward Winslow credit. The snapshot Jury had just returned to David Marr only hinted at his nephew's good looks, probably because a camera couldn't capture the grace with which he moved. Yet, Jury thought that the portraitist had taken the aristocratic bones and bearing too seriously, for though Edward was both handsome and elegant he was also offhand, as if his manner, unlike his clothes, had been pulled off the rack. A designer of men's couture would love to see him in ascot or

117

reefer; Edward himself preferred the wool sweater and collar open at the neck.

He walked into the room with a sort of shamble and an uncertain smile. Then he settled into the corner of the sofa that David had just vacated, and propped his head against his hand. "If you don't mind my saying so, this is all rather strange — I mean, that Scotland Yard would come to Somers Abbas. Oh, sorry . . . " Edward colored a bit, as if thinking that inquiry into Scotland Yard's *own* inquiry were poor form.

Did they all, thought Jury, think of it as a game? Cricket? "You divide your time between Somers Abbas and London, is that right?" asked Jury. When he nodded, Jury asked, "Any particular reason you live here rather than there?"

Edward laughed. "You sound like Mother. Mother says she doesn't want me hanging about, propping her up."

"Your mother doesn't seem in much need of propping, Mr. Winslow."

Edward got up, as David had done, and fixed himself a whiskey, but a very small one. "She does." He drank it off, neat. "Though she hides it pretty well, she does. Since my sister died, mother's been pretty — withdrawn. She — Phoebe — was hit by a car; she dashed right in front of the car; he didn't see her until he was nearly on top of her. Or so he said. It wasn't technically a hit-and-run, since the chap apparently stopped at a call box three blocks away and called police." He looked sadly at Jury. "But I found Phoebe; Hugh was in the house." He paused. "He ran out later."

Jury nodded but said nothing, as he watched Ned Winslow walk about, stopping at the spruce to retrieve the spun-glass angel that winked in the light as he repositioned it on its top branch. Since Ned Winslow had been there — *How did she look? What was she wearing? Did she speak at all?* — he was perhaps doomed to carry the burden, like a tribal memory.

"I'm sorry," said Jury. "Your uncle mentioned you were a poet, a published one, at that. You must be very good."

He laughed. "Well, I suppose you're right — I mean about publication being coincidental with one's worth. And writing poetry certainly doesn't seem like much to be doing, especially to someone on the dole."

"I was wondering," said Jury, "why you go to the expense of keeping a flat in Belgravia when you've the house in Knightsbridge."

"That's simple. My father lives there." He looked at Jury. "I don't get on with him." Ned leaned forward to poke at the fire. A log split and crumbled and a saw-edge of bluish flame spurted up, casting a web of shadow across his face. The color of his eyes, when he looked over at Jury, shifted like cornelian from brown to gold.

"When your uncle called on Monday night, were you here?" Jury watched Ned Winslow, who did not answer immediately.

"No."

"But your mother told you about the call."

"Oh, certainly. After all, it's about the only thing keeping David out of the dock, isn't it?"

Marion Winslow did not take her eyes from Jury as she went to the high-backed armchair.

Neither did Jury move; he kept to the chair beside the center table nearly ten feet away, across the expanse of Kirman carpet.

Her hands rested on the ends of the mahogany armrests; her legs were crossed, a wave of black velvet over the tips of her shoes. She wore no jewelry and little if any makeup. She did not seem to go in for ornaments.

"There's really nothing I can add to what I've already told you, Superintendent. Though I certainly don't mind telling

119

you again." She smiled coolly. "It's the telephone call I imagine you're most interested in?"

"One of the things, yes."

"David rang up, I'd say, close to eleven on the Monday night."

"And you can't fix the time more precisely?"

"No. I'm sorry. Sometimes my husband's answering machine picks up calls and it asks the time. If I'm out of earshot and the servants aren't around, I set it. But that night, I was in the library, reading." She thought for a moment. "I'd say between ten forty-five and eleven or a few minutes past."

"A bit late to call."

She laughed. "Not for David. Not here."

"What did he expect of you?"

With a little smile, she said, "Money. And I suppose a shoulder to cry on. I told you: he'd just walked out on Ivy Childess; he got weary of her nagging about marrying."

"Hadn't he ever intended to marry her?"

"I doubt it very seriously."

"Your brother just doesn't fancy marriage in general?"

She shook her head. "No, in particular. Particularly, Ivy Childess."

"You knew her?"

Her eyebrows arched in mild surprise. "No. I'd *met* her. There's a difference. It was at our house in London. We had some friends round for drinks. My son and brother were there. And David brought Ivy." She shrugged and added: "And Lucinda St. Clair, I remember."

"St. Clair."

"Yes. They live at the north edge of Somers Abbas. A rather rococo house which they've named 'The Steeples.' Lucinda is the older daughter, and we've known her for a long time." Marion rested her head against the tall back of the chair and looked up at the ceiling. "Actually, I think you might want to talk with Lucinda; she's extremely fond of

120

David." She reached out and plucked up a small notebook and gold pencil and wrote rapidly. "Understand, I'm not suggesting Lucinda will give you an unbiased account. Here's the telephone number and address. Though anyone in the village can tell you where the St. Clairs live." She tore out the page and placed it on the table. They were too far apart for reaching.

Marion Winslow was a purposeful woman, thought Jury. No words wasted, no movement embellished. She was, he thought, rather like a fisherman. Everything weighed and measured before thought became act. She gently pulled in the line, took up the slack. "By 'extremely fond' do you mean she's in love with him?"

She nodded. "Yes, and it's too bad. David doesn't return the feeling." Looking again at the fire-shadows on the ceiling, she added, but as if it were of no consequence, "I like Lucinda."

"You're pretty much your brother's confidante, then?"

Again, she nodded. "That's why I wasn't at all surprised when he called late Monday."

"You said you talked for about twenty minutes. Can you be more exact?"

"No. Twenty minutes to half an hour."

That would put Marr in his apartment from approximately ten-fifty to eleven-ten or -twenty, if he left the pub just on quarter to eleven, and *if* it took him Wiggins's estimate of ten minutes to walk to Shepherd Market. The better part of the time allowed for Ivy Childess's murder. No airtight alibi, but better than nothing. He could certainly have walked *back* to the Running Footman, strangled her, and returned to Shepherd Market within the twenty minutes between the pub's closing and the woman's passing with her dog. Twenty minutes, difficult. Thirty, easy. That extra ten minutes could make all the difference. But there would, in that case, remain the problem of why Ivy would have hung about Hays Mews for twenty minutes.

"Your husband spends most of his time in London, does he?" asked Jury mildly.

Marion flinched. "Yes, he does."

"But you yourself don't go to London often?"

"No."

"Mr. Winslow keeps a sort of office here, does he?"

"Yes. He's a financial consultant; I imagine he needs to keep in touch."

Jury thought that "imagine" defined the Winslows' relationship. Marion and Hugh were certainly not one another's confidant. But he asked, anyway, "And did your husband dislike Ivy Childess?"

"I don't remember his ever saying anything about her. One way or another." She shrugged.

"Your husband spends most of his time in London, doesn't he?"

"Yes."

"Though he comes here seldom, does he come — well, regularly?"

"No. Irregularly."

"And you, do you stay at your house there?"

She seemed to be thinking. "Rarely. More often at Claridge's. I wouldn't go at all except to see Ned and David. I don't want always to be dragging them down here."

Jury smiled. "If ever two men didn't look as if they'd been 'dragged' I'd say it was David and Ned."

"Thank you. That sounded like a compliment." She seemed to be studying her hands. "You see — and I'm sure you can understand — I dislike the house in Knightsbridge intensely." She looked up. "Phoebe died there." Her glance shifted from Jury to the table beside him holding the framed photographs.

"I can understand, yes." His look followed her own, straying to the center table. There was a photo in an old-fashioned walnut frame of a small girl, smiling, strands of light hair blowing across her face. Jury studied it. "I noticed there's a painting, a portrait on the landing upstairs. Is it of her?"

"Yes. Phoebe and Rose." She looked away. "Rose was Edward's wife. She left. I wish he'd marry again; perhaps he'd have better luck. How anyone could marry Ned for money is beyond me. But she did; she managed to clean out the account before she left without a word. Yet it's David, not Ned, who hates that portrait. He keeps telling me to take it down. But it's the only one we have of Phoebe, and one doesn't go cutting people out of portraits, does one?"

But one does cut people out of wills, he thought. "You said your brother wanted money. A lot?"

She laughed. "He always does. David's frightfully spendthrift. How he could go through the money he has in the last few years, I can't imagine."

"What about the family fortune? Who inherits what?"

"It's divided evenly, among the three of us. It's about, oh, five million, I expect." She shrugged it off as if it were five pounds. "There is a codicil, though: David inherits when he marries. Our father thought he would run through his share in a year if he hadn't a wife to talk some sense into him." There was a glint of victory in her eyes. "So he'd have every reason to keep Ivy Childess alive, wouldn't he?"

His eye was caught by another photo that looked like an enlargement of the same snapshot he had borrowed from Marr's flat. David and Edward caught suddenly in a moment of laughter. They were wearing tennis sweaters, and Ned's hand held tightly to the handle of a racquet that disappeared over his shoulder. From the position of both Jury guessed they must have had their arms about one another's shoulders. One had won, one had lost, both were happy.

"Edward is very fond of David, isn't he?"

123

"Extremely. *And,* believe it or not, so is David of Edward."

Jury replaced the photo. "Why 'believe it or not'?"

"Only because David so loves to adopt that cynical air. Don't you believe it."

"I don't."

"Because he's got a passionate enough nature to do murder?"

"I didn't mean that."

Jury replaced the photograph; she picked up the bit of notebook paper; a silence fell. He felt somehow awkward, sitting here drinking the dregs of his whiskey — he felt a chump, actually, but didn't know why. He looked from his glass to the silky surface of a Belgian tapestry that seemed to ripple in the light from the high windows like the crests of incoming waves. Through the twilit panes he saw the snow had stopped. The beeches stood in a dark column, but now they were ash-brown. Screened by snow they had looked black. The surface of things could be deceptive.

"Mr. Jury?"

Jury looked up. She had gone to the window to fasten the catch and pull the heavy curtains together, almost as if she hadn't wanted him to see this metamorphosis at dusk. Her head was tilted slightly as if she were trying to see his eyes. "Sorry. I suppose I was woolgathering."

She smiled. "Don't apologize. I do it all the time."

Her attempt to seem at ease was very studied, he thought.

"I'm not trying to get away from you. But I just thought perhaps you had no more questions."

"You're right, none." Standing before the window, her hands lightly laced before her and with her very dark hair and pale complexion, Marion Winslow gave the impression of one whom great misfortune had made very quiet but very sure. Capable, perhaps, of nearly anything. Lying would come easily to her to protect someone, because the old rules no longer applied, the moral element had shifted like sand.

124

He had risen too, of course, and said, "Thank you very much, Mrs. Winslow. I would like to have a look round, if you don't mind."

She nodded. "I'll send Ned along to show you whatever you want to see."

He returned the nod. As she walked in those clothes of mourning, her back straight, across to the door, he thought that Marion Winslow was a woman upon whom society could no longer intrude. She had locked the windows, drawn the curtains, shut the door.

16

THE gallows sign of the Mortal Man creaked eerily in the wind and the snow, lit by a dull metal lamp that lent its sickle-curve of light to the mortality of the sallow-faced figure in the sign. The light spilling from the windows of the inn's public bar was no brighter, no more cheerful. It crept round the edges and through the slits of a boarded-up window, whose shutters banged as fretfully as did the sign. No matter that during the day, the Mortal Man must have belonged to the pretty picture cut by the village green, the duckpond, the row of thatched-roof cottages beyond — here, in the dark and the cold it looked vacant, transient, divested of an inn's life and good cheer.

Inside, this impression was quickly dispelled. There was surely enough life to go round the green and back several times over. A cacophony of shouting voices met him — or rather, blasted past him, in the person of a woman, a youngish girl, a younger boy with a dog. The dog stopped when he saw Jury, as smartly as if he'd run into a wall, ran madly three times around Jury's legs, and continued, yapping, after the boy.

In another minute, this happy quartet rushed back from the other direction, apparently not having solved their logistical problem, if that were the problem. The dog remembered to run around Jury's legs again, in some sort of magical incantation, before it zipped off after the others.

"The common form of greeting at the Mortal Man," said Melrose Plant, who appeared in the doorway of the public bar, smiling broadly, smoking one of his small cigars. "They'll be back; you escaped serious damage this time, but don't press your luck." Plant motioned him in. "The St. Clairs have saved you, possibly, a trip to the Steeples. Count yourself twice fortunate."

Behind the bar, the burly owner appeared to be comparing notes with a tall man who sat with three glasses before him at a nearby table. He was introduced to Jury as St. John St. Clair, and the young woman next to him as the daughter, Lucinda. The gentleman behind the bar, who was slapping his bar towel around, apparently on the track of a fly, snapped it so smartly at the mirror that a patch of the gilt frame fell off.

Jury's offer to stand drinks was met with a sad headshake by St. Clair. He had tried, he said, studying the three glasses before him, all of the Warboyses' stock of Irish whiskey. They had been found wanting. This was, of course, no reflection on Mr. Warboys but on the general instability of that country. The chief difference between the innkeeper and his unhappy guest was that one had a round, red face; the other, a sad, long one. For both, Armageddon was drawing near.

Nathan Warboys lost no time in trying to persuade Jury that, if he had any plans for marrying, he should drop them immediately. "Take my Sally. I mean, I mean, don't think I don't know what that 'un's always on about. Out she goes, every night, dressed like a dog's dinner."

Apparently, the hound had taken this as a call to the front, for he streaked across the room and grabbed St. Clair's walking stick between his teeth with an almighty growl. As he pulled and growled, the handle caught on the narrow table leg, sending table and drinks spilling about. Nathan Warboys picked up a piece of the wood stacked against the counter and let it fly, barely missing Melrose's head, then said someone would be in to mop up the mess.

Melrose hoped not. St. Clair took it quite philosophically, dabbing at his shirt and picking up the conversation where Nathan had dropped it. "You are right, of course, Mr. Warboys. Marriage can be an extremely sad affair, though I can't agree it is the fault of the woman. No, it is the fault of everybody. Certainly, there *are* wives — not yours, not mine, at least not yet — who do cause the most dreadful trouble. Why, look at poor Marion —"

"Marion's never caused any trouble, Daddy."

"*She* hasn't, no. We know of no trouble at all *she's* caused. The fact Hugh stays away must be owing to something else, but we don't want to talk about that. They don't make cloth like they used to; I doubt this stain will come out." He patted his tie with the bar towel. "I'm speaking of that person that poor David is accused of murdering. What a perfectly dreadful mess."

"Did you know her, Mr. St. Clair?" asked Jury.

Nathan Warboys topped up his glass and said, "You want to stay away from them kind, you do."

"No, I didn't. Fortunately. Though I believe Lucinda did."

When Jury turned to her, Lucinda said, "I met her once, Ivy Childess. I hardly knew her. It was at a little party in Knightsbridge." Eagerly, she leaned toward Jury and said, "David couldn't *possibly* have done that. It's just not in his nature to do something so — awful."

There was no question that Plant had been right about Lucinda St. Clair's attachment to David Marr. Jury wondered how far it might take her, that attachment. "Do you visit the Winslow house much, then? Do you go up to London, Miss St. Clair?"

"Hardly ever," said Lucinda.

"Best you don't, my dear," said her father. "And don't forget Edward's misfortune," St. Clair went on, his sonorous voice blending with the hollow sound of the bell in the village church tolling the hour.

Warboys, a toothpick jumping about in his mouth, said, "You mean that there wife of his, a right treat, weren't she? Just up and left and never a good-bye, and never a word since. Well, that were a long time ago, weren't it? Still, it's some way for a wife to act, just leavin' without so much's a word." Nathan then seemed to be reconsidering the merits of this unwifely behavior when his own wife appeared to shout out last calls for dinner.

The St. Clairs left; Plant and Jury walked across the hall to the dining room, while from upstairs came a series of small crashes.

"It's just a Warboys, straightening up your room," said Melrose.

"You are being treated to an evening of the Warboyses in full revel." Melrose Plant repositioned his cutlery and tucked up his threadbare dinner napkin.

Jury squinted his eyes. "Never, *never* have I seen you eat a meal with a napkin under your chin."

"That's because you've never seen me dine with the Warboyses." He lifted his roll, found it rock-hard, and hit it with the handle of his knife. "There!" The roll splintered and crumbled on the plate. "The Warboyses have unleashed my taste for violence."

"Are they joining us, then?" asked Jury, who had reached down to scratch Osmond behind the ears.

129

"Probably." Melrose lifted the edge of the tablecloth to look at the hound, napping happily at Jury's feet. "That dog must be dead."

The dining room was more festive than usual; they were not the only occupants of the room: in a far corner sat a man and woman who had no doubt been lured in by the announcement outside that an "English dinner plus all the trimmings" awaited them. The Warboyses' idea of "traditional" probably ran more to Sainsbury fruitcake than homemade Yorkshire pudding, Melrose thought. He observed that his and Jury's companions-in-adventure were quite silent, looking at the black panes through which they could see nothing but their own reflections. Married, he assumed, and hoped he wasn't stereotyping the couple. But he wondered why married folk always seemed uncomfortable when they dined in public, as if afraid that someone would think they'd just come from a steamy assignation if they looked at each other.

A string of white lights made an arc at the top of the window; the Warboyses' stockings were nailed to the mantel. Melrose had watched Bobby Warboys going at them hell-for-leather, all the while blathering out his complaints, as if he were nailing the entire season to a tree. A small Christmas tree with tiny winking lights sat amongst some souvenirs on a shelf overhead—a flowered bottle of green glass with the legend *A Present from Wells-Next-the-Sea;* several little photos of what looked to be absent Warboyses; one live plant and one in its throes; a stuffed red fox with its one good eye trained on Melrose (the other probably having been shot out by Nathan); a bowl of plastic fruit, whose grapes, Melrose said, must have given this particular wine its special piquancy. By the dining-room door sat a cross-eyed porcelain leopard, bedecked with tinsel. All oddments culled from some jumble sale, it looked like.

"Where's our soup?" said Melrose, twisting round to stare down the kitchen door.

130

On cue, Mrs. Warboys charged through it with two plates of soup. Short, stout, pale, she had been turned by the kitchen catastrophe into a quivering, livid mass. She put Melrose in mind of a mad blancmange. The soup slopped up the sides of the bowls when she set it down and announced the entree selection: "Veal cutlet, toad-in-the-hole, and Bombay duck." She flicked a glance right and left to see how each of them took it.

Melrose looked at Jury who said, "Oh, go ahead."

"I'll try it, though Bombay duck is hardly my idea of your *traditional* Christmas dinner. I was thinking more along the lines of some nice, rare roast beef." He smiled so hard he thought he'd grow dimples.

"Aye, 'tis. But we're out."

"Out?"

Mrs. Warboys nodded over her shoulder in the direction of the couple at the window. "Them two's 'ad the last bit."

"But they're the only others here."

All the while keeping an eye on them, Jury smiled and sipped his wine, a bottle that Melrose had wrestled from Nathan's stock. Everything that the Warboyses owned was considered their personal treasure, from the blind-eyed fox to the indifferent wine. "Toad-in-the-hole for me, Mrs. Warboys," said Jury.

"Yessir." She smoothed out her apron and her frown and nearly curtsied. Then she clutched the tray to her bosom and tramped off, some of the steam having decompressed.

"Toad-in-the-bloody-*hole?* You'll be sorry. It's probably real."

"Haven't had any of that since my days in Good Hope."

"Isn't that the euphemism for that chilly institution you spent your childhood in? It's always sounded to me like a Siberian winter."

"It was."

Since the kitchen door worked both ways, Mrs. Warboys's

131

exit provided for William's entrance. He sped by the table. "You seen Sally?" he asked of them, though he'd never seen Jury until that moment. No, they hadn't. "She's gone and forgot the spuds for supper." He wheeled away.

"Who's Sally?"

"Another Warboys, the woods are full of them." Melrose continued spooning up his soup.

Jury drank his wine. "Give me your impression of the Winslow family."

"I don't think David Marr has much of an alibi, to tell the truth."

"There was a call; we traced it."

"Yes, but there's also an answering machine. Not even Telecom, incredibly efficient as it is when it comes to tracking down delinquent payments, could tell you who or what answered, could it? Only that a connection was made."

Jury was silent for a minute. "And you think Marion Winslow is lying."

Melrose shrugged. "Marion, David, Edward — they'd all lie for one another."

"But if the telephone rang, someone would have heard it."

"No. The servants were gone. You know, I was thinking —" He finished his soup and laid down his spoon. "— that alibis work two ways, don't they?"

At that moment, Sally Warboys scudded across the dining room like gray clouds hurrying before a storm and carrying a brown bag full (Melrose supposed) of the dinner spuds. "Before the storm" was accurate, too, because her father rode fast on her heels, his arms windmilling, unmindful of his clientele. Sally smacked her way into the kitchen, and Nathan apparently didn't think he needed to improve upon the bedlam (a thunderous fall of pans, a rain of cutlery), for he came straight out again. A dusty-looking cat just managed to flash its way through the door and around Nathan's foot before it

132

got mashed by one and kicked by the other. Melrose watched its lightning progress across the room and its skid to a stop by the arched doorway, where it hissed at the porcelain leopard that it had, apparently, never accepted as cousin.

"Here he comes; pretend we're deep in our soup," whispered Melrose to Jury.

Nathan Warboys wouldn't have cared anyway, since he was not a thrifty speaker and demanded no payment in the coin of someone else's comments. With his usual scowl he said, "I mean, I mean, look at 'er, would ya? 'Ow many men you got 'ere? I says to 'er. It's a right treat, innit, and 'er out every night . . . "

Melrose tuned him out; Jury sat there all ears. Melrose wondered under what particular slag heap of Nathan's conversation Jury expected to find the golden nugget. Around Jury a frozen spring became a waterfall, and Warboys was set to run like Niagara. Fortunately, the shrill *brr-brr* of the telephone called him to his duty.

His place was taken now by Sally Warboys, who dealt the dishes round like a card-sharp, knocking half the cutlery from the table before she slopped off to entertain further disasters.

"You were talking about Marr's telephone call. Go on." Jury forked up some potatoes.

"The call provides Marion Winslow with an alibi, too. The impression I got of her was fleeting. But even that left me with the feeling that she's a determined woman. And Edward obviously thinks so, too, loyal as he is. Loyal as they *all* are to one another. Of course, I only saw her for a minute on the stair." Melrose set down his wineglass and inspected his Bombay duck, poking it here and there with his fork. After a moment he said, "Did you notice the portrait of Edward's wife?"

Jury nodded. "Mrs. Winslow said she kept it because of

Phoebe. There's no love lost between her and the ex-wife."
Jury pulled half of a sausage from the pastry blanket.

Melrose leaned over to look at Jury's plate: "I don't see
why Mrs. Warboys had to waste the Yorkshire pudding on
toad-in-the-hole."

"How you do suffer. How's your Bombay duck?"

"It walked from Bombay. You know, Rose's leaving certainly wouldn't sit well with the Winslow family. Neither
would this duck." He held up a morsel.

"Get back to the telephone call. When did she send the
servants away?"

"I calculated it must have been the day of the murder."

"But she wouldn't have known her brother would call; the
servants' leaving wouldn't have been planned because of a
nonexistent telephone call."

"Perhaps it was her intention to go to London without
anyone knowing about it. Of course, she would turn on the
answering machine. She certainly wouldn't want any calls
slipping through her fingers on that particular night. I mean,
of course, if she hopped it to London. And since she often
uses the machine when she's in another part of the house, or
napping, no one would question her not answering. Well?"

"There's the same problem, the problem of motive. Why
would she kill Ivy Childess?"

"Possibly, to protect one of them — David or Edward. That
might be the only thing that would drive her to kill anyone."

"Protect them from what, though?"

Melrose sighed. "You're no fun."

"But this is. Like the plum in the Christmas pud." He
speared the other half of the sausage and held it up on the
tines of his fork. "I rather like your theory, except for something rather obvious."

"I hope you're not foolhardy enough to say things like that
to Commander Macalvie. 'Obvious,' indeed!"

"Take the Beedles over there for example —"

"The who?" Melrose followed the direction of Jury's gaze. The gentleman at the far table was seeing to his bill. "How'd you know their name?"

"Nathan Warboys. Weren't you listening? I've been watching them and their extended silence. Marriage can be very relaxing, I think. No demands to make clever dinner conversation, for one —"

"Why don't you settle down?" Melrose got out his cigarette case, took out a thin hand-rolled cigar, and snapped the case shut.

"I'm talking about the way things seem. Appearance can often be the truth. One needn't interpret their silence as anger or anything at all except a desire not to converse. Sheila Broome and the lorry driver, for instance. Why not assume that Sheila and the driver were acting quite naturally? The quintessential hitchhiker refusing to converse with the person who picks her up? And the telephone call that definitely *was* made, made by David, answered by Marion? And the servants going off to visit a sickbed because someone got sick on that weekend? The killer could have been a woman, yes, of course, and *could* have been Marion Winslow. But as I said, there's still motive to consider."

Melrose took from his pocket Edward Winslow's book of poetry and handed it to Jury. "He's quite good. You know, you say these two killings have one thing in common: the method. Garroted with their own scarves wound about their necks. It makes me think of Porphyria."

"Porphyria?"

"Browning's Porphyria: ' . . . Then glided in Porphyria.' Her lover strangled her with her own hair."

"That's interesting. The Porphyria murders. Macalvie would like that; he's big on repeat killings." Jury checked his watch. "I'm due at the Winslows in a little while and then back to London. Come to London, why don't you?"

Melrose shook his head. "No, I don't think so." He held up one of the two small photographs lying on the table, put that down, held up the other. He held it at arm's length, drew it forward, held it out again. He scratched his head, grimacing. "That waitress at the Little Chef. Exactly what did she say when you showed her the newspaper clipping of David Marr?"

"It was Macalvie showed her. Mary Higgins said he — David, that is — looked familiar. So Macalvie had a good-looking dark-haired cop go in for a coffee, a man about the same height and build as Marr, and she said he looked familiar, too. Macalvie thinks she was trying too hard."

Melrose picked up the picture of the Winslow family again. "It seems strange, though, this Little Chef business."

"Strange, how?"

"Well, it's unlikely the person who killed Sheila Broome would go *in* the cafe, isn't it? But assume he did. This waitress, you said, or Macalvie said, was very observant. Spotting the lorry, the driver, the girl in the rain." He shrugged. "It just seems odd she'd be so vague on the matter of identifying the picture, assuming, of course, there was something to identify. Perhaps, then, to her, it's a bit of a blur. . . . I was going back to Northants tomorrow. But I think I might just go to Exeter, if that's all right."

"Of course it's all right. But why?"

Melrose shook his head. "I don't know. Just a thought. Do you suppose I could have copies of these to take along?" He held up the photos.

"Sure. I'll have them made when I get to the Yard tonight and see you get copies in the morning." Jury turned. "Oh, hullo, William."

William Warboys was standing at his elbow, looking intent. As though the sudden appearance of his master signaled an ambush, Osmond made a dive for Melrose's foot.

Melrose winced. "Good Lord, can't you keep this hound on

a lead?" He moved his foot in an arc, trying to dislodge Osmond.

Ignoring this, William said, "I worked out who killed Weldon."

"Weldon? Who killed Osmond would make a more satisfactory mystery."

"It was Sidney."

"Sidney? Sidney? I thought Sidney was Weldon's best friend."

"Well, he must not be, or he wouldn't have killed him," said William, reasonably. He then turned to Jury. "Want to go out back?"

"And what's out back?" asked Jury.

"Graves. It's a kind of cemetery. When something dies around here, I bury it." William looked down at his notebook. "It's where I get my inspiration."

Said Melrose, "It's where all of you get your inspiration."

MACALVIE sat with his feet on Jury's desk, his arms straitjacketed across his chest. His eyes shifted from watching Wiggins doctor his tea to the screen of a tiny portable television set, where an Oriental was detailing the joys of acupuncture. Wiggins kept the set in a filing cabinet and brought it out at noon every day for the acupuncture report.

"You'd think *someone* would've seen or heard something," said Wiggins, depositing two seltzer tablets into his mug and watching the bubbles sprout over its puce-colored surface.

"Someone did." Macalvie frowned. "What the hell's that, Wiggins? It looks like something's erupting in there." His hand went out for the folder that Jury had just discarded on his desk.

"This headache's fierce; it could turn migraine on me." Wiggins sipped his tea.

Macalvie grunted. "You make it sound like a rabid dog. There are two dozen houses in Hays Mews. Someone's not talking."

"Did you get hold of Andrew Starr, Wiggins?"

"Yes, sir. Said we'd go round to his place late this afternoon."

Macalvie's hat was down but the blue eyes glowed under the brim. "You'd think twice about having me go to Covent Garden, I figure."

Jury's smile was blinding. "Not twice. Once. You're welcome to talk to him once I've finished."

"Thanks. What about this friend of Marr's? Paul Swann?"

"Haven't talked to him yet. He's in Brighton."

Wiggins shivered. "At this time of year." He shook his head slowly.

"You can take off your coat, Macalvie. You won't be contaminated by the local police."

Macalvie undid two buttons. His eye wandered back to the TV, where the squirrel-like gibbering of the Oriental had been replaced by the news at twelve-twenty. Another terrorist attack at the Rome airport; a child drowned in the River Dart; an old man mugged. "Maybe there are things worse than murder," he said.

"Maybe, but I doubt it."

"Dante says —"

Jury looked up, startled. "Dante? You read Dante?" Jury opened another folder from the stack. "I never thought you had time to sit down and read a book."

"I wasn't sitting. An old guy was beaten up in his library. I was going through the books. He — Dante, I mean — puts it below murder: 'Betrayal of friends and benefactors.' Below murder, Jury." Macalvie took his feet from the desk, held out his hand for a Fisherman's Friend.

Wiggins was ripping open a package. "Getting a cold, sir?"

"No. I stopped smoking."

"Good. How long?"

139

Macalvie checked his watch. "Half-hour ago." He picked up a discarded folder. "What about this one? Says he was letting himself into his flat between eleven-thirty and midnight at that end of Charles Street."

"The pub closed at eleven."

"Yeah, but that doesn't mean she was killed at eleven."

"She wouldn't have been hanging round in Hays Mews for an hour."

Macalvie shrugged and tossed the folder on the desk. "No one can fix the time of death that closely. Although your pathologist didn't appreciate my telling her —"

Jury rubbed his fingers through his hair, leaving it standing up in licks. He sighed. "Macalvie, stop prowling the corridors, will you? Leave forensics alone."

Macalvie changed the subject. "This guy David Marr doesn't have any kind of an alibi. The servants were gone, the machine could have picked up the call. The sister's lying."

"Occasionally someone tells the truth, Macalvie."

Macalvie didn't look convinced. He ran his thumb down the stack of folders. "Someone knows something." He rewrapped his arms across his chest.

"What about Sheila Broome? Does someone know something there?"

"Of course."

Jury looked at him. "Nothing's turned up in ten months."

"Something will."

Jury picked up the telephone. "Jury here." The call was from Constable Whicker, on duty in the lobby.

"There's a lad down here, says his name is Colin Rees, says he may have something about the alleged murder in Hays Mews, sir."

Jury could have told it was Whicker from the way he qualified everything. Where Constable Whicker was concerned, "fact" was a relative term, and he always relayed information with caution signs pointing to it as if Fleet Street might be listening.

"Have someone bring him up, Constable."

Constable Whicker turned away from the telephone and there was a murmured exchange. "He appears not to want to, sir."

"Okay. I'll come down." He hung up and said to Macalvie, "There's a kid down in the lobby about the Hays Mews murder."

Macalvie shoved back his hat and smiled.

Two lads. The older of them, Colin Rees, eleven or twelve with faded blond hair the color of Horlicks and eyes like pebbles, small and gray. He carried a cap in his hands that looked several sizes too big for him, which he kept mashing together and pulling apart as if it were an accordion. He had the thin, tense look of a child used to being pinched in the playground.

"You're Colin Rees?"

"Colly, yes, sir." The boy shook Jury's outstretched hand. He was thin, with legs like spindles and fingers like dry twigs.

"I'm Superintendent Jury. This is divisional Commander Macalvie." The boy nodded at Macalvie with the solemnity of an acolyte. "This here's my brother, Jimmy. Say hello, Jimmy."

That Jimmy, who was a stubbier version of Colly, wasn't going to say "hello" was made clear by the head turned to the floor as if the eyes meant to drill a hole through the divisional commander's shoes.

Colly Rees shrugged. "Jimmy never did talk much before Uncle Bub got after him about that lady and now he don't talk at all. Uncle Bub said we was to stay straight out of it. Well, he's not a proper uncle, he ain't, but —"

"Let's sit down, Colly. Jimmy?"

141

Jimmy stood like a stump, his eyes on Macalvie's shoes.

Colly, sitting half-on, half-off one of the leather benches that lined the lobby wall, said to Jury, pumping up his lungs for another go, "What happened was, Jimmy and me was inside the pub —"

"What were you and Jimmy doing *inside?*" asked Wiggins, looking a little fretful at the possibility of a violation of the licensing laws.

"Oh, well, we was just waiting in the kitchen. For Uncle Bub. He kind of caretakes the place and he was closing up. Me and Jimmy'd come from the fillums down in Curzon Street."

Jury looked up at Macalvie, whose silence was being bought at the price of a stare that could have nailed Colly Rees to the wall. "Go on, then," he said to Colly.

"It was Jimmy saw her. He was standing on a bench, looking out through the window at the rain."

"Saw who?"

"This lady, sir. Well, that's what Jimmy says. Now me, I was near the side door that was still open. And I heard someone running. It must have been the same lady, sir." He was crushing his hat up into a ball in his earnestness.

"You heard her. You didn't see her?"

Colly Rees shook his head impatiently and twisted his cap. "It was Jimmy done the seeing. Well, see, we neither of us dihn't think nothing of it, just somebody running in the rain. It was only after we was watching the telly and heard the news about that lady getting —" Colly jerked his scarf about his neck. Wiggins winced.

"Okay. Go on, Colly."

"Nothing to be going on with, except it was a lady."

"Jimmy?" said Jury to the little one's back. Jimmy Rees hadn't moved an inch since he'd taken up his station by Macalvie's shoes. And Macalvie, thought Jury, was making the supreme sacrifice: he hadn't cuffed, slugged, or shouted at him.

Colly said: "Oh, you won't get nothing outta Jimmy, sir. Acts like he's deaf as a post when he wants to."

"Didn't he describe this lady?"

"No. 'The rainlady' he calls her." He looked at his brother, whose head bobbed slightly like an apple on a branch, perhaps by way of confirmation.

Jury looked at Macalvie and back at Colly. "It was raining. Is that what he means?"

"I don't know, sir, do I? Whenever I ask him all he says is, ' 'Twas the rainlady.' He frowned at Jimmy's back, as if this runic message better not pop out inside the walls of New Scotland Yard. "And Aunt Nettie she talked to him something fierce about telling stories, and give him a box round the ears, and give Uncle Bub one, too, for letting us stop in that pub. Said she'd do us both proper if we was to say anything about that night."

"I wouldn't worry about Aunt Nettie, Colly —"

"I don't guess you would. She ain't your aunt, is she? But she says she won't let us watch the telly or have no sweets. Jimmy just loves the telly, that's why he don't talk much. He'd as soon let everybody else do it. I asked him and asked him, dihn't I? And that's all he says. ' 'Twas the rainlady.' "

Macalvie pried his eyes from the downturned head of Jimmy Rees and beamed them on his older brother. "You said you heard running footsteps. How'd you know it was a woman?"

"Well, I guess it had to be, dihn't it, if Jimmy here *saw* a lady?" he said reasonably.

"That's not what I asked: I asked what you *heard.*"

"She was running, sir. I mean, '*it,*' " he added as a quick qualification. " 'It' was running, sir."

Macalvie bestowed upon Colly a smile like splintered wood. "I mean, how could you tell she or he was running?"

143

With his tongue he made a clicking sound against the roof of his mouth: "It was them high heels. I never did know a man to wear them."

"Running?"

"Yes, sir."

"Walking fast, maybe."

"Running."

"Walking."

Wiggins looked from Macalvie to first one boy and then the other. "Sir, does it make that much difference?"

Macalvie glared. "You decide if it's the truth first. You decide if it makes a difference second." He turned back to Colly. "Let's say it was a woman," he graciously allowed. "You wouldn't have heard the tap of the heels; the heels wouldn't have hit the ground if she'd been running. So she was walking fast."

"Either way, she might have seen something, Macalvie." Jury turned to Colly. "Okay, Colly, it was certainly brave of you to come here. Both you and Jimmy."

Jimmy did not respond to pronouncements on heroism. He kept his eyes on the shoes.

"Sergeant Wiggins here can take you home. Where do you live?"

"Near Wapping Old Stairs, sir."

Macalvie was tearing open another pack of gum. "I can do it," he said.

"You?"

"Sure. Maybe get some sweets, some ice cream along the way. What do you say, kids?"

Colly said Jimmy liked chocolate flake; Jimmy did not confirm this.

Jury smiled and shook his head. There were moments when kids were just not going to open up — maybe later, but not now, chewing gum and chocolate flake notwithstanding. "Decent of you, Macalvie."

144

"No problem. Maybe we can have a little talk about this lady."

As if the voice were coming out of the floor and transmitted by the divisional commander's shoes, Jimmy said, " 'Twas the rainlady."

PART IV

Stardust Melody

18

❦

THE house in Knightsbridge faced one of those small green parks surrounded by a wrought-iron fence whose gate could only be unlocked with a key. There was no one else up and down the street and no traffic. Jury often marveled at the silence of such neighborhoods; even traffic kept its distance. Several blocks away cars and buses moved along Sloane Street. Jury looked at the cars parked in front of the house: a white Lotus Elan, dropped, really, like a blossom between the long, black Jaguar and the sable brown Mercedes. As he waited, an elderly woman with two Labradors unlatched the gate of the park and went in.

He looked above the door, at the stained glass and the pediment into which had been carved a coat of arms, now faded. The woman who opened the door, probably a housekeeper, was short and curt. If she was surprised at seeing Jury's warrant card, she hid it well.

Hugh Winslow was a tall, spare man somewhere in his middle sixties who probably kept in shape by regular exercise on tennis and squash courts. His eyes were very blue in the sunlamp-tan of his face, the skin tight over the cheekbones, the complexion like parchment. The body relaxed when he settled into the deep armchair in which he had been, apparently, reading; his manner was that of a man who had solved all of his problems some time back, and he looked at Jury as if whatever had brought police to his door was either inconsequential or a mistake altogether.

"What can I do for you, Superintendent? Would you care for a drink?" He started to get up.

"No, thanks. I'd just like to ask you a few questions, Mr. Winslow, having to do with a young lady who was murdered four nights ago near a pub called I Am the Only Running Footman. Do you know it?"

"No, I don't think I do."

"Your brother-in-law frequented it."

"I've visited David a few times in Shepherd Market, but I've not been to that pub —" He broke off.

"I didn't say Shepherd Market."

Winslow fumbled for both cigarettes and words. "I was simply assuming—"

"I see. Perhaps you've talked with your wife or your brother-in-law?"

"Yes, that's it."

You should have thought of that before I did, thought Jury. "David Marr was, so far as anyone knows, the last person to see Ivy Childess alive. He's in a spot. I wondered if you could tell me anything about him."

"David and I see very little of one another, Superintendent. He comes here infrequently, usually when Ned is here."

"Your son."

"Yes."

"And are you on good terms with him?"

Hugh Winslow's answer was oblique. "He used to stay

149

here when he came to London. Now he's taken rooms in Belgravia."

"But how do you get on?"

"Not very well. He's excessively fond of his mother, though. They both are, Ned and David." His smile was strained.

"What do you mean, 'excessively'?"

Hugh Winslow stubbed out the cigarette and poured himself a whiskey. "I simply meant 'extremely,' that's all. It's not unnatural, especially where Marion is concerned. She's the sort of woman who calls up strong feelings in men."

"In you, Mr. Winslow?"

He looked at Jury over the rim of his glass. "I don't see what this has to do with — Miss Childess."

Jury smiled. "Humor me."

Winslow sighed. "Marion and I are somewhat—estranged. We have been ever since our daughter died."

"I'm sorry about your daughter, Mr. Winslow."

"Yes." He got up and started to wander about the room aimlessly, poking up the fire, moving to the high window. Jury was reminded of Marion Winslow. "It happened just out there," he said, nodding toward the street. "The man responsible wasn't sentenced — it wasn't, I suppose, his fault. He seemed, actually, a decent chap. Wells, or something, was his name."

"Miles Wells. I've checked the accident report. Ten o'clock at night, wasn't it?"

Abstractedly, Hugh nodded, continued his own train of thought. "Yes, I suppose so. It's difficult being thought perfect, you know; that's the way they seemed to think about Phoebe. It must have left her very little room to breathe. Like other children, she had a temper. She was only a little girl, not a holy icon. But everything seemed to change, with that."

150

"Until her death, you and your wife were quite happy, were you?"

"I'd say so, yes."

"Yet, there were other women, Mr. Winslow."

Hugh Winslow had returned to his chair by the fire. It was a dark leather wing chair, and again Jury was reminded of that meeting with his wife. An odd feeling, like déjà vu.

Hugh's smile was a little chilly. "Well, that's true. You might not understand it, but Marion is about the most perfect woman I've ever known —"

"And it was difficult for you to live with perfection."

He nodded. "But if it's David you've come about, you'd be better off asking Marion." He started to pour himself another drink.

Hugh Winslow seemed as isolated as the privileged strollers in the park across the street; it would need a key to get in.

"I have talked with her; it isn't David Marr I wanted to ask you about, particularly. It's Ivy Childess."

The decanter froze in midair. Then he put it down, replaced the stopper, and said, "I really don't know what you mean." It was a poor effort to regain his composure. The key had turned; the gate was open.

"I mean that you knew Ivy Childess."

"I met her once. It was here, at a small cocktail party."

"And you'd met her since, hadn't you? At the Running Footman."

He looked over at the dying fire. Then he turned and said, "Yes."

"But why see her at the pub your brother-in-law often went to?" Jury thought he knew the answer to that.

And it was confirmed when Winslow said it had been Ivy's idea; she liked the place. "But they knew nothing about Ivy and me. Marion certainly didn't."

151

"Are you sure she didn't suspect?"

"Yes. If she had —"

"If she had, she might have divorced you, is that it?"

"Ivy kept up her relationship with David simply so no one would suspect."

Perhaps he really believed that. "Was she holding out for marriage? Did she threaten to make a scene?" Jury knew he was right from the unhappy look Hugh Winslow gave him. "Which is perhaps a price you weren't prepared to pay. Your wife has a great deal of money in her own right."

"I am not exactly a pauper, Superintendent. Oh, you're right, in a way. I wasn't prepared to pay the price. I love Marion; I had no intention of marrying Ivy."

Jury was silent for a moment. His mind had turned to the talk with Stella Broome. *Flash cars and flash men.* Like Ivy Childess, in a way. "Mr. Winslow, about ten months ago there was a young woman murdered in a wood off the road between Exeter and Bristol. Her name was Sheila Broome. Mean anything to you?"

Hugh Winslow seemed relieved that they had left the subject of Ivy Childess. "No, no, I've never heard the name."

"The end of February. The twenty-ninth, it was."

He tried to laugh, but it caught in his throat. "Superintendent, you seem to be asking me where I was."

Jury smiled. "That's right."

Winslow's voice frosted over. "I believe I was out of the country. I have offices in Paris. But I can certainly check my calendar, although I doubt that particular appointment would be noted, were I going to Devon."

"Check it anyway, Mr. Winslow. Is that your Jaguar outside?"

He seemed confused. "Well, no. The Mercedes is mine. Why?"

"Ever own a Jaguar?"

152

"Of course." He shrugged.

Hasn't everyone? Jury smiled. "When was that?"

"Oh, two or three years ago, I expect. But I don't see why —?"

"You said you had no intention of marrying Ivy. That sounds very much like what your brother-in-law said."

Winslow shifted uncomfortably in his chair. "Ivy was — well, she was a terrible opportunist. And I've never known anyone so adept at finding out things. The sort of woman you confide in and wish you hadn't —" He stopped.

Jury thought for a moment. "Would your brother-in-law be likely to confide in her?"

"David? Probably; he's a much softer person than people suppose. But I'm not sure what there would have been to confide; David is very open."

Given that Hugh had been excluded from the family circle, Jury thought him to be fairly charitable. "Mr. Marr seems to have run through a great deal of money, your wife said. And he seems fond of going off to places like Cannes and Monte Carlo —" An image of David Marr's pleasantly sloppy bulletin board came to Jury's mind. "Has he ever been to America?"

Hugh Winslow frowned. "Not that I know of. None of us has. Rose — that was Edward's wife — used to talk about going there. I've always wanted —"

"Yes, so've I. David Marr does not really seem to have expensive tastes, although he talks about gambling, casinos, the fast life. It makes me wonder about the money he's run through."

"I can't imagine David buying Ivy's silence. David's much more the publish-and-be-damned type."

"Depends on what might get published, I expect. And what about you, Mr. Winslow? Are you the same type?"

153

Startled, Winslow turned away. "I imagine I did let Ivy borrow a bit."

"Borrow. How much would a 'bit' be?"

"A few thousand." Hastily, he added, as if it would justify the loan, "She wanted to buy into the shop she worked in as assistant. It's in Covent Garden —"

"Perhaps that's your idea of 'small'; it's not mine. A blackmailer might call it 'small,' of course."

Winslow looked ashen.

"That accident to your little girl happened around ten —"

"What does *that* have to do with it?"

"Perhaps a great deal. At ten o'clock at night, Phoebe ran out into the street. You say she had tantrums. Is that by way of explaining why an eight-year-old would run out into a dark street late at night? Or was there some other reason? Although Edward was here, you say, he wasn't staying here. That meant you were here with Phoebe. And someone else, possibly."

"Ivy was here," he said, his head propped up by his hand, like something broken. "Phoebe saw us." He looked upward, as if visualizing a scene on the floor above. "It was dreadful." His head dropped in his hand again. "But she wasn't blackmailing me, Superintendent."

"Not technically, perhaps. But didn't it come to the same thing? 'A few thousand quid, and I won't tell Marion what happened that night'?"

Winslow didn't answer.

Jury rose and said, "I'll want to talk with you later."

Hugh Winslow saw him to the door, where he said, as if they were still speaking about her, "The price would have been Marion. I'm already a pariah, I expect. They don't communicate much anymore." He looked very weary.

"Yes," was all of Jury's answer. A pariah. Standing in the

hall, Jury looked at him with sympathy, thought of his isolation. They had sent him to Coventry.

He looked back from the pavement to see the man still framed in the doorway, the pediment with its faded coat of arms above him, origins probably long forgotten.

In the little park across the way one or two people walked, enjoying privacy and privilege.

19

~~~

THERE once was a marketplace, but it had been replaced by a grimly commercial double-storied shop-
ping mall with its collection of boutiques, forbidding
health food restaurants, candy shops, card shops, novelty
shops, all of them charging inflated prices because of the address. Jury preferred cabbages and fishmongers. So did Wiggins, apparently.

"I liked it the other way; I liked them selling fresh vegetables and so forth. I wish the Council would just have left it
alone, so what if it was a bit grotty and smelly. That was
London, after all."

"You're right, Wiggins. That was London."

Blue neon shading into silver stuttered out the shop's
name, Starrdust. Against the black background, the last three
letters trailed off into another dimension, dusted with silver.

The shop faced Covent Garden's new marketplace — at
least Jury would always think of it as new. As he stood with
Wiggins and looked into the window, Jury thought Starrdust

might even be a sort of oasis amidst all of this clamor, the rush of rock music rolling in waves from shop fronts; the endless trade in records and jeans and croissant sandwiches.

At first Jury thought it must be a magic shop. Against a cloth backdrop of black velvet (itself sprinkled with silver dust) the window displayed black-coned hats with gold quarter moons, ebony wands topped with fake jeweled stars, silver cutouts of planets hanging by invisible threads. And off to one side was a little house in the woods, and out of this house on an electrified rail came a mechanical Merlin, in his black and starry cape and hat, clutching a tiny wand that he raised once as if in benediction before he rolled silently home.

"Did you see that, sir?" said Wiggins, apparently unaware of the three children that had lately gathered for the wizard performance.

Jury studied the cardboard constellations, names dangling on bits of silver string — Pluto, Scorpio — down through all of the signs of the zodiac. And a sun, giving off a pale wintry light that directed one's attention to a large book, opened, with illuminated writing. And farther down a small gold sign said "Horoscopes and Rare Books." The shop catered not for magicians but for fatalists.

When Jury cupped his hands and looked through the glass of the door (that also bore a sign "Shop assistant wanted"), he thought the place must be closed for lunch, it was so dark. Yet Wiggins had called to say they were coming. He turned the knob and the door opened. Wiggins dragged himself away from Merlin and the three children and followed him.

Like a theater that takes a little getting used to, Starrdust was appropriately cave-dark. Jury blinked. The room was quite long and narrow, and he could not see into its farthest reaches. Whoever had done the place up was highly imaginative. If it was Andrew Starr, he had had the good fortune of never quite growing up. There were lights in the place,

157

bright points of light, that made Jury remember reading under the covers with a flashlight. The room got vaguely lighter. Off in one corner was a child-sized house, painted in the neon blue of the sign, covered with astrological symbols and with a bright sign over its door: *Horror-Scopes.* The three children who didn't look like they'd a pence between them had swarmed in with Jury and Wiggins and made for the playhouse. They were obviously well acquainted with the wonders of Starrdust. Against the long wall several tall book-cases were spaced. Between them on the wall hung silver-framed photos of film stars, long-ago ones like Judy Garland, Ronald Colman. They all looked out of the past amid a spat-tering of stars and little moons. Jury looked at the books and saw they were indeed antiquarian stuff, stacked among the moons and stars like a lunar library.

The pièce de résistance had already been discovered by Wiggins, who was gazing up at a domed ceiling of which the owner had taken best advantage and made into a sort of mock planetarium. "Look at that," said Wiggins again. "Like Madam Tussand's that one is."

"Not quite," said Jury, star-gazing up himself. "See, there goes Venus —" A light dimmed behind the planet. "— and here comes Mars." A light switched silently on. The star-works continued operating its little lights and giving the eerie feeling that the skies were moving.

"Feel like I'm floating," said Wiggins.

From the horror-house came an almost drowsy laughter.

From somewhere in the rear came the Tin-Panny sound of Hoagy Carmichael's "Stardust." But there was no blare, no stereo. Surprisingly the record, which sounded very scratched, was being played on a simple record player. Time seemed to stretch like the room itself. Jury actually checked his watch, although he knew they'd only been here a minute or less.

Out of the well at the rear, two girls of probably nineteen

or twenty came forward. They were dressed in gray cords and black peasant blouses with some sort of silvery thread that winked in the light of the planetarium-ceiling. They both had pale hair held back with star-crusted combs; pale, almost opalescent skin; eyes shaded in blue and silver, pearly-pink lipstick so that the light that washed over them turned to a dissolving rainbow. One might have thought they were twins, though they weren't; weren't, perhaps, even sisters. One asked if they could help. The other giggled slightly. The first gave her a look of warning. Yet they exuded such an air of good humor, Jury couldn't help but laugh himself a little, seeing them standing there straight, each with an arm round the other's waist, like skaters on a pond.

At Jury's response, their clear faces grew even brighter, if that were possible, almost as if the lights behind the planets had switched on behind their eyes. He showed them his warrant card.

"Oh!" said one of the stardust twins. "It's Andrew you'll be wanting to see. See, he told us to look out for two coppers —" She coughed and blushed and said, sorry, "—but you neither of you look nothing like police. . . . "

Jury smiled as her voice trailed off. Wiggins probably didn't look like much of anything except a star-gazer. He was still at it. "Andrew Starr, is it? My sergeant talked to him earlier."

"Andrew, that's right. We'll just get him." The stardust twins apparently did everything in two's. There were fresh giggles, but not from the girls. "It's them kids again, Meg," said one. "Oh, Andy don't mind," said the other. Mind or not, they shooed the children out of the painted house. They trooped about for a bit, looking but not touching, and then came to stand and stare, openmouthed, gap-toothed, up at Jury, who knew not what precisely they were assessing him for, but to take no chances, he plunked down a ten-p piece and took three jelly babies from the glass bowl.

159

They looked at one another, smiled a little, and then trooped out. Another day in the Starrdust.

Andrew Starr had come in on their exiting coattails and looked at them now on the outside staring in at the toy Merlin. He shook his head. "They're here several times a week," he said without introduction. "A few of the regulars. Like a pub, the Starrdust is. It's got its regulars."

Jury looked at Wiggins, still transfixed by the stars, and thought the Starrdust might have added one more to its list.

Andrew Starr was a good-looking young man, slight but well built and well dressed, a person who could make his unexceptionable outfit — tailored cotton shirt and jeans — look as if they came from a bespoke tailor. His hair and eyes were dark, his bones finely structured. He wore a heavy pendant, probably his own astrological sign, and a gold link bracelet, which he habitually turned.

"Of course, it's about Ivy, isn't it?" Starr sat down behind his counter and fished a cigarette from a porcelain mug. He lit up and offered the cigarettes to Jury. Wiggins had finally come down to earth and was getting out his notebook. The stardust twins were shelving books from a crate.

"Ivy Childess, yes. How long had she been working here?"

"Year or less. Had a job behind a counter at Boots before she came here. Ivy was much too ambitious to spend her days dusting eyeshadow on middle-aged women."

"Ambitious?"

"Oh, my, yes. There were three words to describe Ivy. Ambition, ambition, ambition. Of course, she was very good here —"

"What'd she do, exactly?"

"Shop assistant; as you see, I'm looking for another one. Sorry, that sounds a bit macabre. Well, I just can't get all worked up about Ivy. I didn't honestly like her much, but as I

160

said, she was damned good. Besides that,"— Starr reached beneath the counter — "she was a pretty good Madame Zostra."

He had brought out a spangled satin wraparound headpiece, something like a turban, and a large pack of cards, the tarot deck. Jury smiled. "Ivy told fortunes, did she?"

Andrew Starr smiled broadly. "For fun, for entertainment. No attempt to rip off the clientele. Much as she wanted to," he added dryly.

Jury spread out the cards. "You don't believe in all this, then?"

Starr looked a little wounded. "Of course I do. Astrology, that is. And most of my customers I've had for ages." He looked toward the photographs between the bookcases. "Theater, film stars. Well, not them up there. Guess they're all dead. Never did see Marilyn Monroe, worse luck."

Jury smiled. "You'd have been much too young to appreciate her."

"Not for Marilyn Monroe."

"Did Ivy believe in the tarot, astrology, that sort of thing?"

"Oh, good heavens, no. That's probably why she was better at selling stuff. She could sell a pig a silver trough. No, but she knew a good thing — Starrdust *is* a good thing, I can tell you —"

"I believe it, Mr. Starr."

"Andrew. Call me Andrew. Well, Ivy had a bit of money and she kept nagging me to buy in. Wanted to be my partner, she did. I didn't pay any attention to her because I thought she hadn't any more than a few hundred quid — what I mean is, I didn't really bother saying I didn't *want* a partner. Well, she must have taken this as encouragement. Comes in one day with a check for two thousand quid. Then, of course, I put her right off. Said I didn't need a partner. But the damned girl — sorry — Ivy was as tenacious as her name. If she wanted something, she just *went* for it. Power was what

161

she wanted, and money meant power. Take this chap, David, she went about with —"

"David Marr."

"Poor devil. He came in here a few times before closing, hung about, waiting for her. I thought he was a pleasant fellow myself. You know, it's odd the way some people, no matter how simply they dress and talk, simply *reek* of money. Marr was one. So of course she hung on to him. Pardon." He reached behind him and spun another record onto the machine. It was scratchy, like the first. The voice of Dinah Shore singing "Stars Fell on Alabama."

"Ivy wanted to marry him, you think?"

Andrew hooted. "My God, but didn't she. The man was *loaded*. Well, would have been. She talked a lot about what he'd come into. As if she were coming into it too, of course. Only, you know, he didn't seem all that interested. At least not in marrying Ivy. But I suppose she thought she'd wear down his resistance; she'd sit here and flip through the cards and keep saying she'd an 'ace' up her sleeve."

"What do you think she meant by that?"

He shrugged. "Dunno." Andrew twisted the gold bracelet round and round his wrist and frowned. "You know, I think this Marr fellow thought at first he was getting a sweet little shop-girl in Ivy, and then found out she was a grasping, cold-hearted little bitch. Sorry."

"No need to apologize, Andrew. The dead are no more likable because they're dead."

Andrew Starr relaxed and lit another cigarette. "If you want to know what *I* think, it's that her boyfriend really did want to settle down. Probably, in a little cottage in Kent or somewhere—"

Jury smiled. "That's not exactly my impression of David Marr."

"I'm extremely intuitive, Superintendent. Seriously." He

looked round the room. "I've always been fascinated with this sort of thing — when was Marr born, do you know?"

Jury calculated. "Nineteen forty-six. I'd have to check the month and day."

"And hour. Find out that for me and I can tell just what kind of person he is."

Jury had heard of using clairvoyants to solve crimes, but not astrologers. "Thanks. We can use all the help we can get. But do you think he was capable of murder?"

To Jury's surprise, Andrew Starr did not immediately say no. Instead, he gazed up at his mock-planetarium, and finally said, "Oh, he seems very cool, but he's the sort who might do anything — murder, even — if he's terribly disillusioned."

Wiggins looked up from his notebook. "That 'ace' up her sleeve, sir. Would you say she might have known something about David Marr?"

"Possible. In some way she certainly thought she could trump Marr's trick—No. No. No, children—"

This was addressed to the stardust twins, who were in the process of hanging the mirror that had been resting against the bookshelves. One of them stood on a short ladder, the other was holding the mirror at the bottom.

"— a little bit higher. That's right."

It was an odd sort of mirror, a combination of mirror and kaleidoscope. From its fractured center, chips of color turned and reflected in spangles on the twins' faces. "Where'd you get that?" asked Jury.

"Antiques shop in Brighton. I thought it would fit here. The kaleidoscope effect is an optical illusion."

"Brighton?"

Andrew nodded. "Used to live in Hove. I did a fair business in Brighton with horoscopes. You know it's quite famous for looking into the future—if one can put it that way. The place has got a long tradition of astrologers and clairvoyants and so

163

forth. Of course, it's a seaside town, so perhaps that's to be expected. Most of them are honest, I'd say. One or two quite brilliant. I was never one of the one or two," he said ruefully. "Still, I'm honest."

Wiggins was watching the mirror-event with great fascination. "Don't you think, sir, I should just go and give the young ladies a hand?" Without waiting for Jury to agree, he put his notebook on the counter and went off.

"Interesting. We've got to talk to someone in Brighton." Since it was Wiggins whom Jury was going to have do the talking to, he was glad he was out of earshot; Wiggins didn't much fancy seaside resorts, winter or summer. Winter, especially, spelled certain death. "Did you ever know Ivy Childess to go there?"

"Not to my knowledge. As I said, Ivy didn't believe in much of anything but cold, hard cash. Your sergeant seems to be right at home —" He nodded toward the mirror-event. "— if he ever tires of the Met, think he'd like a job?"

Jury smiled. "That's the sign in the window, is it? Speaking of that, have you had any response?"

"Oh, yes. Quite a bit. But they don't really suit, somehow." Andrew shrugged. They're either condescending or crass." He looked up at the planets. "They seem to think it's all a joke, or cleverly commercial, or unworthy of their considerable talents."

"The reason I ask is I have a friend who just might do you. Well, if you can take someone a little bit zany. But hardworking and loyal and very, very pretty."

"Sounds divine. As to the zany, good; that's our style. And as to the *pretty*, all the better. Customers like it, and so do I. A pretty face lifts the spirits, Superintendent, wouldn't you say?"

"I certainly would." He looked at the stardust twins, who with Wiggins's help had hung the glass from the neon heav-

164

ens. The three of them were standing, looking up at it, making fun-house faces, splattered with rainbow-chips. "Are they sisters?"

"Meg and Joy? Oh, no. A lot of people think they're twins, even. I have them dress alike and I suppose again it's a kind of illusion. Most people see what they want to, or at least what they expect to. No, Meg and Joy came in one day when I needed a clerk. They just stood there, looking beamish, and their poor faces fell when I told them I only needed the one. They looked *so* unhappy that I just hired them both. I couldn't bear separating them, I hated to break up the set." He smiled. "But I haven't been sorry. Do you know, they've been here for nearly two years, and in all that time I haven't heard one cross word between them. Plenty of cross words from Ivy, though. And she couldn't stand Meg and Joy. To me that says a lot about Ivy Childess. Not only was I not going to make her a partner, I was going to fire her."

"That bad, was she?"

"That bad. To tell the truth, I'm surprised it wasn't the other way round, her being killed. I mean I'd say she'd have been more liable to kill Marr for refusing to marry her. Poor bloke."

"Did she ever mention any other men, Andrew? Could that have been the ace up her sleeve?"

Andrew Starr thought for a moment. "I honestly can't remember any other man ever being mentioned. He'd have to be rich."

"Or someone who might very well have made David Marr jealous."

"Him jealous? Oh, no, I don't think so. In fact I think Marr and I had the same thing in mind: dump her."

"She wouldn't have taken kindly to dumping." Jury pocketed Wiggins's notebook and got up. "Andrew, I appreciate your help."

"Happy to. And tell that friend of yours to call and set up a time we can get together. Or she can just come round, but the place tends to get very busy." Andrew wrote on the back of a Starrdust card and handed the card to Jury. "There's another number here. Ex-directory. The business line can get terribly tied up. We're closed today, actually. We left the door open for you and your sergeant."

"Well, I'll just collect my sergeant and be on my way." He called to Wiggins, who turned unhappily from the mirror and came back to the counter, in a wake of giggles. The stardust twins went about polishing the mirror.

"I like your shop, Mr. Starr. Bet the kiddies find it a sort of paradise, with all the lights and stars and that little house over there." Wiggins nodded toward *Horror-Scopes*.

"They do, yes. Not been inside that, Sergeant?" Andrew slid a bit of a smile in Jury's direction as Wiggins hesitated, looking at the house.

"Don't tempt him. Thanks again."

"That's all right. I hardly feel I've been questioned by police." He smiled.

"There might be someone coming along to ask a few questions. The Devon police have an interest in this case. Anyway" — Jury smiled — "you might feel you've been questioned by police then."

"I'll be watching out for them. Good-bye, Superintendent. Sergeant." They shook hands as the stardust twins watched. The one on her ladder perch waved the dustcloth.

On the pavement, Jury blinked. "A nice fellow; a nice place."

"You know, sir, all of that fooling about with the mirror — I hope you didn't think I was larking."

"No, of course not. Anyway, we all need a bit of a lark now and then."

They were walking toward the Covent Garden tube station.

"What I was really doing, was asking a few discreet questions of the girls."

"Oh? Did you find out anything, then?" Jury looked away, smiling.

Wiggins walked along deep in thought. To help it along, he drew out his tube of lozenges. "Only that they didn't really know anything, sir. But they did ask me round to their place for tea and a chat sometime. Here, do you need their address?"

"Just keep it handy, Wiggins. You never know. Here's the station." They looked up at the blue and red sign. "It's going to be pretty, isn't it, when they finally finish." He nodded toward the scaffolding outside. "Going to be done in a garden motif. Well, it's Covent Garden, isn't it?"

"True. We're not going to be seeing too much of gardens in the next few days. I want to talk to Marr's friend, Paul Swann, so I just thought we'd go down to Brighton in the morning."

The lozenges might have done for the London market; Brighton, however, hard by the sea, necessitated the drawing out of Wiggins's handkerchief. "Brighton, sir." He blew his nose and, without even as yet casting his eye on the cold sea, or lifting his face to the cold sea air, he looked as if he were coming down with sea-virus. "That's right by the sea, sir."

"I know." It occurred to Jury that not once in the Starrdust had Wiggins gone for nose drops, handkerchief, lozenges. Jury stared up at a sky as unyielding as cement. "Hard falling back to earth, isn't it?"

20

KATE looked up at the high, huge dome, the silver-winged dragon, the star of mirror glass, the open flowers, and the ropes of jewels from which hung the splendid chandelier and wondered what it must have been like when the room was alight. An artificial day created by a blaze of diamonds.

On the other side of the red velvet cord, Kate was the only visitor now. The half-dozen others who had been wandering about were no longer to be seen. The guard at the end of the banqueting table looked bored, impatient to be home, probably; he had ceased long ago to be impressed by gilded serpents and silver dragons and jewels. Perhaps he thought of it as some sort of joke, some hoax, the sort of thing that royalty was always getting up to. He yawned and clasped his hands behind his back.

Her mind, she supposed, was no less mundane, no less homeward-looking. In the midst of this splendor — what exotic dishes must have been served up at that table! — she thought of the meal she must fix, the carrots and cabbage left out. Carrots and cabbage.

Kate dug her hands into her coat pockets, her purse trolling from her wrist, and wondered what Dolly was doing, where she was. They had had another of their arguments about the bed-and-breakfast business, letting the room to a stranger. I beg your pardon, Dolly, but that's generally the sort who books rooms: strangers. Who was he? What did she know about him? Didn't she realize it could be dangerous?

He had hardly looked dangerous. He looked, indeed, quite attractive, quite interesting. Had she told Dolly she had met him in the Spotted Dog — well, all hell would have broken loose. Kate sighed. To meet someone in a pub and offer him a room, knowing nothing about him . . .

A guard was at her elbow, telling her quietly that it was just on five, closing time. How long had she been standing here? As she walked out into the long corridor, the question remained: What did she know about him except that he was charming? Nothing. He came from London, and what did that mean? Perhaps Dolly was right this time. But then Dolly did not share her, Kate's, loneliness.

Under a ceiling divided by small trellises, Kate walked through the reds and blues, bamboo and porcelain, and wondered what sort of man, what sort of king, could build himself this fantasy world. Whose lives had he ruined, whose hearts had he wrecked in the fashioning?

Kate made her way across Castle Square. A light rain lifted and billowed like a delicate curtain and there were few other people in the square, which is why she noticed the man at the far end of the long walk. It was too far away to tell absolutely, but she thought he resembled the man she'd met in the Spotted Dog. He did not move; he seemed to be looking at her.

It made her nervous, although she knew it was ridiculous. He was observing the Royal Pavilion, not Kate. She stopped and turned and looked back. The exquisite architecture of the Pavilion's facade was sorely borne upon by high scaffolding. Most of the workmen had left, but two still sat up there, smoking and drinking from Styrofoam cups. A building full of silver dragons and diamonds and dry rot. She stuffed her hair up under her knitted cap and thought that the reality was the scaffolding, not the silver and gilt. The workmen flicked their cigarettes over the edge, took their belongings, quit, unaware they were patching up a fantasy. Buildings rot, that meant jobs.

When Kate turned again, the man was gone.

21

THREE floors up, Carole-anne Palutski was reeling in the undies pinned to a rope she'd rigged between windowsill and close-hanging branch. The row of bright-colored bikini panties billowed slightly in the wind up there, like flags on a yacht. In the Islington house, there were just the three of them — Mrs. Wassermann in the basement flat, Jury on the ground floor, Carole-anne two floors above, where the rent was cheaper. The middle flat was vacant, and Carole-anne had convinced the landlord to let her "show" it. This was done not simply for the reduced rent it allowed her, but to make sure that if anyone got in, it would be someone who would not upset their clubby three-some.

"Hi, Super!" she called, waving her free hand hysterically as if she didn't see him every day. The undies shot in; the head disappeared.

Jury went up the steps to his Islington flat, first looking to see if Mrs. Wassermann was in. These days, with Carole-anne around, Mrs. Wassermann had become less fearful of the London streets, had taken to going out more to the shops and the butcher's and the greengrocer's.

As Jury went up, Carole-anne ran down, her espadrilles slap, slap, slapping on the staircase, her bottle of bright coral nail varnish in one hand. She had finished one set of fingers and one set of toes. They just missed a collision in front of his door, which didn't surprise Jury; she'd caused enough out in the street. Carole-anne was the only person he knew who could saunter across Piccadilly Circus nonstop. Today she was wearing blinding pink shorts and top that made a surprising blend with her red-gold hair. Only, some of that hair had been dyed an even deeper red since he'd seen her five days ago. Hot coral, brazen pink, brassy orange, fiery licks of hair.

"Hello, Carole-anne; you look like a Tijuana sunset." As they went into his flat, he asked her what she'd done to her hair.

"Now you'll be on about it, I expect," she said crossly, as she flopped herself on his sprung sofa and finished applying the polish to her other toes. Then, "Oh," she said carelessly, unfolding herself and pulling a piece of notepaper from the waistband of her shorts. "Here. It's from SB-stroke-H."

Carole-anne refused actually to *name* Susan Bredon-Hunt, as if by this magical incantation, the person named might appear out of fire and smoke on the spot. Jury looked at the note and its terse message: *eight o'clock.*

Now, Jury knew that Susan Bredon-Hunt was not a woman of few words. He waved the paper. "This all? No flowery tribute to New Scotland Yard and its minions, me being minion number one? No frills and furbelows? No, 'love, Susan'?" He sat down and pulled out his cigarettes and wondered if he had any more beer.

"You needn't get shirty," Carole-anne said, huffing it out.

She was now half-reclining on the sofa, her legs raised in the air, the small of her back propped with her hands. "I'm only the bloody answering service, I am."

Jury smiled. Well, it was true. Carole-anne loved to come in and answer his telephone and play her records on his old record player. He sometimes came home and heard the keening wail of Tiny Rudy, her favorite vocalist, or the calamity-in-the-kitchen sounds (breaking crockery and crystal) of Ticket to Hell, her favorite rock group. Given this access to his flat, Carole-anne had decided three months ago that her favorite policeman should have it redecorated and (naturally without his knowledge) had called Decors, one of the swankiest outfits in London, to come round with their swatches.

Her largess with imaginary money was then forgotten, but the swatches had turned up all the same, in the hand of Susan Bredon-Hunt — tall, model-thin, high-fashion clothes, hair razor cut . . .

It was beginning to sound metallic. All Carole-anne's doing, with her various descriptions of Susan. Her dresses looked like sheet-metal, straight up and down. But then if you'd got nothing up here (the description turning graphic), you wouldn't want to call attention to it, would you? And them cheekbones. She looks like a kite; she's all wings — hips, face . . . One of these days you'll be looking up at my undies and see her fly over.

"You need someone with a bit more bounce," she said now, raising her legs again.

"You're bouncy enough for me. Let's get back to this job at the sleaze joint. You can't take that job —"

"Don't be such an old stick, Super. It's a leg up, init?" Her own legs came slowly down.

"Leg up, hell. From King Arthur's to Soho is leaving a cesspool for a sewer."

She puffed with the exertion of lowering her legs back over

173

her head. "All the Q.T. Club wants is that the hostesses see the clientele don't run out of drinks and chips. You know, for the gambling."

"Oh, don't I know. The whole Dirty Squad knows. You look like a pretzel."

She turned her head and stuck out her tongue.

"That wheel's so rigged you could hoist a mainsail on it." Carole-anne sighed and sat up. "You should see the gown I wear —"

"No, thanks."

Her hands were on her hips. "Lord, you're wors'n an old mum." She tossed her head. It was a poor attempt at hauteur with a pile of red-gold curls spilling across her face.

Jury sighed. He could sympathize with the old mums of this world, trying to convince their kids they shouldn't do what they didn't want to do anyway. Well, he supposed the kids had to beat up on someone because they were mad at themselves at not having the nerve to undertake what was usually some harrowing scheme involving danger.

"You have to be twenty-one to work in that place. You're under."

It was worse than telling her she was ugly. "I'm *not* under. I'm over. Twenty-two."

"No kidding? Last week you were twenty-five when you went looking for that steno job. Twenty-five being the age they wanted. Age melts from thy divine countenance."

She changed the subject. "How long you going to be gone?"

"Five minutes. Long enough to put the Q.T. Club out of business."

"God! Leave off!" She picked up a pillow.

Jury felt a soft thud on his forehead. "And what about the theater? You can't work nights and keep your job."

She flounced back on the couch. "It's not even West End. Camden-bloody-Town! You call that *theater?*"

174

"Just call the club and tell them you regret you must leave town. Say your old mum is dying."

Now she was turned on her side doing quick scissor-cuts with her legs. "Is SB-stroke-H coming over, then?"

"Susan is her name. Yes, for a bit."

Carole-anne sat up again and cut him dead with a look from eyes the color of the Aegean. At least Jury imagined that was what the Aegean must be like, deep shimmering blue blending into the purple horizon. "Tonight we was to go down the Angel." She flopped back, dead.

"I'm really sorry, Carole-anne. I was supposed to see Susan last night and I didn't."

Points for him, having stood up Susan. Carole-anne relented and struck a languid pose, dangling her espadrille on her toes. "You want to go to bed with a frozen lolly, I don't mind."

Jury shut his eyes, not so much to shut out Carole-anne's nattering as to defrost the image of Susan she'd just conjured up. "Who I go to bed with is kind of my business, wouldn't you say?"

No, she wouldn't. She started peeling the new polish from her thumbnail and said, "You gotta be careful of flopping in the sack with just *anyone* —"

"Carole-*anne*." It was the dangerous tone.

Which bothered Carole-anne no more than the sandal she was fitting on her small white foot, Cinderella-wise. "What time is it?"

Jury was suspicious. Carole-anne never cared about time when she was using his flat, for whatever purpose. He felt as if he were living on the time-share plan. "Half-past five. Why?"

She rose and stretched, a sight not just for the sore-eyed but for the blind. "Oh, just thought I'd go for a walk." Arms straight out, she turned from the waist. "What time's SB-stroke-H coming?" Round to the right, round to the left . . .

As if she didn't know. "Eight. Why?"

Her calisthenics continued. Deep kneebends now. She shrugged at the same time. "Nothing." She ended with a split.

"You can be the house cheerleader. Listen, while I'm gone, keep an eye on Mrs. Wassermann, will you? Take her to the Bingo in Upper Street, or something."

Carole-anne stopped halfway down to the floor. "*Bingo?*"

He might as well have asked her to visit a nunnery. "Sure. She's got chums that go there every week."

"Welllll . . ."

"There's a surprise in it for you."

Carole-anne loved surprises. "Sure, I'll take her to Bingo. Don't I always look out for Mrs. W?"

She did, actually. Jury said, "I've found a job for you."

Still split, she took the card he held out. "That's a *surprise?* What's this?" She looked down at the card.

"You'll love it. You get to wear a costume, Carole-anne."

That got her attention. Carole-anne would have gone down the mines if a costume were part of the job. It was one of the reasons she loved acting and was good at it.

"What sort?" Her eyes glittered as she scooped herself off the floor.

"Oh, one part of it's a sort of satin turban. With stars all over it. You get to tell fortunes." He smiled at her own wide smile. Carole-anne was having a good enough time predicting Jury's future. Imagine turning her loose on perfect strangers, knowledge of whose lives would be uncluttered by reality. She'd be moving the planets about to suit herself. In a walk to the Angel pub she'd tried to convince him that the twinkling light on top of the post office building was Haley's Comet.

"Is it a fair, like? Do I have a booth?"

"It's a shop, actually. I'm not sure about the booth." He handed her the little card. "The proprietor wants you to

176

come round right away. Madame Zostra, that's who you're to be," he added. *"Madame Zostra, famous clairvoyant"* . . . where had he read that?

" 'Starrdust,' fancy that," she said, studying the card. "Whatever do they sell?"

Jury smiled. "Oh, different things. Dreams, maybe."

Carole-anne sighed and shoved the card into the band of her shorts. "If SB-stroke-H is coming, you'll need one, Super."

Her espadrilles slapped out and up the stairs.

Susan Bredon-Hunt, who was walking about the room barefoot, in her silky teddies, was talking about a future she seemed to think was theirs. She talked a great deal, Susan did. Immediately she came into his flat, she would undress, but not, he had found, out of a desire to go straight to bed, or even to appear engagingly wanton. She seemed to need to undress to calculate. Prancing back and forth (there was something equine about Susan, who rode to hounds), she smoked and drank her wine. The bowl of the glass she held cupped in her hands like a little crystal ball in which she read their future.

" . . . and it's time you met Daddy, Richard. I just lunched with him today at Claridge's and he wants you to come round for cocktails. . . ."

And so forth. It depressed him to think of it, really. The manor house somewhere in Suffolk. A star-studded family of all sorts of variations of the Most Excellent Order of the British Empire. Here a CBE, there a few OBEs, no lowly MBEs, of course. Daddy, he remembered, was a Knight of the Thistle. Jury imagined that he himself appealed to some sense of recklessness in Susan, the desire to do something shocking like marrying a civil servant, a policeman.

He wished she would stop her pacing and planning and

177

talking about the future they most certainly would never share. Even a fight about the other night when he had left so suddenly would have been a relief, would have made him feel closer to her. But when he had brought it up, she had simply brushed it aside and went on to talk about the future, their future, as if she were dressing a window in some fashionable matchings of escritoires and turkey carpets.

As she paced by his chair, he reached out and pulled her down on his lap, spilling a little of the wine across the peach silk that covered her small breasts. He ran his hands down her sides, from the angles of the shoulders to the bony hips, as she scraped at the wine stain.

"This is brand-new, Richard," she said, pouting.

"I'll buy you another." He buried his face in the curve of her neck —

There was a knock at the door.

He knew who it was.

"Oh, I *hope* I'm not interrupting —" said the tenant from upstairs. Carole-anne Nouveau was wearing a fire-brigade-red dress, down the front of which any man would have loved to dump a cask of wine. The neck was scooped out in a diamond shape, the mandarin collar tightened by some sparkly bit of fake-diamond costume jewelry. The tightness elsewhere didn't need diamonds. He could not believe that she was carrying a casserole, whose steam emitted wonderful vapors. "Your favorite." She smiled sweetly.

He had no idea what his favorite was, but he was suddenly hungry as hell. For drink, food, sex. "Thank you," he said, straight-faced.

"And here's that song . . . " Sweet smile. She sashayed over to the record player, put the casserole down, and took the record from its sleeve. She clicked the button, turned to Jury, and winked, if such a languorous movement of the eyelash could be called a wink. "You remember . . . well . . . "

On an extended sigh she listened to a few bars. *"Of all the girls I LOVED before . . . "* Dreamily, she held Jury's eye long enough for a countdown on a launch pad. "That's Julio. You remember Spain."

The only Spain he'd ever shared with Carole-anne had lasted for twenty minutes in the lobby of the Regency Hotel. He glared at her as Julio remembered the girls he'd loved going in and out his door.

Carole-anne pretended not to notice Jury's black look as she shoved the casserole up against Susan's apricot bosom, and (in a totally different voice) said, "Ten minutes on top of the cooker, dear. Ta."

The steam coming off the casserole could not compete with the steam coming off Susan Bredon-Hunt.

Jury stowed his things in the car next morning and went down the steps to the basement flat. He was surprised to find the door slightly ajar and the heavy drapes open. Mrs. Wassermann had enough deadbolts for a locksmith's display case, and it usually took five minutes just for her to open the door. Not today, though. Since Carole-anne had taken the upstairs flat a year ago, Mrs. Wassermann had lowered the drawbridge of her fortress flat and let in a little light.

"I just dropped in to see if you'd like something from Brighton," Jury said when she came in from the kitchen. Over her navy blue dress she was wearing an apron. Her hair was pulled back from her face and wound in a coil as neat and tight as a clockspring.

"Ah! Mr. Jury, I'm glad you're having a little holiday. Just wait, there is something I have for you."

"Not a holiday, Mrs. Wassermann," he called after her. "I only wish it were."

While he waited, he looked around the flat; with the sun

179

warming the windowpanes and tossing coins of light on the brightly patterned rug she'd brought from Poland, it looked much different from the dark room with the drawn drapes and armored door. But Jury could understand her fears; Mrs. Wassermann had reached her sixties by various escape routes — back alleys, tunnels, blockaded roads, barbed-wire fences. That was when she was young, in what she always called the Big War. It was something they shared, despite the difference in their ages — the loss of her family, the loss of his.

She came in carrying a small parcel tied up with string. "For your trip, I made this. Sandwiches. Breast of turkey, the very best, and a cheese and pickle."

He thanked her and took the parcel. "Keep an eye on Carole-anne, will you? Maybe you could have her down for tea. Maybe you could take her to your Bingo night. She might not show it, but I think she gets lonely."

"Such a sweet child, Mr. Jury." They were walking up the three steps to the pavement. "Isn't it nice about her new job?"

Jury was suspicious. He didn't think Carole-anne could have told Mrs. Wassermann yet about Starrdust. And God knows she would never have mentioned the job she'd meant to take at the Q.T. Club. "New job?"

"You know, in the all-night launderette. Carole-anne said she was to work the late shift and wouldn't be home until the wee hours. Well, I told her she must be careful and to take a taxi."

"The launderette. Yes, I'd forgotten about that."

"So much better than her old job."

The old job was at King Arthur's as a topless dancer. "Yes, much better."

"At the library."

Jury studied the pavement at his feet, then looked up when

the front door opened and the Librarian came out in her skintight jeans and fake-fur jacket. "Much as she likes books, it just didn't pay enough, I expect."

"Ah, so hard it is to find work these days. And at the launderette she gets to wash her clothes free."

"Hi, Mrs. W!" Carole-anne called gaily.

"Hello, dear," said Mrs. Wassermann. "Don't you look lovely!"

"Thanks, Mrs. W. On my way to see about a job." She was looking everywhere but at Jury, up and down the street, at the sky, checking for snow, rain, sun — anything but Jury's expression.

"Hello, dear," said Jury with a mock-sweetness he seldom indulged in. "When you get through with the turban and stars, you can do my laundry."

Carole-anne squinted up at him, slack-mouthed, as if she weren't sure about this unclean stranger on their doorstep. Her creamy forehead puckered; her raindrop earrings stirred. "Huh? Well, I gotta go. Ta." She blew a kiss and hitched her bag over her shoulder.

They watched her go down the street. First one, then another of the male residents coming the other way did an about-face when she passed. Across the way, a small man in a bowler latched his gate and did a quick-step, following up the other two. The postman moved a little more spryly about his duties, stuffing letters any old way through the slots of doors along Carole-anne's route.

"Well, Mrs. Wassermann, there goes the neighborhood," said Jury, with a smile.

PART V

The Old Penny Palace

22

"BRIGHTON is known for the brilliancy of its air," said Jury, looking out over the gunmetal water toward a horizon lost in fog.

Eyes squinted nearly shut in case of sea-spray, Wiggins gave his long scarf one more turn around his neck and looked as if he couldn't care a pence for brilliancy.

Jury flicked away his cigarette and took a deep breath.

"It's not healthy, sir."

"Breathing?"

"The sea air," said Wiggins, adding instructively, "no matter what people say, any doctor can tell you it's not healthy." He then brought out his Fisherman's Friends, a staple in his portable pharmacy ever since the cold, damp days of Dorset. He pushed the packet at Jury. "These'll help a bad throat."

"I haven't got one, Wiggins."

"You will," said the sergeant almost merrily. He put one in Jury's hand.

Wiggins, thought Jury, would have taken shock treatments

184

to ward off flu. "Mind over matter" was not a phrase in the Wiggins lexicon. "There's Paul Swann, or I think it must be." Jury pointed over the railing, down the shingle beach. "Near the Palace Pier."

The char had told Jury that Mr. Swann was not in, that he'd gone down to the beach, to the Palace Pier. Yesterday, it'd been the Royal Pavilion, she said. "Did the east portico. Last week he did the main entrance. He's doing it all, see, inside too," she added, as if Swann did floors.

Paul Swann sat on a canvas stool, looking far down the strand toward the West Pier. Sketchbook and paints sat at his feet, a watercolor rested on the easel before him. He was a man of indeterminate age with a thin face and watery blue eyes.

After Jury introduced himself, Swann suggested they sit on a nearby bench within sight of his painting. An interview in the open air, brilliant though it might be, only made Wiggins cough.

Paul Swann said sympathetically, "Not sick are you, Mr. Wiggins?"

"Not yet, thank you." Wiggins shrugged down into his topcoat.

As they sat down on the bench, Swann said, in answer to Jury's question about David Marr, "I don't really see David that often, so I'm afraid I can't be of much help to you there, Superintendent. Very nice chap, though," he said hurriedly and intently, as if he were concerned that his lack of intimacy with Marr might be construed as his handing him over to police.

"You were in the Running Footman that night, Mr. Swann, weren't you?"

"That's right, I was. Been thinking about it too, trying to remember exactly when he left, what Ivy did, those details." He shook his head. "But I wasn't absolutely sober and I

185

wasn't really paying attention. I think she collected her coat and left just as time was called."

"She said nothing to you?"

"No, nothing."

Wiggins came up out of his shivery cocoon long enough to ask, "How well did you know this Ivy Childess, Mr. Swann?" Turtle-wise, his neck drew back inside his scarf to receive the answer.

"There was a drinks party at the house in Knightsbridge. I went round with David, who had the Childess girl in tow." He stopped and looked up at the sky. "Would you just pardon me a moment." Swann walked across the shingle to collect his easel and palette. "Hope you don't mind. There's just a touch to put to this before the light fades." He continued his assessment of Ivy Childess. "What on earth David saw in that little chit is beyond me. I know that he is not a stupid man, nor a lascivious one — oh, Ivy was quite plump and juicy — and that all of his wild drinking and so forth is merely flinging grit in the eyes." As if flicking a bit of that grit away, he touched the brush, dipped in pale, pale yellow, to the picture of the West Pier.

"Why would he want to fling it, Mr. Swann?"

"I don't know. We all have things to hide, Superintendent. Including the sort of person we really are."

Jury smiled. "Difficult to do with you. I've seen your portraits of the Winslows."

Swann looked up from his painting, smiling. "I'd say that's quite a compliment. Well, I am very good at portraiture, but I will only paint certain people. I'd be a rich man if I took on every commission I was offered; I turn most of them down. I find most people much too shallow or simpering or narcissistic to want to bother with."

"But not the Winslows?"

He smiled. "No, most definitely not the Winslows." Arms folded across his chest, he kept his eye on his watercolor, so

186

intently that he might have been expecting the pier to move, the fog to shift. "That was the only time I'd seen Hugh Winslow, at that party in Knightsbridge. He's the wild card, isn't he?"

Jury looked at him. "Wild card?"

"Doesn't carry the Winslow stamp. I wanted Hugh in that portrait; I thought it would round it out. But when I met him, or when I watched him with the others — especially Marion and Edward — I realized it wouldn't have done. There's this interesting chemistry amongst them, Mr. Jury. Perhaps you've noticed —?"

"Definitely."

Swann, almost as if he were reworking the Winslow portrait, leaned forward, and applied a faint wash of the pale yellow. "That's it, I think. Anyway, when the three of them are together, they become more than the sum of their parts. They *are* a painting, Mr. Jury. They absolutely *are*. I'm sorry I can't help you out in a more practical way — time David went to the Running Footman, time he returned, et cetera, but I just don't know. As for Ivy Childess, it was only on that one evening, and not much of that. I only stayed for half an hour or so. Hate cocktail parties. Much rather go down to the Shepherd Tavern for drinks. I do hope it's not going to go badly for David; I honestly can't see him killing that girl." He shrugged and looked truly sad that he couldn't help out either Jury or David Marr.

"There's another painting there, Mr. Swann, a portrait you probably did?"

"Yes, Rose and Phoebe. Rose Winslow walked out on Edward. You can imagine," he added shaking his head.

It was as though any such behavior on the part of one of them would cause the others to close ranks completely. Jury thought of Hugh Winslow. "Did you hear any talk of another man, someone who perhaps, well, lured Rose Winslow away?"

187

Paul Swann stared at him, and then he laughed. "Lure *Rose?* Good God, I should certainly think it would be the other way round. Poor Ned."

"Did David Marr ever mention her?"

"Yes. He disliked her. Well, she wasn't very likable, you see."

His voice slightly muffled, Wiggins said, "Seems strange they'd keep her picture about, in the circumstances."

"It's because of Phoebe," said Swann. "It's really all they've got left of Phoebe."

Jury looked at the watercolor, the strange milky light of the fog he'd captured that blanketed the pier. "Did you ever hear Marr mention a woman named Sheila Broome at all?"

"Broome? No, never."

"Well, it was just a long shot, Mr. Swann. Thanks."

Wiggins had been studying the watercolor and said, "You know, that's good. That yellow you just put on. Changes the whole thing, really. Makes it look like it's floating."

"Ah, that's just it, Mr. Wiggins. Thank you. You've a grand eye. Do you dabble in the paint pots too?"

"Just a bit," said Wiggins, without a pause. "Sunday painter, that sort of thing."

Jury looked out to sea. Whenever Wiggins found himself in the presence of art, literature, music, a new persona evolved out of the fog, a form taking shape right before Jury's eyes. At any rate, with Swann's speaking to him like a brother, Wiggins had begun to unwind the labyrinthine scarf.

And to include Paul Swann in the elite group of those Wiggins would like to save from certain death. "Care for one, Mr. Swann?"

Paul Swann thanked him and held up the amber lozenge in the fading light. "That is a truly remarkable color."

"I've always thought so, Mr. Swann," he said innocently, holding up its mate in the same way.

Jury scuffed at the broken shells at his feet and was rather sorry his own inartistic eye could identify nothing much but tan beach and gray water. The conversation had switched to literature.

"Sometimes I wonder if Coleridge's dream about Kubla Khan was inspired by George the Fourth and his plans for the Pavilion. The renovation had been going on for ten years when he wrote 'Kubla Khan.'" Paul Swann smiled. "'His flashing eyes, his floating hair.' Can you think of a better candidate for him than the Prince Regent who 'fed on honeydew and drank the milk of paradise'?"

"I never thought of it exactly that way," said Wiggins.

Jury shook his head. If he ever thought of it any way, it was news to Jury.

"And Mrs. Fitzherbert, the only woman he ever loved, according to George, might have also been the perfect candidate for the poor woman 'wailing for her demon-lover.'" Paul Swann sighed and gathered up his paints and sketches and brushes. "Love, love, hmm. I suppose I don't truly qualify as an artist, never having known the turbulence of heart-rending passion. But to tell the truth, seeing all the misery it causes, I just thought I'd give it a miss." He grinned. "I imagine the *crime passionnel* keeps you in work. Do you think this is one, this case?"

Jury said, sadly, "There's certainly enough passion to go round, Mr. Swann."

Swann left them and they walked down the Promenade, past the pub, what looked like changing rooms, a video place where chairs and tables were set up outside for people wanting coffee and soft drinks.

Next door, a fellow was busy slapping paint on the facade of a little museum of antique slot machines, called the Old Penny Palace. He laid down his brush and went inside. Wiggins studied the poster describing some of the machines on display and said, "Look at this, will you?" He pointed to a strength-tester. "Haven't seen one of those since I was a kid. Good for the circulation." He raised his arm, tried to make a muscle. "And over there. Tell your fortune, that does. One of those booths where you pick up a phone and a voice tells you your future."

"A voice from the next world, Wiggins?"

"I know it's just a tape that runs over and over. Still, I wouldn't mind giving it a try. Could we stop here for a minute, do you think?"

While Wiggins talked to the young fellow behind the counter, Jury waited beside the Laughing Sailor. It was dressed in a navy blue uniform and sported a white cap over its sad painted eyes.

"He said the place wasn't open yet, he's trying to get it ready for its opening," said Wiggins.

"Then how'd you get these?" Jury held up a token.

Wiggins counted his tokens, frowning. "Well, I just happened to show him my warrant — "

"Wiggins!"

"No harm done, no harm, sir. Try a few machines; it'll take your mind off things."

"I'm going next door for a cup of coffee." He was looking at the poster near the door listing some of the museum's offerings. "I wonder what the butler saw."

He sat with his Styrofoam cup and a foil-wrapped packet of peanuts. He pushed the peanuts in a circle, assigning to the spokes of this wheel the different signs — Aries, Gemini, Sagittarius. Jury looked at the peanut planets and wondered ruefully if perhaps he should take Andrew Starr up on his offer to draw a horoscope, that in it he might find one or two elusive answers.

Disgusted with himself, he dropped the peanuts into a

190

metal ashtray. Murder wasn't in the stars; it was on the ground, his ground. And it would help, he supposed, if any of the people he'd talked with had been his idea of a proper villain. The thin, plain fabric that had been woven around David Marr and Ivy Childess had now been interwoven with more exotic threads, perhaps obscuring rather than heightening the pattern in the carpet. There was also the disquieting knowledge that Macalvie was right, that solving the murder of Ivy Childess depended upon solving the murder of Sheila Broome.

He stared out at the darkness gathering over the Atlantic and thought about Sheila Broome. Perhaps it was the geography that was throwing him off — connecting her with Exeter when she had, after all, spent a good deal of her time in London. She'd been good-looking, the type Hugh Winslow went for. And if she had threatened, like Ivy Childess, to tell Marion Winslow . . .

Jury rested his head in his hands. Ivy Childess, Hugh Winslow had said, could ferret out anyone's secrets. Jury thought of that bulletin board in David's living room. What if she had ferreted out David Marr's? What had Macalvie said about something worse than murder? *Betrayal of friends and benefactors.*

He felt he needed something, like background music, to silence one part of his mind so that the other could function. Jury drank off his cold coffee without tasting it, started back to the Old Penny Palace.

Through the gathering dusk, he looked down the strand toward the West Pier, floating in the mist.

Then glided in Porphyria . . .

191

23

WHEN Dolly had said this morning that she was thinking of moving back to Brighton, Kate had been astonished.

She was tired of London, she said simply, as if that were reason enough for leaving it, though it meant giving up the decorator flat and the job that she'd clawed her way up to. Kate told her she couldn't understand how Dolly could give up what she'd worked so hard to get.

Maybe you don't want me in the house.

Kate didn't immediately say yes, not because she hadn't wanted Dolly here, but because she was too filled with surprise that her sister, who had for years spoken of Brighton as provincial and dull, would even consider living in it.

When she said it again, that Kate must not want her in the house, the tone was so sad that Kate had to put her hand on her sister's arm and give her a little shake. That wasn't true; of course she did, she told Dolly.

Dolly said they'd have plenty of money, more than enough, even without Dolly's high-paying job, and that Kate could stop all of this. "All of this" meaning her taking in boarders. Dolly made a graceful gesture with her arm (wasn't her every move graceful?) taking in the long drawing room where they'd been having a sandwich for lunch.

But she was used to it, Kate said; she didn't really want to give up her little business.

Dolly had shaken and shaken her head, no. It was degrading, running a bed-and-breakfast.

It wasn't for Kate, though. . . .

The reply had been explosive. Then it's *dangerous.* Dolly's hand was shaking and she brought the silver pot down on the table with a thud.

Dangerous? Surely Dolly couldn't be talking about their prospective roomer. Kate tried to laugh, but it stuck in her throat.

Dolly hadn't stayed to answer. Her Cossack hat was already on, and her boots. She walked hurriedly to the door, where she took up her coat and walked out, the door slamming behind her.

All Kate could do was to gather up the cutlery on the tray. That she might be about to harbor an escaped convict, a criminal, made her want to laugh out loud. Yet Dolly's behavior during this visit had been strange, very unlike her, as if she were stuck in the past, talking of things they used to do when they were children. Dolly would stay out for hours and hours when before she'd spent most of the day in her robe, smoking at the breakfast table. Now she would come back with a report of this place and that — the museum, the Pavilion — all places where their father had taken her, dressed in one of those pastel gossamer dresses sprigged with tiny flowers. . . . Perhaps it was his death. Was he reaching out from the grave to make certain she was still his little girl?

Kate could still see Dolly standing before the window the night their father had died, staring out through the dusk, and the rain blown by wind, great long curtains of it, blowing against the window in waves.

193

WIGGINS was trying his luck on the Love-Test. Its lightbulb display did not seem to be making Wiggins happy; the bulb beside "Amorous" was not lighting up. Jury passed the strength-tester and *What the Butler Saw* and stood looking at the machine called *Midnight in the Haunted Graveyard.*

He put in his token and watched the tiny white figures pop up. A skeleton slid out of an opening grave, a dot of white — a ghost — raised itself behind a headstone; another ghost peered from a hole. A cloaked figure fluttered about in this miniature colony of the dead before it disappeared into the wood. Jury's thoughts scattered as the ground reclaimed its skeletons, the stones and trees their apparitions. *Flash cars and flash men. . . . They all loved Phoebe so much. . . . It all fell apart. . . . "Where have you gone to, Elizabeth Vere?"*

"Just a moment, sir," said Wiggins, his eyes glued to the viewer of *What the Butler Saw.*

Jury slammed his hand over the viewer. "You'll have to

skip the naughty bits, Wiggins." He wrote in his notebook, tore off the page, and handed it to Wiggins.

"Check to see if Plant called headquarters about the snapshot he took to Exeter —"

"But we've already —"

"I *know* we've already. And find Miles Wells."

Wiggins frowned. "The driver of the car that hit Phoebe Winslow? And ask him exactly what?"

"If the lady in the car was Sheila Broome. And why he drove for several blocks and then came back."

"No one mentioned a lady in the car, sir."

"I just did, Wiggins."

"Sheila Broome?" said Macalvie, dragging his feet off the desk in the Brighton police station. "But what the hell? Even if it was revenge, why not go for the driver?"

"That's the point. I think she *was* the driver. She'd been arrested once for drink-driving, Macalvie. If he hadn't taken the rap for her, she'd have been in jail. But to do that, they had to switch seats. Stop the car and switch. I doubt he was simply being a gentleman about it; I imagine he thought it was his neck, too. Better to be booked for an unavoidable accident than for letting your drunk companion drive without a license and run somebody down. The question I asked myself was why little Phoebe ran out into the street."

"So what'd you answer yourself?"

"Hugh Winslow answered. She was angry and frightened; what frightened her was seeing Daddy in bed with a woman who certainly wasn't Mummy — Ivy Childess."

Macalvie looked long and hard at the tips of his run-down shoes, which he'd just planted on the desktop again. Then he said, "So anyone in that family would hold not just Hugh responsible but Ivy. They'd ice her, any one of them, right? Just like Sheila Broome."

"Absolutely. In a way, I suppose, it ricochets: they wouldn't kill him — after all, he's family — they'd kill her."

"Could even have been Hugh himself."

"Yes."

"You're not suggesting it's murder on the Brighton Express, or something? That they were all in on it?"

"No. Only one of them. And I don't think that's the whole of the motive, either." Jury studied the photograph of the Queen hanging on the dull, ocher-colored wall. "I think the motive might be very confused; it has not to do just with the death of Phoebe, but with Rose Winslow. 'Betrayal of friends and benefactors,' that's what you said."

Macalvie sighed. "I wish I'd known what I meant."

Jury sat back, dug his hands in his pockets. "You haven't seen the Winslows; you didn't see what sort of family they are. They're as bonded together as the figures in a portrait. It's unconscious, I think. I doubt the Winslows know what form their punishment takes. Hugh wasn't sent packing, after all. They just stopped communicating. They don't cut you *down*, they cut you *out*. To betray one is to betray all. And David Marr certainly knew that."

"Marr?"

"I'm sure he was having an affair with Rose Winslow. Rose strikes me as being a slightly up-market version of Ivy Childess: selfish, untrustworthy, avaricious. But with enough of a flame-to-moth quality that she singed more than one pair of wings. David Marr's, for example. He's got a collection of stuff in his room — photos, cards. One's from Vegas. He's never been to the States, and according to more than one person, Rose always wanted to go. None of the Winslows, no one, has heard a word from her. So why should David Marr have done, and why keep it a secret?"

"It wouldn't go down a treat with the family. And Ivy Childess found out. Well, well, now Marr has no alibi and a great motive," said Macalvie.

"A touch of blackmail — oh, not for the up-front money. Ivy didn't want to stretch out her days dusting off the stars at the Starrdust. She wanted marriage. Marriage to *any* of the Winslow-Marr family. She'd drop David to pick up Hugh; drop Hugh to pick up David; I'm sure she must have had a bit of a go at Ned, too."

"You're talking jealousy."

Jury raised his eyebrows. "Among *them?* Oh, no. If David had won Ned's girl in a fair fight, or Hugh won David's — the other would have been a gentleman, would have backed out. It's not jealousy; it's betrayal. Betrayal is probably *the* mortal sin with the Winslows." Jury pocketed his cigarettes and said, "Plant's gone to Exeter. He wanted the waitress at the Little Chef to take a look at a photo."

"She's already looked. Something new?"

Macalvie didn't seem surprised. When the wheel stopped, he'd just spin it again.

Jury smiled. "You were right about the connection between those murders, Macalvie."

"That's a relief; for a while, life had lost its music."

"Why in the hell would the killer wait so long? Phoebe Winslow died nearly a year before Sheila Broome."

"So there wouldn't appear to be a connection. But that's just the opinion of your standard, plodding detective."

"If there's anything you aren't, it's 'standard.' " And then it occurred to Jury that he hadn't known Macalvie was even *in* Brighton. But it didn't surprise Jury that he was. The standard, plodding detective would follow a tidal wave if a clue were tossing about on its crest. "Why're you here, Macalvie?"

A police constable stuck his face around the door to tell Jury someone had called about an hour before and left him a message, which he handed to Jury. "He said his name was Plant, sir. Mr. Melrose Plant. That he was leaving Exeter, but that he'd get in touch later. I was careful to write it down, sir, since it was a bit odd." The constable frowned with the oddity of it and ducked out.

"*Weren't they* all *Porphyria?*" Jury read the note to Macalvie, who sighed and said, "Does he have to send his messages in code?"

"Well, obviously he means they were all alike — they were, too: that long, blond hair. Selfish, avaricious." Jury frowned, remembering the photos in the drawing room of the Winslows' house. "And so far as the hair goes . . . even Phoebe Winslow."

Macalvie was drawing a newspaper clipping from his wallet. "My little bit of news comes straight from chocolate flake country." He unfolded the strip of paper and handed it to Jury. "We'd better get the lead out, Jury. There's someone wandering around Brighton who's in considerable danger."

"Who?"

Macalvie turned the newspaper around so that it faced Jury. It was a cutout from the entertainment section. "The Rainlady."

Jury looked at the pretty girl in the picture, at the heart-shaped face and long, blond hair. "You found her. Jimmy Rees finally told you?"

"Hell, no. He's still back there with chocolate flake coming out of his ears. It was the telly, Jury. I was in your office and flicked on Wiggins's set to catch the news. I thought maybe some Fleet Street reporter could tell me who killed Sheila and Ivy. Anyway, the ten-twenty news is supposed to end with this pretty lady coming out in a white slicker and umbrella. It's always raining, see, at ten-twenty. She's the weather girl. Her name is Dolly Sands and she took it with her, in a manner of speaking. Very suddenly she felt she needed a holiday. Dolly Sands lives here in Brighton." Macalvie was shrugging into his coat. "And I think we better find her before she takes a permanent holiday."

25

THE woman who came to the door was tall and attractive, with taffy-colored hair that fell smoothly from a center part to her chin. Once the hair might have been as light as that of the girl in the newspaper clipping. Her blouse was mustard-colored, good silk, but flattering neither in shade nor in fit. She had the diffident air of one who doesn't know how good-looking she is, or hasn't been told it often enough. Most of life no doubt lived in the shadow of her beautiful sister.

"Kate Sandys?" asked Jury, showing her his warrant card. As if uncertain whether to admit to her name, silently she looked from Jury to Macalvie and back to the warrant card. "We need to talk to your sister, Miss Sandys. Is she here?"

"Dolly? No. No, she isn't here. What do you want?" She looked over her shoulder at the hall behind her. It was as if the house belonged to someone else.

Macalvie was standing to Jury's left, leaning against the doorjamb. "To come in, for starters." He put his hand flat against the door and shoved it back.

199

Her eyes widened. "Why? What's happened? Has something happened to Dolly?"

"We don't know yet."

Nervously, she gestured for them to come in. She pushed one sleeve of her silk blouse up, ran a hand over the light brown hair, silky as the blouse. Macalvie brushed by her, stood in the hallway looking round, his hands shoved in his pockets as if he were observing the scene of a crime.

Kate Sandys led them into a large, chilly drawing room. Jury noticed a photograph album lying open on a library table, a coat and scarf across the arm of a sofa, a letter on the mantel above the unlit fireplace. Over the years, Jury had grown more and more aware of the way in which some houses, some rooms seemed to bear witness to the end of something — a death, an imminent departure. Perhaps it was the closeness to the sea here that intensified that image. The sea, the photographs of old Brighton on the wall, the watercolor of the deck of an ocean liner, dim figures by the rail waving, an attempt to be gay and lighthearted amidst the flutter of colored streamers. He glanced around him, almost expecting to see the furniture sheeted, the steamer trunk packed, the cab at the door in the fog.

In answer to a question from Macalvie, Kate said, "She's gone out."

"Out where?"

"I don't know."

"Think."

She didn't answer; instead she kept her gaze fixed on Jury's face, as if it were the more hospitable of the two. "You still haven't told me why you want her, or what's happened."

"Your sister Dolly may be in big trouble, a lot of danger," said Macalvie.

"*What* danger?" Her hand went to her neck, fingers worrying the thin gold chain on her breast.

Jury told her about the Hays Mews murder. "We think

your sister might have seen something, might have seen the killer even —"

Kate sat down suddenly. "You mean he's come *here*, to Brighton? But how would he know who —?"

"Easy," said Macalvie. "Dolly Sandys walks right into his living room every weekday night. Three days ago she calls in sick to the studio, packs a bag, and comes here. It was your name and address they had in case of emergency. And we weren't the only ones that had come inquiring after her. So you'd better think very hard."

"That's why she's been so moody; ever since she came I've been wondering why and what's wrong with her."

"Have you seen anyone hanging about, Miss Sandys? Any strangers?"

She looked up anxiously. "No. Well, yes, in a way. There was a man in the Spotted Dog, that's a pub not far from here. We got to chatting; he mentioned he was looking for a room. . . ." She spread her hands. "I told him about our house." Her voice was strained. "Later, when I thought about it, I wondered if he was the man I'd seen earlier, when I went to the Pavilion. When I came out and started walking across Castle Square, I saw him standing down at the end of the walk. It was unnerving; he seemed to be watching me. As if he was following me."

"What'd your sister say when you told her?"

"But I didn't, you see. Dolly left the house early in the afternoon to go to Pia Negra's. She's a fortune-teller, a clairvoyant with a place in the Lanes. I know she came back because she changed coats — she left the fur and took the rain slicker. But I haven't seen her."

"You say she went to this fortune-teller. Exactly where in the Lanes?"

"Black Horse Lane."

Macalvie wrote it down. "Okay, where else could she have gone? Favorite pub? Shop? Restaurant?"

Kate shook her head.

"You better think it up, Miss Sandys. Your sister's out there with a killer."

She flinched as if he'd slapped her. "I'm trying to think." She rolled the gold necklace between the palms of her hands. "I thought it was a man, that she was having trouble over a man."

"She is. Big trouble."

26

HE watched her as she stood in the weak arc of light coming from the entryway to the Old Penny Palace. She was standing there, pulling the collar of the bright, white slicker round her throat, considering. Her face was pale, filtered through the drizzling rain that had started a few minutes ago. Perhaps she was looking for shelter. She went in.

Except for the pub farther down, everything else was shut up tightly along this causeway of amusement arcades underneath the arches of the King's Road, between the two piers. There was no one about. From the direction of the West Pier came the barking of a dog, excited perhaps because of its proximity to the water. But he saw no one, nothing. The only illumination came from the sodium lamps above, along the King's Road; that, and the sickly yellow light shining out from the Penny Palace.

Except for her, the museum looked empty. Someone must have been spiffing it up, for there was a bucket of marine blue paint on the counter with a brush across its top. The owner or whoever was doing the painting was gone, perhaps gone along to the pub under the arches for a drink. There was no one but the two of them, nothing but the wooden figure called the Laughing Sailor inside his wood-and-glass cage, there beside the entrance to greet the customers if they had a penny to make him laugh.

When she had left the house on Madeira Drive, he'd followed, as he'd followed her twice before. Those times, though, it had been daylight, and she'd led him in the other direction, away from the seawall toward the center of the town and the brick-paved alleys of the Lanes, a maze of narrow streets like a spiderweb.

It had been difficult watching the house; there were no newsagents, no shops or restaurants he might have gone into, as there'd been in Exeter. So he had watched from several different vantage points from King's Road and the seawall, leaning against a railing, pretending to read a newspaper or to look out over the sea. And the surveillance — at which he felt he was no good at all — had to be interrupted by going off for a meal, or to the toilet, then coming back, then going off again.

He had considered going up to the house when the other one had gone out. The sister. They looked enough alike to be sisters. Older, a little taller, but without that strangely compelling presence that made the younger one so popular. How odd that he should recognize a television personality; that news broadcast with its trendy little weather report was the only thing he watched. Otherwise, he would never have found her. And whether it was her face or whether that white slicker she always wore, he didn't know. As he followed her, he watched men turn as they passed her, turn and stare.

He moved closer. There was a counter for making change, dispensing the big pennies that were necessary to work the machines. He watched her moving about through the thicket of machines, stopping to look at the crane in its fancy glass enclosure. She must have had some of the pennies with her from an earlier visit or perhaps she'd nicked a few from the counter, for she reached in her pocket and in a moment he saw the crane move. After a moment she moved away, circled some more of the machines, sometimes cupping her hands around her face and peering through glass. Against the far wall was a player piano; she studied it for a moment, slugged a coin into it, and soon the tinny, broken sounds of music filled the night.

He stepped back into the shadows of the awning of the place next door that housed video games and a coffee bar when he saw someone coming along the Parade, hurrying now. Probably the owner or whoever had left the machines untended. He could hear voices, brief laughter. It would be difficult to be angry with her; she was too pretty. And probably whoever was in there was bored, maybe lonely.

He listened to the rattling, broken-sounding notes from the piano, remembered the words: " . . . *trade it for a basket of sunshine and flowers.*"

"Pennies from Heaven," it was called. Where had the sunshine gone, and the flowers? He looked up at the night sky, black as lacquer, studded with stars, and thought how much it was like that other night long ago. Darkness, stars, music . . .

He heard her say good-bye. On the way out she — or perhaps the painter — must have dropped a coin into the wooden sailor. There was a short, guttural, donkeylike laugh that stopped suddenly when the music stopped.

And in a few moments, she came out. Stood, looking up at the black sky, as if calculating how long it would be before the rain got heavy, turned up the collar of her white raincoat, and walked on into the darkness toward the steps that led up to the King's Road.

205

He passed the Laughing Sailor, its wooden jaw locked, mouth hinged in a permanent grin.

Kate Sandys was weeping; Jury knew she couldn't help it, that she was frantic with trying to think of the first place Dolly might have gone to. Macalvie had convinced her that there might not be time to find a second.

She dried her eyes and looked down at the small photo of David Marr. It was a horror; she had actually been going to let him a room.

"It'll be all right, Kate." He leaned toward her, took her hand. "Try to relax."

"I've always been — envious of her, always said she was spoiled. I don't know now. I know I should have taken her more seriously."

"Great," said Macalvie, who was still standing. "That's great but it's not finding her." He snapped shut the photograph album he'd been looking at. "The Brighton police will have gone to everyplace you've mentioned by now — but that doesn't mean she'll be at one of them." He held up the album, frowning. "You leave this here?"

Kate wiped her eyes and looked up. "No. Dolly must've."

"She was going through her childhood pictures, mostly of the pier and the sweet stands and stuff along the oceanfront. Does she go in for it still?"

"The King's Road Arches arcade. Dolly loved the arcade more than anyplace."

"Let's go, Jury." Macalvie started for the door.

Jury put the album in Kate Sandys's lap, wondering why he thought that would be any comfort. Yet, she wrapped her fingers round it as if the memories were real, staring straight ahead.

Then he picked up and pocketed the picture of David Marr. He shook his head. David hadn't been there, he hadn't seen it. And he thought Plant was right about their all having run together, in the mind of the murderer, as the faithless Porphyria. He looked again at the photo he'd been holding of David Marr. But it wasn't the first time, he supposed, he'd been wrong. And God knows, it wouldn't be the last.

She didn't walk up the steps to the King's Road after all; instead, she left the paved walk for the shingle beach. She stopped for a moment to look out to sea, shading her face with her hand, as if it were broad daylight and one could actually see out there, as if she were looking for the bright, bobbing head of a bather. She picked a pebble from the shingle and threw it and continued down the strand, the white raincoat dazzling in the night, a long, yellow scarf fluttering behind her.

He had carried a gun before and he carried it now. At this time of year, though, a woman could be depended on to wear a scarf, and she wore hers as the others had done, ends dangling down the back.

She was walking slowly enough that his catching her up might seem natural to her. Apparently it did, for when he spoke, she merely turned and looked at him, brushing back her hair with her hand.

He told her he was sorry if he seemed to be following her, that she looked so much like someone he used to know.

And did he look familiar to her? he wondered. He could not believe that his face was not engraved on her mind, etched on her eyes the way the victim is said to carry the image of the murderer.

Yet she looked at him almost sightlessly and for some moments. There was a strange expression in her blue eyes, a look of acceptance — he might even have said of complicity. The scarf was unwound, removed. It too was white, and it trailed from her coat pocket. It wasn't a yellow scarf fluttering behind her, but her hair. How could he have mistaken one for the other?

She said that a lot of people took her for someone else; she said she looked like the woman on the telly who did the weather report.

There was nothing in her manner to suggest she recognized him; her voice was flat, expressionless.

Did she live in Brighton? Did she like it?

All of her life, she said; lately she'd been living in London, but she thought she would move back. Then she looked out to sea, said she remembered it the way it was when she was young.

When she was young. Of course, she must have meant when she was a child, but it was still an odd thing to say, as if youth were lost to her, had receded like the wrinkled waves drawing back from the shore.

Looking up at him, she said, *Dolly Sands.* That's who she reminded people of.

Rose, he said. That's who you remind me of. She did not seem to think it was odd that he had said *Rose.*

Then he was silent. That was wrong, somehow. Phoebe, it was Phoebe he was thinking about, wasn't it? Phoebe with all of her flaxen hair spread out in the street.

His hand reached toward her hair; she drew back. As he turned his head, he saw the lights of cars, blue domes whirring up there along the King's Road. A voice hailed him and was carried off by the wind.

Someone screamed. And then she broke from his arms and started to run. There was shouting, torches burning and circling like little moons, people scrambling down the steps.

Before he raised the gun he had time to think of the irony of this. That he hadn't meant to hurt her; she hadn't even known who he was.

The voice that had hailed him called out again: *"Ned!"*

He felt the gun heavy in his hand. Strange that he hadn't felt angry with David. But he shouldn't have told him he was coming here; he should have known David would follow him.

Ned heard the explosion, felt nothing, saw a terrible white glare — stars showering like meteors, moon breaking like a mirror, raincoat flying down the strand.

The Deer Leap

To the memory of my father
Was it a pleasant Day to die –
And did the Sunshine face His way –

A Wounded Deer – leaps highest –
I've heard the Hunter tell –
'Tis but the Ecstasy of death –
And then the brake is still!

The poetry quoted in this book is by Emily Dickinson

PART 1

Good Night!
Which put the Candle out?

One

Una Quick had been searching for two days for her dog, Pepper.

Whenever anyone in Ashdown Dean came into the post-office stores (of which Una had been purveyor of goods and stamps for forty-five years) she would ask the same questions over and over, thereby delaying the dispensing of letters, tinned goods, and half-loaves for as long as she could keep the benighted villager's attention. Everyone in Ashdown knew Pepper's habits in tedious detail.

"Probably just run off or someone picked him up. And don't forget that lab," added Sebastian Grimsdale with his usual compassion. Over the two torturous days, Sebastian finely tuned this theme with references to dog- and catnapping, never forgetting to toss in references to the Rumford Laboratory, where, according to Mr. Grimsdale, they did all sorts of dreadful experiments. Having reduced Una Quick to tears, he would then tell her not to worry, and leave with his post and tinned tomato soup. This he would later reduce to something slightly thicker than water but considerably thinner than blood for the guests of Gun Lodge.

Blood was, indeed, his milieu: Sebastian Grimsdale was Master of Foxhounds and Harriers and his own huntsman. The only persons he actually paid were his one maid-of-all-work, and his head keeper, Donaldson. Donaldson was a great stalker. Like most of them, from Scotland. But Grimsdale preferred Exmoor, the game being much larger. That was through now until spring, damnation. This put Grimsdale in an even more insufferable mood than was usual for him. He was cheered only by the thought of the meet in five days — though running a fox to ground was no comparison to the stag at bay. Well, in the meantime, he could take his shotgun out to the pond and see what flew by....

With poor Una Quick clutching at her heart — she had a "heart," as she described her condition — most of the Ashdown villagers offered far gentler and happier prognoses. "Pepper'll be back, you'll see, dear," said her neighbor, Ida Dotrice. "You know the way they are. Just turn up at the door like always...."

Una was not sure the way they were after going missing for two days.

Little Mrs. Ashley, whose baby sat with its moon-face half covered by a cloud of white blanket, consoled Una by telling her the tale of "those dogs and that cat that went for hundreds of miles, or something, and finally got home." Mrs. Ashley panted slightly, as if she had just made the journey herself, while shoving marmite and bread into her carryall. She went on about these animals: "... all the way from Scotland or somewhere, I don't remember. Didn't you read it? Well, you ought, one was a Siamese, you know how smart they are.... How much do I owe? Oh, that much. Things get dearer every day. And what they charge for just *dog* food.... Oh, sorry, Miss Quick. You must get that book." She could not remember its name. "Don't you worry now. Ta."

Siamese cats trekking through Scotland did not console

Una Quick at all. She grew paler with every chime of the steeple bell that reminded her that everyone would pass to his reward, including Pepper. The vicar, a tiny man who walked as if he had springs on his shoes, had not helped Una with references to all of us going to our reward.

On the third day, she found Pepper. The liver-spotted dog lay stiff as a board in the tiny shed behind her cottage where she kept her few gardening supplies, one of them weed killer. The door had been secured, she was positive, by a stick driven through the metal clasp.

Una collapsed. Ida Dotrice, come to ask to use her telephone, found and revived her. Una was barely alive.

It was the first time the post-office stores had been closed during the week, other than half-day, when Pepper's funeral was held in the backyard of Arbor Cottage. Una, wearing black, was supported by Ida and her other neighbor, Mrs. Thring. The vicar had been persuaded to read over the small grave, and he did this, but somewhat springily.

Paul Fleming, the local veterinarian and the assistant administrator of the Rumford Laboratory, had said, yes, it was undoubtedly the weed killer. Una asked him how Pepper had managed to work the stick out of the latch. But Una was known to be slightly absentminded. Paul Fleming had shrugged and said nothing.

Ⅺ

The Potter sisters — Muriel and Sissy — were well known in Ashdown Dean, largely because hardly anyone knew them at all. They were famous for keeping their curtains drawn, their doors locked, and themselves behind them. Groceries were delivered by a local boy, and there was never any post. When they did appear, one was always dressed in black and one in mauve, as if in the first and second stages of Victorian mourning. It was considered an event when they had gone up the High Street to the Briarpatch tearoom to sample the proprietor's famous pastries.

After all of these years of shuttered living, the Potter sisters were seen leaving their house the day after Pepper had died, their cat wrapped in a blanket, and getting into their ancient Morris.

Sissy drove hell for leather up the street and out of town, where Dr. Fleming's office was situated.

They returned without the cat and locked the door.

〇

Gerald Jenks, a surly man who kept a cycle shop on the edge of the village, also kept a spitz as surly as Gerald himself. The dog was chained to a post outside the run-down shop like a guard dog. What there was to guard, no one knew. Only Gerald could have found anything of value in the tottering stacks of wheels and parts and pieces.

The day after the Potter sisters' cat had died from a heavy dose of aspirin, Jenks found the dog caught in a rusty bicycle chain, its efforts to escape apparently having strangled it.

If it hadn't seemed impossible, one would have thought the animal population of Ashdown Dean was methodically killing itself off. Or being killed.

〇

Una Quick lay in bed three days later, not having risen since the funeral. Stiff as adamantine, hands clasped over her bosom, a votive candle burning beside her.

The vicar hadn't wanted to read the service over Pepper, she was sure. Beneath him. *Him.* Fidgety old fool, he was. Some just didn't understand how you got attached to an animal.

Here in her tiny cottage in Aunt Nancy's Lane — two up and two down — she'd nursed a crotchety mother for twenty years. And forty-five years keeping the post-office stores. Little enough thanks had she got from the villagers for *that*. Selling soup and sorting post. So what if she had her bit of fun with it. That taint of perfume on letters to Paul Fleming. Handsome, thought he was God's gift.

The candle guttered in a tiny gust of wind. She had held one at the funeral, and when that went out she had lit another and then another. Keeping watch. In that breeze she smelled a storm coming. Una thought of it waiting out there, like Death.

When the steel band gripped her below the breast, she winced. The beat of her heart was uneven and ragged as her breath. Dr. Farnsworth had come and gone directly after the funeral to check on her again. Would he be annoyed if she called him on the Monday? Tonight? Instead of Tuesday?

The band loosened and the constriction eased. No, she mustn't fall prey to the habit of some patients. He had laughed, pleasantly enough, his arm round her shoulder, and told her to stop dwelling on her heart, as it only made matters worse. But it had almost killed her this time, what with Pepper's passing away. Arsenic. It must have been horrible....

Across the room the telephone rang, and she wondered if she should make the effort. It persisted. She dug her feet into slippers and went to it.

The voice was strange. Strangled, almost.

The message was stranger.

She wiped beads of perspiration from a brow cold as pearl.

Two

Ordinarily a person who could be rendered speechless by the public in general, Polly Praed was ready to strangle the woman in the public call box. At least she thought it was a woman; it was hard to tell in the rain pouring down the call box, soaking Polly's yellow oilskin, water flung like sea-spray against her eyes. A sudden beak of lightning turned the blood-red box a livid yellow, but the damned fool just nattered on.

Had she not been *in extremis*, Polly Praed would no more have thought of pounding on the glass of the door than she would have considered giving a speech at the annual Booker Award ceremonies. Not that she'd ever get the chance. The trees that lined the High Street could have accepted the award better than Polly Praed. Ten minutes now. Ten minutes. She wanted to scream.

Unfortunately, screaming was out, too. She had failed her est course in London. When commanded to fall on the floor and scream, she had sat like a rock.

She had failed her Assertiveness Training course in Hertford, too.

218

Any call from her editor threw her into paroxysms of fright; he would call to "check on her progress." In his sly, friendly way.

About the only people she could manage were a few of her friends in Littlebourne, and she was cursing herself for a fool for not staying there in the first place.

The rain poured, the lightning clawed, and that odious man at Gun Lodge had had the nerve to tell her the Lodge telephone was for private use only and directed her up this hill to the call box.

She felt like throwing herself against it, toppling the damned thing and the person inside who must be calling everyone in Ashdown Dean. Fortunately, it was a tiny village. Probably only another twenty calls to go.

If her editor hadn't phoned her to "check on progress," she'd never have set off on this harebrained literary excursion in the first place. Canterbury first, then Rye, as if the imaginations of Chaucer and James might fall at her feet like cathedral stones or tiles off roofs. Then up to Chawton and Jane Austen. Not even Jane could make the wheels start turning.

Had she stuck with Assertiveness Training, she would simply have told that Grimsdale person — *demanded* — that she must use his telephone. Then, of course, the storm hadn't risen to gale force. So she had trekked up here.

Raining cats and dogs.

She wouldn't have minded if it had rained down her own cat, Barney. That dreadful person said no animals allowed. Barney was used to the car, having made this literary pilgrimage with her. And she had gone sneaking out after dark to bundle him in.

Only Barney wasn't there.

If she hadn't got kicked out of est, she would have been able to go to police, rout out whoever was around. But she knew, instead, who to call and who would give her advice, since he had been so free with advice over the last two years whether she wanted it or not.

Finally, in a furor, Polly put her hand in the metal pull and yanked the door open.

"I'm *sorry!* It's an *emergency!*"

The woman responded quickly enough. She fell backward across Polly Praed's feet. Her hand was still holding the receiver and the cord lay snakelike, half in, half out of the call box, as the lightning knifed again and showed a waxen face.

It was too much like her stories to be believed.

Here she sat in the police station on a hard chair waiting for Constable Pasco to come back. Polly, having done a great deal of research in the course of writing her mystery novels, knew that rigor mortis had either passed off or not yet started in the body whose head had used her feet as its cushion. Having gingerly removed those feet, she had had no choice then but to step over the elderly woman and ring up the local police. The lonely public telephone in the rain had quickly become a carnival of whirling blue lights and villagers materializing out of Ashdown Dean's cottages and narrow streets.

For a good twenty minutes she had been sitting on this chair, waiting. Since Constable Pasco was the single local policeman, he had sent to some town five miles on another edge of the New Forest for reinforcements. Polly had been surrounded at the call box, questioned, plunked down here.

And no one cared about Barney. She told herself not to worry. Barney had probably just crawled out the window. Barney wore a red neckerchief and would have got the gold medal in Assertiveness Training. . . .

Literary inspiration. Good God.

She was absolutely stuck for a plot and she had that contract staring her in the face, promising January delivery of a book that she hadn't even started. And it was October

220

twenty-second. All the way from Canterbury to Battle she'd contrived a plot around six people in a first-class train compartment making bets on which of them could tell the most interesting story before they got to their destination. She had been killing them off one by one as each had to leave for the toilet or somewhere. She didn't know who was doing the killing or why . . . the Chaucer scholar, perhaps, who had thought it up.

Battle had scratched that plot when she saw the Battle Rolls in the Abbey and wondered if a murder incorporating William the Conqueror might not be instructive. But think of all that research. . . .

Then Rye. Henry James. Inside Lamb House she wondered how a mystery in which several people have achingly endless, convoluted conversations over tea and biscuits, all of them knowing there *was* that body in the solarium but, with their Jamesian sensibilities, making such oblique references that no one knew if anyone knew if he or she knew. Including the reader. Her fascination with the endless possibilities of this grew. It would break new ground in the mystery world. A mystery within a mystery. A cobweb-covered windowpane. Her editor wouldn't know what was going on, but would of course have to pretend he did, being a man of Jamesian sensibility himself.

But her hopes were dashed when she picked up *The Awkward Age* and tried reading it over tea and cakes and realized that, although she couldn't make head nor tail of it, Henry James probably knew what he was doing. Damn the man!

Why hadn't she stayed in Rye for dinner at the Mermaid, as she'd been tempted to do? Or spent that extra day in Canterbury? Or never left Littlebourne, where she would be just settling down in bed with somebody else's mystery, hoping there might be something she could nick?

Thus did Polly Praed, like a film running backward, retrace her movements over the last three days. After leaving

Jane Austen's imagination in Hampshire (where she now was), Polly had planned to motor along and make a casual stopover in Long Piddleton, Northamptonshire, though she didn't see how one could merely be straying by the family seat of the Earls of Caverness. Well, he kept *asking* her to visit, didn't he?

Half an hour. No police. Constable Pasco had questioned her quite thoroughly and, she thought, with some suspicion. Why hadn't she used the telephone at Gun Lodge? Because that Grimsdale person wouldn't *let* her.

Finally, he came in, and she found a sliver of steel in her spine, enough to say, "I'm allowed one call."

Feeling a fool for all of the times she'd heard that on American television programs, she blushed. Pasco, a tall, laconic policeman, merely plunked the telephone on the counter and told her to go ahead, miss.

Pleased at least by the *miss* — Polly had left her "miss" days behind her like a string of pop beads — she picked up the receiver. If he was so plentiful with advice and succor, let him advise and succor his way out of *this* mess.

In this way, Polly Praed decided to dump the whole thing on the former Lord Ardry, eighth Earl of Caverness, pretty much like she dumped her hastily written books on an unsuspecting public.

PART 2

What Inn is this
Where for the night
Peculiar Traveler comes?

Three

"*ime!*" called Dick Scroggs.

The publican of the Jack and Hammer called for last rounds at ten. The deference he showed his occasional overnight guest was absent with his regulars, not even bothering with the *please* or the *ladies and gentlemen* to announce the closing hour.

Considering the lack of variety of ladies and gentlemen, all but one of whom were gathered at a table in a small bay window, Dick might be forgiven his abruptness.

Marshall Trueblood, who lent what variety there was, glanced at his watch and called back to Dick, "Isn't it a bit early, old sweat? It's only just gone ten. Since when did you start locking up before the half-hour? Let's have another round, anyway." Marshall Trueblood nodded in the direction of Mrs. Withersby, asleep by the fire. A pistol shot wouldn't have bestirred her faster than a shot of gin.

"Of course, *you* needn't worry," said Lady Ardry to her nephew, Melrose Plant.

Melrose Plant lowered his crossword puzzle and raised his eyebrows. The comment had come, unhooked to previous conversation, a tail without a dog. She had been rustling the financial pages of the London *Times*, having put by the *Telegraph*.

Lady Ardry's presence here at this latish hour was testimony to all that the dregs of the beer, of the day, and most probably of the autumn had been reached. She could generally be counted on to turn up here or at Ardry End throughout the day, but she had always stoutly announced that for her, morning was at seven. She was no layabout, like others. Always in bed by ten.

"About what needn't I worry, dear aunt?" He did not wait upon her answer: the comment had been loaded, he was sure.

"Funds, Plant, funds. Investments. Money. About which you needn't worry, not with *your* inheritance."

He did not bother to answer. That the seventh Earl of Caverness, his father, had not left at least one wing of Ardry End to his sister-in-law Agatha would forever put Melrose Plant in the company of rogues and bounders. Nor did she seem to recall that Melrose's father had left her provision in the form of a cottage in Plague Alley and an annual allowance. She must have been squirreling it away, though, considering the high teas she consumed at Ardry End, family seat of the Caverness line.

"I want something safe for one. Something that will allow me capital gains should I decide to sell. Something that will not fluctuate with rising and falling markets. Something absolutely stable." She drank her shooting sherry. "I'm considering precious metals. What do you suggest?"

"The Holy Grail," said Melrose.

"Antiques, old trout," suggested Marshall Trueblood, Long Piddleton's single dealer in them. "I've a fine jade dragon, Ming Dynasty — give a century, take a century — that I'll let go cheap — to you." He flashed her a smile and lit up a pink Sobranie. As usual the cigarette was an extension of the costume. Trueblood was wearing a safari jacket, a flamingo

neckerchief and a chartreuse shirt. On the table was a pan-
ama hat. In October. Left over from Guy Fawkes Day, perhaps. Melrose calculated that Trueblood could clear the
jungle just by stepping out of the bush.

"You could buy my house," said Vivian Rivington to
Agatha.

"*That* old falling-down place? You've left it go too long,
Vivian."

Trueblood snorted. "Falling down? It's the handsomest
cottage in Long Pidd, and you know it." He turned to Vivian.
"But really Viv-viv, you do keep putting it up for grabs and
then taking it off the market."

Melrose could not stand this absurd chatter over his aunt's
"investment potential" a second longer. The only thing
Agatha would ever invest was time — a large part of it spent
before her nephew's fireplace consuming tea and cakes. He
slapped his checkbook open, uncapped a thin gold pen.
"What do you want for it, Vivian?"

Vivian Rivington looked from him to the checkbook and
said, in a small voice, "Whatever are you talking about,
Melrose? *You* don't want my house."

"True. But at least you'd have it sold, and then you
wouldn't always have to be zipping back and forth between
Northants and Venice." He smiled obligingly. "Sixty thousand. Seventy? We could avoid all the rigmarole of estate
agents, et cetera." The pen was poised over the checkbook,
calling her bluff.

She cleared her throat. "Well . . . it's not *certain* I want to
sell. . . . I mean, Franco's been talking about keeping the
place. For a bit of a holiday now and then . . ."

Melrose returned pen and checkbook to pockets. "Count
Franco Dracula will find Long Piddleton bereft of nubile
maidens or convenient crypts in which to stuff them —"

The usually quiet Vivian flared. "I *told* you to stop calling
him that."

"Yes, really, Melrose," said Trueblood. "Viv's looking absolutely grand since she got back. Not pale at all."

Her hazel eyes flashed Trueblood a warning, too. "Both of you make me sick." She started to wrap her terribly de la Renta scarflike thing about her, preparatory to rising.

Trueblood was right: she did look quite different whenever she returned from Italy — but it was a difference Melrose could have done without. He suspected the fiancé (who'd been hanging on for some time now) had a good deal to do with her highlighted, upswept hair, her lacquered nails, her fashion-plate clothes. Why was that crushed-leather belt, for instance, riding down somewhere round her hips? Melrose sighed. It would take a couple of weeks to get her back into the old Vivian-rut of twin-sets and nice, shiny, shoulder-length hair.

"Oh, sit down, for heaven's sake," he said crossly.

She sat. "Dick's closing up, anyway."

"Well, he'll have to deal with Withers, first."

Mrs. Withersby, although her longevity in the Jack and Hammer might have earned her the sobriquet, could not be called a pillar of the pub. At the moment she was sprawled across the hearth, out cold.

Scroggs, who seemed to have forgotten his call to arms of nearly a half-hour ago, was holding out the telephone receiver. "For you, m'lord," he shouted across to Melrose Plant.

Plant frowned. "Me? At this hour . . . ?" It would be Ruthven, he thought. Ardry End, like Manderley, must be burning.

Ⅺ

The connection was dreadful. Cracklings all along the line, as if someone had indeed sent out the fire brigade.

It was a trunk call, much to his surprise.

228

More to his surprise, from *Polly Praed.* He could not believe *she* was calling *him.* "What are you talking about, Polly? You fell out of a call box?"

On her end, Polly Praed wanted to throttle him. *"No! I* didn't fall out, *she* did . . . no, no, no!" As if Melrose could see as well as hear across the miles, she shook her dark curls in a frenzy. "I wasn't *in* the call box with her, you idiot!"

Melrose smiled. "Idiot" was a backhanded compliment. Melrose seemed to be the only adult this pathologically shy woman could confront. Around children, animals, and the Natural World, she did well. He had first met her in her village of Littlebourne, in colloquy with a tree. "Look, this line is awful. Can you hear me?"

"Enough of you."

He wondered what that meant.

She spaced her words out carefully, as one does when talking with the demented. "This woman just fell *over* me."

"Where are you?"

Irritated beyond belief, she squeezed her eyes shut. She'd told him twice. Through clenched teeth, she spelled it: "A-S-H-D-O-W-N-D-E-A-N. Borders the New Forest. They won't let me leave —"

When Constable Pasco turned a questioning glance on her, she slid down the counter, putting the telephone on her lap, and whispered.

"Did the police *tell* you she was murdered?"

"Well, good Lord, what else could she be?"

"Try to be calm, Polly. Now, I take it you want me to come straightaway."

"If you like."

If he liked. How gracious. The New Forest was over a hundred miles away.

"I was just thinking ..." Polly sat there on the station floor, winding the telephone cord round her finger.

Silence.

"You were just thinking," said Melrose, "that I could get Superintendent Jury down there." Under pain of death, Polly could never have called Richard Jury herself, though she knew him well enough. "No." Melrose had to hold the receiver away from his ear.

When she was through yelling, he brought it back. "Jury has probably the usual mess of pottage on his platter — rapes, murders, thefts — and, anyway, he couldn't go to Hampshire without a formal request from that constabulary, which I doubt will be forthcoming."

Silence again on her end. He sighed. "Polly. Have you *any* idea what happened?"

"Yes," she snapped. "The lady didn't pay her bill and Telecom did her in!"

Smash went the receiver in Ashdown Dean.

four

etective Superintendent Richard Jury was not, on that same evening, working on a case and might have welcomed an interruption of the little seduction scene taking place in the bed-sit directly above his own flat.

Carole-anne Palutski (a.k.a. Glo Dee Vine, her "stage" name), whom he had first met a month ago when she was wrestling an armchair up the narrow steps of the Islington terrace house, was bending down to a minuscule table for a couple of bottles of Carlsberg, gyrating her Sassoon jeans with a toss or two not absolutely necessary for the task at hand. On one of the rear pockets was an appliquéd *Smartass*, and when she turned, Operation Carlsberg successfully completed, the little heart appliquéd on the crotch fairly throbbed. Carole-anne believed in advertising fore and aft.

"Want an Elephant, love?"

Since she was holding up the Carlsberg, she meant beer. Jury wondered what the answer would have been from someone with less restraint — or not old enough to be her father, as Jury certainly was. Twenty-two was what she said she was.

231

He let it pass, mentally ringing up nineteen. "One more and I'll run downstairs like Niagara," he said. "You look a little wobbly yourself, Carole-anne."

She lifted a skintight-jeaned leg. "It's only the shoes, love. Four-inch heels these ones must be. And call me 'Glo,' " she said, probably for the umpteenth time that evening.

"No. It doesn't suit you."

Carole-anne pouted and set about decapping the Carlsberg in such a way the beer foamed over and ran down the tank top that didn't need anything more to let him know how little lay between thin cotton and skin.

"Now look what I've gone and done," she said wonderingly, as if she hadn't for a minute meant to go and do it. Beer was snaking down her naked torso to the jeans. Where the "waistline" was supposed to be, only Sassoon knew: it seemed to ride her pelvis at the moment, the belt holders threaded with some silky stuff that ended in little balls cavorting with the red heart.

"Come here," said Jury, who was seated on the lumpy daybed.

The false lashes lowered over deep blue eyes, her whole expression saying *at last*. She swayed over to him, still holding the beer bottle, and landing the viscous torso right in front of his mouth.

Jury took out his handkerchief and wiped her stomach.

Her mouth fell open and her arms fell down, clutching the bottles as if she'd wring their necks. He took one from her and swigged it.

The empty hand went to her thrust-out hip. "Well, ain't you a hoot and a scream, then? You can't be queer, so what's the argy? I mean, I ain't exactly an old dripper."

"Not since I wiped the beer off." Jury smiled.

Her face went red and he thought she was going to yell, but instead she fell down on the bed giggling. "Takes all kinds." She sighed and leaned her head on his shoulder. "You're my first failure."

"Maybe I'm your first success."

All she did was screw her face up and look at him as if he must be crazy.

"Men are thick on the ground, Carole-anne. You know what I'd do if you were my daughter?"

"Nah. What?"

"Kick your little Smartass right across the room. Maybe buy you some Gloria Vanderbilt jeans — at least the swan's harmless — and a cashmere sweater. Loose."

"You like kinky sex? That it?"

Jury put his forehead against the Carlsberg and laughed. That was the only way she could look at anything.

"Well, I was only trying to pay you back," she said. "You know, for helping me with the furniture and all that."

"For God's sake, Carole-anne, can't a man help you without your having to go to bed with him?"

She thought that over while she picked at the bottle label. Carole-anne shrugged. "Tits for tat."

☿

The odd-lot furniture hadn't taken a removal van to bring it, just a lad driving an old pickup. Her earthly possessions were vested largely in herself. She was gorgeous. Navy blue eyes, waist-length hair, a shape that would show through potato sacks. He'd helped her stow the furniture, turn the tiny bed-sit into some sort of home, and then taken her out to one of the locals for a bite.

On that warm-for-September moving day, she'd been wearing bright blue sateen shorts, cut up above the line where buttocks met legs, and over this, as if for modesty, a short skirt of the same material. The modesty was very mild, however, since the skirt was slit up both sides, thereby em-

233

phasizing the legwork underneath rather than hiding it. The weather hadn't been *that* warm, but he doubted Carole-anne dealt much in coats.

Whether you started at the floppy sandals and worked your way up, or at the spaghetti straps of the cut-off blouse and worked your way down, the effect on the men at the bar was unanimous. Heads moved in a synchronized turn that would have done a chorus line proud.

Studying the chalked specials on the little blackboard at the serving bar, Carole-anne didn't give the starers and hopeful-gropers a second thought. "Cottage pie, couple of Scotch eggs, chips, salad." Then when she saw Jury was ordering sausages, she added, "And one of them ones, too." She left Jury to see to the filling of the plate and slapped her sandals over to a little table, stuffed next to a banquette. Moses parting the Red Sea couldn't have made more space than this vision in blue sateen.

"You're a *what?*" said Jury, halfway into his sausage, watching Carole-anne stuffing in cottage pie.

"You needn't get huffy. A topless dancer." She shrugged a shoulder in some unidentifiable direction. "Over to King Arthur's. Never been?"

"That sweatshop? Only when I was nicking one of the dips that works the passage."

"You? A superintendent? Lower yourself, don't you?"

"This one's a personal friend. Listen, you shouldn't be doing stuff like that. What in hell would your parents think? They probably don't know."

"Listen to him, would you?" She appeared to be addressing the Scotch egg. "Mum's dead. And Da—" She shrugged. "Who knows? Anyway, I can't even remember him." She said it matter-of-factly.

"I'm sorry. But you must have *some* family."

234

Her deep blue eyes looked up, slightly puzzled. "Why? There's lots don't. Do you?"

"Not much of a one. A cousin. Lives in Newcastle. How've you been getting by, Carole-anne?"

Again, those blue eyes regarded him, this time with a sparkle. "You kiddin'?"

Jury said nothing.

She sighed. "Oh, okay. I'm not into that. What I want to be is a dancer or actress."

"Thought you were one," he said.

"God, you're wors'n a dozen mums. I mean a *real* actress. Tried out for *Chorus Line*. Almost got a part, too."

"Well, if you didn't, the casting director must have a Seeing-Eye dog."

She hesitated and then laughed. "Thanks."

"That's your ambition, then? West End musicals?"

"West-bloody-End musicals? Well, it'd do for a start. What I'm really good at is the straight stuff. You know. Like that Judith Anderson or Shirley MacLaine, maybe."

"You sweep the board, that's for sure. Had any lessons?"

"Some. Need a bit of training." Her look was quite serious as she scrutinized her Scotch egg.

"A little, at least. I've got to get to work. I'll see you back to the house. I'm keeping an eye on you, Carole-anne."

Shrugging a creamy shoulder toward the bar, she said, "So what else is new?"

¤

"Polly? Polly *Praed?* In a phone booth — ?" Jury had left Carole-anne's flat after checking the dead-bolt lock and fixing the loose chain. (*"You going to bolt me in, Super?"*)

Just as he entered his own flat, the phone rang. He wasn't on rota, so it shouldn't be New Scotland Yard, but, knowing his chief superintendent's tendency to ignore who was first,

235

second, third down, he fully expected one of Racer's late-night calls-to-arms. That didn't mean anything was happening in criminal London that demanded Jury's attention, only that Racer's club and the pubs were closed.

So Jury was pleasantly surprised to hear the voice of his old friend Melrose Plant on the other end.

"Yes, I'm working on a case. Racer makes certain my hands are either full or tied behind my back. Where is this place?"

Jury wrote it down. "Okay. What else did she tell you? . . . Hmm. Well, you must bring out the best in her." Jury smiled. "I'll see you there tomorrow. Unofficially, that is. The Hampshire police wouldn't appreciate my coming along uninvited."

Hung up on him, had she? Jury shook his head, looked at the dull paperwork in his hand, tossed it back on the desk. From his memory of Polly Praed, getting her to talk about anything at all was like being stuck at a party of clams. She struck him as extremely shy, unless the subject got around to murder.

five

U na Quick, according to Dr. Farnsworth, had died of
cardiac arrest.

It was the storm and Ida Dotrice's account of Una's
habit of calling her doctor, who signed the death certificate,
that provided the Hampshire police with a reason for the accident. Dr. Farnsworth, whose practice was in the nearby
town of Selby, examined Una Quick every month, like clockwork. It was unfortunate (Farnsworth had told police) that
Miss Quick had not had a clockwork heart. Could go at any
time.

Una had told Ida Dotrice that Dr. Farnsworth insisted she
call him once a week — every Tuesday after office hours to
report on her condition. How the latest medication was af-
fecting her, or how the old ticker was doing, or whether she'd
been going against his orders and drinking more than her
limit of two cups of tea, and so forth.

But the storm Tuesday evening had brought down a telephone line and she hadn't been able to ring up the doctor
from her cottage. So she had stupidly taken the walk up that

hilly High Street to the call box dutifully to report to the doctor.

The call had never gone through; Una had passed out in the kiosk and instead of slumping to the floor, as one might have suspected, she'd been supported by the telephone box itself. Must have thrown her arm across it — as police reconstructed the case — to keep from falling.

Dr. Farnsworth did not appreciate the irony of his patient's death put down to a gradual but nonetheless steep climb to a call box to report on the state of her health.

Ⅺ

It was morning and Barney was still missing.

Melrose Plant would be here at any moment. Now, of course, she was hideously embarrassed that she'd got him all the way down here to Hampshire under false pretenses. Perhaps she could suggest they take a nice drive through the New Forest or have lunch somewhere. Or something. Polly scrunched down in her chair in the dining room of Gun Lodge.

Why she felt perfectly comfortable talking to *him* — he who was, or had been, one of the Earls of Caverness, and Viscounts Somebody, and a baron, and who knew what else, and had given it all *up* . . . Polly knifed the table mat as if it were one of the defunct titles. Not that she gave a fig for a title. She simply disliked people acting in a way contrary to what she would have them doing in her books. Earls and dukes and marquesses were supposed to stay that way.

"Ma'am," said a spindly girl who seemed as shy as Polly herself. The girl had waited at table last night, had brought her early tea this morning, and seemed to be the only employee in Gun Lodge. She deposited a bowl on the table.

"What's that?" asked Polly, peering into the bowl.

"Porridge, ma'am," said this pathetic breath of a girl, who then scurried away.

238

Polly had no appetite anyway. Not with Barney gone.

The girl was back. *Go away,* she thought with the embarrassment of one who doesn't want to be caught crying. "A gentleman to see you, ma'am."

She looked down, listened to the approaching footsteps, said a brief (and rather surly) *Good morning* to Melrose Plant's *Good morning, Polly,* and without preamble, told him: "Coronary occlusion, that idiot doctor said. Well, maybe it was, but why was she in that call box anyway?"

Melrose Plant put his silver-knobbed stick on the table, sat down, and said, simply, "I don't know. Why're you crying?"

"I'm not," said Polly, his obvious sympathy breaking a log-jam of tears, which now flowed freely. "My cat's missing."

"Barney?"

That was the trouble with him. He even remembered the name of her cat. Not only that, but he seemed more interested in her cat than that she'd got him here on a wild-goose chase. She wiped her face with her napkin. Why he seemed actually to *admire* her was beyond her comprehension. She was off-hand, rude, demanding, and temperamental. "You're a masochist," she said, sniffling.

"Obviously," said Melrose, looking at the bowl. "So must you be if you're eating that." He took a spoon and stuck it in the porridge. It stood there.

"Don't touch it. You may never get back to Ardry End. I was met at the door by a gray-mustached, dreadful man who seemed to want a full accounting of my life before he'd rent me a room."

"Why did you stay, then? There's a perfectly good little pub with rooms a bit farther along."

Polly looked up, enraged. "He told me there *wasn't* any other place."

Looking round at the prison-gray walls, the plastic place-mats, the porridge, Melrose said, "How else could he get cus-

239

tom? Never mind. You can have my room at the pub and I'll stay here.."

"I can't. See, Barney might come looking for me."

Remembering Barney's battle scars, more likely he was out looking for a leopard to fight.

"Don't worry. We'll find Barney."

He was rewarded with a deep look from Polly's violet eyes. That he had been dragged all the way from Northampton-shire to Hampshire was nothing in the light of eyes like amethysts. The rest of her was ordinary enough. But who would bother looking at the rest of her? Melrose had to look away. "I take it you are thanking me?"

She churned the spoon in the awful gruel and more or less shrugged, dropping her glasses back in place. They often rode on her head. "Thanks."

"Ah, the bliss! The everlasting gratitude! The hundred-mile drive — !"

"*Do* stop being dramatic. You know you've nothing much to do."

"How gracious. Except find your cat." She deserved to be humbled a bit. "Well, not to worry. I called Superintendent Jury. He should be showing up in —" Melrose paused for a bit of drama with his gold watch "— in an hour or two."

Medusa couldn't have done a better job of turning someone to stone than did the eyes of Polly Praed, now a stormy purple, staring into the green ones of Melrose Plant. "*What?*"

"Why are you looking at me as if I'd just marshaled the Coldstream Guards? *You* were the one who hung up because you were so blasted angry I wouldn't call him. So, I called him." Melrose poured himself a cup of lukewarm tea and asked if she minded if he smoked. From her look, he could have gone up in flames, and no one the sorrier. "Look, I *did* what you wanted."

"Well, *this* is just wonderful. The poor woman keeled over from a coronary. But she didn't keel, that was the trouble.

There I was, thinking it was a live person making a call —"

"Not an unreasonable assumption. But you mean this is why I'm here?" He could see that her mind was somewhere on the A204 tracking Jury's car. Melrose might have been dragged from his own deathbed — that wouldn't worry her.

"How am I going to explain to Superintendent Jury that I'm not up on a murder charge — ?"

"The way you're pointing that knife, you soon might be." He moved the blade away. "I don't know," he said, smiling wonderfully. "Poor Jury. Dragged all the way from London on a missing cat case —"

Polly Praed slapped her napkin on the table and slid down in her seat, still staring at or through him.

Then she said, to his surprise, "Why didn't she have an umbrella?"

PART 3

Children—swindled for the first
All Swindlers—be—infer—

Sir

S he wore a washed-out blue denim pinafore over a white jumper, sneakers faded like the denim, and no socks. Her hair was nearly platinum in the slant of sun breaking through the drizzling rain and the trees that surrounded Ashdown Heath. The shine of her hair made up for the lack of light in her face, a pale oval, glazed with rain. Her eyes were the same wash blue, faded like the rest of her. She looked like any other ordinary fifteen-year-old, except for the .412 shotgun butted against her shoulder, as she squinted along the barrel at the two boys thirty feet away.

"Put the cat down," she said.

Billy and Batty Crowley had been stopped in the act of pouring the can of petrol on the ginger cat. It had a red bandanna round its neck and looked almost like a cartoon cat — eyes white and huge with terror, fur sticking out like pine needles. Batty Crowley was just about to strike a kitchen match.

She had walked softly up behind them, a quarter of the way across the heath, and they'd been so absorbed in their game they hadn't heard her until she'd said it: "Put the cat down."

They turned and stared at her, their own eyes frozen over now like the cat's. When they didn't react as fast as she liked, she cocked the gun and released the safety catch.

Then she said: "Take your shirts and sweaters off."

They looked at each other and then back at her as if she were the mad one who'd contrived the merciless game in the first place. "What the bloody hell you mean?"

"Take your shirts and sweaters off. Now! Wipe that petrol off with the shirts."

Both of them, each holding a leg of the squirming animal, bellowed with laughter —

Until she fired. She fired into the dirt of the cleared-off place where they were going to barbecue the cat. They ripped off shirts and sweaters and started wiping the cat down. They were sweating, half naked in the cold of the October morning.

"You're —" screamed Billy Crowley. He must have thought better of telling her what she was when he saw the shotgun come up slowly, aimed somewhere in the area of his forehead.

"You got the petrol off?"

They nodded, squatting down and wiping for all they were worth. The cat screeched and clawed Billy.

"Wrap those sweaters round the cat so it can't lick itself and put it in that box you brought it in." When she motioned with the shotgun, they cringed. "Bring the box here."

"What — ?"

The gun moved again; the question went unasked. It would certainly have gone unanswered.

Billy wrapped the sweaters around the cat and stuffed it — screeching and clawing — back into the box.

"Here."

They did as commanded, setting the box about six feet

246

from her. Rustlings and bumpings came from the box that looked as if it were moving by itself, a trick box.

"Now you just run like hell across the heath and I'll just stand here till I can't see you any longer."

They didn't look back.

She didn't wait. She broke the gun, took out the other shell and dumped it with the box of them in her pocket. Then she picked up the cat, hid the gun in some bracken, and ran through the trees until she reached the road that led out of Ashdown Dean. Where she ran even faster.

Seven

Polly Praed was still staring malevolently at Melrose Plant three-quarters of an hour later when he had moved them from the dining room of Gun Lodge to the more pungent airs of the Deer Leap. Since Melrose had taken a room here, the publican, John MacBride, was only too happy to open the bar at ten.

"It's a point, certainly. No one would have gone out in that storm without an umbrella." He looked around at the chintz-covered cushions of the chairs and window seats, the windows once again lashed with rain; at the inglenook fireplace; the pewter and brass mugs hanging above the bar; the copy of Landseer's painting of a stag hanging above the fireplace. "But I'm not sure what it means."

Neither was Polly, so she changed the subject. "That Grimsdale person nearly shut the door in my face for even suggesting the Lodge wasn't the Ritz."

"Um. Well, don't worry too much about your predicament. I expect the superintendent can clear you when he gets here."

"That's so funny I can hardly contain myself. I'd like an-

248

other Guinness." She shoved her half-pint toward him, former earl, present lackey.

Melrose pretended not to hear her and looked at his watch. "He should be here any time now."

Forgetting her Guinness, Polly started collecting her umbrella. She was still wearing that yellow mac and hat. "Give him my regards."

"If you think you're leaving after all of the trouble you've caused, you're quite wrong. Anyway, my dear Polly, it's too late."

Melrose watched her die a thousand deaths and knew exactly what was in her mind — she sat there in that ridiculous oversized hat and mac, gum boots to match, looking as if all she needed was a small boat and a large net and she might come back with a crocodile.

Actually, he rather enjoyed her dilemma, even if he couldn't say he enjoyed the reason for it. Polly was absolutely gaga over Jury, but Melrose was intelligent enough to know that gagaism didn't add up to love.

He leaned across the table and whispered, "Don't you remember that love means never having to say you're sorry?"

"Having some trouble, are you, Polly?" asked Jury, after he'd greeted Melrose Plant. He and Detective Sergeant Alfred Wiggins pulled out chairs and sat down. Wiggins smiled and blew his nose by way of hellos all round.

Melrose looked at the stag in the painting, both of them mere innocent bystanders.

Turning her glass round and round, she managed to get out a strangled "Yes."

Melrose watched as she tried to outmaneuver conversational possibilities. To him, she had detailed the odyssey of her journey round the Kentish coast and up through Chawton like Ulysses. Now, of course, she was tongue-tied.

Jury waited. Nothing doing. Ectoplasm in a yellow oilskin.

249

He cued her: "You found this body in a public call box, or at least that's all I could get out of Mr. Plant."

Melrose sighed and looked up at the stag. The innocent always suffered. He turned to Wiggins. "How are you, Sergeant?"

Wiggins merely shook his head. "Caught a chill. It's pneumonia weather. Runs hot and cold. And the rain doesn't help."

"Quite right," said Melrose. "It's hell."

"Wet hell, sir." Wiggins said he was going to the bar for a buttered rum. Would the superintendent care for anything?

"Pint of bitter, thanks. Miss Praed — Polly?" She might have been out like a light. "Tell me exactly what happened."

"What happened? Well — didn't *he* tell you?"

Jury smiled, and Plant thought he should have known better. The smile only made her shrink further into her slicker.

"Okay. I'll tell you what I know and you supply the missing details —"

"Barney." She looked down into her empty glass. "Is a missing detail."

"Your cat."

Quickly, obliquely, she ventured a glance from under her brim. "You remembered."

"Your cat? Who'd forget him? I think I'd be afraid more for anyone who crosses his path. Go on."

"No, you."

Good heavens, thought Melrose, sighing hugely, they might have been playing Patience. That was certainly Jury's game. Why didn't he simply reach across the table and shake her till her teeth rattled — dragging him all the way from London. But no, he would never lay a hand on a woman; he would just sit there with that damned smile . . . no wonder they melted at his feet.

250

As now. "Okay. You opened the door of the call box and an elderly woman fell at your feet. That sum it up?"

She beamed. "Perfectly. But she didn't have an umbrella."

Jury looked puzzled. "Is that significant?"

Polly raised her eyes to heaven. "It was *rain*ing."

"Good heavens, Polly," said Melrose. "I wouldn't take that tone with the superintendent, here."

The eyes dropped as Wiggins returned with Jury's drink and went back for his own, which he had to wait for, since he wanted it medicinally hot.

"That *is* odd. Good for you, Polly. . . ."

Jury's voice purred on. He might have been petting that damned moth-eaten cat of hers. It really wasn't fair, thought Melrose; *he* had gone to all of the trouble —

"Oh, sorry, sir," said Sergeant Wiggins, breaking the spell of those violet eyes riveted on Jury's gray ones.

"Hmm?"

"Your glass, Mr. Plant. Let me get you another." His racking cough was somewhat more convincing than Polly's little throat-clearings. But then Wiggins had had years of practice. He looked at Plant's empty bottle of Old Peculiar and shook his head, frowning slightly. "I'd suggest a nice hot buttered rum, sir. Never seen such weather. Ran straight into the eye of a storm coming here —"

He would turn it into a monsoon. "Just some more Old Peculier, thanks."

As Wiggins slouched off (still in coat and scarf), Polly was becoming slightly more voluble, probably hypnotized by the grey eyes. Anyway, it was either talk or burn.

Plant just sat there turning his small cigar round in his mouth. She hadn't arrived at the doctor's report yet. Thus far, the only criminal activity was the catnapped Barney.

Under other circumstances, Jury might have appreciated Polly's epic, himself being a lover of Virgil, but even the su-

251

perintendent's patience had its limits. He was already into his second pint when he finally asked the Fatal Question: "How was she murdered, then?" When Polly simply studied her hands, Jury asked, "What did the medical examiner say?"

An indrawn breath. "Well, this woman wasn't *exactly* murdered."

Jury looked at her. Wiggins looked at her. Plant studied the picture. Neither the stag nor Polly had a chance.

It was Wiggins who finally said, "Not 'exactly.' Could you explain that, miss?"

Polly blew out her cheeks. "Yes. Well, it more or less looks like she died of some kind of heart-thing."

Melrose offered helpfully: "There wasn't a knife or a bullet in the heart, Superintendent. Not that sort of heart-thing."

That got him a gum boot in his shin.

"Coronary?" asked Jury, his expression bland.

Polly nodded and nodded, bobbing her dark curls. She had, during her tiresome exposition, at least removed her ridiculous hat.

There was rather a lengthy silence as Polly slowly scraped at a dried bit of food on the tabletop.

Melrose, eyes narrowed, watched Jury watching Polly. There it was, that damned slow smile. Instead of beating her about the shoulders with a table leg as she deserved, she having hauled him — or, worse, got Melrose Plant to do her dirty work — all the way from New Scotland Yard where there would be hell to pay when he got back . . .

"Not to worry," said Superintendent Jury. "You never know. It sounds pretty strange; police might be jumping to conclusions. . . ."

Vigorously, she nodded. "That's just what I said."

She'd said nothing of the kind.

"And Barney missing." Now she slumped back, tearful.

"We'll find him." And then, hemming in that smile, quite

252

deliberately, Plant knew, Jury said to *him,* "But really you should have got more of the facts before you called. . . ."

Polly's smile at Jury was dazzling.

Melrose shut his eyes. Why didn't they just stuff him and mount him like a deer?

Eight

aul Fleming's surgery was a half-mile outside Ashdown Dean, along the road which Carrie had just run, the cat sliding back and forth like a boulder in the cardboard box.

She watched Dr. Fleming, who was, unfortunately for him (Carrie thought), the village "catch." He took the cat out of the box. Wrestled it out, rather. The cat in the red bandanna wasn't looking with any more kindness on this second helpful member of the crew than he had on her. As the veterinarian more or less tossed and held it on the examining table, she wondered if animals, like humans, remembered their torturers and could go after them later, for she surely would like to set this cat on the trail of Batty and Billy Crowley.

Paul Fleming was sniffing the air. "Where'd you find this one? Smells like it's been dumped in a petrol pump."

Carrie scratched at her elbows. She never believed in giving out any more information than absolutely necessary. Constable Pasco would be bad enough, and she intended to get to him before the Crowley boys' aunt did; that way she might get off with the usual lecture, instead of jail.

"It has been. Someone put petrol on it. I got off what I could but I didn't know —" She shrugged.

She held the cat steady while he got soap and water. "How long's it been? I mean since you found it?"

"Fifteen minutes maybe. Just soap?" She nodded toward the pan of water.

"Castile. Beef fat. The petrol defats the skin. You wrapped the sweaters round him?"

Holding the cat still, she merely nodded.

Fleming looked from cat to Carrie. "To keep him from licking at the petrol? That was clever. Apparently, it didn't get any in its system; I'd hardly call this cat lethargic." The cat took a swipe at the towel. "Hold on, you big thug. Two sweaters. You must've been cold." He glanced up at her.

No reply.

"Where'd you find him?"

"On the heath."

"Well, what the hell was he doing running round out *there?*"

"*I* don't know, do I?"

Her refusal to give out the details had nothing to do with wanting to protect the Crowley boys. She wished they'd burn in hell. In petrol, in hell. Carrie simply didn't believe in telling any more than she had to. Not even to Dr. Fleming, whom she supposed she could stand being around for ten minutes at a time, which was saying a lot for someone who walked on two feet. But she didn't approve of his work at the Rumford Lab. She never lost a chance to remind him of that.

"Off work, today, are you?"

He looked at her. "You don't call this 'work'?"

Carrie looked at him. "I mean from the lab."

Fleming looked as if he was just barely controlling himself. "Let's not have another go at that, if you don't mind."

"The RCVS doesn't seem to be doing much to improve things." She rolled her eyes ceilingward to avoid looking into his. "I mean, they change the language around and so forth. 'Termination condition.' That's pretty good. Why don't you say what you mean?"

Paul Fleming glared at her. "Listen, if there wasn't any animal experimentation, what about this cat here? That ever occur to you?"

She looked at the big tom. "I suppose so."

"Thanks!"

"Kill fifty cats to save one." Slowly she nodded. "I suppose so."

"You do *not* know what you're talking about! God! Why aren't you up there with the rest of the demonstrators, torching away?"

"It's against my principles."

He looked at her and shook his head.

Carrie knew it upset him, just having her walk in. Too bad. He was pretty nice. And Gillian Kendall was probably in love with him.

Poor Gillian. Carrie watched him as he worked and had to admit he was handsome, also good with animals, also unmarried. He'd be better off to stay that way, and so would Gillian. Carrie was a reader, and was constantly amazed at how few books could get by without the Big Love Scene. These scenes neither embarrassed nor repulsed her; she merely found herself grandiosely indifferent to the intermingling of lips and bodies. It was their unlucky lot to be caught up in a fate worse than death.

"Instead of standing there mooning, help me," he said, handing her a towel.

"I never moon." She wiped the cat.

"Bring in a jaguar next time, will you?"

Carrie liked the way the cat's pupils spurted in the light like red-hot coals, probably a reflection up from his red bandanna.

"God, is that a *smile* I see?" he asked, wiping the cat's fur down.

Quickly, she erased whatever giveaway look had been there. She hadn't known he'd been watching her.

"Gone," he said, sighing heavily. "Well. I suppose you'll live, tiger."

That the cat would not only live but probably outlive them both was clear. It wrestled with Fleming as if they were both on the mat and then flung itself on the floor.

"Oh, for heaven's sake," said Carrie, picking him up and plunking him back in the box. "You got one of those cardboard cat-carriers?"

He sighed. "You're already into me for three of those. One pound apiece."

From her pinafore she pulled some pound notes and slapped three on the table.

Paul Fleming reddened. "Look, it's okay —"

"I robbed Nat West."

"All right, all right, don't give me that stormy look." From a low shelf he pulled out the cat-carrier and unfolded it, handles upright. He smiled again. "Ten pounds is the usual fee. But for you —"

"That all you think about? Money? You know I'll pay you."

Again, he smiled. "Just a penny. For your thoughts. What *do* you think about, Carrie?"

She picked up the carrier, just as much of a boulder, but quieter. "Fates worse than death. Thank you." She walked out.

Too late.

Police Constable Pasco slammed down the telephone and glared at her, so she knew Amanda Crowley had already rung up. Probably the reason it took Amanda so long was because she knew Billy and Batty were guilty. "I'm reporting a crime," Carrie said.

"That so?" Pasco folded his arms across his chest and plunked his feet up on his desk.

"Batty and Billy Crowley got hold of a cat and were going to burn it." She put the cat carrier on the ledge between his desk and the tiny entryway. "Here he is."

Pasco pointed to the telephone. "*That* was Amanda Crowley on the phone just now. She said you aimed a gun at those kids."

"What was I supposed to do? Let them burn up the cat?"

"This is the eighth time —" He looked up at a huge calendar with pictures of grazing sheep on it. Carrie wondered why he'd want to look at sheep or cows or anything else on four feet. He didn't care about animals. "No, tenth — *tenth* time — you listening?"

"Yes." She lowered her eyes as though in sorrow and shame but actually to look at the copy of a manual put out by the RSPCA on his desk. The constable must have been doing his homework. He kept count on the calendar of how many times she'd been in here on some complaint from a villager.

"Well, you better, Carrie. Just because you got the protection of the Baroness —"

That, thought Carrie, *was a giggle.*

"— doesn't mean you can go round untying dogs, stealing cats —"

"If you mean Mr. Geeson's beagle, he kept it on a chain morning and night and that's against the law." She held up the blue manual, slapped it back down.

His blue eyes narrowed. "*It's against the law to threaten people's lives!* This is the last time —"

"You want the fumes of roast cat ponging through the village?"

He closed his eyes, pained. "Don't think I'm not on to you. Don't think I don't know who unstopped earths during cubbing season. If I get one more complaint from Grimsdale —"

She tuned him out. Sebastian Grimsdale was Master of Foxhounds and Harriers, one of the shining stars in the Ashdown Dean social heavens.

Disgust stamped on his face, Pasco drew a pad toward him. "What's its name?"

Carrie frowned. "The cat's? Batty didn't introduce us —"

"Clever." He pointed the pen like an arrow at her. "Fifteen and so damned starchy you probably sleep standing up. What's it look like, then?"

"See for yourself. He has a red bandanna round his neck. He doesn't live in Ashdown Dean —"

He told her to keep the thing *inside* the box. Then he swiveled in his chair and picked up the phone. As he dialed he said, "Know every cat and dog and pig and fox in town — *Hello?*" He asked for someone named Prad, it sounded like. He left a message they'd found her cat.

"The cat belongs to a guest at the Lodge. One of these days, Carrie, big, big trouble —"

Again, she lowered her eyes. "Yes." She picked up the carrier.

"Leave it here," commanded Pasco.

"Finders, keepers," she said, running out the door with the carrier before he could stop her.

ℼ

As she walked past the blue sign with the white *P* that told all of Ashdown's villagers where to find help, Carrie reflected that, taken all in all, her relationship with Constable Pasco wasn't so bad. She'd certainly been in his company often enough to know.

Coming along the walk toward her was Donaldson, Sebastian Grimsdale's head keeper. He was a Scot, supposed to be a brilliant stalker and harborer, and she loathed him. How he could have lowered himself to come here and help Grimsdale with his bagged and kenneled foxes, Carrie couldn't imagine. And another supposedly good-looking one with his copper hair and square face. Carrie had heard he was having an affair with Sally MacBride, the publican's wife of only a year.

"Ah, and if it isn't wee Carrie."

Wee Carrie, indeed. She could have belted him.

He stood directly in her path and when she tried to get round him he did a sidestep first one way and then another. She refused to ask him to let her pass. Carrie simply stood her ground and stared straight through him. There were times when she honestly thought slime like Donaldson was not solid, that she could reach out and stick her hand right through him. If he was soulless, why wouldn't he be bodyless?

His smile was one of the most unnatural, one of the most twisted she'd ever seen. He made a grab for the carrier, which she moved quickly out of reach, behind her.

Looking her up and down in what was supposed to pass for a lazy, sexy glance, he said, "Y' should do yerself up proper, lass; y'd be a looker."

Still she said nothing nor did she move.

"Got nowt to wear but that damned faded pinafore? It hides too much." His own eyes stared at her breasts, or what he could see of them, their bloom deliberately obscured by the sweater and shapeless pinafore.

Of course, he was trying as hard as he could to unsettle her, to make her nervous, to make her strike back. She just stood and stared.

"Aye, and I can stand here all day if needs be."

Carrie said nothing. He wouldn't have the patience to stop here another minute, if she knew him.

She did. Now disdaining her, he said, "Think y'r really the princess, don't ye? Just because you live with that old nut, the Baroness." Then he shouldered Carrie out of the way as if the pavement weren't big enough for the both of them.

As she kept on toward Gun Lodge, she thought of how different he was around Sebastian Grimsdale, M.F.H. Donaldson was like toffee. You could hardly get him off your fingers, he was so sticky-nice.

Sebastian Grimsdale was one of the Baroness's favorite guests, not because she liked him; she liked his posturing. He was forever at her silly *salons,* the most prominent of her guests — at least, in his own eyes. In Carrie's he didn't even reflect.

She was walking along the riverside that skirted the village, and came to the old playhouse behind the Deer Leap. The pub was built of chequers of local stone and knapped flint and had been simply a pub, until John MacBride's new wife decided to open up a room for paying guests and call it an inn. Sally MacBride was another one Carrie had no time for. She wouldn't let her niece have any pets at all. Carrie had thought of a way around that.

They didn't use the child's playhouse much anymore. It was awfully small and had no windows, but it had been fun when Carrie was younger. There were gardens at the rear of the inn, even an herb garden with peppermint and pennyroyal. Lupines nearly as tall as Carrie herself, roses, daisies, and all the rest "clumped" (said the Baroness) "all together with no respect for design, pattern, nor grace of movement."

Carrie could not quite understand why a garden was only good for the thought of oneself moving through it, but the Baroness probably imagined nothing else. In her own mind she would see herself by one of her reflecting pools; or walking with her parasol beneath an arbor of white roses; or reclining "gracefully" upon one of the many benches of white-painted iron. Carrie had once found her outstretched beside the privet hedge, drunk as three lords. It was nice to enjoy one's surroundings, she supposed.

The cat had been so quiet, she looked into the carrier to see if he was all right. He was peacefully dozing. Despite Dr. Fleming's care, you never knew. Turn around and you might find something dead. Besides: she did not understand how a veterinarian, who was supposed to be in the business of taking care of animals and saving their lives, could have anything to do with the Rumford Laboratory.

The laboratory lay over a mile from Ashdown Dean, a long low gray fortress surrounded by a chain-link fence. Carrie saw it as a long scar on a blighted field.

There had been demonstrations; she had walked there to watch them. But she didn't participate. The lab had been torched once by the Animal Freedom Front, and she couldn't for the life of her figure out their reasoning, since several rabbits had died from smoke inhalation. That aside, burning things down that you didn't like was against her principles.

Walking on to Gun Lodge, she kicked up the fallen leaves, wishing she could make a great pile of them and dive straight in. Cover herself up and lie there hiding for a while. Her arm was wearying with the weight of the cat, and there was an old oak tree by the river, one that looked as if it had been lightning-struck. It hadn't; there was a natural division that made a space just large enough to shove a small length of board into. She had found some wood to fit it and she liked to sit in the tree.

Although she knew she should get the cat back to the guest, she was awfully tired from the morning's work. So she put the carrier on the ground and sat down, drawing her legs up with her sneakers against one part of the trunk and her back against the other. The sunlight that in September had filtered through the leaves had weakened to cast pale rivulets across her legs. *And did the Sunshine face His way?*

Carrie twisted her face and flattened it against the tree bark to keep from crying. Childhood amnesia. Her mother and father were probably dead, but she would never know.

That was a line of poetry from somewhere. Carrie had been to an East End school off and on, mostly off, and hated it. What she knew she'd taught herself. She did not go to school now. When social services came round to find out why, the Baroness had told them Gillian Kendall was her tutor (which she wasn't — she was the secretary), and when threatened, the Baroness had counterthreatened with a verve and energy that could only come from the fourth drink of the afternoon. They always said they'd be back, but there were no return trips.

The Baroness might be a little nutty, at that. That was fine with Carrie, because all of the sane people she'd known hadn't been God's gift.

Getting down from her tree perch, she picked up the box, and once again looked up at the hazy sunlight, the sky like pearl. *Was it a pleasant Day to die — And did the Sunshine face His way?*

She squeezed her eyes shut. In a hasty moment, she had even had to name herself and had no idea why she came up with Carrie Fleet.

Nine

Sebastian Grimsdale stood at the window of Gun Lodge, his hands clasped, or, rather, wrenching themselves behind his back, watching her come around the stables. This morning when he had awoken at six, all had been covered with hoarfrost, dew frozen on each dying blade of grass, and he had known a moment of rare exhilaration. Hunting was the only thing that brought that on. Certainly the girl coming across the court didn't. Nor did that Proud woman. No, Prad. Something like that. And here came the Fleet girl carting the damned cat. Police, mind you! Had they nothing better to do with their time than go about the countryside looking for cats?

"I assumed Barney could stay in my room —" the Prad woman had had nerve enough to say.

Well, he'd scotched *that* plan mighty quick. Told her she'd have to leave the cat in the car, and when she'd turned to find lodgings elsewhere — nearly flung down the pen, rude woman — he'd taken thought about the eight pounds and told her the veterinarian could board the cat. The woman had seemed easy enough to subdue.

A cough behind him turned Mr. Grimsdale from the window to confront two of his guests. Archway, or something like. And his bleached-blond-haired wife who looked enough of a floozy to be in some West End musical. There she was now, dabbing lip-rouge on. Wondered how the husband, who had a face like a biscuit and wore rimless glasses, ever wound up with *her*.

He dragged his eyes away from her frontage, which was ample, and said, "Yes, Mr. Archway? What is it?"

"Archer. We were just wanting to pay our bill."

They were supposed to have stayed another night. Wasn't it awful enough that lean circumstances had forced him to turn Gun Lodge into a guesthouse (he refused to refer to it as a B&B) without those guests breaking their promises. "It was my understanding you were to stay two nights. *Two."* The indictment made the husband redden, but the woman snapped shut her compact and said in her dreadful East End accent, "That room's as cold as a virgin's —"

Fortunately for her, the husband silenced her. An elbow in the side. Well, if they insisted on being difficult ... "Checking-out time is at noon. It is now one o'clock." A long case clock in the entryway bonged the fatal hour.

And as if in tune with the sounds of doom, the giant iron knocker was raised and lowered once with a deadly crash. That Fleet girl. No respect for anything. "I am sure that you would not wish to pay for a night's lodging without the privilege of using it. No one has complained about the heat before," (actually, quite a few complaints along those lines had reached his ear) and here he sighed wearily — "however, I shall see Midge puts an extra heater in your room. Now, if you will excuse me."

Carrie Fleet stood on the wide doorstep and looked without expression into the eyes, hard as knuckles, of Sebastian Grimsdale. "I've come with the lady's cat."

There was a movement from within the box.

Grimsdale looked at both of them with the same disdain. "Just leave it."

"Here on the doorstep?"

"*I* will see she gets it."

Carrie, who seldom registered emotion, allowed herself the luxury of hating Sebastian Grimsdale, not only because she found him personally hateful, but doubly so because of his being Master of Foxhounds and taking the greatest pleasure in hunting anything (within the law) on the wing or on four feet — pheasant, rabbit, deer, grouse. Indeed, the only time she ever noticed him smiling was when he was tramping along with a gun in his hands.

"No," said Carrie.

"No? No what?"

"*I'll* see she gets it." Her tone was merely determined, but the major would take it as rank insolence. His face turned beet red. "Can't I come in and wait? I'll sit in the kitchen." If he let her in at all, she knew that's where she'd have to sit, anyway.

He glared at her, nodded curtly, and told her to go round back and Cook would let her in.

The delivery boy's entrance was okay with Carrie. She took the cat around to the back of the house, a big ramshackle brick place with a stone wall encircling it like an iron band.

When Polly Praed and Melrose Plant walked into the big kitchen of Gun Lodge, Carrie Fleet was drinking tea from a mug and Barney, out of his box, was dozing peacefully by the hearth. The cook, Mrs. Linley, had paid no more attention to the rules smartly laid down by Sebastian Grimsdale than did anyone else in Ashdown Dean: the greengrocer, the butcher, the librarian.

Polly rushed to the hearth and gathered up the intractable Barney, who seemed to prefer to sleep rather than be found. Barney had never been putty in Polly's hands. It was a bit embarrassing the way he squirmed to get back down to the tattered little rug on which he'd been toasting himself at Carrie's feet.

Polly momentarily put him down and said to Carrie, "Wherever did you find him?"

"On the heath." She shrugged. "It's near where I live. I guess he got out of your car and just wandered around."

"How can I thank you —?" Polly, with the aid of Melrose's handkerchief, wiped her eyes and blew her nose, which then looked frostbitten. She scrabbled about in her handbag, drew out her purse, and held out some folded notes.

Carrie frowned slightly. "I don't take rewards for stuff like that. It's against my principles." She put down her mug and got up.

Melrose Plant had been about to take out his wallet when she said that. The frown disappeared like a shadow's sudden passing and her face took on a lunar quality, something rather above it all, the expression calm as a nun's, though he felt there was something very unnunlike in its placidity. He had to admit here was someone under thirty who held a certain interest for him. He looked at his wallet, and turned back to see her pale blue eyes look quickly away from him. "That's certainly very kind of you."

Barney was again in a death struggle in Polly's arms, not impressed with the great reunion scenario. "He smells funny—well, soapy, or something." Polly sniffed the cat's fur.

"That's the vet's soap. Dr. Fleming. You can pay him if you want."

"A veterinarian? Was he hurt?" Polly started inspecting Barney, who let out an ungrateful growl and managed to struggle down to the hearthrug.

Carrie Fleet seemed to be considering. "No. But I didn't know whose cat it was; except for the bandanna, it could have been a stray. You don't have a collar on him."

There was a definite reproach in that word *collar*.

"So I thought it'd be a good idea to take him to Dr. Fleming."

The girl was chewing her lip, and her quicksilver glance from the one to the other of them suggested to Melrose that there might be more to her story than she was saying. But he let it pass.

"But — well, that was so *good* of you. What's your name, then?"

"Carrie Fleet." She brushed the pale hair back across her shoulder and started for the door.

Polly Praed didn't know what to do about Carrie Fleet. "Where do you live? In Ashdown?"

Carrie Fleet turned. "Yes. With the Baroness."

And with that as explanation, she walked out the door.

¤

As Carrie walked back along Ashdown's High Street, she realized how stupid her story had been and that the lady would go to Dr. Fleming and find out about the petrol.

Maybe a stranger's going to Constable Pasco and complaining would finally convince him that Batty and Billy were holy terrors around anything that couldn't defend itself. Maybe Batty couldn't help it, being the way he was, but Billy ought to be in borstal.

A family of ducks rowed up to the edge of the pond, probably hoping for lunch, seeing her there. But she had no bread today. She turned out her pockets in mute explanation, but the ducks didn't take the hint, and bobbed there, shoving one another about, each wanting to be first.

"No crumbs," said Carrie. "I can't *always* have crumbs, can I?"

She remembered Batty had been here one day, tossing in pieces of bread, and when the ducks came up close to the edge, he'd tried hitting at them with a stick until he saw Carrie and started backing off. She grabbed the stick and gave him a small whack across his bum, just the thing his aunt should have done. Even though she hadn't hit him hard, this assault had landed her yet once again in front of P.C. Pasco, being lectured to by Amanda Crowley. *"Poor Batty only trying to play with the ducks and you come along—"*

"Billy probably told him to do it," was Carrie's answer.

That had not gone down well at all with the aunt, who had always considered herself a martyr first-class.

Carrie loathed this tall, slim, buckled-down woman. She always seemed to be wearing riding gear of some sort. Tight pants, tight boots, that day a jacket closed with metal clasps. She had a mouth like a clamp that barely opened when she spoke in angry little spasms. Her hair was metal-gray, but fashionably done, pulled back in a fancy chignon from a round face, slightly jaundiced from too much passing about of the hunt cup, probably. It reminded Carrie of a poached egg. Amanda Crowley considered herself very county, loved to hunt and shoot, and was rumored to have her eye on Sebastian Grimsdale.

A wonderful pair, Carrie had thought, listening to the spasmodic voice of Miss Crowley. The two of them might mistake the rustles they made in the woods and shoot each other.

"The Baroness will have to be told." The Baroness was often approached by certain of the villagers who did not appreciate Carrie Fleet's ministry. It was always with that *you must be told* excuse, though no one apparently ever thought Amanda Crowley "must be told" about her own two.

This going to the Baroness always made Carrie laugh inwardly. The Baroness sometimes would, and sometimes wouldn't, invite the complainants in. When she allowed them an audience, it was in her withdrawing room, where she promptly withdrew her attention.

Thus while Amanda or Mr. Geeson or whoever happened to be that day's visitor was issuing an ultimatum, the mind of the Baroness was far away, strolling through an avenue of limes and plum trees, ripe fruit fallen underfoot, sunshade twirling slowly, milky hand lying on the arm of the Baron. That, or the faraway look had something to do with the gin in her teacup.

Carrie enjoyed imagining the Baroness's imaginings. Perhaps she embellished upon them in her own mind, she didn't know. But she had seen so many old photographs of what "La Notre" had once been — its summer house, its Grecian columns, its grounds and gardens completely out of place in Ashdown Dean.

There were times when Carrie's own arm replaced the Baron's as she accompanied the Baroness on her rambles through gardens long gone to seed or strangled with vines and grounds gone to moss and trees lichen-drowned. But the Baroness seemed to see in this adumbration of some garden Armageddon a mere need for the gardener to "see to" a few things. The cold stalks of dahlias she aimed her walking stick at and told Carrie to tell Randolph to see to them. Randolph was in his dotage and saw to nothing. Occasionally, Carrie had observed him leaning on a rake or a hoe and performing about as effectively as the crumbling statue at his back. Randolph also had a faraway look, but this was directed to the turf accountant's in the market-town of Selby. He would roll out his rickety bicycle and wobble off down the long drive, headed for Selby.

Given the Baroness's predilection to absent herself mentally from the felicity of the Crowleys of this world, it was left to Carrie herself to sit there and accept the hard coin of their complaints, like a parishioner passing the collection plate, as she literally passed the cake plate. And all the while marveling that none of the Ashdown Dean crowd had twigged it: the Baroness Regina de la Notre was either in a waking dream or dead drunk.

Although, of course, when she held her salons, Regina came up for air out of the past to join the present.

These were Carrie's reflections as she looked blindly across the bright water at the Church of St. Mary's and All Saints. The ducks, everlastingly hopeful, had been joined by two swans. She had the money for the Baroness's gin in her shoe, and would buy a half-loaf and come back.

Carrie started toward the sub-post-office stores, her mind again on the lady and man at Gun Lodge.

She allowed herself the vain thought that she didn't know which pair of eyes, deep violet or glittering green, she would have given her soul for. She had always hated her eyes, faded like her denim dress, hated her hair, her pale face — all of her. It was shameful, perhaps, in a world full of suffering, to want to be pretty. Carrie wanted to be absolutely smashingly beautiful. That was worse.

As she neared the store, she thought, well, at least she could buy bread, and that was more than a lot could do.

Ten

ry as she might, and huge as were the grounds of "La Notre," it seemed impossible for Carrie Fleet to circumvent the Baroness Regina. At eleven-thirty, the Baroness should have been taking her late coffee and brioche on the vine-tangled terrace overlooking the duck pond.

The Baroness was as unpredictable as her history. Her maiden name was Scroop, a Liverpudlian. The Baron Reginald de la Notre had made himself a fortune in fine leather gloves and it was indeed behind a glove counter in Liverpool that he had discovered Gigi Scroop. And had been bewitched (according to the Baroness) by her hands. Carrie had often been treated to the look of her graceful, beringed fingers when pouring another tot of gin or lighting another cigarette.

It wouldn't surprise Carrie at all if they'd married because of their names — Regina and Reginald — so they could call each other Reggie. "Gigi" had been the diminutive in Regina Scroop's family. Carrie wondered how she had got the Liverpool accent out of her speech. She even knew French; or enough of it to make people believe she even knew French.

"La Notre." What a stupid name in an English village,

Carrie thought, as she walked through the deer park, one part of her mind checking for signs of poachers. (The only person allowed to carry a rifle on the grounds was Carrie, an allowance made to herself by herself.) Before the Baron had got his chubby fingers on the property, the old house had been called "The Grange." The Baron (dead these fifteen years) had seen (according to the Baroness) the incredible possibilities of both house and grounds — the "estate" through whose history she had boringly sifted so many times that Carrie wondered there could be any more grains left on the mental beach. The Baron was a descendant of that famous gardener who had done Versailles. Carrie had been treated to enough pictures of famous gardens to make her feel like going out straightaway and trampling the lobelias.

Yet, she was sometimes sorry the Baron had passed on to his long line of flowery ancestors, for it would have been a lark to find someone else both as silly and determined as was the Baroness. To watch them take walks together, probably arm-in-arm, up and down the paths, past the Roman statuary, round the pools and ponds. What a team they must have been. She could not understand how anyone could have taken the simple *before* picture of "The Grange" and turned it into this enormous, ugly building of dark gray stone, bay windows bulging inappropriately underneath the battlements, a building that sat on a swell of ground overlooking the pretty green of Ashdown Dean, like a king of the toads on a lily pad.

Carrie walked in the covering shade of willows and immense dahlias, screened from the terrace, when suddenly a sun-hat popped up amongst the begonias and larkspur and asked her where she'd been.

Carrie answered with her own question. "What're you doing out here *gardening?*" making it clear that no occupation of Carrie's could match in idiocy the Baroness's being caught with shears in her ringed fingers.

"One must have an occasional bout with exercise." She

273

made it sound like flu. "Gillian didn't do the flowers *again.*" Snip. "You haven't answered. What've you been up to? Here, take these, will you?" She handed Carrie a rough-cut bunch of wilting lupines.

"You always think I'm 'up to' something."

"You always are. What's in that box? Oh, God, don't tell me." The sun-hat disappeared, reappeared, a few roses browned at the edges like burnt toast in her hands.

"A stray. I found it in the woods."

Beneath the sunshade of her giant hat, Regina squinted. "I think you call them like spirits from the vasty deep." Her shears stopped, midair. "That could be poetry. Did I invent it? How wonderful."

Although Carrie had quickly put it down so the Baroness wouldn't notice, the kitten was mewling. To divert attention, she said, "You want me to get you some fags in the village?"

"Don't use guttersnipe words like that. It's moving."

"What is?"

"You know what. Oh, never *mind.*" One of the cigarettes she ordinarily plugged into her ivory holder was dangling from the corner of her brightly painted mouth. The Baroness pulled some money from her coverall pocket. When she dressed for something, she dressed for it, and always, for some undisclosed reason, carried money. The diamond earrings seemed a bit out of place, however. "Did you bring the Gordons?"

Carrie nodded. "But there was a fight with Ida. Over me being too young to buy it."

"So what? You always win."

¤

The first thing Carrie Fleet had seen of the Baroness Regina de la Notre two years ago was a silver-buckled shoe on a sheer-white-stockinged leg, followed by a mauve and gray-blue dress, and then a matching hat. This mannequinlike display had descended from a cab outside of the London Silver Vaults. The face above the dress, however, was running on a different time schedule from the shoes, dress, and hat. It was painted and powdered to erase the difference, a good twenty years of it. The Baroness had (as for two years she had been advising Carrie to do) "taken care of herself." Avoidance of sunlight was important, she was always saying. A similar avoidance of gin and cigarettes might have had the same effect, allowing the sixty-year-old face to run neck-and-neck with the forty-year-old body.

As the woman disengaged herself from cab and cabbie, Carrie was further intrigued by her having a Bedlington terrier on a rhinestone studded lead — mauve, like the dress. And since the Bedlington was grayish-blue, it blended perfectly: a dog chosen to complement the ensemble.

Carrie, seated on her portable canvas stool, had already taken on a whippet and a poodle. Round her neck was a plastic-covered card. "You can't take the dog inside, madam."

The formidable woman stared. "Who are you?"

"I mind animals." The brief blaze of the look Carrie Fleet shot Regina de la Notre could have melted the glove leather shoes on her feet. "For a pound an hour."

The Baroness looked the situation over. The Alsatian was having a nap in a pool of sunlight. The poodle was doing the same beneath the canvas stool the girl sat on. Neither seemed to care that its owner had gone. Nor would, apparently, the Bedlington terrier, straining at the lead when the girl held her hand toward it.

Probably a witch, thought the Baroness. Covens of them all over England. "I find this amazing and, surely, illegal."

"Here's a constable coming. You can ask him."

Strolling slowly, hands behind him, seeming to enjoy the unearthly spring sunlight, the policeman looked as if he too might just curl up on the sidewalk and nap. The Baroness looked from him to the girl. "Kickbacks, probably. I suppose you want your money in advance. Or do you just hold the animals for ransom?"

"No, madam," said the unflappable girl. "Like I said, pound an hour."

As if to turn her words to gold, a handsome couple walked up the steps from the vaults and collected their whippet. The gentleman plucked two pound notes from his money clip. The girl took them and opened her little purse and returned fifty pence.

He seemed embarrassed. "Oh, heavens, my dear child —"

There was a look that the Baroness rather liked on the face of the dear child. It reminded her of the flower girl being taught to speak properly.

"You were only gone for just over an hour." She handed him the lead to his whippet. The dog seemed nervous and baffled; its sleep had been disturbed and, worse, it was to go back to the same old routine, the same old people, to be hauled about like a dog. It gave its temporary keeper a beseeching look. The girl returned the look, but let it go, like the realist she was.

The Bedlington was clearly ready to take the other dog's place in the sun.

Regina's tobacco-brown eyes followed the couple and the dog. "Part of the setup?"

Carrie Fleet flicked her a smile like someone tossing pennies. "If I may say so, madam —"

"You may not. Very well. Here's Tabitha, and you needn't wince. It's as good a name as any."

Tabitha lay down at Carrie's feet and the Baroness started down the steps. Then she turned, curious. "What were you going to say, anyway?"

"You don't seem to trust people much."

"Aren't you clever. I don't."

"Neither do I," said Carrie Fleet in a tone like dry ice.

There was forged between them an immediate bond. Mutual curiosity and reciprocal distrust.

She was the first interesting thing that had happened to the Baroness since the Baron had died.

Eleven

The negotiation for the life of Carrie Fleet was carried out in a run-down street near the East India Docks, but not in that dockside area lately running toward chic, where warehouses and crumbling waterfront properties were being bought up by the sorts of people who usually lived in mews in Kensington or Chelsea and realized that proximity to Harrods no longer did much for status. Decorators were followed by artists, actors, and retired brigadiers.

Although the general ambience of the Crutchley Street house had a certain warehouse flavor — orange crates doing service as tables — the Brindles, Joe and Flossie, weren't fortunate enough to have one of those properties the moneyed were looking for. It was one of several on this mean little street, where doorjambs and window moldings had been tarted up by Pakistanis and Indians with more of a flair for color — especially marine blues and rusty reds — than had the Brindles. They had decided to let well enough alone, a decision which extended both to their property and themselves.

⬡

The Baroness was sitting on an orange crate covered with an India-patterned spread and drinking tea the color of coffee from a permanently stained mug.

The cab at the door, from which the Baroness and Carrie had exited, had been regarded through the windows by several pairs of eyes. Probably, the last cab at the door in this street had been a hansom.

"Now, then," said Joe Brindle, the vest undulating over his loosened belt, "you're sayin' you was thinkin' a findin' a bit a work for our Carrie here?" He gave Carrie a friendly smack across the buttocks that made the Baroness, well traveled and used to the various breeding practices of many countries, somewhat uncomfortable.

Flossie, drinking a bottle of Bass, one thin leg tucked under her other on the sprung couch, said (for the dozenth time) "Well, I never." She kept curling and recurling a ringlet around her index finger. "Whatever'd you want t'do that for?"

The question that the Baroness had wanted to ask ever since she'd put her silver-buckled shoe out of the cab was: Whatever had *they* been thinking of when they took the girl in in the first place? Mercy and succor did not seem to be the Brindles' strong points. Sex and avarice would have beat them out by several lengths.

Then there were the others — children, dogs, cats — the last two categories fallen apparently into the hands of Carrie, and the Baroness hoped they knew how lucky they were. The dog Bingo, a rat terrier missing half a leg, had yipped and yapped and got up in a strange dance on its good legs like a circus animal the minute Carrie came into the house. It was the sort of animal that made the Baroness shudder — but then she had no interest in animals, anyway. Even the Bedlington did not belong to her, but to a friend in Eaton Place. She had thought it rather chic. The other dogs and cats could have been regulars or casuals; it was hard to say. A couple of them were growling over a dirty bone. That got them a boot in the side from Brindle. A one-eared cat got the same when it wound too close to his whiskey glass.

There was a young girl dozing under a pile of old blankets on another sofa, its springs coming through as on the one on which Flossie Brindle sat, a matched set. The girl was perhaps three or four years older than Carrie and hadn't moved at all except to wave a buzzing fly away and wipe her nose.

"Well, Joe, I'll be a monkey's." And she took another swig of Bass Ale and rewound the curl. "I knew we done the right thing when we found her."

Carrie might have been an investment in stocks.

"So where'd you say you lived, then?"

"Hampshire," said the Baroness crisply, only wanting to pay them off and be gone.

He scratched a closely shaven head, tugged at his ear. "Hampshire. Near that place — what's it called, Floss? Stonehenge, that's it."

"Stonehenge is in Wiltshire. The Salisbury Plain. I live in a village near the New Forest."

"New Forest. That's where you live?"

"Not *in* it, no. I would find that rather discommodious. The New Forest is more room than I need." She sipped the strange fluid and over the rim of the mug saw Carrie's mouth flutter in a tiny smile that quickly died. It made the Baroness think of a butterfly with broken wings.

Brindle blinked and then laughed. "Hear that, Floss?" he boomed, as if Floss were stone deaf. "More room — that's a good one. Okay. So you want Carrie here to come work for you. That it in a nutshell?"

"In a nutshell, Mr. Brindle."

"Well, I'll be a monkey's," said Flossie. "Imagine. Us findin' her wanderin' in the woods round Hampstead Heath, and here was you lookin' for her all this time."

It was the story the Baroness had given out, that Carrie was her younger sister's third cousin. "It's a small world," said the Baroness, taking out her silver cigarette case (which she watched them appreciate) while Carrie stood there, saying nothing, contradicting nothing.

Watching, thought Regina de la Notre, the world go by. Regina could have told the Brindles that Carrie was sister to Prince Rudolf of Ruritania and Floss would still simply have been a monkey's.

Of course, the richer the bird, the harder the fall when the Brindles brought it down with buckshot.

"That makes us some kind of relations-in-law." Joe winked.

"No, I don't think so."

He slid down in his chair, squinted up at the ceiling as if the price of one Carrie Fleet were printed in its spidery cracks, and said, "A course, Carrie puts bread on the table. Good girl, is Carrie. What'd you make today, luv?"

"Six pound. Pounds," she corrected herself. The Baroness Regina had noticed that Carrie Fleet's accent bore no resemblance to either of the Brindles', one East End, the other vaguely Northern.

"Jesus, you do better than them down t'the Sailor's Mate," said Flossie, swigging her ale.

The Baroness did not stroll her imagination down to the Sailor's Mate, where she imagined Flossie strolled often enough.

"It will also be one less loaf," she reminded Joe and Flossie.

He looked puzzled. "What's't?"

"Mouth to feed, Mr. Brindle."

Flossie stopped curling her hennaed locks and looked a bit sharper at the Baroness. "You don't mean you'd just take the girl away without no renumeration." She leaned forward. "Listen, we been seein' to Carrie here for five year, *five.*"

The United Kingdom had been seeing to Carrie Fleet. It

281

was obvious they were all on the dole. The giant color television and video machine would have attested to that. Extra money for the poor little orphaned girl.

"Remuneration, of course. I shouldn't think of taking away your chief means of livelihood."

Brindle had his eye so hard on his mark that he didn't even get the insult. "How much were you thinkin', then? Not, a course, we'd want to lose Carrie. Means a lot to us, Carrie does."

"A thousand pounds perhaps?"

He pretended to think it over. Looked at Flossie, whose finger was frozen in midcurl. Slapped the arm of his horsehair chair and said "Done!" Then quickly added, unspilt tears choking him, "Meanin' if it's okay with you, Carrie. She could give you lots more than we ever could."

Carrie looked around at all of them and when she spoke, her breath might have frosted the April air. "Maybe."

The Baroness was ambivalent in her feelings toward that reply.

ᴉ

The Brindles wasted no time the next morning in handing over Carrie Fleet. Flossie's hand was busy with a wadded hanky at her eyes, but since that took only the one hand, she had one left over for her can of Bass Ale.

Joleen, the girl who had been snoring on the couch the day before, appeared either sad or simply cross to see Carrie leaving. The other children — stairsteps of two, three, and four — did not appear to comprehend the solemnity of the affair and were chalking graffiti on the sidewalk.

Only the animals seemed upset. Carrie said good-bye to each one.

Breaking her vows of silence, Carrie remarked as they drove across Waterloo Bridge, "You could've got me for

282

less." There wasn't a touch of pathos in her voice. Or humor, either. It was simply matter-of-fact.

The Baroness twirled a cigarette into a carved-ivory holder. "No doubt. A case of whiskey and several of Bass would probably have done it." She glanced at the shiny, battered hatbox Carrie was holding on her lap. There were airholes stuck in it. It seemed quiet enough. "A three-legged cur wasn't part of the bargain, however."

"You wouldn't want me to leave Bingo behind?"

"Yes."

"In case you're interested." Carrie stopped there, as if it were the end of a lengthy exegesis.

The Baroness waited. Nothing further was forthcoming. "Well? Interested in *what*, my dear girl?"

"Why Bingo's only got three legs. Wasn't born that way."

"I had inferred as much. Hit by a car, or something?" She tapped ash out the window. Frankly, she wished the rest of him had gone the way of the fourth leg.

They had spanned Waterloo Bridge, and she was thinking nostalgically of the old one, and poor Vivien Leigh standing in the fog. Or was it poor Robert Taylor? Both, probably. . . .

They were in Southwark, now, on the other side of the Thames and headed for Waterloo Station.

Carrie drew her companion's attention to a skirmish outside a dilapidated building, where several boys were throwing stones at a couple of mongrel dogs that had been searching for their breakfast in an overturned dustbin. "I found Bingo in an alley, round back of the docks. One of his legs was practically chewed off. That's the way it looked, anyway."

"How revolting. Don't bother with the details."

The details were forthcoming. "It wasn't chewed. Somebody'd beat it with a spanner. Or something like." Carrie's face was turned around, watching, while the cab was stopped at a light.

And then she looked at the Baroness. "I don't suppose you want to go back?"

"Back?"

Carrie hitched her thumb over her shoulder. Her expression was as hard as the stone that hit the dog. "There."

"I most certainly do *not.*"

The girl was rather alarming. But she said nothing else, just sat staring straight ahead. The Baroness took in her profile. It was, actually, quite good. Straight nose, high cheekbones. Magnificent pale blond hair. "Once we get you in some decent clothes," she said, enjoying her morning cigarette and hoping the train had a *real* dining car, "and scrubbed up, you'll be quite presentable."

"I'm not a potato," said Carrie Fleet.

The Baroness chose to ignore this. "You're not going to get that animal in a first-class car, you know. He'll have to go third."

Carrie Fleet was still looking back over her shoulder. Then she turned around. "You could just buy up all the seats in the car. Then there wouldn't be no — *any* —" she'd squinted her eyes like a person with a stammer "— bother from people."

"Good God! You *are* the most stubborn person I know."

"Second most," said Carrie Fleet, with her butterfly smile.

Twelve

The whitewashed cottages of Ashdown Dean straggled off like roses on a trellis, up the hill-rise of the High Street and down the other side, with winding roads as narrow as stems branching off, one of which was Aunt Nancy's Lane, where Una Quick had lately lived.

The bizarre incident of the death in the call box explained, Ashdown was returning to its daily rounds, with Ida Dotrice filling in at the post-office stores. Thus Jury knew that Constable Pasco was merely indulging the superintendent's whim. If he wanted to waste his time in the overcrowded cottage of an elderly woman, Pasco didn't care.

Pasco was leaning against the cluttered mantelpiece, chewing gum, as Jury stood with his hands in his pockets and looked around. "Certainly liked knickknacks, didn't she?" Pasco apparently felt the answer to this quite obvious, given the bits of shells, little stuffed birds, blown-glass animals, Presents from Brighton, the Isle of Man, and Torquay, their greetings written in flaking gold script across shaving mugs, gilt-edged cups and saucers. The little parlor was stuffed with memorabilia. "No family?"

285

"None I ever heard of," said Pasco, lazily chewing his gum.

Jury smiled. The constable's duties in Ashdown Dean were probably limited to stopping motorists going over the thirty-mile limit and checking locks at night.

"Why am I mucking about here, you're probably wondering." Jury was looking at a silver-framed photograph. A group in bathing costume, arms round one another, laughing by the seaside.

Pasco smiled sleepily. "True. But if you want to, I guess you have a reason."

Jury replaced the photo, sat down and lit a cigarette. He tossed the pack to Pasco, who took one and tossed it back. The constable, Jury thought, under that lethargic manner was nobody's fool. Maybe lazy or simply bored, but when he wasn't doing his sleepy act, you could see the blue eyes were very sharp.

"Did you think there was anything strange about Una Quick's death?"

The eyes opened; Pasco paused in the act of bringing cigarette to mouth. "Strange how?"

"That storm last night. It took down a couple of power lines and apparently Miss Quick's phone service with it. No one else on the phone nearby? Ida Dotrice?"

Pasco shook his head. "Una couldn't really afford one —"

"Who can? Go on."

"— but she was so nutty about her heart that she had one put in. In case something happened. And to call Farnsworth."

"You said she reported to him religiously, as he told her to do, by calling his surgery every Tuesday. Dr. Farnsworth must be an extremely dedicated doctor, to do that."

Pasco smiled. "If Farnsworth is dedicated to his National Health list, I'm the Chief Constable."

"No money in it."

286

"But a lot in private patients. Still, according to Una, that's what he told her to do."

"But she *did* have a bad heart."

"Damned right. When her dog died ... Pepper, its name was. Poisoned on some weed killer." Pasco threw the butt of his cigarette into the cold grate. "It nearly killed her."

"Where was it found?"

Pasco nodded in the direction of the rear door. "Potting shed. Claimed it was locked, but Una was pretty absent-minded."

Jury thought for a moment. "Ashdown Dean goes uphill and the one call box is at the top. Not a very steep incline, maybe. But a woman with a heart condition whose pet had just died —? The storm and the hill. Would you've done it, Constable? It's pretty ironic, isn't it? The very effort of calling your doctor kills you. And there was that comment Miss Praed made about the umbrella. Why wasn't one found in the call box?"

"That storm came up pretty suddenly. She must have left before."

"Then that's even stranger."

Pasco frowned.

"That means, given the time of death as Dr. Farnsworth puts it, Una Quick was in that call box for at least a half an hour."

The constable looked around the cottage, still frowning. "The storm took out the service at the vicarage and the post office. They're working now." Pasco moved to the other side of the room and lifted Una Quick's receiver.

"But hers isn't," said Jury.

Thirteen

"Ididn't insist she should ring me, Superintendent," said Dr. Farnsworth as they sat in his surgery in Selby. "It was, if anything, the other way around." He rolled ash from a Cuban cigar that must have come from some secret stock; it hadn't come from the local tobacconist. Indeed, the doctor's surgery had not been decorated by the National Health. Not with a Matisse on the wall and a marble sculpture of a fish on a desk whose polished surface the fish could have swum across.

"You know," continued Farnsworth, "the way many cardiac patients are. Obsessive about their hearts. Phobic. Which adds to the problem. She did ring me on Tuesdays, that's true, but not at my insistence. And not last night."

"Then Una Quick was lying?"

Dr. Farnsworth leaned back in his leather swivel chair, another gift from a private-patient list that Jury imagined was extensive. After showing his warrant card to the secretary, whose receding chin seemed to pull in even farther, turtlewise, Jury had told her he'd be happy to wait until the two

288

patients present had seen the doctor. The one who had just left had been wearing silver fox. The two remaining wore fashionable suits that hadn't come off the rack. All three were women. And as Jury sat observing Dr. Farnsworth now, he guessed that most of his patients were women. Farnsworth was a trim sixty-plus who had had his arm around the shoulder of the middle-aged patient he had escorted to the door (no buzzers here, apparently), giving the shoulder a reassuring pat.

His manner with men — certainly with Jury — was somewhat more brisk, somewhat less unctuous, somewhat less full of direct eye-contact. Jury didn't put this down to his being a policeman. He bet that was Farnsworth's general manner with men. All of his women patients were probably in love with him.

"I merely meant that many patients do become obsessed with their illnesses and want to believe you've a particular interest in them."

Jury did not bother to point out that Una Quick's story about the telephone calls was much *too* particular to be explained in that way. But he dropped the point for the moment.

"Why is all of this so important, Superintendent? And why would Scotland Yard be interested? Do you question my diagnosis?"

Farnsworth's expression was like becalmed water, not a ripple crossed it. If he was at all worried about Jury's visit, he was doing a superb job of hiding it.

"It was a friend of mine who found her," said Jury.

"Ah. The lady at the call box." He shook his head. "Devil of a thing to happen to a visitor."

Jury smiled. "I suppose it'd be a terrible thing to happen to a local, too. Were you surprised, Doctor? Cardiac arrest apparently from climbing up that hill?"

Farnsworth continued to roll his cigar in his mouth as his glance strayed about the room, a room he obviously took some pride in. "Una could have gone at any time."

Although the doctor did not appear to resent Jury's questions, still he was doing precious little by way of answering. Jury approached the central problem in another way. "Miss Quick must certainly have had a lot of faith in your patience, then, to call you every week like clockwork. And after office hours."

"It's not much trouble answering a phone call, Superintendent," said the doctor, expansively. "Wouldn't you do the same in your line of work for someone who went in fear of her life?"

"Yes. I might even insist the person call."

Farnsworth stopped rolling both the cigar and the chair. "I have a feeling you don't believe me."

"Sorry. The only other person who'd know is dead."

The doctor frowned. "Good God, Mr. Jury. Why would I lie about something so innocent as having a patient telephone me?"

Depends how innocent it is, mate, thought Jury. But all he said was, "It's true that Una Quick would have more reason to embroider — self-aggrandizement, maybe. What sort of person was she?"

Dr. Farnsworth shrugged and shoved the ashtray into line with his gold pen set. "Ran the sub-post-office stores, lived alone. No relatives except a cousin or two in Essex or Sussex. Perfectly ordinary old woman with an old woman's complaints. No kind of person, especially."

It was that comment that rather encapsulated everything Jury disliked about Dr. Farnsworth.

♊

The same could not be said for Dr. Paul Fleming, the veterinarian, whom Jury called round to see next.

290

His offices were Spartan and his patients on a lower social scale than Farnsworth's. But at least their fur was their own.

Paul Fleming was scraping a mass of tartar from the teeth of a large black tom while he talked to Jury. "I only knew Una, really, in relation to her dog. I s'pose that's the way I know most of the villagers. Haven't been here all that long. It was a terrible thing, that — I mean the dog. And you've heard about the poisonings?" Paul Fleming shook his head. The cat lay quiet, anesthetized and into another night as dark as the one he apparently had come out of. Fleming had found him, he said, on his doorstep, like a patient come to call.

Jury started to take out a packet of cigarettes and remembered where he was and put them back.

"Later," said Dr. Fleming. "When I'm through with him we can have a smoke and a drink. I feel like I could drink the whole flaming bottle." He lifted the cat from the porcelain table and put it in a cage. "Okay, mate, when you wake you'll be able to eat again."

Now they were sitting in Fleming's small, crowded parlor — books stacked about, magazines on veterinary science. They were passing the bottle back and forth, topping up their glasses.

"You work hard, Dr. Fleming."

"Paul. Yes. I'm also an administrator at the Rumford Laboratory about a mile outside of town."

"Animal experimentation, I think."

"I love the way you put it. Sound like a bloody member of the Animal Freedom Front. There's research and research. A lot of people don't understand that."

Jury wasn't sure he did himself.

Fleming went on. "I suppose people think they can save themselves. From cancer. From thalidomide. After all, what's the life of a baby compared with a dozen cats?"

Jury smiled. "Several hundred, more likely."

Fleming just looked at him.

Jury changed the subject. "There was Una's dog, and, I understand, a cat and the bicycle-shop owner's dog. How do you explain it?"

"Accidents, that's all. The Potter sisters are known to be a bit 'peculiar,' to say the least. Their cat died from a dose of aspirin."

"Aspirin?"

Fleming nodded. "I'd given them some pills for the cat's allergy. Flat, white. They were screaming at one another that the other one — Sissy is half-blind — gave the cat the wrong pills." He shrugged. "It would take more than one, though." Fleming looked doubtful. "So someone had to make the mistake several times."

"Let's suppose none of these deaths *were* accidents."

"Hard to suppose. But I guess I'd probably bet on those Crowley kids — though that'd be going a bit far even for them. And they'd have to gain access to the food." He shrugged. "They said the cat got fed on the back step. Someone could have got at it, I suppose. Some animal-hater. Grimsdale, maybe."

"The one who owns Gun Lodge?"

Fleming nodded. "M.F.H. Real snob, worse because he hasn't got the cash to keep the place going without turning it into a B-and-B. He nearly went bonkers when he found old Saul Brown's dog turning up the rosebushes. Actually got out his gun." Paul Fleming leaned his head back against the worn leather and considered. "There really aren't that many possibles. Amanda Crowley — Billy and Batty's aunt — maybe. Loves horses but that's all. And she's phobic when it comes to cats. But that would be a point in her favor, wouldn't it? She'd be terrified to get near one. Must play bloody hell with her in Ashdown. There're so many of them. I remember Regina — the Baroness —" He turned to Jury. "Have you met her?"

Jury shook his head. "Haven't had much of a chance to meet anyone yet."

Paul Fleming laughed. "You're in for a treat if it's your plan to go about questioning people. Anyway, the Baroness de la Notre, as she calls herself, unaware of Amanda's phobia, had a couple of cats wandering about during one of her salons. Amanda started screeching and fell into Grimsdale's arms. Maybe it was just an act, at that. But how anyone could be attracted to him is beyond me." Fleming stopped in the act of refilling their glasses. "Of course, the same could be said of *her*.

"So if you haven't met Regina, you haven't met Carrie Fleet?"

"Haven't had the pleasure, no."

Paul Fleming burst out laughing.

fourteen

eahle Meara had pulled the covers up over her face,
body stiff and straight, pretending to be Dracula. It
was difficult with the kitten rising and falling with
every breath. It would be nice to be able to sink long fangs
into Sally MacBride's neck. It was dark. Dawn was just
breaking outside the dormer window nearly strangled in
creepers, but no light filtered through the covers over
Neahle. It was also cold. Sally made Neahle wonder if death
really might come in bat-form and pick you up with its talons
(Sally's were long and lacquered) and take you off.

But it would have to drop you in a wooden box. That's the
way her father had been buried. She lay there and tried to
think how it felt — but he couldn't have felt, could he? Being
dead? It was four years ago, but she remembered the wake
and the sitting up and the singing and drinking and found it
very strange they were having a party when her da was dead.
It's not a party, Neahle, her gran had explained, it's but the
way we see your dear father is taken into Heaven. Her
mother had died giving birth to her. Her da she had loved
because he was always in such a good humor and telling her

how pretty she was, how her eyes reminded him of the lakes of Killarney.

It was supposed to be such good luck for her to have this English uncle with his pub in Hampshire who was so happy to take her in. For he could offer her so much more. And get her out of Belfast. Neahle remembered Belfast vaguely as a place full of bright shops on the one hand, and broken glass and boarded-up houses on the other.

Uncle John had the Deer Leap, and things had been all right for a couple of years until he had gone up to London and come back with a new wife who did not like Neahle Meara at all. Neahle was there before Sally, sitting at John MacBride's hearth. How did Sally MacBride know that she hadn't also been first in his heart?

Neahle sighed. Uncle John had changed a lot since Sally had come on the scene. And under the covers when Neahle sighed, the kitten rose and fell. The kitten was very small and probably not interested in what coffins were like and slept on, darkened over by covers though it was. Carrie had found it just yesterday and said she'd keep it part of the time with the other animals. Meanwhile, she'd fixed up an old book bag with air-holes at the bottom so that Neahle could smuggle it into the Deer Leap and up to her room. Carrie had even brought over a supply of Kit-e-Kat that she'd put in the play-house. No one ever went down there except Neahle, and you couldn't see it from the house. It was a perfect place to play with the kitten.

Neahle was not permitted to have pets. Only the chickens and hens in the henhouse.

"How can you call chickens pets?" Neahle argued. "You can't take them to bed with you or play with them or anything."

It was Sally who had laid down that law. It was always *that'll be enough of that, miss.* And turning to John Mac-Bride, *Such sauce.*

"Maybe I could have a fish, or something."

"Well, now, love," said Uncle John. "I don't see anything wrong with that, do you, love?"

This *love* directed at one of the most unlovable things Neahle could imagine.

They had been sitting round the dinner table, a dinner that Neahle herself had cooked, wearing an apron that hung nearly to the floor. Even at nine she could cook rings around Sally MacBride (née Britt) because her gran had started teaching her when she was five. They were having fish, which was what made Neahle think of it.

Sally, who had large horselike teeth, was picking at them in a most unladylike way. "A fish is it? One of those goldfish in a bowl to stink up the place. No, thank you, miss."

Neahle went round the table collecting the plates. Washing-up was also her job. "I was thinking more of a shark," she said, and ran from the room, jangling the cutlery on the plates just to make Sally MacBride turn sharply in her chair and yell *"Brat."*

Now this morning there was the problem of feeding the kitten, so she must rise from her coffin and dare the daylight before Sally the Bat came round to whoosh at her door and tell her to get up and fix the breakfast.

Then Sally would go back to bed, leaving Neahle to make the porridge and eggs. And there was Maxine Torres, a sullen Gypsy-like maid, who came in around eight, and would tell the world if she caught Neahle. She worked for the Baroness, too, sometimes, but Neahle liked the Baroness because she was kind of crazy and let Carrie do all the things that Sally MacBride would never let Neahle do. Most places Neahle was not supposed to go, but that made no difference to her, since if she only went where she was supposed to, she'd have to sit in a chair or stand at the stove all the time. But Neahle's visits to "La Notre" were different, for Sally believed in currying favor with those who might be useful or who lent to Ashdown what she called "tone."

Neahle left the kitten under covers scooped up for air and slipped her feet into her felt slippers. Light streaked the small windowpanes and cast its skeleton-finger across the dark floor. On the wardrobe door was a mirror in which Neahle could see herself in her white nightgown and, squinting her eyes, could imagine herself sliding ghostlike down the hall, quiet as the grave.

Д

Melrose Plant awoke in the chilly dawn light and pulled the duvet up to his chin. It was too short and left his feet uncovered, and the room was both cold and stark, but his brief encounter with the proprietor of Gun Lodge was enough to convince him that taking rooms anywhere else would be preferable to the steely gaze of Grimsdale over his morning gruel.

Porridge and toast as cold and hard as shingles was Sebastian Grimsdale's interpretation of Full English Breakfast.

Melrose wondered if he would fare better at the Deer Leap and lay looking at his feet, deciding he didn't like them, and contemplating rashers of bacon and fresh eggs and fried bread. The dinner last night had been quite presentable. Good English fare. When he told the MacBrides to offer his compliments to the cook, the wife had found this worth giggling over. But, then, she found a great deal to giggle about, whishing her brandy glass.

He was getting hungrier every moment and wished they did early teas. He had generously offered to give up his room to Jury, but Jury had had no qualms about dealing with Mr. Grimsdale's porridge — to the speechless delight of Polly

297

Praed. Anyway, Jury and Wiggins needed two rooms, and Melrose very much doubted Sergeant Wiggins would live out the visit.

Melrose frowned and pulled the duvet down over his feet, having considered them long enough to know he didn't like them; no more did he like the proximity of Polly Praed to Superintendent Jury. The violet eyes that regarded Melrose as a fly on the wall were simply dazzling turned upon Jury. Jury, fortunately, was not bedazzled by Polly. He found her seeming inability to knit words into sentences whenever she was in his presence puzzling. Melrose had always wondered at Jury's lack of awareness at the effect he had on the female sex. He only wished it would rub off on him. Plant closed his eyes and pondered. Certainly, he was rich enough, probably intelligent enough, even good-looking enough. Had he not thrown the Earl of Caverness and Viscount Ardry out the back door of Ardry End, he would even be titled, and *more* than enough. He tried to punch the pillows up, but they were too thin. It had annoyed Polly Praed no end that he had given up his titles, because she hated the titled family in her village of Littlebourne and would have loved to refer to *my friend, the Earl of Caverness.* Again he pulled the covers up to his chin. Perhaps it was his feet. He sighed and yearned for tea.

The welcome he had received at the Deer Leap was considerably warmer than the one at Gun Lodge, since there hadn't really been one. Though Grimsdale would have loved to rent the room, he somehow made it clear he'd rather not have anyone actually in it.

Here, however, the proprietors were all warm welcome, especially Mrs. MacBride, to whom he might have been a sailor returned from the sea. Looking at her, and getting her London bearings (Earl's Court out of East End, perhaps), Melrose imagined she might have had some experience in welcoming returning sailors. Sally MacBride, though not ravishing, appeared willing to *be* ravished. Though a bit overblown, she was still a looker, if you liked the type. She offered Melrose and Jury double brandies, a tight skirt that looked welded above her knees, and the story of her life. Or at least up until the early twenties, when her husband, John, a mild-mannered publican, twenty years older than his new wife, must have decided that Mr. Plant was not Boswell and stopped her. But heartily laughing at her escapades and peccadilloes all the while.

What miscrossed stars had brought the two together Melrose could only imagine: Sally was getting a bit long in the tooth and John MacBride had a nice, cozy business — the only pub in a pleasant village. But he did not appear to be a man of great sexual appetite. The wife, with all that flaxen, waxen-sprayed hair and pouty red mouth, was certainly one a lot of men wouldn't have minded having a bite of.

As his mind turned to Una Quick's death, Melrose was aware of something moving along the corridor. He decided to investigate and rose and tied his dressing gown. Anything would be better than lying in an old brass bed six inches too short for him.

Nothing, he thought, would take the chill out of the air, until he saw through the crack in the door a small, white figure, arms outstretched, coming down the hall. Apparently, It had heard his door open, for It stopped dead. The arms dropped as the little girl turned and fled with a look of horror back down the hall. Melrose saw a coal-black kitten getting shoved inside the room to the right of his.

The girl in the white gown disappeared, too.

He stood in the doorway to his own room and thought about this little scenario. The world of childhood was a world he felt best left to children; generally speaking, he did not engage in conversation, unless forced to do so, with anyone under twenty, and certainly had never himself *initiated* a meeting with an eight- or nine-year-old (for at such did he put her age). But in this case, curiosity overcame tradition.

He passed the MacBrides' room, where the door was slightly ajar and a night-light burning. Sally had had terrors of closed places ever since being locked in a closet, and her husband had leaned over to Melrose and whispered, *Claustrophobia, I call it.* Melrose heard the snores of John MacBride. The next room was the one into which the child had disappeared. He tapped on it; the door was open a crack, as if she had expected him, with his hood and sickle, to come calling. Given the look on her face.

Her head bent to the kitten in her lap, its coat as shiny-black as her bobbed hair, she said, "Now, I suppose you'll tell."

"Tell? Not only do I not know *what* to tell, I do not know *whom* to tell it to. Consider yourself safe."

There was a moment's scrutiny — a penetrating appraisal of his face — from eyes of such a rich blue one was surprised to see tiny knives in there. Then she looked at the window and the panes growing smoky white and put the kitten from her lap. "Okay. Maxine's probably not here yet, so let's go."

The carpet slippers slapped past him and as he hesitated, she motioned impatiently with a tilt of her head that he was to follow. He wondered if they were both to glide, arms outstretched, down the hall to their crypt.

"Where?"

"To the kitchen," she whispered over her shoulder, putting a finger against her mouth.

The kitchen. Tea. He followed down the narrow back stair where he felt the rising damp almost like tendrils of fog.

"What are we doing here?" He looked to see if there was a kettle on the hob.

She was busy sticking her head in a large fridge — there were two of them in the pub's kitchen, in addition to a large freezer and a huge butcher's table in the center of the room.

The floor was stone and icy-cold. Now she was dragging out milk and bits of cheese and things that she stacked along her arm. "It's got to be fed. You can carry some of this."

"I see. But why were you walking along with your arms out?" Melrose extended his own, in imitation. "Were you sleepwalking? Or, I mean, pretending to?"

"No. Here." She handed him a knife and a small plate. "Cut up the cheese in little bits. Thank you." This was added as an afterthought and without so much as tossing a sweet smile in his direction.

"You had your arms out —" Melrose was determined.

Crossly, she said, "We've got to be quick about this or Maxine or somebody'll come in. Can't you cut the cheese faster? You haven't done it at all. I'm nearly finished with mine. Do you eat venison?" She was looking toward the big freezer. "I think it's awful to kill deer and eat them. You must be the guest." She did not stop for confirmation or even temper her speech long enough to be surprised that the Deer Leap's single guest was down here doing scullery duty around seven A.M.

"For my labors, I would appreciate a cup of tea," he said, cutting the cheese in bits.

"We don't have time. Can't you make those pieces littler?"

"We're not feeding a mouse; it's a cat," he said.

"It's only eight weeks old. I'll get the milk and you run down to the playhouse and get the Kit-e-Kat." Her head was buried in the fridge.

Run to the playhouse. That made as much sense as anything in this dawn patrol. "I do not feel like running to the playhouse —" How could such rich, almost navy blue eyes give him that look full of splintered glass? "Oh, for heaven's sake. I shall do it only if you put the kettle on." Must he wheedle this person? "And *where* is this 'playhouse'?"

She looked as if she could have wiped the floor with him,

301

but her slippers slapped on the stone as she got out the kettle. "Just down the walk behind those trees. And don't dawdle, please."

Dawdle? Outside in his dressing gown? "Just have the water boiling," he commanded.

The playhouse was just that: a tiny place where he expected to find the seven dwarfs. As he turned the knob on the door he was thinking of Snow White. Hadn't she had trouble with her bed, too?

It was dark and musty in the little place, and his eye fell on the supply of Kit-e-Kat in the corner.

Unfortunately, it had to travel over the body of Sally Mac-Bride on its way.

Melrose needed no warning about dawdling on his way back up the path. The sprite had probably tired of waiting — he had spent perhaps thirty seconds assuring himself the woman was, indeed, dead — and the kettle was whistling its long, screeching note.

He shoved it off the burner and went for the telephone.

fifteen

There was so little room in the playhouse, they kept bumping into one another, or at least Wiggins and Pasco did. Jury managed to keep his own space clear. Pasco had called the Selby station. They would try to get hold of Farnsworth, the doctor they seldom needed to call in as a medical examiner. If not him, someone from the local hospital.

"Not a mark, except for the hands." Jury got up. "Leave it until the M.E. gets here." He shook his head, looking around the single, square room. Perhaps twelve by twelve, he figured. Tiny. The few scraps of furniture — rocking chair, small bed, lamp, table — were clearly leavings from the dustbin men or unwanted sticks from the pub.

"MacBride's little girl's place?" He saw a sack of catfood in the corner.

"Niece," said Pasco, still looking wonderingly at Melrose Plant, now wearing a Chesterfield coat over his dressing gown.

Plant was getting damned irritated. "Constable Pasco. I *wish* you'd stop looking at me that way."

"I just can't figure out what *you* were doing down here — getting a can of Kit-e-Kat, you said?" Pasco gave him a flinty smile.

"Hell," said Melrose.

"Stop it, both of you." Jury was not happy.

Neither was Plant. "Look, what I really wanted was *tea*. So I followed the ghostly child to the kitchen —"

"Neahle," said Pasco.

"What? What sort of name is that?"

Pasco, used to sleeping in until nine, yanked from bed before eight and with another death on his hands, was not happy either. "Neahle Meara. Irish."

"Nail? What an awful name for one so young."

"Spelled N-e-a-h-l-e."

"Oh. Rather pretty."

Jury had picked up an enamel doorknob, handkerchief wrapped around it. "Bag this, Wiggins."

Sergeant Wiggins had been standing hunched in the doorway. There wasn't room for a fourth. He took a plastic bag from a supply he carried about like cough drops. "Shouldn't we wait for the Selby —"

"Probably, but I'm afraid of too many more feet mucking up this place. We've probably done enough damage as it is."

Plant said, "Look, I didn't touch anything."

Jury smiled up at him from his examination of the metal stem from which the knob had come off. "I know that." He got up. His head nearly brushed the ceiling. "You only came for the Kit-e-Kat."

Pasco smiled. Melrose smiled back.

Pasco was kneeling where Jury had kneeled, looking at the inside of the wooden door. "Terrible. It looks like she was trying to claw her way out."

"Claustrophobic," said Plant, frowning. "You remember how she was talking about cracking their bedroom door at night." Plant bent to look at the marks. Splintered wood and blood.

Jury could tell from the state of the fingers where the streaks of dried blood on the door had come from. "Absolute panic." He frowned and turned to Pasco. "Why would she be down here, anyway, Pasco? How well did you know her?"

Although Pasco's *about as well as anyone else*, was casual enough, Jury noticed the flush spreading upward from his open collar. "I don't know why she'd be down here."

After the Selby police pathologist had examined the body and it had been zipped up in a rubber sheet, he put the cause of death down to heart failure.

"Like Una Quick."

"Brought on by fright, from the looks of it," said the pathologist. "If she was, as you say, a claustrophobic."

Detective Inspector Russell, from the Selby C.I.D., shook his head. "I'll be damned." He looked at Jury unhappily, whether from having Scotland Yard here or from a second death in this tiny village, Jury couldn't say. "What the hell was the woman doing down here?"

"We don't know. Any objections to my being here? It was a friend of mine who discovered Una Quick's body."

Inspector Russell didn't seem to mind; indeed, he looked relieved. If Scotland Yard wanted Selby-Ashdown corpses, they could have them. "I'll check it with the Chief Constable. That door —" Again he shook his head. "Knob just came off?"

"Maybe."

Russell took out his handkerchief and tried to twist the stem. It was old and rusted and wouldn't give. "She couldn't get it back on." The iron fitting inside the porcelain was broken, making it impossible to fit the knob to the stem. It was a very old doorknob.

"Let's go talk to MacBride. Does he know?"

"I took the liberty," said Melrose, "of informing him there'd been an accident. In a word, yes. He knows."

"Would you mind if my sergeant went along?" asked Jury, who was looking around the tiny house, his gaze finally fixed on the chair and the lamp. "And Mr. Plant?"

"Your sergeant, yes. And Pasco." He squinted at Melrose Plant. "But I don't see why —"

"He found the body," said Jury.

"Okay. What about you?" A mild suggestion that Scotland Yard was leaving the dog's work to the Hampshire constabulary.

"I'd like to talk to the girl — what's her name?" he asked Pasco.

"Neahle Meara."

"Ask her to come down here." At Plant's look, Jury said, "No, I won't show her the inside of the door. I want to talk to her, away from the others."

Then Jury added, "And tell her to bring her kitten and a can opener." He grinned.

Ⅺ

She stood framed in the doorway, clutching a gray cloth coat around her and holding what looked like a schoolbag.

Jury was surprised by her black hair and deep blue eyes, now smudged underneath and looking scared. He hadn't seen her in the Deer Leap; although he knew she wasn't the daughter, he'd expected someone with MacBride's washed-out coloring. This little girl was definitely not washed out; she was beautiful.

"Hullo, Neahle," he said. "Is the kitten in the book bag?"

Wordlessly, she nodded and chewed her lip. Then she stepped over the sill and said, with as much defiance as she could muster, "You can't take him away. He didn't do anything."

"Good God, whatever made you think I'd want to do that? I just thought maybe you'd like to give him his breakfast."

"Lunch. He had some cheese for breakfast, and milk."

"Lunch, then." Jury smiled. They might have been here for no other reason than to confirm the kitten's eating habits. It poked its black head out of the bag and blinked.

Neahle pulled it all the way out and set in on the floor, but made no move toward the catfood. "I heard about Sally — Aunt Sally."

That she didn't want to call her "aunt" was clear. And that she wasn't sorry the MacBride woman was dead was equally clear.

That, unfortunately, meant guilt could fall on her perhaps suddenly like a brick, hard and fast.

She was sitting in a troll-sized chair, picking at the flaking blue paint. "It's too bad." She did not look at Jury because she couldn't work up the appropriate tears, he bet.

"Yes. I thought you could help."

She looked up, then, interested. "I've got the can opener." She said it as if the Kit-e-Kat might be by way of helping.

"Toss it here." She did. Jury pulled a can from the bag and opened it. Then he put it down for the kitten, who obviously had had its fill of cheese.

"Why do you carry — what's its name?"

"Sam."

Jury nodded toward the book bag. "That's got holes in it for air."

"I know. That's to smuggle it in and out of the house. Sally"— and she inclined her head again —"wouldn't let me have pets. Said they just dirtied the place up."

It sounded consistent with the little he'd seen of Mrs. Mac-Bride. "That was clever of you."

"Oh, I didn't think it up. It was Carrie. She's my best friend. She found the kitten in the woods and fixed the bag. It was yesterday."

It was almost as if the fact of the kitten, Sam, had brought about this tragedy. Now she was groping in the bag and brought out an apple. "Would you like this for your lunch?"

"Thank you," said Jury gravely, as she handed it over. It was the first bribe he'd ever taken. "I don't know Carrie. I've only heard her name. Is she a school chum, then?"

Neahle laughed and put her hand over her mouth, which she smoothed out as if she were smoothing out her coat. Laughter in the house of death was hardly right. "No. Carrie doesn't go to school. The Baroness's secretary teaches her, or something. She's lots older than me. Fifteen. I don't know why she likes me."

Best friends, like kittens and aunts, could disappear easily in this world, her worried look said.

"I can't imagine why she wouldn't. Age doesn't make any difference."

"How old are you, then?"

"Quite old," said Jury solemnly. Thinking of Fiona Clingmore, he smiled and added, "I'll never see forty again."

Her eyes widened. "You don't look *nearly* that old."

"Thank you. Listen, Neahle. You know your aunt — Mrs. MacBride — was found in here."

Solemnly, she nodded, watching Sam now batting a tiny ball of wool she'd tied to the lamp cord for him.

"Did you ever know her to come down here before?"

"No. No one comes here but me, and sometimes Carrie."

"Okay. When was the last time you were here?"

"Two days ago."

"Did you keep the door closed?"

She looked puzzled.

"I mean, was the knob missing from the inside of the door? Fallen off its iron stem?"

She frowned. "I suppose so. I didn't much notice." Neahle scratched her ear. "It was dark."

If there'd been wind, it could easily have banged the door

shut. "Would you have been scared if you'd got locked up in here?"

She seemed surprised. "Me? No. I like to come here and read and sometimes I go to sleep on the bed there." She was watching Sam the kitten, now clutching the wool and swinging like a metronome from the lamp cord. "You could scream if you got locked up in here, but it's so far from the house —" She stopped watching the kitten and put her head in her hands.

"There was a wind last night, too. Neahle, you can't love everyone you think you should. When they won't let you have pets, and have you do the cooking. Why should you?"

She looked up at him. Then down. "You didn't eat your apple."

"Did you ever know Sally to come here?"

Neahle shook her head. "Why would she? She didn't even want *me* to."

"Maybe she would to, say, meet a friend."

"Like men?" Neahle was trying to look worldly-wise.

Jury smiled. "Like men."

Neahle scratched her ear. "Well, there's that Mr. Donaldson. He's creepy. Carrie says so. He works at Gun Lodge."

"Anyone else?"

She chewed her lip and shook her head.

Wouldn't have mentioned Pasco, even if she'd known. Jury picked up her apple and rubbed it on his raincoat. Her look seemed to ask, Are you going to do something magical?

He crunched the apple, leaned back in the chair, and watched Sam swinging. Sam dropped from his perch and came over to sit and stare up at the new person.

Neahle started to cry.

"Not to worry, Neahle." Jury picked up Sam and put him in Neahle's lap, where its shiny black fur was wetted with her tears. Then he sat back and simply waited until the worst of it was over.

309

The end of the cord from which Sam had been swinging led up to a socket and a blue-shaded lamp. "You came down here a couple of days ago, you said. Did you come down at night?"

Neahle chewed her lip.

"I won't tell." He nodded at the books. "Did you read, then?"

"Of course." She nodded to a little stack of books. "*Sam Pig*, that's my favorite. I named Sam after him. I suppose you can name a kitten after a pig." She seemed doubtful. "Anyway, I sneaked out of bed."

Jury turned his head on the back of the rocker. "What happened to the light bulb, then, do you think?"

⊐⊏

None of them, particularly John MacBride, had been sitting very comfortably in the bar during the questioning of the husband.

Wiggins pinched the bridge of his nose and said, "Going up to London, was she? For how long, Mr. MacBride?"

"Few days. To visit a cousin."

Wiggins wrote down the name of a Mary Leavy who lived, said MacBride vaguely, "Somewhere in Earl's Court."

Melrose could have constructed any number of scenarios, taken from all of those mysteries he'd suffered through for the sake of Polly Praed. It was such a cliché. Wife going off to London, then mysteriously "disappearing." Fun for Crippen and Cream. But not, it would seem for MacBride, who seemed to be crumbling like the huge log sparking and splitting in the fireplace.

Detective Inspector Russell's smile was tiny. Melrose could almost read his mind. It's always the family. Dead wife, find the husband.

"And how was she to get there?" asked Pasco.

310

"How?" MacBride's eyes were glazed when he pulled his head from his hands.

"Yes. You said she was going to London, John."

"Oh. Train from Selby this morning."

Pasco prodded him gently. "But to Selby?"

MacBride wiped his hands over his thin hair. "Someone at the Lodge going to drive her. Donaldson, I think."

How nice, thought Melrose.

"Mrs. MacBride suffered from claustrophobia, I believe," said Russell.

MacBride nodded. A shadow like a raven's wing passed over his face as if the thought of Sally's being trapped in that house were too much for him.

"I'd have thought," said Russell, "when that door closed and she couldn't — well, let's leave it for the moment." He must have seen the look on MacBride's face, too.

Pasco put it in a more roundabout fashion. "You can't see the playhouse from the pub, not with that screen of trees. And I expect you can't hear — it's a bit far, there by the river."

MacBride only nodded.

Melrose put in: "There was a howler of a wind last night, too."

Wiggins couldn't have agreed more, but Russell was looking at Plant as if he couldn't imagine this guest in the Deer Leap offering anything of substance. The testimony of someone who would wander out to a playhouse at seven in the morning to get catfood . . .

"Splintered wood," said Russell, "long marks as if she'd tried to —" Again, some more humane instinct took over.

"Sorry, John," said Pasco. Light filtering through the fussy chintz curtains scooped out hollows in MacBride's cheeks. "Maybe you should lie down, John. We can talk to you later."

"Where's Neahle?" asked MacBride, looking a bit wildly around.

"Asleep," said Wiggins, snapping shut his notebook.

Wiggins might have had more sense than all of them.

Sixteen

Jury wondered when the driveway would end and who had managed, in what couldn't have been more than an eighth of a mile, to devise the tortured approach to "La Notre" that in its twists and turns must have been like a Disneyland adventure-game. He expected something to jump out at every turn.

And at that moment in his thoughts, he had to veer and brake, barely missing an old man on a bike careening around one of the curves and not seeming bothered at all about scrapes with death. Must belong to the place, must be used to it, thought Jury, starting up again.

The surprise-package at the end of his deadly drive through deep rainpools and littered branches was a huge house whose towers he had seen from the Ashdown Dean road not far below. It was architectural gimcrackery at its worst. Where the original house left off was clear. It had played its part innocently enough as an old manor house or a draughty vicarage. Its design was pleasant and traditional, mullioned panes set in slabs of gray stone, ivy-bound. But to this house had been added towers, oriel windows, and cathedral windows, these last with a topping of painted bargeboards, like icing on a cake, utterly out of keeping with anything else. English, Italian, medieval, ecclesiastical all jousted for first place.

To round it off, from what he could see when he got out of his Vauxhall, there must have been a large expanse of Italianate garden behind the house. Jury just glimpsed a statue, a pagodalike bridge, a Corinthian column in the far distance.

None of this marvel, which made him want to laugh despite the reason for his visit, had been seen to — neither house nor grounds — in what must have been years. The ivy crept, the stones crumbled, the branches fell. Round those mullioned panes were cracks that must have let all the weather in Ashdown Dean come to settle here at "La Notre."

His card was taken on a plate of tarnished silver by a waiting maid in a cockeyed cap, hastily pinned on for the occasion.

While Jury waited for an audience with the Baroness, he looked around the commodious entryway. Here England, Greece, and Italy competed. Between beams of dark wood, Grecian-like columns held sculpted heads (that reminded him unpleasantly of those once stuck up on Traitors' Gate). The ceiling moldings were graced with cupids and garlands. The floor was green marble, the wide staircase mahogany. "La Notre" made up in money for what it lacked in taste.

Jury was admitted to an enormous room to his right, out of keeping with the hall, all breezy and bright, a sort of solarium, with plants everywhere. On the walls left and right, two identical *trompe l'oeil* murals. They seemed to be a reflection not only of each other, but of the real scene between them — on either side of a marble fireplace, french doors led

314

to separate stone paths that in turn led to the wide gardens beyond. Jury blinked. It was worse than seeing double.

"Fools you, doesn't it?" said the woman on the green chaise of watered silk.

Her smile was as tricky as the mirror-image of the murals. Jury returned the smile. "You're the Baroness Regina de la Notre?"

"No. I'm her double. Two of everything. Good idea?"

"Maybe. Only one of me, though."

"Pity," she said, looking him up and down. Then her eye drifted to the card she held. "A superintendent, no less." Waving the hand that held the card, she invited him to sit.

Her dress was not his idea of eleven in the morning, magenta with a sprinkle of sequins, a violent shade that matched her lipstick and rouged cheeks. The bones were high and aristocratic.

From her velvet chaise (in keeping with herself, but not the plant-gorged room) she said, "A Scotland Yard superintendent. I'm impressed."

That it took one hell of a lot to impress the Baroness was quite clear from her tone.

She seemed as much a part of her surroundings as had the tricky driveway, the crumbling walls, the deceptive vista of the *trompe l'oeil* murals. Her smile was slightly unpleasant, not the result of ill will, but of dull teeth. Too many cigarettes, and, he supposed, catching a whiff as he had shaken her hand, too much gin. As she looked at the wall behind him, she said, "The Baron — my late husband — was fond of that particular school of French painting."

And, thought Jury, the Italians, the British, the Greeks . . .

She leaned forward, offered him a cigarette from a pedestrian crumpled pack rather than the gold box. "It's Una Quick you've come about, I expect. Wasn't that heart of hers at all, was it? Murdered, wasn't she? Not surprising, is it? It's her Nosy Parker business with the post, isn't it . . . ?"

315

Jury cut into the barrage of questions. "Why do you think Una Quick was murdered?"

"Because you're here, obviously."

Again, Jury smiled. It was a smile unmarred by tobacco stains, cynicism, deviousness, or anything else that might make a witness or a suspect throw up a guard. It had the opposite effect: they let down the guard. "I came here because of a friend."

Regina de la Notre stopped being arch. She merely looked at him and said, "Perhaps, but I'm not the friend, so you're poking about for other reasons. Una Quick was a simpering little mouse of a woman who ran the post-office stores and had a right rave-up with other people's post —"

"You're suggesting she read the villagers' post?"

"No, I'm *assuring* you she did."

"How do you know?"

"Because I posted a letter to myself from London that I got someone else to write — as I'm quite sure Una knew my hand — and turned the second page upside down. When she read it, she quite naturally had to turn it and forgot to turn it back. Or, even if some part of her little sewer of a mind took note, it discarded the notion that such a small thing might be important."

"That's very interesting. A different impression of Miss Quick than I'd got so far."

"Only because most of the people in Ashdown are idiots. Tea?"

She raised a silver pot, which had to be cold by now. Jury refused and she reached behind the chaise. "Gin?"

"Sounds better than tea." He smiled.

"I thought you'd think so." She poured some into a teacup. "Always knew that business about policemen not drinking on duty was bunk. How the hell would you get through a day of your line of work without it? Here."

Jury took the cup of gin from the beringed hand. He was

rather surprised. Though he wasn't going to drink a cup of gin, at least it had been offered with something like sympathy, something he doubted she plied to excess. The Baroness continued with her fund of information as she stuffed a cigarette into a long holder. Also sequined. "And now there's the MacBride woman."

The sip of gin Jury had taken burned his throat. "And just how did you know that? Her body was discovered only a couple of hours ago."

She raised her gin and eyebrows at the same time. "God. In a couple of hours the Ashdown Dean scandal could travel to Liverpool and back. My hometown. You probably noticed I am not French." Two possible murders did not seem of much more account than her Liverpudlian background. "Carrie Fleet told me."

"Carrie Fleet?"

"My charge. More or less. Neahle Meara came running up the drive an hour ago. She tells Carrie everything. Though I doubt she understands most of what she tells. I'm still debating whether MacBride was sleeping with our constable or that oily head keeper, Donaldson. Or both." She raised the pint of gin in invitation.

Jury shook his head. "Why don't you tell me what you know, then?"

Having poured herself another tot, she screwed the cap back on the bottle, and looked up at the ceiling through tendrils of smoke. "I'll try and condense it. Otherwise, you'll be stopping here all day. I told you about Una and the post. And that MacBride piece of fluff. If someone killed her, I'm quite sure it wasn't John. That, I believe, was true love, worse luck for him. I myself made a marriage of true love. No man since Reginald — the Baron — has interested me. Had you come along twenty years ago, things might have been different. Loaded with charm, aren't you?"

Jury smiled. "I only just got here."

"How tiresome." She sighed. "Charm, like a falling star, can be seen in a flash."

"Thanks. Continue."

"Well. Amanda Crowley is hot on the trail of Sebastian Grimsdale, though I imagine he'd rather sleep with a horse. I hope you do not think our Constable Pasco is stupid *or* lazy. That's all an act. Farnsworth, on the other hand, is both, which is not to say he's not capable of murdering the entire village. Paul Fleming, our veterinarian, is exceedingly clever, handsome, unmarried, and my secretary appears to be in love with him. Her name is Gillian Kendall. I expect you've heard the names of these people if you haven't already met them. As for myself, I prefer to keep behind the battlements here, in regal splendor, and let the others make asses of themselves. Occasionally, I invite some of the asses here. To what I call a salon. I don't really know what that means, but Grimsdale and la Crowley appear to think I am loaded —" quick smile "— I mean with money. And that allows me a certain ascendancy when they come to complain about Carrie. The local RSPCA. She turned the Baron's arbor into a sort of animal refuge. I am not fond of animals. That's where I found her. Outside the Silver Vaults —"

This enigmatic statement was cut short by Jury's looking up, suddenly, to see a girl and a woman appearing like dream figures at each of the french doors. Again, he thought he was seeing double: they might have been figures in the mural, each of them coming to a dead stop with her foot just over the sill when she saw Jury.

Regina turned her head and looked from one to the other as if they were party-crashers. "Oh, it's you. Gillian Kendall, Superintendent Jury."

The woman came in, holding out her hand. The other arm held some Michaelmas daisies. "How do you do?"

"Original as always, Gillian."

318

Gillian Kendall gave her employer a tiny smile. Used to her put-downs, probably. Jury couldn't help staring at her, though she was not a beauty. Except for the Grecian nose, her features were unexceptionable — mouth too wide, eyes narrow. But her hair and eyes were a lustrous brown — hair more of an auburn — and the very plainness of the prim gray dress with its high neck and long sleeves drew attention to the body underneath it. He wondered if she knew this. He watched her arranging the flowers, brown-tipped from frost, in a vase. No beauty, but the most sensual woman Jury had seen in a long time.

He turned to see the girl staring at him. But she hadn't moved from the frame of the french door at whose sill she stood, dead still.

"Oh, don't be such a stick, Carrie." Regina waved her impatiently into the room. "Carrie Fleet, Superintendent." She turned to Carrie Fleet. "Superintendent Jury is with Scotland Yard."

That announcement brought to Carrie's face no hint of surprise, pleasure, bewilderment. But she did come in. Not, Jury thought, because of the command; she might have come or gone as she chose. She did not offer her hand. Jury felt the air stir when she walked in, felt a subtle change in the atmosphere — a pause. Gillian had stopped in her act of arranging the poor bouquet; Regina drew her lap rug a bit more closely. And all the time she had kept pale blue eyes on Jury.

"Well, good lord, girl, at least say hello."

"Hello." That she said no more was not a deliberate slight. Perhaps this was the way she marshaled her forces, moving carefully from trench to trench, gaining a bit of ground here, another inch there. Jury wondered only what the battle was. She made the single movement of brushing her long hair back across a shoulder. It was platinum, the sort of blond hair that made one think it could turn, overnight, to pure silver. She was a marvel of self-control. Indeed, for those few moments she had controlled the room. Involuntarily, Jury looked at the clock to see if it had stopped.

After telling the Baroness she needed money for more chicken feed, she turned and left through the french door.

Regina topped up her gin-laced tea and said, "What a trial."

Gillian Kendall smiled slightly at the vase. "She's the only one you like, and you know it." Then she excused herself and left through the door to the foyer.

"God," said Regina, screwing a cigarette into her holder, "you can imagine how sprightly the conversation is round the dinner table."

"They both did seem rather shy." That was certainly not the word for Carrie Fleet.

Nor did Regina think so. "The girl has been called in to our local police station over half-a-dozen times."

"Why?"

"Because she *will* go wandering about the village seeing which cats and dogs are receiving what she considers adequate attention and which are in their death-throes. She did not care for the way Samuel Geeson kept his mongrel leashed in his backyard, and unleashed him and took him along to Paul Fleming and got him to call the RSPCA." Regina rolled the ash from her cigarette. "I found her in London. She had been living with a couple named Brindle. The Brindles had in turn found *her*, wandering in a wooded area of Hampstead Heath. Amnesia, they said. The Brindles knew where the dole money was. One thousand pounds I paid them, and they're putting the bite on me for more. Why on earth they think I'd be ripe for blackmail, I've no idea. Of course, I suppose they *could* claim I'd abducted her." Regina arched an eyebrow. "I really think *one* abduction is quite enough for one child, don't you?"

320

She reached round to a majolica jar and drew out a letter. "Here, have a look. Perhaps you can do something."

The two pages — a bit grimy and just edging toward literacy — took first a whining and then a honeyed tone. Jury said, "You didn't tell me she'd been given a bad blow to the head."

"Dear Superintendent, I did not know. I believe they are playing it for tears. Presumably, that accounts for the amnesia."

"It's a rather odd letter." Jury turned the pages over. Nothing on the back.

"I can assure you, the Brindles have their odd little ways."

". . . so we thought, taking enclosed into account, another five hundred might be worth your time. I remain, truly yours . . ." and a flourish of a signature. "What does he mean?"

Busy measuring out her gin, Regina just looked at Jury. "That he wants five hundred pounds, Superintendent. Even my spongy brain could ascertain that."

"Mind if I keep this?"

She waved the letter away. "By all means. Poor Carrie. Her name isn't even real. So there it is, she came to me with no documents at all."

"You make her sound like a purebred dog with dubious credentials."

She laughed. "Ah, Carrie would like nothing *better* than that comparison."

Jury smiled. "What about Gillian Kendall?"

"She's a Londoner and was having morning coffee in the local tea-palace when she overheard a conversation that I was looking for a secretary. I was beginning to bore myself, though that might be hard to believe, and when she came up the drive to offer her services six months ago I said yes on the spot. Couldn't stand to advertise and have half of Hampshire on the doorstep. But I'm not sure I care for her very much. I dislike people who walk on tiptoe and always seem to be carrying something in their hands — vases, decanters, flowers. Who knows but underneath there might not be a knife or a gun?"

Seventeen

ard to believe that Gillian Kendall had a knife or a gun hidden under the cardigan she kept drawing more closely about her.

They were walking between the privet hedges that made up the maze, another of the Baron's practical jokes, she told him. "It's very carefully constructed," said Gillian Kendall.

"Isn't that the idea behind all mazes?" Jury thought Regina's assessment of Gillian Kendall was off the mark. She did not walk on tiptoe, nor did she seem nervous. On the contrary, she struck Jury as composed. Composition. It was the right word, if one were an artist. An extra brushstroke here and there would have colored over the too-pale cheek, brought a spark to the eye that would have doubled its effect.

"It's quite intricate," she went on. "For one thing, it's round. It can't help but give the impression a person is going in circles."

"Metaphorically speaking, a person usually is."

She stopped and looked at him. For a moment he thought she might be going to say something less oblique. But what she said was, "I've got lost here several times. The Baron apparently wanted to make sure that once his wife got in here, she couldn't get out. Oh, no malice. None. He liked games. This one I imagine would be sexual hanky-panky." Gillian looked away. "Funny. She speaks of him with surprising devotion. I would have thought she'd only have done it for the money."

"You don't care for her very much, I take it."

A gust of wind whipped her hair, even in this privet-sheltered place. Hiding the little row of buttons that marched up her prim dress by pulling the cardigan closer, she said, "I honestly don't know. She's like a wine that hasn't aged well." Gillian laughed. "A sixty-five Bordeaux, perhaps."

"A bad year?"

There was a pause as she picked at the hedge. "A very bad year."

Jury didn't think she was talking about wine.

Gillian looked along the curving path they had taken, one they could have continued along, or taken another to their right. "We've got three options," said Gillian. "Go on, go back, or go right. I leave it to you. Which way?"

There was an arched opening in the hedge. Through that he could see several others, like a series of archways down a long hall. It was much like the mural. "Well, that vista is a trick, I'd say. It appears so obviously an escape that it probably leads straight back to the center of the maze. So I'll take the fourth option."

"There are only three. Back, forward, out."

"There's also down." Jury enjoyed the feel of her arm as he pulled her to one of the benches they'd passed. "Strategically placed. Let's sit."

Shaking her head, she sat down. "Not fair."

"I disagree. Perhaps we can talk our way out. Or I can. After all, you know the way, and you've been leading."

The eyes she turned on him were cool. "You think I've deliberately led you into a trap?"

Jury smiled. "Yes."

"I don't understand. What have I said?"

"It's what you haven't. You've been having a hell of a good time walking round here, telling me about the Baron and his little practical jokes. But I would think that, knowing I'm from Scotland Yard, you'd wonder why I'm here."

"Why are you, then?"

"You must have known Una Quick."

She frowned. "Everyone did. But you're not here on her account —"

Jury interrupted. "A few days ago her dog was poisoned."

"That's right." She shivered and pulled her cardigan closer. "It was awful for Una. She was a sick woman, anyway. Paul — Dr. Fleming — he's the local vet . . ."

"I've met him. What about him?" Given the way she hesitated over the name, Jury wondered if the handsome Dr. Fleming was the reason for another bad year.

"Only that he said Una claimed the door to the potting shed was locked."

"Do you put that down to Miss Quick's forgetfulness? Or a local animal-hater?"

"That's hard to believe. But if I had to, I suppose I'd say it was the Crowley boys. They're awful. One truly is retarded, and the other acts as if he were. I can't think why Amanda doesn't put Bert — they call him 'Batty' — in an institution, instead of that 'special school' she sent him back to."

Looking through the corridor of openings, Jury said, "Institutions can be pretty grim places." He remembered his own years in the orphanage the social services had put him in after his mother had been killed in the last bombing of London. He had been six, but he would still, in his mind, walk the cold corridors, sit on the brown-blanketed bed, taste the watery potatoes. "Maybe she loves the boy too much."

"Amanda loves Amanda." Her profile, above the collar pulled up around her chin, was like the sculpted profile of one of the statues. "It allows her to play the martyr. It also allows her to play with several thousands of pounds a year. Twenty, Regina says. Amanda's the executor of the will. The father knew the youngest — that's Batty — might be put in some sort of institution right after he died. So the bequests, he made were contingent on that." Gillian turned to Jury, her smile sardonic. "I imagine most people could put up with a few pranks for twenty thousand a year, don't you?"

Gillian Kendall did not seem especially cynical. Her face had a wasted look right now, the expression of one who's gone down for the count once too often.

Jury changed the subject. "Who collects the post?"

She looked puzzled. "Well, it depends. I do, Mrs. Lambeth does sometimes; she's our cook. Randolph, who's supposed to be gardener. Carrie Fleet. Whoever happens to be near the post office."

"Did the Baroness Regina ever mention her suspicion that Una Quick was reading people's letters?"

"Oh, yes. I'm quite sure she's right, too. I sent Paul — Dr. Fleming — a note that he was positive had been opened. He laughed about it."

Her face burned. *She* hadn't laughed about it.

Jury asked her point-blank. "What's your relationship with Dr. Fleming, then?"

Another pause. "Nothing." She looked at him squarely. "I'm not sure there ever was."

"That's hard to believe."

She looked away.

"The Baroness says you've been here for about six months. Are you really her secretary or just good company?"

Gillian laughed. "I'm really her secretary. She enjoys having me read her morning post to her. That way, she can hold on to both her cigarette and her coffee, spiked, as you saw, with a tot of gin. As for company, I doubt I'm much company for anyone."

"I'm not having a bad time."

It was the first genuine smile he'd seen from her. "And if you pull that cardigan tighter, I'll be forced to take off my coat and put it around you. Did you see this letter?"

She looked at the one Regina had handed over to him. "*Those* people. Yes, I saw it —" Gillian looked a bit startled. "They can't actually *do* anything about Carrie, can they?"

"No. Extortion isn't held in much esteem by police. Didn't you think it peculiar? Brindle's saying 'the enclosed' ought to be good for another five hundred quid. What was 'enclosed'?"

Gillian frowned. "I don't know. There was nothing." She read the letter through. "I supposed he was talking about the rest of the letter. The trouble and worry — the poor girl'd been attacked, apparently. Doctor's bills —" Gillian shrugged.

"Brindle? From what I can see he's a tuppenny-ha'penny crook. Probably on the dole. Social services would have seen to all that. Well, never mind."

But she looked as if she minded very much, and Jury asked her if she'd heard about Sally MacBride.

With surprising bitterness, she said she hadn't. Jury wondered how many men Mrs. MacBride had got on her list. Fleming, perhaps?

Jury told her, and her look changed quickly.

"*God!* How awful! I didn't know her that well. I've been to the Deer Leap a few times, talked to her a bit, but that's all." She shaded her eyes with her hand, gazed up at the cold blue of the sky. "What's going on in this village?"

"Good question." Jury got up. "I think I'll have a word with Carrie Fleet."

She smiled. "A word is about what you'll get." And she rose from the bench, too.

"You'll lead me out of this maze, I hope."

She looked at him as if she wished she could.

327

It had once been an arbor, now bricked in, ivy-bound, and moss-encrusted. The stone mason had done rather a sloppy job of it: there were cracks, some of them stuffed with rags against the weather. Though the weather today was fine, a throwback to spring.

The building was long, and at first he saw not her but the wooden crates and metal cages. Some were empty, unused perhaps, or temporarily vacated by their tenants.

Their keeper must certainly have been a virtuoso performer. Cats, dogs, a rooster scratching in the dust, and in the largest compartment — more of a horse box — was a donkey. And on his walk through the grounds he had been startled to see a pony that definitely bore the stamp of the New Forest. It chomped at grass in a patch of woodland behind a statue with a broken arm. It had looked at him for some few moments, apparently used to the occasional two-legged animal, and then returned to its grazing.

Jury's appearance in the doorway caught her by surprise. She had been forklifting hay into the donkey's stall. He tried to remember where he had seen such an expression before; it might have been struck from metal, and that was where he had seen it, on all of the coins bearing the profile of the Queen.

A black and white terrier with a missing leg stayed close to her as she went about her work.

"Now, what's a New Forest pony doing roaming through the woods of 'La Notre'?" Jury smiled.

He was surprised to see her blush before she turned back to the donkey. "It got hit by a car. Tourist, probably," she added without rancor.

"But how did you get it here?"

"Pickup truck."

He leaned against the doorway of the dark hutlike place and simply shook his head. If she shot, no reason to be surprised she drove.

"Doesn't the Forestry Commission take care of them anymore? Those ponies are protected."

"Nothing's protected," she said evenly. She stepped back and surveyed the donkey. "I got him from a tinker. I had to pay him twenty pounds. Him, his caravan, and everything in it wasn't worth that. But I didn't have a gun."

"You usually carry a gun?"

"No. Mostly when I'm in the woods. Poachers, see."

"Most people don't go along with the idea of somebody carrying a shotgun around, you know."

Carrie opened a cage door in which some mourning doves cooed, put in some feed, and turned to look at Jury. "Especially policemen."

"Especially."

There was a long silence. She stood there in her blue dress with a sweater underneath, very straight, like a lightning rod. Jury thought that in that place she was quite firmly grounded. And the longer she looked at him, the deeper the blush. She turned the high color of her face away and took a cat out of its cage. It was a rather ugly black tom with one eye permanently closed.

"Blackstone," she said. Carrie put him down and hunkered down beside him. "Blackstone, come on." There was a combination of command and kindness in her tone. He had heard that quality occasionally in good leaders. The cat didn't move; he seemed afraid to move. She put something a little way away from him. A toy catnip mouse it could have been. It was dusky in the arbor, which had been wired with one bulb. The cat sprang. Carrie smiled.

"I thought he'd have to do something. He was getting pretty bored."

Blackstone flicked the mouse with his paws all round the

dirt floor of the arbor. The terrier watched and then joined in. It was a game.

"Well?" asked Carrie. "I s'pose you came out here to ask me questions."

"If you don't mind. We could go sit down somewhere."

"I have too much to do to sit." Noisily, she rattled a cage door, trying to open it, disturbing a badger in its rest.

Jury could feel again the turbulence in the air and wondered if it was his proximity that bothered her. He did not think she wanted, as in the case of the tinker, to go for her gun.

"Okay. I don't want to bother you if you're busy. Maybe later."

He turned to go.

"No!" One of the crates toppled and she quickly righted it. The gray fox inside ran round in circles. She smoothed her hands down her dress, brushed her hair over her shoulder, and locked her arms across her breasts. "I mean, go ahead and ask."

Jury smiled. Carrie looked away. "Thank you," he said, with a bit of a try at formality, respecting the distance she put between them. But he was not sure how to go on with her. Not with that look of woe she tried to let pass for either indifference or patience with uncomprehending adults. "First thing, Carrie: you came on the Crowley boys with Miss Praed's cat with a gun in your hands. You don't deny that, do you?"

Carrie hadn't moved her eyes from his, and not a flicker of denial had crossed her face. She was fingering a very small gold chain around her throat.

Jury felt stupid. It was as if he were back in detective training school trying to get a handle on the ways to question witnesses. All he could bring to mind was the stare. Stare the buggers down. They'll come round.

Carrie stared back.

"You shot that gun at them." Jury knew she'd shot it into the dirt. But she didn't bother correcting him.

And still, she'd talked to him about the animals. He'd been stupid, taken the wrong path. "Okay. No one ever poured petrol over me and started lighting matches." Her look shifted like sand. "What'd you have done if they'd gone ahead, Carrie?"

"Shot their kneecaps," she said, reasonably.

"Constable Pasco would have pulled you in pretty quick for that."

"I'm used to him." In an old cage, a finch with a bandaged wing uttered its weak double note. It must have felt there was something worth singing about.

"What's the finch's name?"

"Limerick. Neahle was born there. Before they moved to Belfast." She opened the cage. "You can come out." But the bird still sat, swinging gently on its perch. She closed the cage. "It doesn't like strangers. I s'pose you're going to do something about the shotgun, aren't you?"

Jury smiled. "I suppose if the Baroness wants a game warden, she has a right to one. It's not up to me anyway, is it?"

To that she simply answered, "I can shoot a gun, too. The Baron liked to hunt and used to do target practice on the grounds. Probably shot off a couple of statues' arms." She put Blackstone back in his cage, along with the mouse.

"Where did *you* learn to shoot?"

"I taught myself. And the Baroness loves to go to Clint Eastwood films. I like the way he holds the gun with both hands." She paused, considering, chewing at the corner of her mouth. "He's handsome, Clint Eastwood." She blushed and shrugged it off. "I mean if you like that type. The Baroness claims the Baron looked like him," she said, hurrying along to cover up her compliment to anyone who might be a policeman. "But I've seen enough pictures of the Baron to know how true *that* is."

"Would you do me a favor and come sit down on that bench?" Jury nodded beyond the opening to the arbor.

"When I'm finished," she said crisply.

Jury smiled inwardly. Might as well try to move a Stonehenge monolith as move her. As she went about her business of feeding her animals, he watched her in the filtered light that cast narrow bands of green across the arbor walls and across her face. Paraphrasing the poem, Jury thought: *A green girl in a green shade.* The poet might have been describing Carrie Fleet, much as she might have hated to be thought a pretty figure in an old romance.

Eighteen

hen they were finally seated on the stone bench, with the dog Bingo lying underneath, Jury took out his cigarettes.

"You going to smoke?"

"Do you mind?"

"It's not my lungs."

There was a lengthy silence as Jury smoked and Carrie Fleet meditated. Finally, she said, "For a policeman, you don't talk much."

"For a fifteen-year-old, neither do you."

She shrugged. "Talking's just a nervous habit."

Jury smiled. "Do you mind if I ask you a few questions?"

"No. I'm used to police."

"I understand you've had one or two talks with Constable Pasco."

She bent her head and counted on her fingers. "Eight. Though he makes it out to be more like a hundred and eight."

"That much trouble, is there?"

Now she was gazing at the sky. It was an ice-blue, a frozen-over lake of sky, like her eyes. "Not for me."

"Just for Pasco."

Carrie didn't, apparently, think a response necessary.

"You knew Una Quick and her dog. And seem to know everyone else's dogs and cats. What do you think's been going on?"

"Not accidents."

"Why not?"

She was scuffing the toe of her sneaker in the dirt. "Two dogs and a cat. And two people. That's an awful lot of accidents to happen in a week."

Of course, she would put the cat and dogs before the people. "Have you any ideas?"

"Maybe."

"Mind telling me?"

"Maybe."

Jury looked down at the stub of his cigarette, smiling. "I'd rather question the Queen."

Her blue eyes widened. "Have you, then? What'd she do?"

"Nothing." He laughed.

Interest in Scotland Yard evaporating like the wispy smoke of his cigarette, she sighed and turned away. Jury glanced at her profile — quite perfect, but she didn't know it. The child who'd emerged suddenly was hidden again.

"Given the animals, I think I imagined you'd have done a lot of thinking about it. Because you'd have cared more."

Still scuffing up dust, she looked away. "Maybe."

This time, the word caught in her throat, one syllable pulling the other along. She turned back. "It's someone in the village."

In the act of grinding out his cigarette, Jury stopped, surprised. "Why do you think so?"

"*Because* —" Her tone was loaded with disgust. "— I don't think somebody would come up from London to poison the Potters' cat or Una Quick's dog. And if I find out who —" The tone was grim.

"I suggest you tell the police."

She just looked at him. Hopeless.

"Have you got a list of suspects, then?"

"Haven't you?"

Jury took out his notebook. "Haven't lived here as long as you. Only got into town yesterday afternoon. Would you mind telling me?"

"Yes, I'd mind." Shading her eyes with her hand, she looked up at the sky. "Probably going to have frost, and I know that'll please Mr. Grimsdale to death. He can hardly wait to get hounds out. Going to be a meet in a couple of days." She sighed. "It's so much *work*."

"What work?"

Her blue eyes glazed his face. "Unstopping earths."

Jury smiled. "What do you do? Follow the earthstopper when he goes out?"

"Don't have to. I know where they are." She nodded toward the arbor hut and rough-cut wooden sign nailed to it, on which was printed *Sanctuary*. "That's his fox I've got in there. It's a little sick. I'll let it go in a couple of days."

"Good God." Jury laughed. "Can't imagine Grimsdale letting you play nurse."

"I stole it." When Jury opened his mouth, she sighed. "Here it comes. Lecture. It was one of those foxes he bags. If you think it's okay to bag foxes and keep them in a kennel, lecture away."

"No lecture. Does he know?"

"Maybe. But he can't go into my sanctuary. It'd be like trying to drag some thief or someone out of a church."

"If Grimsdale doesn't try, I'd put it down more to fear of broken kneecaps than God."

Her smile was small and faded quickly. He had never seen such a determined chin, such an adamantine gaze. Again, she was fingering the gold chain, its links so tiny they were gossamer. Jury wouldn't have thought Carrie to be much con-

335

cerned with finery. Part of the necklace was under the jumper, and she drew it out. There was a small ring attached, an amethyst. It was too small to fit her fingers.

"That's very pretty."

She nodded. "I wish *I* had eyes that color."

Jury looked away, smiling. Obviously, she'd seen Polly Praed. "Is it a special ring?"

Carrie held it toward him. "Can you read what's inside? The writing's so small I can hardly make it out. I think my mother gave it to me."

Jury squinted at the initial *C* and the tiny words *from Mother*. He knew she only wanted confirmation, or to share some knowledge that he doubted she herself had. "That's what it says, all right. Do you remember her?"

She shook her head, put the ring back under the jumper. End of subject.

They sat there for a minute, and Jury said, "It would be helpful to know who's going round killing off the animal population."

"And the people," she said calmly. "Una Quick and Mrs. MacBride. I wouldn't be surprised if there's more." Her face turned once again to the sky, as if it were her main concern. "Frost."

Nineteen

manda Crowley was wearing whipcord trousers and a tweed jacket. Jury wondered if she was always scenting, like Sebastian Grimsdale and hounds, for the cold and the frost that foretold the hunt. The Crowley cottage reminded him a little of a rather fancy tack room. It smelled of polish and horses.

It was the first thing she mentioned after the most abrupt of social interchanges. "Hunt starts soon, too bad the boys aren't here." Then she looked about her, as if mildly surprised by their absence.

"Too bad, yes. They've gone back to school, I understand."

"Just two days ago. They'd been on a brief holiday. . . ." Her voice trailed off.

Been sent down, you mean, thought Jury.

"I really haven't much time, Superintendent. I'm expected at Gun Lodge in a few minutes. Can't imagine why you're here, anyway."

Again, he smiled, betraying in Amanda a response she no doubt resented. She fell for it. She pulled down the jumper beneath the jacket and ran her hand, like a comb, over her smoothed-back hair. The body was thin and the hair silvery; still, she would have been attractive except for the creases about the mouth that suggested a crotchety temperament.

"I was wondering how well you knew Sally MacBride." Jury held out his packet of cigarettes.

She took one and rolled it between her fingers for a few seconds, then accepted his match. There was another brief silence. "Scarcely at all. It's a dreadful thing to happen. Poor John."

Amanda crossed her legs. From thigh to ankle, in the tight trousers, it was clear they were well-shaped but taut, like the rest of her. She reminded Jury a little of the riding crop she had absently plucked from the table and was running up and down her leg.

Nicely Freudian, he thought. He wondered how she got on with Grimsdale. "What's 'scarcely at all' mean, Mrs. Crowley? That you spoke to her only to say 'hello,' or 'nice morning'?"

"Well, of *course*, I chatted with her. I often go to the Deer Leap. Don't we all?"

Jury shrugged, rested his chin on his hand, and said, "I don't know, do I?" The tone was mild. No belligerence, except for what she might infer.

"I don't understand all of this. Why are you asking about Sally?"

"What about Una Quick? Now, you *did* know her rather well?"

The little lines around her mouth seemed etched in acid. "*Everyone* knew Una Quick. And I *still* am asking you what's this all about?" She flicked her wrist, looking at the watch with its sensible leather strap, as if she'd give him another one-half minute.

"Gossip," said Jury.

338

Her eyes narrowed. "I am *not* a gossip, Superintendent. I've better things to do."

"Didn't say you were. But I'd imagine Una Quick was, especially running the post-office stores as she did." Jury looked around the room. Wood-paneled, a couple of saddles — one on a mock-up of a tailor's horse — riding crops, boots, even two brass 'ones guarding each side of the small fireplace. The glass out of which she'd been drinking was etched with stirrups. "In three days, two accidents. And :hat's not even mentioning the dogs and the cat. Fatal. Doesn't that make you wonder?"

Her eyes, stone-gray and stone-hard, regarded him. "No, it doesn't. Una had a bad heart; Sally had the misfortune to get trapped in that playhouse." She had the grace to shiver, rubbing her arms up and down. "Probably the wind banged the door shut. Awful to be claustrophobic —"

"You knew she was?"

"*Everyone* knew she was. Was on a train that stalled in the tube and she fainted. Had to sleep with a light on, that sort of thing."

"Don't you think it strange that Mrs. MacBride would be going out to Neahle's playhouse at night?"

Her smile was knowing. "An assignation, perhaps, Superintendent?"

Not much sympathy was being wasted on the dead woman, certainly. "With whom?"

"I can think of one or two. Donaldson, for instance. Only I thought those meetings were generally held at *his* place. And then there's our constable, isn't there? And, perhaps, even Paul Fleming. Too bad for Gillian Kendall."

Jury's jaw tightened. Then he smiled. "Since you're not a gossip, Miss Crowley, perhaps you might know who is."

"Well, I dislike speaking ill of the dead. But certainly Sally MacBride seemed cheek to jowl with Una Quick."

"Ever heard of rumors of Miss Quick's tampering with people's post?"

"Well, Billy and Batty — Bertram — *did* mention —"

She quickly dropped the subject of Billy and Bertram and Jury just as quickly picked it up. "That incident with Miss Praed's cat —"

Her diversion was to say she had no idea who Miss Praed was. "The woman staying at Gun Lodge whose cat was taken from her car —"

Amanda interrupted. "You've been listening to Carrie Fleet, of course. She's hardly to be taken seriously."

"According to her, your nephews were about to burn Miss Praed's cat."

Amanda crushed her cigarette so forcefully it looked like a splayed bullet. "I'm suing that girl for slander."

"You'd have to sue the Baroness. I don't think you'd win. Dr. Fleming saw the cat."

"That *doesn't* prove my boys —"

Jury was losing patience. It was an effort not to show it. "Miss Crowley, I'm not here to press charges about the cat. I'm interested in the deaths of Una Quick and Sally Mac-Bride. And the motive for their murders."

She stared at him through the gloom of the little sitting room. "*Murder?* Their deaths were accidents."

"I doubt that."

"Dr. Farnsworth signed Una's death certificate."

"She was phobic, really."

Amanda shrugged. "I'd hardly call a bad heart that."

"I would. If your behavior was so compulsive you had to call your doctor every Tuesday to report. That's pretty phobic."

Again she shrugged. "I wouldn't know."

Jury got up. "Don't you wonder about your own, Miss Crowley?"

Sharply, she looked up. "My what?"

"Phobia. Cats." Jury smiled and said, "I should be careful, if I were you. Thanks for your time."

She did not bother to rise as he opened the door. Her mouth was still open.

Twenty

The Deer Leap was closed except to guests of the inn and police, though the sanguinity of John MacBride had been replaced, behind the bar, by the sanguinary looks of Maxine Torres.

When Jury asked her for a double whiskey, he almost expected her to say *I don't do windows.* And her sullen though sultry look at Wiggins, who asked for a hot buttered rum, would have been enough to make anyone less determined to stave off a bout of flu forget it.

Maxine was happy to forget it. "Kitchen's closed," she said. "You want beer, gin, whiskey, okay. Sherry, okay. Nothing that means cooking."

"Heating up a bit of water and butter hardly means cooking," said Wiggins.

"Yeah? To me, you have to put it on a stove, it cooks." Even under the heavy lids, the Gypsy eyes stared him down. Then she recited the litany of drinks she would fetch. This time she left out the sherry. She'd have to travel down the bar for that. The optics were directly behind her.

Wiggins gave in. "Brandy."

"Brandy," she repeated, ran a balloon glass under the optic, and plunked it on the bar. All in one motion. Should have been a flamenco dancer, thought Jury.

Wiggins was certain he was coming down with a disease unknown in the annals of medical science. On the way back from Fleming's laboratory, he'd sneezed his head off and asked Jury if there might have been something back there he was allergic to. Only cat or dog dander, Jury assured him, knowing Wiggins could even talk an allergy into something terminal.

He sat beside Jury now, as determined to believe he'd caught something as Maxine Torres was determined not to help him get rid of it. She sat at the other end of the bar, wetting a finger, slowly folding back the pages of a fashion magazine, her interview with Russell apparently not having dented her complacency, and the death of Sally MacBride having turned her attention to a new wardrobe.

The door opened and Polly Praed came in together with a gusting wind that made Wiggins shiver. Maxine looked up, sulking, and informed Polly that the Deer Leap was closed. Respect for the dead. Looking around at the three of them, she made it sound as if only Maxine had any.

"I'm meeting Lord Ardry," said Polly. Jury heard Maxine mumble something, but having taken on the job of temporary publican, she was forced to serve her.

When Polly asked for a sherry, Maxine gave her a look that could stop a tinker's cart, and moved down the bar, Polly calling after her, "Tio Pepe."

"No got," she said, not about to search through the various bottles. She returned with the one nearest to hand, Bristol Cream.

"I don't *like* sweetish sherry."

Maxine shrugged and didn't even look at her. "Don't drink it, then."

"Isn't she a charmer?" said Jury.

Polly braved a look at him in the mirror, adjusting her big glasses. "Oh, hello."

Jury shook his head. "Hello, Polly." He asked Maxine for a pint of best bitter. Fortunately, the beer pull was directly in front of her.

"Hello, Sergeant Wiggins." Her greeting was absolutely sunny. He returned it. "I'm meeting Lord Ardry," she said to the mirror, then let her gaze wander all around the firelit room — at the horse brasses above the bar, at the painting above the fireplace — everywhere but directly at Jury.

"Polly, why don't you stop with that 'Lord Ardry' stuff. You know he dropped the titles." He watched her color and snap open her bag and rummage relentlessly through it, as if looking for proof of Plant's peerage. Looking at his reflection in the mirror, she said, "I can hardly call him Melrose, hardly knowing him as I do. Or don't." She fumbled with her sherry glass.

"Good God. After all the time you spent with him in Littlebourne?"

She was silent.

"You *do* remember your own village, Poll? The murder, the letters —"

"*Poll?* You make me sound like a parrot."

Jury smiled again and shook his head. "You're not nearly so talkative."

It was at this moment that Melrose came down the stairs. He had been looking glum but brightened when he saw Polly.

"Hullo, Polly. Ready for dinner?"

Maxine looked up in alarm.

"Oh, *don't* worry. I wouldn't ask you to boil water."

"I just did," said Wiggins.

π

"Liberty Hall, back there, isn't it?" Plant was surveying the decor in the recommended restaurant in Selby. The town was charming, the restaurant, or *taverna*, was not — at least in the judgment of Melrose.

"You're always complaining," said Polly equably as she drank her wine.

"I? I beg your pardon. Seldom do I complain. I simply do not care for defrosted *spanakopita*. And this retsina tastes like fish oil" — he made a face as he took another sip — "and I believe all of the waiters and Mama Taverna are really the rest of the Torres family. They're Greek Gypsies." Melrose poked at a stuffed grape leaf. "This reminds me of that horror movie about the body-snatchers —"

"Leave it," said Jury. "You're putting me right off my meal."

"Sorry. Didn't mean to be rude. I just want to go back to England."

"I have to get back to London. Although Racer probably doesn't even know I'm gone yet." He looked at Polly. "I'd pretty much guessed Una Quick wouldn't have made that trek up the hill unless it was damned important —"

Polly looked crestfallen.

"— But the umbrella; that I missed completely."

Polly's violet eyes glimmered. "You can't be expected to notice *everything*, I expect. I write mysteries; I've trained myself to notice things."

"Scotland Yard, of course, hasn't," said Plant, holding up a hand to signal a black-eyed waiter, who was irritated at having his rattling conversation with the other three broken by the customers.

Polly ignored him, chewing a bit of crusty bread. "She'd come out before the storm." Polly frowned.

Jury waited for her to go from A to B. But she only shrugged.

"It wasn't the storm that pulled down the telephone wire," said Plant. "Which means, then, someone tampered with it —"

"You're so clever," said Polly, irritably. "That's just what I was going to say."

"Good. Then you would also have deduced that someone knew Una Quick would have to make a telephone call and wanted to force her to walk up that hill."

"That's certainly a chancy way of trying to kill someone," said Polly.

"Like the dog."

"What?" Polly looked suspiciously at the plate of hummus.

"The dog," Plant repeated, asking for the wine list. The retsina had been Polly's idea.

"Don't you agree?" asked Plant, over Polly's head.

"What's this stuff? It looks like something I feed Barney."

"Cats and dogs," said Jury. "The death of that terrier, given the terrible state of Miss Quick's heart, *could* have brought on an attack that would kill her. But it didn't. Next thing, force the old woman right after the poor funeral to huff up the hill to the phone box."

"Still chancy. Polly, will you stop coveting my shish kebab? Eat your catfood."

"Not if there was someone on the other end of the line," said Jury.

Polly reached over quickly and forked a succulent piece of lamb from Melrose's plate, saying, "You mean Una Quick *was* making a call?"

"I'd say she'd been told to call someone at exactly such-and-such time."

"Farnsworth," said Plant. "Everyone in town knew that she called him on Tuesday evenings."

"But that doesn't mean she was calling Farnsworth."

Polly, having helped herself to half of Melrose's plate, stopped chewing and sat back. "What you're saying is that it wasn't a soothing statement about her heart that did it."

Jury nodded. "More likely something quite venomous. Deadly. A threat, perhaps."

346

" 'I was the one who killed your dog and the same thing is going to happen to you, Una,' " said Plant. "That ought to do it."

"I'd say so. It might have done the job even over her own telephone. But forcing her to physical exertion beforehand would make the result pretty much a dead cert, wouldn't you say?"

Polly, having pretty much polished off Melrose's dinner, was sitting back, wearing her glasses again, staring up at the ceiling. "What an absolutely marvelous way to kill somebody —"

"Really," said Melrose, studying the wine list. "A bottle of blood, Polly, perhaps? Couldn't taste worse than the fish oil."

"No, I mean it —"

"I know you mean it. Here's your moussaka. I'll just have some —"

She slapped his hand away from her plate. Melrose ordered a bottle of Châteauneuf-du-Pape and the waiter, who in truth might have been Maxine's relation, looked at him as if he were crazy. "We got the retsina, house wine, the . . ." He named two or three others.

"Then why is the Châteauneuf-du-Pape on the wine list?"

"Who knows? Have the house wine." He moved off.

Polly continued. "It *is* ingenious. The murderer disguises his or her voice, doesn't get near the victim. So even if it *doesn't* work, the worst that can happen is that Una says she was threatened. And the storm becomes simply a lucky accident for the murderer. Makes it look as if *that's* what knocked out Una's telephone wires, when they'd already been cut."

"Sally MacBride?" asked Polly, well into her moussaka.

"I believe I'll have some shish kebab," said Melrose.

She stared at him. "You just did."

"It would be very much the same thing," said Jury, as

347

Plant signaled the waiter, disengaging him once more from the interminable conversation going on at the rear of the Taverna. "Probably a number of people knew about that phobia, her fear of the underground, her sleeping with a light on and the door open —"

The waiter had ambled over, yawned, and stared at Plant. "Another shish kebab, if you please."

"You just had some," said the waiter, glaring.

"That's what I told him," said Polly, eyes now on the list of sweets.

"I know I just had some," said Melrose. "Instead of your skewer —" He reached around and picked up his silver-knobbed stick, clicked a button, and the ebony stick disengaged immediately. "Use mine."

The waiter stared at the swordstick and stood back. He gibbered something in Greek and quickly walked away.

"That's illegal," Polly said to Jury.

"Uh-huh. May I go on? A lot of people knew — Sally was a great talker. Gossip would be a better word."

"She was talking about the Underground," said Plant. " 'You couldn't get me down there on a bet,' she said. Said the train got stuck once and she nearly fainted. Same thing happened on an elevator."

The shish kebab appeared so suddenly, Jury assumed Plant was right. Everything was pre-prepared. The waiter bore it on a plate, the skewer flaming. He doused the flames, put down the plate, and scuttled off.

"The service has picked up." He speared a cube of lamb and studied it, frowning. "Now, the playhouse. It's very unlikely Sally would have any interest in going there."

"Someone could have persuaded her," said Polly.

"True. Or it could have been done far more easily. Take, just as an example, Grimsdale's kennel master? Or even Pasco? Isn't it more or less general knowledge that Sally MacBride had something going with maybe more than one man in Ashdown? The husband being the last to know. What about a midnight tryst before she leaves?"

"Or," said Jury, "someone sending her a note from one of them. 'Please meet me at the playhouse . . . Vital.' That sort of thing. That little house is accessible to anyone. And screened from the pub. There could be a dozen different ways to get the MacBride woman there."

"But why would she have gone *in* the place? And if she didn't, it wouldn't have looked like an accident."

"If she'd been led to believe the person she was to meet was already there, or would be at an appointed time, she'd have gone in. Too late then."

"You mean the killer is waiting, immediately shuts the door. And leaves."

"Probably. Having knocked off the inside doorknob and taken the bulb from the lamp."

Polly shuddered. "Clever, but God, what a thing to do. Baklava," she added.

"What?"

"My sweet. And coffee." Without a pause, she went on. "The thing is, both of these deaths play on a victim's weakness. Heart. Closed places. The killer doesn't have to *touch* a weapon, so there are literally no traces, except for footprints in the dirt, or something."

"You read too many of your own mysteries. I doubt *this* person would have been so stupid as to leave that sort of trace," said Plant.

Polly glared. "I *never* leave prints in the dirt."

"And what about the other animals — the Potter sisters' cat and the other dog?" asked Plant.

"Red herrings, I'd guess. To call attention away from Una Quick's dog. I wouldn't be surprised if the killer actually thought the death of that terrier would finish her off."

"Funny. If I were going after animals, I'd hit that animal sanctuary of Carrie Fleet's."

Jury smiled. "The *last* place I'd hit would be Carrie Fleet's." He took the letter from Brindle from his pocket. "What do you make of this?"

They both read it. Polly shook her head. "More money?"

Over his gold-rimmed spectacles, Plant said. "What's 'the enclosed' refer to?"

"My question, too."

"Something's been left out," said Plant.

"Taken out, wouldn't you say?" Jury put the letter back in his pocket. "I'm going up to London tomorrow. Take my room at the Lodge, would you?" he asked Melrose.

"Your room? Why?"

"Because I want you to keep an eye on Sebastian Grimsdale, Donaldson, Crowley, the lot. Wiggins is there, but I'd rather have two of you. I mean three of you," he said to Polly's downcast eyes. "Tell Grimsdale about your stag-hunting days."

"*Hunt* a stag. I've never even seen one."

Said Polly, finishing off her baklava. "Just lie. You're good at that."

"Fox-hunting, then. You were up on a horse in Rackmoor. Remember?"

"Very well. Cold toast and gruel is my lot in life."

⬩

It was not the maid who opened the door of "La Notre," but Gillian Kendall. "Oh!" She stepped back suddenly.

"I'm sorry. I know it's late."

Gillian smiled. "Not for us. We're more or less night people. But the Baroness is out."

"At this hour? Where's she gone? To the films in Selby?"

Looking rather sheepish and trying not to smile too broadly, Gillian said, "My joke. I meant out like a light. Sorry."

"Why? It was you I came to see, anyway. Lucky for a change."

Somewhat nervously she fingered the row of buttons on the dress she'd been wearing earlier. When she saw Jury watch the fingers, she dropped her hand and blushed.

He laughed. "I haven't come to take you to the nick. You actually look relieved. The guilty flee when no man pursueth. What've you done?"

"Come on in and I'll tell you." She smiled.

Jury stood in the Grecian-English-Italian foyer and said, "I'd rather have a walk. It's a fine evening, and I'm going to London early tomorrow."

"I'd love it. You're not thinking about the crazy maze, are you?"

He grinned. "It's probably more interesting at night than by day. I may never make it up to London."

Taking a wool stole from a peg, she said, "I doubt anything could keep you from your job."

The Baron had stationed little lights, hidden really, at different places in his circular maze, and they threw up a dim, unearthly glow on her face whenever she and Jury passed one before winding into darkness again.

"So go on, tell me. Any confession will do."

She tightened the stole about her in the same way she'd tried wrapping the cardigan. He put his arm around her. "Why in hell don't you wear warmer clothes?"

"So people will be tempted to put their arms around me."

"Oh. Fair enough. Let's sit." They'd come to another of the wrought-iron benches. "Go on."

"With what?"

"Paul Fleming. I just wanted to know before I went to London, that's all."

351

Her head lowered, she plucked the fringe of the stole. "Why? Who's in London?"

In the dark, Jury grinned, thinking of Carole-anne Palutski, trying her best to act the role of pro-tramp. "The most beautiful girl in the world."

It was Gillian's turn to say *Oh.* It was a very sad *Oh.*

His arm around her, he gave her a little shake. "For God's sake, Gillian, you know I'm kidding. There is a beautiful girl. She's nineteen and I'm her father-figure." Jury paused. "More or less."

Laughing and hiding her face in the stole, Gillian said, "Probably more."

"Less. You think I'd take advantage of a nineteen-year-old?"

She looked at him straight. "No. Would you, though, of a thirty-five-year-old?"

They looked at one another for some time, until Jury said, "I think I could give it a go."

The bench was cold and unyielding. Jury wasn't.

When he had carefully looped up each one of the buttons, she said, and he thought it very odd: "It was I, wasn't it, who was supposed to save you from the maze?"

"Like Theseus? The Minotaur hasn't got me. So how do you know you haven't saved me?"

She laughed. It was the first genuine show of joy he'd seen in her. "Oh, it would take a *true* Ariadne for that. Not I."

Jury raised her chin. "Who's the real one, then?"

Gillian thought that over. "Carrie Fleet. She could get you out."

There was for Jury an odd sensation that Carrie Fleet — the way he remembered her standing there in the french door with Gillian at the other one — might be, after all, an Ariadne.

It disturbed him. It disturbed him for no reason he could think of.

But all he said was, "I like older women. Even ones tied in some sort of knot over some other man. I can wait."

He kissed her good-bye.

part 4

You—too—take Cobweb attitudes

Twenty-one

The Brindles' downtrodden row house on Crutchley Street was not in the moneyed section near the Thames. What prettying up Flossie had attempted had been quickly besmirched by weather, trampling kids, and lack of attendance.

To put Carrie Fleet in this milieu was hard for Jury; it was like a picture with a figure cut out.

Joe Brindle was not at all happy with police on his stoop — to say nothing of New Scotland Yard.

"I won't be long, Mr. Brindle." That was the truth.

Jury wouldn't have sat down even if asked. Though the Brindles were glowering from two tufted lounge chairs, neither of them had suggested he sit. Given an older girl, snoring on the couch-mate of the lounge chairs, there weren't too many choices, anyway. "I just wanted to ask you a few questions about Carrie Fleet. This letter that you wrote to the Baroness —"

With a shaking hand, Brindle put his Bass Ale on the floor and looked at the envelope. "So? We had the care of her all them years, din't we? *We're* the ones found her, wandering round in that woods."

Flossie Brindle wanted her turn. She almost rose from her chair, found it too much effort and went back down again, a diver going for another look at an ocean floor of ale. "A hard case, Carrie was. Never ever said anything; didn't help with the kiddies; only the animals." And as if in a bout of nostalgia — which Jury thought might very well be real — punched her husband's arm and asked, "What *was* that old terrier she fancied so much?" She looked at Jury. "Three legs it had. Can you beat it? Didn't go in much for beauty, did she?" Flossie plumped up her home-permed curls and gave Jury another look at her knees.

Not much for beauty, Jury thought. "The letter, Mr. Brindle?"

Brindle looked at the envelope, shrugged, handed it back. Then he rose from his chair, a little unsteady on his feet, his manner defensive rather than threatening. "Look, that girl was a burden, there's no reason we couldn't ask the old lady for a bit more."

Where Brindle made his mistake was in thinking Jury knew as much as Brindle. "A thousand pounds wasn't enough, Mr. Brindle?"

Joe Brindle's body heaved, the belly protruding even more over the unbelted trousers. *"No!"* He tried to swagger it off. "You come in here, about that little bitch —"

Although Jury's reflexes were usually in control, he knew that if Flossie Brindle hadn't jumped from her chair and thrown the rest of her Bass in her husband's face, Jury would have hit him. *"Fooled around with her, you did. Bloody liar.* Thought I didn't know," she said to Jury.

Jury supposed he'd known it, but still he felt sick. He waited. Flossie wanted her revenge.

Brindle was wiping the wet from his face, mumbling how he'd never got anywhere. Carrie was too quick for him.

Something to be thankful for, at least. "This letter, Mrs. Brindle —"

Flossie interrupted. "Called herself 'Baroness.' That's a hoot. Manchester or Liverpool's more like it. Well, we neither could believe it. Why would anyone want Carrie Fleet?" She shrugged, lay back again in the dark blue chair, and said, "So Joe, here, he thought why not try for a little more of the ready." She uncapped another bottle.

"Why don't you shut your face, Floss?" His eyes were glazed over; Jury could hardly believe it was from remorse — or any other emotion. He shrugged. "Nothing come of it." And he looked around the room, the pile of dirty clothes a thin cat was making dough on, the snoring girl on the couch, the velvet painting of a deer, as if nothing had come to much.

Flossie, at least, could be counted on for nostalgia, even if it was ale-sodden. She'd taken the letter from its grimy envelope, handwriting like that of a child. "Guess she kept the snap." She took another swig from the bottle.

Jury tensed.

"I'll tell you this," said Joe Brindle. "Flossie here's got a temper, but she ain't no fool." He almost smiled. "Recognized that uniform straightaway, she did." And he gave her a friendly little cuff on the arm.

Jury sat down, smiled, and said, "Do you think I could have one of those, Flossie?" He nodded at the Bass Ale.

There was clearly nothing she'd like better than a chance to serve the superintendent. It allowed her to adjust her legs, the black-patent-leather belting in swells of flesh, and to play Hostess. She even brought him a glass.

"Thanks. I suppose you kept a copy?" Brindle would be smart enough not to send the original off without making one. Or keeping the original and sending a copy. After drinking down half a glass and keeping his smiling eyes on Flossie, he said, "Mind if I have another look?"

"The maid? Yeah, why not." Flossie left and returned with a snapshot. It had curled at the edges, not very clear, apparently taken on a rainy day. There was a young woman, in a dress and cape that might well have been a "uniform," trying to restrain a blur of an Alsatian that seemed much more interested in the nearby gaslight than in her. Her head was back; she was laughing at this trial.

"Amy Lister," said Flossie.

"You knew her?"

Flossie shook her head. "It's on the back."

Jury turned the picture over. The name was printed there. Brindle said it again: "Smart girl, is Flossie."

"Why didn't Carrie take this picture with her?"

Flossie shrugged. "Dunno. Maybe after all these years she forgot it was there. The purse lining was ripped and the snap was in between it and the outside."

She lit a cigarette, tossed the match more or less in the direction of an ashtray, and said through the rising spiral of smoke, "See that lamp? The one the dog's trying to piss on? Well, I knew where that was. It's one of the last gaslights left in England. Off the Embankment it is. And then I got t' thinking." She paused, perhaps to demonstrate that particular power. "See, I used t' work at the Regency Hotel. I waitressed there. That gaslight, it's near the Embankment and right down that narrow street from the Regency." Her eyes grew misty. "The tips you could make. I mean, that Regency! You had to be nearly rich as the Queen —" She pointed her cigarette at the snapshot. "I didn't know her, but that Amy Lister's wearing a maid's uniform from the Regency. You got the money, you could get one of them maids or the porter t' walk your dog. Now, I says t' meself, what's this Carrie Fleet doing with this snap?"

"And you tried to trace Amy Lister?"

Here she gave her husband a smart slap. "Joe here did. Worse luck."

360

"You went to the Regency?" Jury was looking down at the young laughing woman. A nice person, he thought. Out there on pavements sleek with rain, getting wet herself — well, if Flossie was right, the payment might have been worth it. "Didn't find her?"

For the first time, Joe seemed to come back to the real world. "You don't know sod-all, Super. And you being Scotland Yard." He leaned toward Jury, his ale-laden breath spanning the distance between them. "I took some money, not much — well, we're on the dole, ain't we —"

Jury looked at the video recorder. "I'm sure."

"— and gave twenty quid — *twenty* — to the old coot worked the desk, white gloves and black tie, think the help was all going to a bleedin' ball. Anyway, I paid him to give me the dope on the maid in that picture." Brindle appeared to delight in holding Jury hostage to suspense, for he took the moment to uncap another bottle, light another cigar, blow a smoke-ring.

"Turns out, he couldn't remember her name was Lister, but he did her face. Said far as he knew, she went into service in Chelsea, so I goes *there*. Right proper little bit of sleuthing, 'ey?"

"Depends. What'd you find out?"

Brindle waved the question away with a figure eight of cigar smoke. "Nothing, yet. She'd left, no notice." Furrows of simulated thoughtfulness crossed his brow. "But I ain't stupid. I'll find her."

"That'd be the day." The voice, almost ethereal, as if it inhabited no human form, came from the couch. Jury hadn't noticed the snoring had stopped.

The Brindle daughter had turned. Her eyes looked, through the smoky light, directly into Jury's. "She fed the cat, she did. And she never asked for nothing, and she never tried to put herself in between me and them. Not that there's much between. But Carrie never tried."

361

The girl — he didn't know her name. She was still lying, but leaning on one elbow. A change had come over the room, as if a tomb had opened, the voice of one long dead frightening the living. Directly at Jury she looked, and he saw, to his surprise, she was very pretty. Buried as she had been under coverlets and blankets, he had merely imagined some greasy-haired child, dull and inarticulate.

"I thought about it a long time, that snap," she said, nodding toward it. *"Him,"* — and with a deprecating nod of her head, she motioned toward Joe Brindle — "he never did sort it out. Come back from this Chelsea place, no, couldn't remember no Amy working for them."

Brindle lowered his head.

The look the girl gave Jury was near pleading. "How could they remember? It wasn't the maid. Amy was the dog."

The girl lay back, flung her arm over her eyes, and said nothing more.

Twenty-two

Through the open door of Chief Superintendent Racer's office, Jury could just glimpse the cat Cyril — only his head, since he was sitting in Racer's leather desk chair — carefully washing his paw. The usual mists and drizzle of October had given way to a sunlit afternoon, the light of which beamed through the chief's window and spangled Cyril's coppery fur.

Cyril, unlike his keeper, savior, or whatever one might call Racer's secretary, seemed concerned only that cleanliness, not beauty would get him through those pearly gates. Fiona Clingmore was far more convinced that the art of nail-varnishing was the heavenly priority. More to the nails she was holding up for inspection than to Jury, she said, "He's out."

Jury nodded toward the Racer's door. "Obviously. The Met has been left in better paws than Racer's. When's he coming back?"

That Racer came back at all was a mystery to the Metropolitan Police. At least twice a year there were rumors of the chief's imminent departure, which never materialized. There were even worse rumors that he would be kicked upstairs to

363

an assistant commissionership. Fortunately for the safety of Greater London, the kick never landed.

"He's at his club. Been gone since eleven, so I dunno." Her eyes squinted. She inspected her index finger. A flaw. Carefully, she just touched the tiny brush to the nail. Satisfied, she recapped the bottle and waved her fingers in air to dry them. Now she could concentrate on smiling at Jury.

"You wield a mean brush, Fiona. Matisse wouldn't have stood a chance."

"Had your lunch?" It was a ritual question. Jury always had some excuse. Not that he didn't like Fiona; indeed, she fascinated him in many ways. Right now she rested her elbows on the desk and let the fingers hang down, nails purplish-black like talons. Her lipstick was the same color, which rather washed out her already pale skin. The silvery strands in her blond hair she put down to frosting. Nails dry, she now stood up and took the opportunity to display a laddered stocking, which she turned and presented for Jury's inspection. "And I just bought them." Her half-turned, hand-on-hip position also showed the curve of the hip-hugging black skirt and the beruffled blouse, sheer black like the slightly laddered stocking. Just a tiny one at the ankle that she held up in case his eyes had gone bad in the last three days. Jury loved the way Fiona tried for the demimondaine and only ended up seeming old-fashioned. He could imagine her carefully washing out her undies at night, before rolling up her hair and creaming her face. Suddenly, he felt sad.

He hadn't time for lunch, he told her. She accepted this, as always, with grace.

"He's in a right temper," she said, nodding her blond curls toward Racer's office. "And seeing that cat there won't help it along. *Cyril!*" There would be hell to pay if Racer found Cyril sitting in his own kingly perch. "He says he's going to garrote him."

Cyril paid no attention to commands or to threats on

364

whichever of his lives he was enjoying. Racer had nearly got him one day with a letter-opener.

"Cyril knows what he's doing. Did the Hampshire police call?"

"Well, they didn't *complain*. I listened on the extension. Of course, he'll say they did." Fiona ran a blank page in her typewriter and called for Cyril again, who just kept washing. She checked her tiny bejeweled watch. "Been down at that club two hours now —"

The subject under discussion just that moment walked in, the tiny red lines on his face rather like the laddered stocking, red turning to blue nearer the nose. Jury guessed about three doubles. And brandy to follow. Savile Row–suited and boutonniered, Racer looked more as if he should have been in a window of Burberry's than in a New Scotland Yard doorway.

"It's Superintendent Jury. Well. I haven't interrupted your little Hampshire holiday, have I?"

Fiona, her face expressionless, was banging her newly painted nails on the typewriter.

"Got those letters done, Miss Clingmore?" he asked smoothly.

"Nearly done," said Fiona, equally smoothly. "Just the finishing touch here and there."

"Well get the here and there into my office quick, girl!" He snapped each syllable out as if he were shooting rubber bands. "Come on, Jury!"

The cat Cyril had slipped like cream from the chair and now lay in wait in the corner under the desk.

As soon as Racer planted his feet there, Cyril slid himself around the knife-pleated trousers, then whipped out and whizzed toward the door Jury had been careful to leave open a few inches.

A few expletives and a paperweight followed Cyril on his way.

"Miss Clingmore! Throw that beast out of the window!"

The Cyril-ritual always ended on this note.

As did the Jury-ritual end on one much the same, except that paperweights and letter-openers were not for him. No fate was mean enough for Jury. Being roasted on a turning spit would probably have been the chief's choice, largely because he thought Jury, rather than Cyril, might be sitting in that leather chair one day.

That Jury would rather sit on a curbstone in a blinding snowstorm did not occur to Racer. Naturally, anyone with Jury's rank *had* to be after the chief's job.

"The Hampshire police are raising holy hell, Jury. Just how did you manage to slip this one over on me?" He did not stay for an answer, but turned on the mental tape that had detailed Jury's egregious errors and derelictions of duty over the years.

"They seem to welcome my presence, actually. Sir."

Racer always noticed the infinitesimal pause and glared at him. "You're larking about in Hampshire investigating a couple of accidental deaths —"

"Maybe."

"*Maybe?* Even Wiggins can tell the difference between accident and murder. I think."

"I'd like twenty-four hours. That's all. You can surely do without me for twenty-four hours."

That would put him in a bind, thought Jury. Racer had a way of reminding him the Met could do without Jury forever. Into the brief silence where Racer must have battled with this problem, Jury jumped. "I was wondering if you could do me a favor. After all, you have *influence.*" The flower girl on the steps of St. Paul's couldn't have plied her wares so well.

"Certainly I do. Would I have got where I am — ?" Then seeing the weevil in the boll of his career, Racer rushed on. "What sort of favor?"

366

"You lunch at the Regency rather often . . . ?" Rather seldom, Jury knew.

But it worked enough to make the chief superintendent smile his thin-as-a-penny smile. He flicked his lapel, as if a crumb of some privileged repast and all its perks still clung to his garments. "When I've the time. Why?"

"Know anyone named Lister?"

To cover up his obvious lack of knowledge, Racer asked Jury what made him think this Lister would get into the Regency? "You know what sort of place it is. Not just *money* gets you in. Privilege, that's the ticket. And as far as getting information out of the management goes, forget it. Manager'd be on the phone to the A.C. unless ten guests had just been knifed over their Rémy. Or Armagnac."

One thing Racer knew was brandy.

One thing Jury *didn't* know was the name of the manager. Which was what he wanted to know. Jury didn't give sod-all about the manager's calling the assistant commissioner. He just didn't want him or her calling Lister. And given his plan, he certainly hoped it was a man. Too much tradition at the Regency, he was sure, for a woman in that job. "One of the best in London, he is," said Jury, hoping Racer would rise to the bait.

He did. "You mean Dupres?"

"Umm."

"Just how do you know Dupres? Been nosing about?"

No. You just told me. "Heard his name somewhere."

"Georges doesn't deal with People."

Thanks for the first name, thought Jury.

"There's an assistant for that."

"I should imagine. Now, about that twenty-four hours —"

Racer waved his hand. "Hampshire can have you. I've got work to do."

Jury left. As he walked out, the cat Cyril slipped in, gliding noiselessly and almost invisibly across the copper carpet.

His first stop was at a costumier's off St. Martin's Lane used by theater people and the rich who wanted to do Marie Antoinettes and harlequins at drunken fancy-dress parties.

" *'Ello*, luv," fluted a voice.

Jury turned to see a youngish woman with fire-brigade curls eyeing him, the eyes outlined in black. She looked as if she was just making up for that party herself. There was a velvet coral band round her neck tricked out with a cameo, and between that and her waist, not much of anything. Slash-and-dash must be the fashion this year, he thought.

"I wanted to hire a costume."

She looked him up and down. "Come to the right place, you did. What sort?"

"Actually, just a few pieces of women's clothing —"

Her smile altered.

"Not that kind, dear. No whips and chains, either."

She giggled. "It'd be hard to believe anyone looks like you —"

Jury broke up that encomium, but still smiled. "I'm stupid when it comes to fashion. Do you have anything that you'd say would look particularly French?"

"Inside or out, ducks?" Her tongue, coral like the band, ran round her lips.

"That's cute. I'm talking about a dress. Dignified but sexy —"

By now she was leaning on the counter, fingers intertwined, chin resting in them. The case housed some spangled masks and Jury wondered if it wasn't rather cold on her breasts, since nothing much supported them except the glass top. She looked at him as if this were absolutely the most fascinating request she'd ever got. "That's a tough one, luv."

He was getting impatient. Running the gamut of female enterprise could be tiring sometimes. But he only smiled more disarmingly. "Not for you, I bet. Say a size —" He gave her the once-over, just to please her. "No, a little bigger."

She leaned farther. "Where?"

"More or less where you're leaning, love."

Again, she giggled. "Ain't you a caution?"

Jury didn't think so and wanted to get on with it. The only problem was the dress and hat. He'd already eyed a short sable cape he wanted. Probably cost him a month's salary to get it for a day.

He followed her through hangered garments and he had to say she knew her business. She judged the size as a ten. "Bust okay?" She held it against her own.

"It certainly is."

Tiny white teeth glimmered at him through coral lips. The dress was a draped crepe de chine, silky green, low-cut waist . . . well, it was hard to find the waist. "Perfect."

He'd decided against a hat; why cover up the hair? "There's a sable cape, short, back there. How much?"

"How long?"

"Half a day, maybe."

She was bagging the dress, wrapped in tissue paper. "We can only rent for a whole day. For you, hundred quid."

"Good lord." He took out his checkbook.

"Oh, you get some of it back. Deposit, see. We wouldn't want just anyone walking off with *that* little number."

He took the parcel and asked her her name.

"Doreen," she said, hopefully.

"You're good at your job, love." Jury took out his warrant card. "So'm I. You don't have to worry about the sable."

She stared. "Crikey!"

Twenty-three

Jury's foot had barely scraped the stone step of the Islington house when the window flew up above him on the second floor, and a bolt was thrown back in the basement flat.

"Super!" shouted down Carole-anne Palutski. He looked up.

"Pssst! Mr. Jury," whispered Mrs. Wasserman. He looked down.

Carole-anne was not on the telephone, so he'd called Mrs. Wasserman — for whom the telephone was a lifeline, little as she went out — to make sure Carole-anne was there. Jury had already been ninety-percent sure. Daylight began at noon for Carole-anne.

They both had been eagerly waiting his return. He shouted up to Carole-anne, dressed, or undressed, in her flimsy nightie, to pull herself back in; he'd be up in a minute. Then, carrying his parcel and some flowers, he went down the several steps to Mrs. Wasserman's apartment.

Or fastness, he should say. The bolts thrown, the chain unlatched, all she needed was to lower the drawbridge, metaphorically speaking, to let him in. *To be on the safe side* had little meaning for Mrs. Wasserman, for whom safety was a passing condition, something that quickly faded when she got used to the installation of Jury's last lock or window-guard. Always, she could find another possible means of entrance for the intruder who never came (and, Jury knew, never would). But the Feet followed her, she was sure, when she went out, and had done ever since the Big War.

From her stout, neat frame, today clad in navy blue lawn, came her breathless account of the past few days. Her plump hand pressed to her heaving bosom, she might indeed have been running down long streets, fleeing her shadowy pursuer. Patiently, Jury waited, leaning against the wall, nodding, nodding.

"... right to keep an eye on *that* one. Such a child she is, innocent, you know what I mean, out at all hours, and, of course, you know I don't go out at night — I apologize, I cannot follow to see she gets into no trouble. . . ."

"I hardly expected you to do that, Mrs. Wasserman," he said to her outspread arms, her look of mournful apology, the failed policewoman who could not keep an eye on her quarry. "I really don't think Carole-anne is getting up to anything."

"Ah!" Mrs. Wasserman closed her eyes in pain. "Would I suggest *that?*"

No, but it wouldn't be a bad idea. He hid a smile.

"And her men-friends — she says they are cousins. But such a large family? Twenty-four she says she is —"

Carole-anne had aged two years in three days. My.

"— but truly she looks only eighteen or nineteen. And her clothes, Mr. Jury." Sadly, Mrs. Wasserman shook her head. "What can you do with one who wears sweaters down to here and *such* tight pants. Like skin, they are."

You can do plenty, thought Jury. "That's why I wanted you to, you know, give her a cuppa, chat her up a bit. . . ." Jury shrugged.

Mrs. Wasserman's small black eyes grew hard. Even her tightly pulled-back hair had a determined look about it, as if she'd nearly pulled it out in thinking about Carole-anne Palutski. "I have had her in for tea or a coffee. And she has kindly returned the favor, though it is difficult for me to walk up three flights. I say nothing against the child; the soul of kindness. Just — what can I say? She says she goes to the films. Every *night*, Mr. Jury? There are not that many films in Islington. You do not think she takes the Underground into the West End . . . ?"

It went on, interrupted only by Jury's handing her the bunch of roses he had picked up outside the Angel tube station. "You're doing a good job, Mrs. Wasserman."

She was overwhelmed. "For *me?* Roses." She might never have seen one in her life. And she was spieling off her thanks in Czech or Lithuanian — Jury remembered she spoke four or five languages.

French. Jury smiled. "Would you do me another favor?"

"*You* ask *me?* After all that you have done for me. Name it," she added, with a sort of special-agent crispness.

"You speak French."

Her eyebrows slanted upward. Didn't everybody?

"Mine's very rusty, what I ever knew." He had his hand on the door. "Would you mind staying in for a half-hour, an hour? I'm bringing Carole-anne down."

He had asked her if she'd "mind" only to give her whatever spurious support there was in his thinking she was free as a bird, one who flew at will all over Islington, London, wherever.

"Indeed I wouldn't, Mr. Jury. But why this French?"

"You'll see." He smiled. "Bet you don't recognize her."

⚵

372

Jury certainly did. It was mostly naked skin that had hung over the windowsill, and although it was now covered, it made no difference. The body would turn a suit of armor to a pane of glass. There was just no way of hiding Carole-anne.

She threw herself at him as if he might be one of the many long-lost fathers, brothers, cousins that had accumulated on the stairway over the past weeks. "Super! How's about a kiss, then?"

"Sure," said Jury, giving her one right on her soft lips. "Oh, cut it out, Carole-anne," he said, dragging her up from the floor and out of a pretended swoon.

"Nearly fainted at that one. Let's have another go." Before he could stop her, the arms were like steel bands around his neck, and she seemed to have maneuvered parts of herself into every crevice of his body.

He pulled her arms away. "You kiss your dad like that?"

Meltingly, she looked up at him. "Ain't got one. Just you, Dad." And she tried it again.

He shoved her back. "Who're all these men been trailing up and down the stairs like a school of sharks?"

Carole-anne's already pink cheeks turned crimson, as if she'd just dabbed on rouge. "You mean *she* told you?" She pointed toward the floor. "Well, bloody damn. I never —"

"Mrs. Wasserman only told me you had a brother and a father. She thought that was very nice. Thought you were being taken care of."

The fire that flared, died. "Oh. Well, had to tell her *something*, didn't I? So bleedin' innocent she is. Nice old bag o' bones, but she sticks to that flat like glue. I did what you said and got her up here for tea and biscuits." Carole-anne's mouth puckered. Tea was not her drink. "So she couldn't come up here, so I go to her place. Tried to get her to come down the Angel pub with me, but you might as well try to get the street lamps to walk —"

373

Jury burst out laughing. Mrs. Wasserman going down the pub.

Carole-anne was miffed. All her good work should have rated more than a laugh. "You did a great job, love. She likes having you round. Puts some life into this old pile of bricks, she said."

"Oh. Well." Carole-anne sat down beside him. "Lay on a cig, Super, okay? I'm out."

No matter what she said, it sounded like sex. He got out his pack of John Players, lit one for both of them, and said, "I've got a job for you, Carole-anne."

"How much do I have to take off? I stop at —"

"I don't want to know what you stop at. Actually, this involves putting *on* clothes." He'd been unwrapping the parcels, and when she saw the sable she shot up from the sofa. "And there's some money in it for you, Carole-anne."

With her eyes glued on that sable, she said, "There's some positions I don't do, and no ropes and tie-ups —"

"Shut up!" He knew she talked like that just to get a reaction. Carole-anne Palutski probably hadn't gotten many reactions that didn't have a tab on them. It came to him with a small shock, that thought. For a brief moment, his command had penetrated the Glo Dee Vine mask, and he saw what Mrs. Wasserman saw, however misled her vision of it. Carole-anne looked innocent.

He thought of Carrie Fleet and his blood ran cold.

"Work, love."

A half-hour later he was tapping his coded knock on Mrs. Wasserman's door, and he had to admit, he didn't think he'd have recognized Carole-anne Palutski himself.

Of course, she looked gorgeous, as he'd known she would. Though the dress was draped, there was still that tiny strain across the bust, but the rest of it hung in such gentle undulations that the body underneath was plainly not advertising.

Jury thought of Gillian Kendall and tried to brush that thought away. But it was the paint job that was a marvel. Nothing flamboyant, she had gone at that makeup case with the eye of a surgeon. Outliner like a scalpel, lip-liner incised. Blusher like the real thing. Absolutely perfect. To top it, she looked ten years older than the ages she'd been doling out.

"French?" she squealed, on their way downstairs. "You crazy?" But her eyes and hands were all for that sable cape.

"Mr. Jury! What a surprise!"
It was. Mrs. Wasserman stared at Carole-anne with squinty eyes, eyes trying to adjust themselves to a totally different light. "How do you —?"
"Hey, babe," said Carole-anne, chewing inexorably away at the gum Jury told her she'd have to park beneath a bench or behind her ear.
"Carole-*anne?*"
Carole-anne was pleased at the shock of recognition. "One and," she said. "Come for the lesson. Only French I know is *bonjour.*"
Mrs. Wasserman smiled. "You pronounce it that way, dear, they will think you are Japanese."
Carole-anne giggled. "You're a right caution sometimes." Then, from her queenly height (fortunately, she'd had the right shoes) she deigned to look at Jury. "*He* thinks I can learn to talk like a frog in ten minutes."
"Right now you talk like a frog, dear. But French, you do not sound."
Carole-anne giggled again. They must have been getting on like a house on fire.
Mrs. Wasserman fluted, *"Bonjour, monsieur. Il y a long-temps, Georges."* Arms folded, she looked hard at Carole-anne. "Repeat, please."
Carole-anne had parked the gum. She repeated.

"Again."

Again.

" *'Il faut que je m'en aille.'* Repeat."

Carole-anne did so.

"Again. Three times."

Three times.

After a few more phrases and few more repeats, the lesson was over.

"Thanks, Mrs. W.," called Carole-anne, as the bolt shot home behind them in the basement flat.

Jury had reckoned on an hour. A phrase here and there. It had taken only fifteen minutes.

No wonder Carole-anne wanted to be an actress.

Twenty-four

Jury had parked the police car illegally near the Charing Cross Station, and Carole-anne reminded him he'd get a ticket. He handed her a card.

"A bloody baroness. Wherever did you get this? Is this me, then?"

"For the next hour. Then the coach turns back to a pumpkin."

"You call this a coach, Super?"

He helped her out of her side of the Ford and watched, as they walked the two blocks down the narrow street, the looks of the men. And of the women, too. But the men tended to stop dead. Some of them were wearing bowlers.

Carole-anne could have stopped a beer lorry in the middle of the M1. She didn't even seem to notice the effect she was having. Then Jury noticed her lips were moving. Probably in the silent gutturals of the *r*'s that Mrs. Wasserman had so easily rolled from her throat.

In the marble foyer of the Regency, which was an unpretentious-looking, narrow building with only a brass plaque to bear witness to its name, a name that could be singled out by the select — which certainly didn't include C.S. Racer, but miracles would happen. On its opposite wall outside was one of those little blue plaques which announced that a famous writer had written his classic novel on these premises. (A page of it, perhaps, thought Jury.)

There was, in the foyer, one of those old-fashioned sedan chairs in which now dozed the doorman. But he came to right swiftly when the door whished shut behind them.

Carole-anne whispered, "Bleedin' morgue, it reminds me of."

"Quiet," said Jury, wondering if this could possibly work.

He felt almost remorseful for underestimating Carole-anne's powers of persuasion. He certainly hadn't underestimated the effect she had on the young man in white gloves behind the rosewood desk. At her *Bonjour, monsieur,* and its accompanying smile, the pen with which he'd been filling in something in a daybook stopped in midair.

"Ah, my'ah Anglais, ees not, you know, *perfect.*" Here came a tiny, deprecating shrug, as she handed him her card.

The bow dipped his head nearly to the counter. "Madame." Meltingly he looked into her sapphire eyes. "If I could be of service." Jury might as well have taken his place among the palm fronds and the marble statuary. If any question arose, he was to be her uncle.

"*Mon ami,* I weesh to speak with my old, ah, friend, Georges Dupres. He ees, how you say, manager?"

The young man — at least young, Jury thought, for the high-powered job of assistant manager at the Regency — seemed at a loss. "Madame! Please forgive me, but . . ." And then he flew off into a torrent of French as Carole-anne arranged her décolletage more winningly over the counter and looked sad.

What in the hell the fellow was saying, Jury didn't know, and was afraid this would dish it right here —

378

No. Carole-anne put her hand, in what might have been a forgiving gesture, on his arm. Jury was sure her eyes were silvered over with tears, given the way the assistant manager looked at her. She shook her head, she sighed, she said, turning to Jury, "*Mon oncle.*"

And then she went to sit on a damask dais, removing from her small bag a lacy handkerchief.

Mon oncle went over to her, smiling sweetly, patting her on the shoulder, and saying, "What the hell are you doing?" It was out of earshot — though lord knew the way he stared at the new Baroness Regina de la Notre, the assistant manager might have had far-reaching antennae.

Through her brimming eyes, Carole-anne smiled soulfully up at Jury and said, "Why bother with George-bloody-Dupres? Not with this other one locked up."

She rose, she turned, she waved a sad farewell and, to Jury's amazement, started toward the door.

The assistant manager might have been wearing electric shoes, the way he sprang from behind the desk and grabbed her arm. Then let his hand fall, aware that he might have contaminated a guest of the Regency. "If there is some way *I* can be of assistance, madame?" Oh, the look of hope.

"How kind of you," said the baroness, throatily. And then mumbling, ". . . *il fait un temps . . .*" Carole-anne shook her head, probably wondering how to use up her short supply of French phrases.

"Anything, madame."

As if it were but a sudden inspiration, she snapped her leather-gloved fingers, and drew from her purse the picture of the servant and the dog. Jury didn't think there was much chance of the *assistant's* going back eight years but what the hell?

The man could barely take his eyes from Carole-anne long enough to glance at the picture. He shook his head and said he was sorry, but . . .

"Ah, ees the, how you say, livery of the Regency. Uniform. She was maid? Waitress? *Non?*" Carole-anne flipped the snapshot over. *Amy Lister.*

To Jury's surprise, the penny dropped. It was gratitude more than surprise that registered in the assistant manager's face. He remembered. He even allowed himself a chuckle. "Of course. The Listers." Then he looked like a chicken with its head in the wringer. He'd got the Listers straight, but . . . "It wasn't the maid you were wanting? You're right, that is our livery, but I've never seen the maid. Only the dog, the Alsatian. It was always with the Listers. That's what I remember."

Carole-anne gave him such a lovely look as she shook her glowing, chignoned head, that he started rattling on about the Listers. He stopped rattling when he saw her drop her head in her hand —

For Christ's sake, Jury wanted to shout. He's telling me what I want to know. What are you on about —?

Again, Carole-anne put her smooth little hand on his arm. "Ah, *mon ami* . . ."

She was going to do that stupid phrase to death. He felt like trampling on her tongue. He stood there, instead, her smiling *oncle.*

". . . eet ees the Baron Lister I look for —"

Oh, bloody hell! The silly little twit was so much into her role she didn't even know why she was there anymore.

The manager looked confused, sad, displeased with himself for not being able to produce the Baron Lister. "I'm most dreadfully sorry. Far as I know, there was never a *Baron* Lister. Would Lord Lister do?"

Lord Lister. Address, Carole-anne.

Her smile was small, sad. She raised her gorgeous face to the heavens and said, *"Si."*

Si? Oh, wonderful.

Blushingly, she changed it. *"Oui.* Myself, *mon ami,* I travel so much, I sometimes forget which country I am in." A batting of thick eyelashes went with this.

Jury envisioned the coast of Spain. Ocean. Shoving the Baroness Carole-anne right into it. Inwardly, he laughed at himself. What he really wanted was to see Carole-anne in a bikini. What the hell was she doing now?

She had handed the assistant manager a tiny address book. He was writing in it, sending up furtive looks to those jewel-like eyes. He nearly clicked his heels as he handed it back. "Ma'am!"

Jury felt if he didn't sit down he'd fall down at this breathless leavetaking. How'd she got his name?

"Henri. *Mon ami* . . ."

I'd rather talk to Racer.

". . . *Vous serez toujours dans mon souvenir.*"

Henry swayed and as she called over, flutingly again, to *Oncle Ricardo*, Jury again imagined the Costa del Sol. But Uncle Ricardo, having done nothing at all, merely smiled, and said, together with the baroness, *"Bonjour, mon ami."*

It was all of that thinking of Sunny Spain that had left him sun-mad, he knew. She sat there, gibbering away in the car and jouncing her gorgeously stockinged leg, and poking him in the ribs.

"So how'd I do, then, Super? We got the goods, right?"

"We did, *mon amie.*"

Mrs. Wasserman was peeking through her heavy curtains. Jury wouldn't have been surprised if she'd been watching out ever since they'd left.

Carole-anne scooted from the car and down the stairs to the basement flat, Jury following.

"Bonjour, madame," said Carole-anne, unwinding her sable cape with a bullfighter's expertise and dropping it on a

convenient chair. "'*Ello*, Mrs. W. Lemme get these bleedin' heels off. I could drop where I stand."

Mrs. Wasserman clasped her hands together, looking at her star pupil. "You did well, Carole-anne?"

"Perfectemente. Right, Super?"

"Perfectemente."

Carole-anne, shoes off — and apparently dress coming off, before Jury stopped her — said innocently, "But I thought you had to get this stuff back to the false-face shop." She stopped in the middle of unzipping.

"Later, Carole-anne. Right now I have to get *myself* into Lord Lister's good graces and back to Hampshire."

"You was to take me to din-dins, Super," she said, pouting.

Mrs. Wasserman gave him a look that might have been scathing, but she snatched it away.

"I'll take you to din-dins when I get back. Keep the gear"— Jury was writing on the back of one of his cards — "and tomorrow, love, go to this chap. *Adios, señora, señorita.*"

He could hear the gaggle of voices as he ran up the steps. ". . . a bloody the-*at*-rical person. 'Ere now, Mrs. W. Is he pulling my leg?"

"Never would Mr. Jury do that . . . but he might like to . . . ."

Their mixed laughter could be heard even as Jury got into his car, smiling. It was the first time he'd heard Mrs. Wasserman return to her girlish, giggling youth. *Bless your heart, mon amie*, thought Jury, pulling away from the curb.

ᴨ

Before he went to Woburn Place he called New Scotland Yard and got a run-down on Lord Lister: Aubrey Lister, granted a life peerage in 1970, chairman of the board of one of London's most powerful dailies until he retired ten years ago.

382

And Jury sat at a red light, engine idling, thinking his brain was too as he looked up the road marker on the side of a building.

Fleet Street.

Some part of Carrie's mind had unearthed, like a fox's covert, that scrap of memory. Though she must have no idea why she'd chosen a name that everyone in London connected with the world of newspapers.

Jury put his head on his overlapped hands on the steering wheel while the Mercedes behind him got very impatient.

Twenty-five

he house in Woburn Place looked as if it had remained unchanged through decades of Listers, kept to its original brass fittings, its stained-glass fanlight, newel post, rosewood table in the entrance-room sitting on a Belgian carpet so silky it reflected the dim light. The room's only concession to the present was converted gaslight, frosted tulip lampshades, the fixtures within now electrified.

The maid who admitted Jury was dressed in starched pearl-gray and a lace cap. It was to her he had shown his warrant card — just routine, of course, he'd said. He'd like a word with Lord Lister. The maid had been well trained to register no surprise. Vagrant, Minister, Scotland Yard — whoever appeared on the stoop at Woburn Place would be dealt with calmly. Still, looking up at Jury she had to adjust both her expression and her Victorian cap. "Have you a personal card, sir?" She smiled.

"Sorry. Of course." Jury dropped one of his cards on the salver on the marble table. She nodded. "Shan't be a moment, sir."

Whatever the maid's origins — the fens, the North, Manchester, Brighton — traces of that accent had been overridden by the West End. She had gone into a double-doored room on his left, carefully pulling them shut behind her.

In a moment she reappeared. It was almost a smile of relief she gave him, while telling him that Lord Lister would see him now.

If it was merely a conferred, a life peerage, one would never have known it from the demeanor and bearing of Lord Lister. No matter he was a smallish man, thin and drawn and in his seventies, his confidence spread, like the fan of sunlight coming through the high windows behind him. And he was, as all powerful men would have you think, a simple man.

"How interesting, Superintendent. Haven't a dog's notion why you're here, but it makes a change. Tea?"

He did not wait upon Jury's acquiescence. Lord Lister pressed a button on one side of the marble mantelpiece.

"Thank you. I could use it." He doubted Aubrey Lister was a man who wasted his time over small talk. "It's about this snapshot, sir." Jury took the snap, creased by now, from his pocket and handed it over. "Nothing that's a police matter, maybe. Only, I'm interested."

Lord Lister, who had reseated himself on a sofa covered in watered silk, took out a spectacle case and said, "Not a police matter." He smiled over his spectacles. "Yet here you are, Superintendent."

Jury smiled. "We lead other lives, Lord Lister."

Jury had caught the old man before he'd barely glanced at the picture. His tone was kind, but he said, "Then we should not lead them on police time, should we?" The corners of his mouth twitched.

Jury was glad he was enjoying himself. He did not want to upset this man, living here alone as he did — if one discounted a plethora of servants belowstairs. But he especially did not want to upset him on the errand on which he had come.

"I'm sorry. I do not recognize this picture. Should I?"

"Not necessarily. I was hoping you would." Jury immediately put out his hand for the snap, pretty sure the snapshot would be withdrawn. And that his lordship would look at it more keenly.

"Turn it over," said Jury.

Lord Lister adjusted his spectacles as if that might clear the cobwebs from his mind. " 'Amy Lister.' " He looked up, his glance around the room leaving out Jury, falling on the mantelpiece and a small collection of gold-framed pictures. Then at Jury. "You've found *Carolyn?*"

"Sir?" All Jury could do now was play the innocent.

"My granddaughter, Carolyn. Amy was Carolyn's dog. This is Carolyn's Alsatian. And the woman —" He shrugged. "A servant of some kind. What do you know about Carolyn?"

"I'm not sure I know anything."

Lord Lister tapped the snapshot. "Then how'd you come by this?"

The tea was delivered by the amiable, if starched, maid. The maid poured, asking Jury how much sugar he desired.

"A couple named Brindle found a little girl years ago in a wooded area on Hampstead Heath, dazed. They'd gone there for a picnic. She didn't seem to know how she'd got there, who she was. All she had was a small purse containing a few pence and this picture. And a very bad head wound."

Lord Lister was clearly shocked. "We supposed she'd been abducted. You're suggesting someone tried to kill her?"

"I don't know."

Lister looked again at the snapshot. "I wonder why the person responsible didn't take the picture?"

"It had got between the lining and the purse itself. The Brindles only found it recently." Jury put down his cup. "When was the last time you saw Carolyn?"

His chin rested on the hands overlapped on his ivory-knobbed cane. "When her nursemaid had taken her to the zoo. In Regent's Park." His sharp eyes looked across his cane at Jury. "The nursemaid returned empty-handed."

A rather sardonic attitude to take toward the disappearance of a child.

"You didn't report it to Scotland Yard, and you kept it out of the papers. How —?" At Lord Lister's tight smile, Jury remembered. The "how" would have been quite easy for the old man. He was chairman of the board of one newspaper and influential with others.

"Penny dropped, Superintendent? How do you think I got my peerage? Apparently, the Queen thought I had done the country some service by keeping a series of especially grisly crimes, the plans of certain drug dealers, and so on, out of the newspapers. I have a certain — influence." His smile was thin. "My son, Aubrey junior, was miffed that the title would last only for *my* lifetime. I told him if he wanted a title, he could damned well go out and get his own."

"You thought that spreading Carolyn's disappearance across the paper would work against her being found — so no reward was offered."

Had there been, Flossie and Joe would certainly have turned up with Carrie in tow.

"Of course, that's what I thought. And I did not want to contact police for the same reason. Kidnappers are rather . . . touchy on that point. That was quite clear when the ransom note appeared two days later. The kidnappers weren't especially greedy. They only asked for twenty-five thousand. Which I delivered personally to the Left Luggage place in Waterloo Station tucked into a suitcase full of clothing. And the stub I left in a paperback mystery in a W. H. Smith's. At the end of the stack. I assumed I was being watched all the time."

"But Carolyn wasn't returned."

"No." He pinched the bridge of his nose and shook his head. "Nor was the money ever collected. I immediately hired two very good private detectives. They turned up nothing. Apparently, the kidnappers did not want to take the chance of showing up. Perhaps Carolyn was already dead. Perhaps—" Lord Lister shrugged. "— anything."

"And the maid, or nurse? What was her story?"

"She'd gone to get them both a cold drink. It had taken only a few minutes, but when she returned, Carolyn wasn't there. She grew more and more afraid as she searched. Carolyn never wandered off, and the servant felt sure she'd been abducted. Straightaway, she came back to the house."

Jury had taken out his notebook, and Lord Lister said, "Oh, don't bother. The nurse is dead. She can't help. She was fired on the spot, of course."

"Did Carolyn's parents go along with your plans?"

"Parent. Carolyn was illegitimate. The father is dead. My daughter Ada is dead, too. Died when Carolyn was three or four. I thought she should have a name."

"It does help one's sense of identity."

Lister looked at Jury sharply. He had not touched his tea. Still with his hands on the cane, he turned his eyes toward the high window, and spoke like a man from whom most emotion had been wrung. "They're all gone, the children. Didn't find the house too — salubrious. Ruth and Aubrey. My sister Miriam finally left, too."

"Gone where, Lord Lister?"

"They do not keep in touch. The last I heard from Ruth, she was —" His glance traveled around the room, came to rest on the pattern in the Oriental carpet. "India, I think. Miriam. I should like to see Miriam again." He looked up, thoughtfully. "We were close, though she was some fifteen years younger."

"Have you pictures of them?" Jury nodded toward the mantelpiece.

He shrugged. "Help yourself. Those are very old."

Old and faded and rather fuzzy. There was one who certainly looked like Carrie. "Her mother?"

"Ada. Yes." Lord Lister seemed disinclined to deal in the past. He looked at Jury. "You think I was a tyrant, that I drove them away?" He sighed. "My dear Mr. Jury, they are merely waiting for me to die." The thin lips pursed. "Money, Superintendent, money."

"People like that usually keep very much in touch. So you'll know where to send it."

Lord Lister actually laughed. "Oh, I like that. No. They know they're going to get it. What's eating at them is that Carolyn is getting the lion's share."

That surprised Jury. "You were fond of her."

The statement seemed to have to pass, like a memo to the board, and come back with stamps of approval. Lord Lister took a long time considering. "Yes. I was fond of her. You see, I felt a bit like Lear. Not that I would hold a mirror to her lips to see if she lived still." His eyes, when they looked at Jury, were like polished silver. They were glazed with tears. "But Carolyn, unlike the others, never *wanted* anything from me. Aubrey and Ruth are selfish and shallow and opportunistic. Actually, Carolyn took after me. And Miriam, perhaps. Resolute. Undemonstrative. Stoic, really. Her mother was like that." He leaned toward Jury, as if he felt it were important the superintendent understand: "*That* is simply something I was never used to. Greed was the major component in the makeup of the other children."

"May I ask how much money is involved?"

"You may. For Carolyn, a million."

Jury stared.

"For the others, a hundred thousand apiece. If Carolyn *is* dead . . ." He looked away. "Then her part of the inheritance would go to them. Evenly divided. But there must be proof of actual death. If she is declared simply legally dead, her inheritance will go to several charities."

So the others would be waiting not only for the death of the old man, but the death of Carolyn Lister. "I don't imagine that made Carolyn overly popular with your son and daughter. And your sister."

A glimmer of a smile. "Not precisely."

"But Carolyn disappeared over seven years ago. Wouldn't that suggest she's dead?"

"Yes. Except that now you've turned up with that picture, haven't you? The young girl who had it *could* be Carolyn. The tale you relate of this family finding her would fit the facts."

"You have other pictures — of the family?"

Lord Lister shook his head. "Of my wife, quite a few. And the children when they were very young." He looked toward the ceiling. "An album, perhaps, somewhere in the attic. I do not go into attics, Superintendent. Like the mind, they tend to be dark and filled with cobwebs. I am not a sentimental man." He paused. "Is the girl you refer to happy?"

Jury thought for a moment. "It's hard to say. But I doubt one could be very happy who has no memory of her childhood."

"Ah. Is she well provided for?"

"Yes."

"Good." He shrugged. "Unfortunately, there is no proof. . . ." He looked at Jury, then around at the luxury of velvet draperies, Georgian furniture, less resplendent now in sunlight grown sluggish. He smiled that thin smile — not so much insincere as one learned from years of dealing in confrontation. "That's up to you, Superintendent."

"She wears a ring, a small amethyst. That mean anything to you?"

Lord Lister leaned his chin on his hands and thought. "Am-

390

ethyst. I am not positive, but I believe her mother might have given Carolyn one. A birthstone. Yes, that would serve as proof, I'd say."

Proof? "That she's alive?"

"Or dead."

Jury felt a sudden chill. "And if this girl is Carolyn. And if, by some chance, something should happen to her —"

Lord Lister raised his eyebrows. "Unlikely. She'd be quite young now."

"She was quite young when she was left for dead on the Heath," said Jury bitterly.

The old man said nothing.

Jury went on. "Why wouldn't part of that fortune go to the person who's been taking care of her — not the Brindles. I mean the one she now lives with?"

"I suppose it could." Lord Lister seemed puzzled.

Jury waited for the questions. *Who is taking care of her? Where?* . . . But there were no questions. Jury put away his notebook and thanked Lord Lister for his time.

With the help of his cane, the old man rose. "Of time, I have aplenty, Mr. Jury."

Jury smiled. "Then if she were to come here, perhaps your memory would bestir itself. Perhaps hers would. I imagine, living alone as you do, you'd be happy to have her back."

"You don't understand, Superintendent. I do not like attics. I do not want the past back. I do not want Carolyn."

After the pleasant maid saw him out, Jury stood for a few seconds on the stone step. All for nothing. He had done nothing to help Carrie Fleet, who, in a sense, had no past. Million quid or no, she had been truly swindled. He himself could have gone to the attic, taken whatever mementoes he could find, perhaps helped her piece it all together.

391

But how do you do that when the end of it is that no one wants you back?

He went down the steps and saw, as he turned, a velvet drape drop back in place.

Shutting it all out.

PART 5

Now it is Night—
in Nest and Kennel—

Twenty-six

elrose — now "on" as Earl of Caverness — stared up at the picture of Grimsdale, in the forefront with a few of the favored staghounds. In the background was a stag at bay about to be taken. And beneath this, and above the mantelpiece, was a hunting horn.

Melrose had a great deal of difficulty in looking at it, much less with admiration. But a job, he supposed, was a job.

"Absolutely nothing like it," said Sebastian Grimsdale, standing beside Melrose Plant in the Lodge's trophy room. Grimsdale sighed with pleasure. "Prince of Wales killed a stag by sweeping the knife upward. Instead of merely slitting the throat."

"That is certainly a lesson in the art of venery, Mr. Grimsdale. It must have been a wonderful sight."

Grimsdale started, slapped his hand on his thigh, and laughed. "Well, I'm not quite *that* old, sir." He grew more serious, as if almost reluctant to say, "Even if I'd been there, I wouldn't have got near the stag. Too dangerous, you see."

"Oh. Sounds a bit like a bullfight to me."

"Good God, Lord Ardry. That's not *sport.*"

Melrose lit a cigar, offered one to Grimsdale, who was so lost in the picture that he merely shook his head absently. "Never done any stag-hunting, then?" Melrose shook his head. "Nothing like it," he said again. "I remember one sprang up from the heather under the very nose of my horse. Ah, well . . ."

There was a pause for nostalgic reflection. "Season's over in Exmoor now for stag-hunting. But if you're here again in the spring—"

"I rather doubt it," said Melrose, trying on a smile. Looking at the stag at bay, the smile didn't quite fit.

Grimsdale noticed the weak reflection of a smile. "Oh, oh. You've been taken in by all that old Landseerian rubbish, *Monarch of the Glen*—sentimental nonsense. They're a nasty sort of beast, the stag. Do you know, one would push another out to take his place, if he was being hunted down."

"Really."

"Absolutely." Grimsdale seemed determined to convince him that the stag was not a family man. "Push out another and lie right down in its place in the heather. Or mingle with hinds. No scruples."

"None."

"None," repeated Grimsdale in a satisfied way. "Too bad you've not hunted stag. Hills, huge distances, awful streams, bad weather—"

"Sounds inviting."

"Well! If the Devon-Somerset pack's out, at least you can hunt with the Buckland. New Forest. Fallow deer, there. Nothing to compare with the red." Grimsdale checked his watch as if the hunt might begin at any time. "Nearly ten. Donaldson will be doing his rounds. Trying to start my own pack of staghounds. Those two staghounds you saw, handsome brutes, drafted those from one of the best foxhound kennels—"

"You've got your own pack of foxhounds. I should think that would keep you busy enough, Mr. Grimsdale."

Whatever hint of disapproval there was in Melrose's tone was lost on Sebastian Grimsdale, who simply said there could never be enough hunting.

Melrose could see that. He was surrounded by the efforts of more than one taxidermist — he doubted *one* taxidermist would have had the time, even if he'd had the interest in working in so many different media: gray fox, pheasant, woodcock, badger — a few of the smaller displays. All under glass. While Grimsdale was lost in wonder at the larger of the mounted heads of stag and buck, Melrose picked up one of the glass cases, looked at the blue-tipped wings. Beautiful bird.

Grimsdale turned. "Ah, I see you like birds, Lord Ardry." The tone suggested that Lord Ardry *must* have a passion for some sort of gunplay.

Alive, yes.

"Shoveler drake, that is. Hardly ever see one in these parts. It's when the weather gets so bad up country they want a warmer climate." Grimsdale gazed at the drake with satisfaction, rubbing his pipestem against his cheek.

"This one found it, I guess."

The sarcasm fell wide. Grimsdale picked another bird, mounted on a a limb, from the mantelpiece. "Teal. Dozen of them took off from the pond —"

"Pond? I didn't see one."

"Round back." Grimsdale laughed. "Not supposed to see it, Lord Ardry. Just luck it was there, surrounded by trees, bracken, rushes. Absolutely perfect. I keep the mallard there. That draws the others."

Melrose was eyeing the shoveler drake, sorry for it, but feeling he'd warmed up Grimsdale enough, both with brandy and talk, to get round to the real subject.

397

"Hunting and shooting's not my line —"

"Worse luck for you, sir." Grimsdale laughed.

"But doesn't the forestry commission slap a ban on shooting wildfowl if they're *driven* by weather to the south?" He knew he shouldn't have said it; he was usually more controlled. When he looked at this rosy-cheeked, iron-haired, smug Master of Foxhounds and Harriers, he couldn't help himself. The look on Grimsdale's face, as if he'd lost an old poaching-partner, told Melrose he'd have to make up the points if he wanted information.

"That's quite a stag there, Mr. Grimsdale." Melrose raised his eyes to the twelve-pointer, the one Grimsdale himself had been admiring. "Where'd you get that one?"

"Auchnacraig. That's in Scotland."

"I've heard of it," said Melrose, without the trace of a smile. Nice to get the geography lesson along with how to shoot just about anything that walked or flew. But Grimsdale was bathing so much in his own glow, he didn't notice.

"Ah yes. Twenty-one stone. Nearly got a silver on that one."

Melrose assumed he meant a medal. He smiled bleakly. "Wonderful. Where do you hunt the stag around these parts, Mr. Grimsdale?"

"Exmoor. For your red deer, that's the place. For buck, the New Forest. Donaldson's one of the best harborers there is. He's the one out at first light to find a warrantable stag. Can't get on without a shrewd harborer."

"Right. Just as the superintendent can't go without his sergeant."

For some reason, Grimsdale thought this rather rich and slapped his arm around Melrose's shoulders. Given the multiple brandies he'd had that evening, the ruddy glow of his complexion could have competed with the rather remarkable sunset they'd seen a few hours before.

"What did you think of Sally MacBride?" asked Melrose, suddenly.

The arm dropped just as suddenly away. "The MacBride woman?" The irritation gave way to feigned remorse. "Incredible thing, the way she died." He shook his head, drank his brandy, gazed up at a broad beam of antlers, and repeated it. He might have been talking about the stag.

Melrose was sick of this dismissal of the death of the woman. "What do you make of the dogs and the cat?"

"Cat? Dogs?" he said, as if he'd never heard of anything that didn't run with a pack. "Oh, you mean, the Quick woman's dog. And the others? Well, what about it?" He answered his own question about Gerald Jenks's dog. "Good riddance. Tore up my damned rosebushes." The glow deepened to the ruddier flush of anger.

"How well did you know them — Una Quick and Sally MacBride, I mean?"

Grimsdale was still looking at the stag, smiling. What was the life of the odd villager or two compared with twelve points and twenty stone? Then he refilled his glass and offered Melrose another. Melrose shook his head, wondering if the man were stalling, or merely dreaming of Auchnacraig and Exmoor. If dreaming, he seemed to waken suddenly to the distinct oddity of Lord Ardry's questions.

"I don't understand. I knew Miss Quick — she was postmistress, after all, everyone knew her. And Mrs. MacBride. I go to the Deer Leap, don't I? Only pub in the village, unfortunately." He looked about at his own superior accommodations smugly. "They'd — he'd do better to fix it up a bit. But of course, *she* was such a layabout —"

Grimsdale stopped, coughed. Whether he saw the unintended pun, or simply thought it rude to speak ill of the dead, Melrose didn't know. But he did know the conversation would stalk all over hunt country if Melrose didn't get his eye off that hare Grimsdale was now hefting in his hand. "What would you say to these women having been murdered, Mr. Grimsdale?"

The stuffed hare was replaced with a thud. "*What?*" Grimsdale looked slightly wild and then he laughed. It was a hearty laugh. "*Murdered?* Murder in Ashdown Dean?"

"It could,"said Melrose mildly, "happen anywhere."

"Not here," said Grimsdale, his eye now caught by a gray fox.

"Why do you think Scotland Yard is here, then? To investigate a case of cardiac arrest?"

"But that's what it was, man! If the damned fool woman didn't know enough not to go out in a storm up to that call box . . ." He shrugged.

"Her telephone wasn't working, apparently. Was yours?"

"Mine? Damned if I know. I wasn't making any calls around that time."

"What time?"

Grimsdale stopped his inspection of the hare, looked sharply at Melrose, and said smugly, "You're asking questions like police, sir. But you can't catch me out with that old ruse. *Everyone* heard about Una Quick falling out of that call box close on ten. After all, one of my guests was the person she fell across. Praed, her name is. But you know her. Has some monster of a cat that's clawed up half the curtains in her room. See she pays for 'em, there'll be no mistake. Have to get a decorator in. Or get Amanda Crowley to sew a new batch."

He stood there, apparently dreaming away about how he could stick Polly for the price of the curtains, while getting Amanda to volunteer her talents as a seamstress.

Melrose lit up another cigar, trying to think how best to lie to get at the truth. "Ridiculous, of course, but you're probably aware there's been some talk in Ashdown about you and Mrs. MacBride."

Grimsdale's face seemed to take on all the hues of the fire in the grate. Eyes electric blue and sparking, cheeks like licks of flame, iron hair like volcanic ash. *"That is a lie!* What in God's name would I be doing with the likes of that common . . . Anyway, Amanda and I —" He stopped short on that one, and quickly asked, "Where'd you hear it?"

"Here and there. She was known to take that little river walk at night that ends up, I suppose, at your pond. With the tame mallard." Melrose smiled briefly.

Sebastian Grimsdale collapsed in a chair, and Melrose thought some confession was forthcoming. Then he sat up. "If you must know, there's been talk about the MacBride woman and my kennel master. Thought Donaldson was smarter than that. I'd see a light in the stable house. Wondered what he'd be doing up at that hour. I let him live in that place just back of the kennels."

Having reached his own solution to his satisfaction, Grimsdale sat back and lit up a cigar, shaking and shaking his head. "There it is, then. Fancy."

"I imagine the superintendent might want to have a talk with him, then."

"Can't imagine *why*. Donaldson's from Scotland. Got nothing to do with these people. He's just here for the season."

Melrose laughed, "Well, one can get up to any number of things waiting —"

He was interrupted by one of the most terrible rackets he'd ever heard.

"My God! *What's that?"* Grimsdale shot out of his chair and looked wildly at Melrose. "Sounds like hounds rioting."

It did indeed. Before Melrose could put down his glass and chuck his cigar into the fireplace, Grimsdale had rushed from the trophy room through the french windows and out into the court.

Melrose followed in the direction of the kennels and stableyard, where a soupy fog closed around him. In the midst of the chorus of foxhounds came the eerie sound of the deep baying of Grimsdale's staghounds.

And as Melrose tried to make his way through the fog, he thought that mixed with all of this riot was the sound of a scream that no hound would make.

The handsome Donaldson was handsome no longer. He lay inside the kennel, ravaged by the staghounds, one of which lay beside him. In the light of Grimsdale's torch, Melrose saw the other hound stagger and fall, its light markings now blood-smeared.

Then he heard feet running across the courtyard. Wiggins. Polly.

Grimsdale, having stood frozen, looking down at the bloody kennel floor, suddenly shouted, *"Get Fleming!"*

And that, thought Melrose, turning to stop Polly in her tracks, pretty well spoke the man's obsession. Call for the vet, not the physician. Though Farnsworth couldn't have done Donaldson any good now, neither could Fleming help the staghounds.

Wiggins took the torch from Grimsdale's hand as Melrose practically had to wrestle with Polly to keep her away. "Nothing for you to see, old girl —"

"Oh, shut up." She broke from his grasp, peered through the fog along the tracery of torchlight, and was back in an instant. "For once, you're right." Polly buried her head against his shoulder.

Across her dark head, Melrose squinted. A form seemed to emerge from the mist at the other end of the stableyard. It seemed to undulate as it came toward them, became a ghostly blob, finally turned into a recognizable form. Carrie Fleet.

A very dirty-looking Carrie Fleet.

402

When Grimsdale saw her, he stared for a few seconds and then slowly raised the rifle.

Melrose disengaged himself from Polly, but Wiggins, fortunately, was quicker. With a judolike kick, he knocked Grimsdale's rifle arm upward and the shot went wide, broke glass somewhere — possibly one of the stable house windows.

Calmly, Wiggins took the gun. "I think that'll be enough, sir. I really think that'll be quite enough."

Carrie Fleet just stood there, motionless.

Grimsdale screamed. *"You devil! Always trouble —"*

Melrose clamped his hand around Grimsdale's arm. If anyone were possessed, he thought, it was Grimsdale.

"What're you doing here, Carrie?" whispered Polly.

Carrie Fleet jerked her thumb over her shoulder toward the edge of the New Forest. "Unstopping earths. I heard hounds." She walked over to the kennels and peered in at the body of Donaldson and the dead hounds.

She shook her head and shook it. Then she looked one by one into the several cages housing the beagles.

Then she turned and walked back into the fog that closed round her like a glove.

No one tried to stop her. The night was deathly quiet.

"There's no way of knowing for sure until I do an autopsy —"

Grimsdale, a large balloon-glass of brandy in hands that might have been palsied with all of their shaking, said, "They'd never have turned on Donaldson. Never."

"We seem to have evidence to the contrary," said Melrose coldly.

Wiggins, in the absence of Jury, wanted to get down to business. "Dr. Fleming — ?"

"I was about to say. It could be one of several drugs, administered anytime from minutes to days or even weeks before. Something like fentanyl. But that's not easy to come by — unless you're a doctor or a vet. Then there's benzodiazafine. Valium. Easy enough to get hold of." Fleming shrugged. "I'd have to do an autopsy."

Wiggins made a note of that and said, with a frown, "That would mean that *whoever* went into that kennel would have been torn apart."

"Yes," said Fleming.

"But there were only two people who did," said Melrose. "And Mr. Grimsdale, here, wouldn't have gone into the kennel for any particular reason, not until tomorrow."

Polly Praed, sitting in the trophy room in her old brown wrapper, chewed at her lip. "And that's the third one. The murderer could have been anywhere when it happened. What a bloody awful way to kill a man."

Melrose's thoughts were on Polly Praed's head on his shoulder when she added, turning those amethyst eyes on Wiggins. "But aren't you going to get Superintendent Jury back here at the double?"

Twenty-seven

"**A**nd where do you think *you're* going?" asked Polly Praed the next morning. She had just walked into the Lodge's breakfast room to see Melrose finishing a sumptuous — by Gun Lodge standards — breakfast. The piece of toast she plucked from the toast rack was actually warm. So was the piece of bacon she plucked from his plate. "It's only just gone nine."

Then, apparently having lost interest in Melrose's designs, she looked around the room. "I should have thought he'd be here by now."

He meaning Jury. Melrose sighed. "According to Wiggins, the superintendent had rather a full schedule yesterday. But he might come walking in at any minute, so I suggest you get dressed. Not that the robe is unbecoming; I'm sure Sherlock Holmes would have loved it. Sorry I ate my breakfast," he added, seeing her staring at his plate. "But I imagine the Grimsdale cook, unobstructed by Grimsdale, will provide you with one."

"Where is the awful man?"

"In the trophy room, last I saw. With Pasco and Detective Inspector Russell. Grimsdale does not look at all well."

"He shouldn't. He should look like death. He was going to *kill* that child. If it hadn't been for Sergeant Wiggins ... Where *are* you going?"

"To 'La Notre.'"

"At this hour? Don't baronesses and so forth sleep until noon?"

"I have no idea. But she might rise to see the Earl of Caverness."

"Impostor," said Polly, chewing the last piece of toast.

꠸

To see her, however, one ran the gamut.

Melrose's Silver Ghost probably hastened the running of it, he guessed. A little maid in a cockeyed cap stared at it and then at him and the card he handed her, uncertain as to which of the three was the most impressive.

"I don't mean to bother the Baroness Regina at this rather ungodly hour —" Melrose smiled. "I thought perhaps I could see —"

"Oh, I'm sure it's no bother, Your Grace —"

He laughed. "I haven't reached those heady heights. Only an earl."

"Hullo," said a voice from the shadows of the foyer. "Gillian Kendall." Gillian put out her hand. "Regina's secretary."

"Miss Kendall." She had been sorting the post on a silver plate, rather tarnished. "Sorry to be dropping by so early." If nearly ten could be so considered.

She replaced the post and said, "That business last night at the Lodge. That was absolutely dreadful...."

"Carrie told you?"

Gillian Kendall looked puzzled. "Carrie? No. What did she have to do with it?" Then she smiled. "Though she does have a way of turning up when there's an animal crisis."

406

It was Melrose who was puzzled now. "I'd call it more of a Carrie crisis. She didn't tell you —?"

Before he could finish the statement, a vision, if not precisely of loveliness, but a vision nonetheless, came sweeping down the staircase. "How very kind of you to call, Lord Ardry. Coffee in the salon, Gillian?"

"Yes, of course. But what about Carrie?"

"Carrie? Carrie?" said the Baroness, attempting to upsweep her hair and hold it with the hairpins in her mouth. The mouth had been rather quickly painted; lipstick bleeding into the tiny pursed lines around it. Regina de la Notre apparently had no compunction about completing her toilette in public. "Carrie is always in trouble." She sighed and stopped with her hair-pinning. "*Now* what's she done? And to a peer of the realm, dear God."

"It's more what's been done to Carrie."

"Well, dear God! Why are we all standing here?" She said it as if chairs should materialize out of the very air, and looked sharply at Gillian, as if her magic act were rotten.

Gillian opened the doors into the salon and Regina swept in. Her dressing gown was definitely the sweeping sort, blue brocade and ivory insets and a long train.

Having arranged herself on a chaise longue and accepted a light for her cigarette, she was ready for the day's disasters. Gillian still stood. "Now, what is all this?"

"Grimsdale nearly killed her last night. If it hadn't been for Sergeant Wiggins, I doubt she'd be alive — I can't imagine her not telling you."

Both of them looked horrified, Regina enough that she seemed pulled from her chaise by invisible wires. She started pacing. "Blast and damn that man." She whirled with quite an exquisite movement of pulling the train of brocade with her hand. "I trust the police have got him."

"Questioned him, yes. Got him —?" Melrose shrugged.

"Assault with a deadly weapon — Gillian, will you please not stand there like a stick, dammit. Coffee!"

"Don't you think Carrie takes precedence over coffee?" Gillian said, icily.

Fortunately the little maid was back, given instructions, and Gillian went out through the french doors. Despite the greater concerns of the morning, Melrose could not help but be fascinated by the *trompe l'oeil* murals.

When the Baroness had stopped her pacing, and restored herself to the chaise and another cigarette, Melrose told her what had happened.

"*Donaldson?* Killed by those beasts of Grimsdale's?" She shuddered. Then she turned to Melrose. "I've been visited by a Scotland Yard superintendent. What on earth is your particular interest in all of this?" She plucked up his card from the table beside the chaise. "Earl of Caverness."

Melrose smiled. "More or less."

"I beg your pardon?"

"My name is really Melrose Plant."

"Mine's Gigi Scroop. From Liverpool. I am actually a *real* baroness, not that it gets me much but lording it over the village. Why do you pass yourself off as an earl, then?"

"It's not quite that. I simply gave up my titles."

A well-plucked eyebrow shot up. "I'll be damned. *Gave* them up? Well, to each his own tastes. Now, Grimsdale is done for, I hope. That should get him five to ten, wouldn't you say?"

"Possibly —"

Gillian was back. "She's with her menagerie. Not talking. It doesn't surprise me. Bingo — that's her dog — is missing."

"Then I can imagine she'd be worried."

He stood up. "Mind if I have a word with her?"

"Of course you may," Regina swept her arm toward the french door. "It's her sanctuary. Displaced-animal thing. I

408

don't mind, if that's what keeps her happy. I only wish she'd get rid of the damned rooster. I'm not Judas."

"No coffee, Mr. Plant?" asked Gillian.

"Later, thank you."

As he started for the door, she said. "You're a friend of the superintendent?"

Melrose turned. "Yes."

She colored slightly. "You wouldn't know when —"

"He's coming back?" He smiled wearily. "Sometime today." Certainly, she was a good-looking woman.

Not that that would get *him* anywhere.

ꭥ

She was taking a black cat out of a makeshift cage when he stood at the door to the little house. Or "Sanctuary," he supposed, looking up at the rough-cut sign above the door.

Given the cat, an elderly Labrador, two badgers, a rooster, and what he could have sworn was a pony that had peered at him out of the trees, Melrose had to admit that Carrie Fleet didn't play favorites. It didn't even have to walk on all fours, apparently, given the rooster clawing at the dirt floor with its bandaged leg.

None of the animals seemed in terribly good repair — the Labrador looked as if it had been hit by a lorry. It lay quietly in a wooden box with slats, eyes blinking, breathing slowly.

"Oh. Hullo," said Carrie, in the act of putting a much-abused stuffed mouse at the other end of the room. Hut would have been an apter description than "Sanctuary."

"Hello, there." He waited, with a warm smile, supposing her own greeting, not awfully friendly, but certainly not cold, to be the forerunner to a lengthy conversation about animal welfare.

It wasn't. She had squatted down to give the cat a small push, apparently trying to work up interest in the mouse.

409

There was something wrong with one of its hind legs, and it seemed resistant. "Go on, then," said Carrie, giving it another little push.

"Well. I suppose it needs a bit of exercise, that it?"

She nodded.

It was as if the events of last night hadn't happened. She just crouched there, running her long silvery hair behind her ear, watching the cat. Eventually, it got interested and made its clever play for the mouse.

She got up then, looking relieved.

"You have a way with animals, certainly. . . ." And then he felt an absolute fool as she looked at him with those milky-blue eyes almost devoid of expression.

"If you call not hitting them with cars and sticks."

Almost a whole sentence. He wondered what it would take to get a smile out of her.

"Generally, of course, I don't bother about the drover and his sheep. Just plow the car right through them." Melrose's own smile was brilliant.

It went unanswered.

He coughed. "Look, couldn't I talk with you for a minute?"

"You are." She opened the cage where the dog lay, ran her hand down its back, not so much petting it, but more in the manner of a doctor whose fingers can feel what the eye can't see nor the ear hear.

Damn. Melrose would have hated to report to Jury he couldn't get the girl to talk. "I'm a friend of the superintendent —"

That should get a reaction. And the usual question.

"Is he coming back?" There was a hesitancy, though, as if asking it gave something away.

"Of course. Today, I'm sure."

"Then maybe he can find Bingo."

"Bingo — oh. Your dog. I'm dreadfully sorry he's missing."

410

She came to the door of the dark little hut, blinking in the morning light. "At least you didn't say, 'He'll turn up.' "

Had Melrose's long-standing habit of refusing cheap condolences actually done him some good? "Don't you think he will?"

Carrie squinted off toward the horizon and was silent, as if her eye scanned the hill for some sign of Bingo. She was perfectly still, fingering a narrow gold chain around her neck.

There was a bench there and Melrose sat down. "Would you mind sitting?"

She shrugged. Standing, sitting — little difference.

"Sebastian Grimsdale's in a good deal of trouble about last night. I can't imagine a man being so obsessed —" There had been very few times in his life when Melrose blushed. This was one.

But all he caught was a flicker of a smile. "He's awful. With him, it's either a huntable buck or trash." She leaned over, her elbows resting on her knees.

"I had rather a long lecture on the intricacies of stag-hunting."

" 'Nasty beasts,' he calls them. Probably didn't say anything about what deer do to escape. Like jump over cliffs. Try to swim out to sea —"

If Melrose thought he'd got a long lecture from Grimsdale, it was nothing to what he was getting from Carrie Fleet. Silent on other matters, she was extremely voluble on the subject of animals. It ended, the list of deer-hunting atrocities, with the story of a buck that had fallen under a van and got pulled out by its antlers and its throat slashed in full view of the villagers.

"And he bags foxes," she went on, staring straight ahead.

He was taken with her magnificent profile. Who had been this girl's forebears?

". . . see the one there?"

Melrose shook his head to clear it.

411

"I'm sorry. The what?"

"Fox. He keeps it in a kennel. He'll let it go and set hounds on it. That's what he does, and it's against the rules. I've read the rules."

Melrose could believe she'd *written* them.

"What he does is, if a fox goes to ground and he can't get a badger or terrier to get it out, he does it with tools and has a bag. That's how he got the one he has now." Carrie looked at Melrose, her pale blue eyes like glistening ice. "When a fox goes to ground and finds a rabbit hole or something, that's supposed to be sanctuary." Suddenly, she got up. "I've got to look for Bingo."

"Carrie, just a second. Pasco will be round, of course. You'll be asked to press charges." She seemed not to comprehend. "You know. Against Grimsdale."

"Why? Because he almost shot me?" She shrugged, still scanning the horizon. "He'd have missed, anyway."

Not at that range. "Are you saying you're not *going* to? It was assault with a deadly weapon."

"Someone killed his dogs. I guess I'd get pretty upset too."

Melrose couldn't believe it. "But you *loathe* the man!"

Her face was again without expression. "He's not warrantable. He's trash." She started to walk off and turned again. "When Mr. Jury comes back . . ."

The sentence hovered there, unfinished.

ӿ

Jury was, at that moment, sitting in his flat, smoking, turning over pages of reports he had accumulated from various branches of New Scotland Yard. They told him next to nothing. Brindle had been nicked once for extortion that hardly seemed worth the trouble. Probably he had tried it on several times, maybe got away with it, maybe not. It seemed to be the way he spent his leisure time when he wasn't watching the telly and drinking.

412

As for the Lister family, nil. What the old man had told him was confirmed by the odd newspaper report — about the Listers, not about Carrie Fleet. Or Carolyn, assuming they were one and the same. They had to be — there wasn't a break in the chain of events that had led up to that accidental meeting with Regina —

Jury shook another cigarette out of the packet that lay on the arm of the chair. A family far flung, the Listers. Son, daughter, a couple of cousins. And a sister. He had mentioned a sister near his own age.

The match burnt Jury's finger as he thought about Gigi Scroop from Liverpool. He took Brindle's letter out again. ". . . well, Floss and me thought, having the care of her all them —" And the *them* crossed out, *these* printed in above it. Extortionists have to be careful of their grammar; Jury couldn't help but smiling over this. "— years, that this ought to call for just a bit more, don't you think, Baroness?" Probably the title had been suggested by Flossie. Add a touch of class, even though she'd already forgotten what the class was.

Jury dropped the letter atop the other papers and frowned. If Una Quick had taken the picture, she might have had blackmail in mind. But how could she put this particular two and two together? "Amy Lister" would have, in Una's mind, no association with Carrie Fleet.

But in somebody else's mind?

Someone in Ashdown Dean was smart enough to put Carrie Fleet into that picture and see there was money in it —

He was shaken from this brown study by a knock at the door.

Carole-anne stood there, dressed again as only Carole-anne could, meaning she looked undressed. Skintight leathers she was wearing today and a parrot green T-shirt. And behind her, clutching her black handbag to her black bosom, Mrs. Wasserman, all smiles.

Carole-anne draped herself in Jury's doorway, all smiles

413

herself. "Took your gear back, Super. I mean, can you see me in sable?" From her ears dripped long, bluish-green bits of glass, like tears. "Mrs W. and me" — she nodded at Mrs. W., behind her — "we're going down the pub. *Come* on, then."

Jury stared, blinked, stared like a man who'd just had the bandages taken from his eyes. "Mrs. *Wasserman?*"

"It's more fun you need to have, Superintendent. We were just saying that maybe we could get you out."

Carole-anne smiled her syrupy little smile and winked slowly. "Don't be such an old stick, Super. Down the Angel for an hour and you'll look near human."

"Down the Angel for an hour and you'll have to carry me back. I've got to —"

Carole-anne rolled her heavenly eyes toward heaven. "Oh, God. You've *always* got to." She was pulling on his sleeve. "We need an escort, right, Mrs. W.?"

"Absolutely, Mr. Jury. You would not want unattended women going to the pub." She slid a glance toward Carole-anne and winked at Jury.

"See. Outvoted." Carole-anne lounged and chewed her gum.

Jury laughed. "Half an hour."

"Oh, hell, how wonderful. *Vous serez toujours dans mon souvenir.*"

Mrs. Wasserman was clicking the clasp on her purse open and shut, nervously. "This one, she has an ear, a real *ear* for languages. I tell her if she studied, the Common Market would hire her as a translator."

Carole-anne plucked at her teardrop earrings. "Just what I always wanted."

Twenty-eight

The note was delivered on the silver salver, along with the rest of the post.

Carrie, sitting at the luncheon table, had been staring blindly at her salad, thinking about Bingo. She hadn't seen him since last night, when she'd been out unstopping earths.

"He'll turn up, Carrie," said Gillian, but without much conviction in her tone.

"Like the others?" Her face, her tone were void of expression.

Gillian handed the Baroness the post, and said, "Animals *do* wander off, Carrie —"

"How would you know?" There was no inflection, no bitterness in the tone; it seemed only a mild question.

It was true; neither Gillian nor Regina had shown interest in the sanctuary: the infrequent visits they made to it were born of curiosity, nothing more.

The Baroness, at least, had the sense not to offer cheap comfort. Or perhaps she was simply more interested in her letters. As she smoked and drank her coffee, Gillian read two of them to Regina. Then she frowned and handed Carrie a small envelope. "It's for you."

Carrie, who never got any letters, was as surprised as were Gillian and Regina. It had been posted in Selby. Carrie wondered who in Selby would be writing to her — Neahle, perhaps? Maxine might have broken down and taken her on market day. The scrawl was childish, large loops of letters. But why would Neahle —?

"Aren't you going to open it, for heaven's sake? It might be some news."

Regina sounded really concerned.

Bingo. It was not a word; it was a small picture of a bingo board. The entire note consisted of pictures. Cut from a book or magazine, more likely a child's playbook, was one of those maze-puzzles. Then — and here Carrie's iron control nearly broke — a snapshot of the Rumford Laboratory. Taken at night. Floodlit on that empty field, it looked all the more like a prison.

That was all. Carrie stared past Gillian, who looked at her anxiously, as Regina asked, "Well, what *is* it?"

Carrie was about to say something and then stopped. For she knew, she knew with the swiftness of Limerick taking to the air, and with the surety of a lock clicking closed on a cage, that whatever this was, it wasn't some silly game Neahle was playing. That whoever had done it, with the exception of the address, was being incredibly careful not to give away the sender's identity. It was a warning. Or a direction . . . ?

Regina had just jogged her arm impatiently. "Carrie?"

Carrie shrugged and said calmly, "Oh, it's just some silly pictures Neahle sent me."

"Neahle? Good grief, I didn't even know she could write."

Carrie had pocketed the envelope and paper. "Maybe she

416

got Maxine to do it. Maybe just to cheer me up. May I be excused?"

"I don't know why you bother to ask. I'd have to chain you to a chair to keep you from doing what you want to."

"I suppose so," said Carrie, pushing back her chair.

Not until she was out in the sanctuary did she take the paper out again. Almost absently, she fed the animals — misfeeding the Labrador, who let out a whine. No wonder, she thought. She'd given him chickenfeed. *Keep your head,* she told herself. *Keep your head or Bingo's going to die.* She let Blackstone out and gave him his food and the mouse. Her jobs done, she sat down to study the threat.

Through the opening of the old folly she looked at the maze. Why? Why would someone want her to go into the maze? She knew every inch of it. Carrie looked back at the picture. What she thought had been meant as the "La Notre" maze was not that — this one was square, the sort of thing scientists run rats and mice through with some kind of reward at the end.

So it was merely another pointer to the lab. And when she had been there those weeks ago, the demonstrators, several of them, had been taking pictures by torchlight.

All right. Carrie sat on her stool, perfectly still. Someone either had or was going to take Bingo to the lab.

The only person she knew of who had access to it was Paul Fleming. She frowned. She didn't like him much, really, because of his work, but what on earth would he want with Bingo? Why would anyone want to hurt Bingo?

Sebastian Grimsdale. For revenge, maybe. But would he have poisoned the Potter sisters' cat and killed the two dogs? Carrie frowned. Una Quick had died and Sally MacBride. But nothing had happened to the Potters or Gerald Jenks. She saw no connection.

It didn't make sense. She had the funny feeling that what she held in her hands now was all she was going to get. This person wasn't going to chance another note, and was depending on her to be clever enough to solve what she had right there.

What she was supposed to do was go to the Rumford Lab, at night. No way to tell which night. So she'd have to go every night until she knew what was going on.

♊

Sebastian Grimsdale, although still showing the effects of the previous night, was coming round to his old self. His chief concern appeared to be that what had happened had resulted in there being no meet.

Jury had got back to Ashdown Dean to find Wiggins dredging up totally unnecessary apologies for not having got hold of him sooner. Plant had credited Wiggins with saving Carrie Fleet's life. Hardly a need for apologies, Jury assured him.

"If anyone's to blame, I am. That you couldn't reach me. Where's Grimsdale?" he'd asked as the three of them had stood in the large foyer of Gun Lodge, overseen by several racks of antlers.

Between Grimsdale and Amanda Crowley, it might have been a wake. Amanda was dressed in her usual breeches, stock perfectly done up. Her tweed jacket was slung over the arm of the chair. Grimsdale had had plenty of brandy and was in the act of telling her to stay to dinner when Jury and the others walked in.

"I don't think Mrs. Crowley will have time for that," said Jury.

As they stared at this bizarre infringement upon their freedom, Jury looked at Amanda Crowley. In that gear, eyes the color of dry sherry. Lips, although touched up, equally dry. "Sergeant Wiggins would like a word with her."

418

Since Wiggins wasn't sure what word he'd like, Jury tore a page from his notebook and handed it to the sergeant.

Grimsdale sputtered. Jury overrode whatever objection he was going to make. "And I'd like to hear your story, Mr. Grimsdale."

Amanda remained seated. "I've no idea what this means."

"You will," said Jury in a voice that lifted her from her chair. Then, escorted by Sergeant Wiggins, who, ever the gentleman, offered her a throat lozenge, she marched from the room.

"I'm sick of being dogged by police." He reddened at his own pun.

"That's too bad. I'd like to hear your story," Jury repeated, sitting and helping himself to the cigarette box on the table.

"I've told it often enough —"

"I'd like to hear it, Mr. Grimsdale."

Grimsdale reluctantly told him what had happened the night before, piecemeal. Of course he hadn't aimed the rifle at the child. Although he was quite sure she had something to do with it —

"Carrie Fleet? Probably the only person who wouldn't."

"She despises me, despises hunting — the whole lot."

"Please be logical. It's just for that reason she *wouldn't* have harmed those staghounds. But it is very likely you *would* have harmed her."

Trying to drag a red herring across the path, Grimsdale said, "And it's *illegal*, Superintendent, to go about unstopping earths!"

He took a pull at his brandy.

"What was Mrs. Crowley's relationship with your keeper? Donaldson?"

"I beg your pardon?"

Impatiently, Jury shook his head. "You know what I mean."

419

"I know what you *mean,* and I resent it."

"Unfortunately, resentment means sod-all to me." He smiled.

"There was no . . . *relationship.* Good lord, man, everyone knew Donaldson and—" He stopped.

" 'And.' Go on." Jury smiled inwardly. Plant had used the same trick.

Jury merely wanted to confirm the rumor.

"It would be ungentlemanly of me."

"That's a shame. Be ungentlemanly. Your keeper and Sally MacBride were having an affair, that it?"

"That was the rumor. I pay no attention to rumors."

Jury bet. "Whose time do you want to waste, Mr. Grimsdale? Mine or the Hampshire C.I.D.'s?"

Grimsdale waved him back into his chair. "Oh, all right, all right. He had his separate digs in the stable house. That's where they met."

"Cozy. Anywhere else?"

"How should I know? Listen, you've no right to browbeat—"

"I'm not. But I could. You tried to kill a fifteen-year-old girl."

Grimsdale shot up. *"And were you there, Superintendent?"*

"No. With three witnesses, I hardly needed to be, did I? Now, tell me if you're familiar with the name Lister."

In the act of lighting a cigarette, Jury nearly dropped the match when Grimsdale said, "Of course."

"What?"

Moving impatiently in his chair, Grimsdale said, "Can't imagine why you'd be interested. You know the way we name hounds. Use one letter a lot of the time. Lister's one of them. Then there's Laura, Lawrence, Luster—"

"I see. I was thinking of a *person.* A Lord Lister."

"Person? Oh. No, I never heard the name."

"Tell me about Amanda Crowley, then."

420

"What about her?" His tone was convincingly indifferent. "Been living in Ashdown ten, maybe a dozen years. I don't keep *count.*"

Jury watched his eye travel from stag's head to buck's to birds under glass. He certainly did, of some things. "She has money of her own?"

"I don't know."

"She doesn't seem to do any work, Mr. Grimsdale. One would assume she has money of her own. An allowance? A trust fund? Something like that?"

Grimsdale leaned forward, brandy glass clutched between his hands. "Are you suggesting I'm a fortune-hunter?"

Jury smiled. "Why not? You hunt everything else."

"Nothing, sir." Wiggins flipped through his notes. "She was here this morning because the hunt didn't meet at the Deer Leap, and she rode over to find out what was happening. Been here ever since."

"How convivial. Breakfast, lunch, and a supper we interrupted."

"Yes, sir. But given the food in *this* place . . ." Wiggins shuddered. "Never had such stiffish oatmeal, sir, and then —"

"Too bad, Wiggins. The name Lister —?"

The sergeant shook his head. "Claimed it meant nothing to her. Never heard it before." Wiggins folded the bit of paper and slid a lozenge into his mouth. "Believe me, I watched her responses sharp as a cat."

"Unfortunately, people can be sharp as cats too. But not to worry. I didn't expect much." He paused. "In my next report, you can bet what you did last night will be detailed."

Seldom did Sergeant Wiggins laugh aloud. Now he did. " 'Next report,' sir? Do you ever make them?"

"Intermittently. Where're Polly and Plant?"

'At the Deer Leap, for some food. I expect even Maxine could put something together better than what you get here.

As long as she doesn't have to cook it," he added glumly, and then sighed. "Poor Miss Praed." Seeing Jury putting on his coat, Wiggins pulled his scarf about his neck.

"Why 'poor'?"

"Got all scratched up. Trying to get that hulk she calls a cat from running up the Lodge's curtains."

"Hope he did a good job. On the curtains, not on Polly. She should take a lesson from Carrie Fleet."

As they let themselves out into the cold dusk, Wiggins said, "That reminds me. Mr. Plant wanted me to tell you. The girl Carrie's dog. It's missing."

"Bingo?"

"Yes, sir. She wanted, Mr. Plant thought, to see you. Though she didn't say it directly."

"She wouldn't."

Twenty-nine

"Damn the man! Revenge! You can bet on it!" Regina de la Notre had dropped her languid air and paced about the salon trailing behind her a vermilion coat of Chinese silk and in one hand a bottle of gin, which she used to top up her glass. She had been pacing now for a good ten minutes — back and forth, back and forth, mural to mural — and Jury wondered whether her turns at each wall and the passing of herself in front of the huge mirror might not have been done as much for effect as angry tirade. The bottle of gin didn't quite fit that image.

She went on ranting. Wiggins, notebook out and handkerchief on the little Sheraton table, looked gratefully at his cuppa and unhappily at the gin. They had been there nearly an hour and the bottle had been in more or less constant motion. *Cocktail hour,* she had said when they walked in, inviting one and all to join. Where was Lord Ardry? Charming man. Jury thought he and Miss Praed had gone to the Deer Leap for a meal. How utterly revolting, and who is Miss Praed?

To Jury's questions about Woburn Place it was no, no, no.

No, she had never heard the name Lister; no, she knew nothing about any sort of Alsatian; no, she had never seen Carrie before the meeting at the Silver Vaults, and what in *hell* were all of these questions about? She seemed to blame not Jury, who was asking them, but Wiggins, who was writing down the answers.

All of this was taking place amidst pacing and sweepings of silk with her hand, and interspersed with the continued harangue. "*Grimsdale* — that odious creature — has done something to that terrier of hers, what does she call it?" The Baroness snapped her fingers as if in a fit of forgetfulness and addressed this question to Gillian.

"Bingo."

Jury thought the look Gillian gave her employer was close to loathing. As if she thought the Baroness might, after all this time, at least remember the name of Carrie's dog. Which, Jury was pretty sure, Regina did. She merely strived for effects.

As now she clutched her fists to her handsome silk coat (one fist still around the neck of the bottle) and exclaimed: "He could actually believe Carrie — *Carrie* — had a hand in those damned dogs of his being poisoned? The creature's round the twist, ought to be put away." Distractedly, she looked about her like a woman gone quite mad with the news (which Jury was sure she hadn't; it merely made a change) and asked, "Where's Carrie? Where is she?"

"Looking for Bingo, of course. Or in her animal hut, brooding. What would you expect?" said Gillian. She was now standing in front of the mirror, thus blocking Regina's view of herself. Between the twin doors, the twin *trompe l'oeil* murals which again doubled the doors and the view outside, and the mirror facing the mirror on the back wall, Jury felt he had fallen, perhaps like Alice, into a world of reflections.

424

Regina, by now quite drunk, though carrying it off to a fare-thee-well, ran her hand in a tragic gesture across her forehead. "She must be back for dinner. She knows we dine at eight-thirty."

Gillian raised her eyes to heaven and shook her head. Her dress tonight was a grayish brown, different from the other only in its style. Had she been asked to play down her own looks in order to enhance Regina's, she couldn't have done a better job. But colorless as the dress was, it was draped across breast and hip in such a way that — like the other — it could hardly hide what lay beneath.

"So your meeting with Carrie Fleet was accidental," said Jury mildly. The Silver Vaults were famous, well visited. It was possible that anyone in London might have gone there. No particular reason to be suspicious, but all the same... Liverpool could not be accounted for in the accent and aristocratic cheekbones of Regina de la Notre.

The Baroness stopped in her tracks and came to look down at him as if he, too, like Grimsdale, must be insane. "I *beg* your pardon? Accidental?" She bent slightly over Jury, who could have filled a shot glass from her breath alone. "Of course not, Superintendent. I traveled from Woburn Place to Eastcheap to Shoreditch to Blackheath to Threadneedle Street to the Old Curiosity Shop to the Silver Vaults. Just *searching*, my dear, for a thirteen-year-old animal-minder. *Good* God!" And she was back to pacing again.

Gillian was trying to look everywhere in the room but at Jury. "Your friend —" and now she paused for a name.

"Lord Ardry," said Jury, easily.

"Lord Ardry, yes. He was talking with Carrie this morning." She looked down at her intertwined hands. "I wonder if she told him about the note."

"What note was that?" Jury shifted uneasily, drank his whiskey.

425

"It came with the morning post. She said it was just some silly thing from Neahle Meara. I wondered about it; Carrie never gets letters."

"Never? No one in her past—" He turned to Regina. "Didn't you ever wonder, Baroness—"

"Regina," she corrected him, throatily, as she studied the mural before her.

"— about Carrie Fleet's past?"

"For God's sake, my dear, she hasn't a past."

Jury looked at her, bleakly. She was right.

Gillian ran through one of the french doors, calling over her shoulder she was going to look for Carrie.

As Jury got up to follow her, the little maid announced dinner.

"Well, my dear Sergeant, shall we . . . ?"

If there was any more to that question, Jury didn't hear it.

Gillian was standing at the door of the sanctuary, peering into blackness when Jury came up behind her.

"She's not *here*," Gillian wailed. It was hard to know if her face was wet with rain or tears. "She's *not here!*"

Jury put his arm round her and his hand on her satiny hair and held her. "Then she's looking for Bingo—"

"You don't understand, you don't understand, you don't —" And the weeping grew with every repetition. Jury drew her closer, as she kept shaking her head against his coat.

"Gillian. What was in that note? Why're you so upset?"

The silky head kept shaking back and forth, back and forth, like Regina's pacing. "I don't *know*. But something's wrong. Something's *wrong!* Carrie's so disciplined—" And she moved her head from Jury's shoulder to look up at him. "You don't know her. She really *likes* that old devil—"

It was obvious she meant Regina.

"Sorry. I didn't really mean that. But if dinner's at eight, Carrie's *there!*" She was breathing in great, sobbing breaths.

426

"I know . . . you don't . . . believe me. Jealousy . . . something
. . . but oh, where *is* she?"

Jury pulled her back again, head against shoulder. "I'll find
her. Right now, I want you to have some brandy and lie
down. I'll take you up —"

She seemed not to hear him. He shook her. "Gillian. We
can stroll through the maze. Then I'll take you up and tuck
you in. Fair enough?"

He thought the bad joke might be lost in the wind and the
rain, but she did smile a little. "Fair enough. But no stroll.
I'm too done in."

As they walked away from the arbor, she kept stopping
and looking back, so that he had to urge her toward the
house.

♊

After he saw that Gillian was in bed and drowsy from
brandy and a sedative she'd taken from a small bottle, Jury
went down the hall, looking for Carrie's room. It wasn't hard
to distinguish it: snapshots of Bingo and other animals —
possibly the ones at the Brindles', one with the Brindle
daughter in it. Had they then been mates of a sort? Had
it been, for all of her posture of indifference, a painful
parting?

Jury sat on the narrow, white-counterpaned bed, in the
narrow room, white-walled. No ruffles, no ribbons, no nonsense. He was sure the lack of ornament and the size of the
room had nothing to do with Regina's pinching pennies. It
was definitely a Carrie Fleet room.

He searched it. No note, no letter, but he hadn't really expected to find one; she was too smart to leave something important lying about, or hidden in a drawer. He opened the
cupboard. The few garments hanging there — another
sweater, another dress like the one she'd worn when he met
her, a coat. He went through the pockets. From the pinafore

427

he drew out a snapshot. A shot, taken at night of a building, nondescript looking, nothing he'd seen.

But no note. And he was sure the note had been important, otherwise she would have told them, at lunch, what was in it. Her dislike of talk Jury did not put down at all to secretiveness: he put it down to despair.

Despair. A feeling that would be disallowed by adults and turned into something like "just going through a stage." But Jury remembered sitting on a bed very similar to this one, only in a row of beds when he was a little younger than Carrie. For him, when his mother and father were killed in the Second World War, it had been an orphanage until an uncle had rescued him. For Carrie, it had been the Brindles, until the Baroness had rescued *her*.

If rescue it had been.

♊

The scene in the dining room was a delight. The Baroness at one end of a long rosewood table, Wiggins at the other. They seemed to be getting on like a house on fire, a lively conversation in progress, probably owing more to the three wineglasses at each place than to Wiggins's verve and wit.

He could have asked Regina about the snapshot, but thought better of it.

"Sergeant," said Jury, interrupting.

"Sir!" Wiggins stood up, his napkin falling to the floor.

Jury sighed. It was one of those times when Jury was the drill sergeant.

"My *dear* Superintendent! Please join us. My cook is superior —"

"Thanks, but I'm not hungry. It's after nine, Regina. Aren't you concerned about Carrie?"

"She's still looking for Bingo." Regina sighed and put down her wineglass. "I'd hardly expect her to report for dinner spot on eight-thirty."

"If you're finished, Sergeant —"

Leaving Regina sighing over Gillian's absence — and no one to talk to — Jury and Wiggins got into their coats and then into their car.

"Where're we going, sir?"

"The Deer Leap. To find Plant. And Neahle Meara."

Wiggins turned in surprise. "The little girl, sir?"

"The little girl, yes."

☿

They sat around the table in the saloon bar, used for the odd serving of meals, since few were served.

"I don't know," said Neahle. "*I* didn't write anything."

Jury smiled. "Didn't think you did. But what do you make of it, Neahle?"

The brown eyes looked from the snapshot and back at Jury. She shrugged. "*I* don't know." Her voice was tearful.

"It's all right, Neahle. Never mind then. Go on to bed."

But she sat like a rock now, her small chin in her fists. "Where's Carrie?"

"And what," asked Melrose Plant, "makes you think something's happened to Carrie?"

She looked away, toward the fire that had burned down to sparkless ashes. "Because you're all here asking funny questions." Then she slipped from her chair. "*I'm* going to bed." She ran out of the room.

The snap was passed around and around again. "Pasco? Maybe he'd know."

"What makes you think it's somewhere around here?" asked Polly. "Maybe it's near the East India Docks."

"What a vivid imagination, Polly. All of that ground — looks just like the Thames."

"Call Pasco, Wiggins."

Wiggins left.

Plant took the picture and reluctantly headed for the bar, where Maxine Torres was wetting her finger, preparatory to turning a page in her magazine. Sullenly, she looked at Plant. *"Again?"* Obviously, she was referring to his pint of Old Peculiar. Plant, the raving alcoholic.

"No, Maxine, not another pint. It is your gorgeous black eyes I am interested in." He brought the picture near the eyes. "Recognize?"

She shoved it back. "Am I blind?"

"Don't know. Do you recognize this place?"

"Yeah. It's that lab outside town. Outside Selby. Mile, two miles." She was not interested in the snap or in the question. Or in Plant, certainly. Not having to refill his pint, she went back to the magazine.

"Directions, please."

Maxine squinted at him. Directions were not part of her job as temporary publican, at least not until Plant tore a page from her magazine, plunked his gold pen beside it and repeated his request.

She drew a few lines for roads and an X marking the lab. Then she gave him an evil look and shoved page and pen at him.

"Don't worry. I'll get you a subscription."

Wiggins had come back to say that Constable Pasco wasn't at the station and wasn't at home.

"Neither place?"

"Neither, sir."

Jury was silent for a moment. "Call the Selby C.I.D. See if they know where he is."

Polly shoved her glasses up on her head, as if that gave her a compass bearing. "But *why?* What makes you think Carrie would go there?"

"Because that's where she thinks someone took her terrier and I'm not going to sit around here arguing. No, not you," said Jury as Polly gathered up her coat.

430

"What do you *mean*, not me? I was here before either of you!"

"That makes a lot of sense," said Plant, buttoning his Chesterfield, picking up his stick. "We're not exactly queuing for a bus."

"It's a police matter, Polly," said Jury.

That made her drop the ugly glasses down over her eyes. "Then why're you taking *him*?"

Because I need him. But Jury didn't say that. He leaned over the table and gave Polly a wonderful smile. "Because if I leave him here with you, you'll have him in that Silver Ghost driving at eighty miles per out to that lab, dear Polly." He kissed her cheek.

Her glasses steamed up.

PART 6

An Amethyst remembrance
Is all I own—

Thirty

From a clump of bracken she had been watching the dark lab for an hour or more and wished she'd brought the binoculars, but it would have been too much to carry along with the torch and shotgun.

No one. At least no one had gone into the lab from her range of vision, so perhaps it wasn't tonight. Carrie got up from the ground, which was squelchy and cold, and walked toward the long building, dark except for one amber light inside. She couldn't understand that.

Of course the gate was locked, but the fence was easy enough to scale, and she did, dropping first the gun and then herself on the other side. The ammunition was in her pocket.

Because of the demonstrations, there had been talk of surrounding the whole building with barbed wire or electrifying the fence and getting a guard. The lab itself was hardly impregnable; if she couldn't get in by way of a door, she could by way of a window. Three of the doors needed keys to get in. But one small one at the end was padlocked. Joe Brindle hadn't been good for much, but he had taught her how to listen to the tumbler on a padlock, information he'd picked up from his safe-cracking days. *Acute hearing's what you got, girl.* She turned the knob, her ear close to the lock, and heard the nearly inaudible clicks. Carrie opened the door.

She had never come into this building, despite Fleming's invitations — again, she thought of Dr. Fleming. The staff were the only ones with keys, and whoever intended her to come here certainly must have a key, unless the person intended to break a window, not having had the benefit of Brindle's teaching. The single bulb at the other end of the corridor made a misty alley of light, showing rows of doors down both sides. The first ones were labeled "Restricted." Carrie turned her torch on one and tried the knob. It wasn't locked and she went inside.

What she found was an antiseptically clean room, with cats in separate cages, most of them asleep. A few were awake, or had come awake when the light swept over the cages and they sat up. The doors of the cages were mesh, and she went from one to another, looking in, putting her fingers through the mesh. Some of them backed away into the shelter of a dark corner; others clawed at the mesh. At least, she thought, they hadn't been declawed. The room was equipped with ultraviolet lights. Her hands took on a strange bluish glow. On the other side of the room were cats inside plastic bubbles. Carrie supposed by being in here she was contaminating the place.

There was a lightswitch on the wall, but she was afraid to turn it on; it might attract attention.

That was what she had found strange: the whole building should have been floodlit.

She loaded the gun and in her soundless sneakers made her way to the door, stiffbacked against the wall, peering as well as she could down the corridor. Not a sound.

She looked back at the cats in their cages. Carrie would have expected the yowlings and meowings of animals upset by a change in routine, if nothing else. But they were still silent. Blood tests, Dr. Fleming had said. Fifty percent of them would probably die, just to see how big a dose it would take to kill them.

One by one she opened the cages, being very quiet. It was almost as if the cats were cooperating, not letting whoever was in the building know where Carrie was. But it was really that they were scared, too scared to make a noise. The window was barred, but locked only with a simple latch. A high table beside the window she shoved beneath it. Then she peered down the corridor, still empty, stepped out, and closed the door.

In the next room were rabbits. On a long table she saw the harnesses. These weren't blood tests. Carrie knew what this was all about and she felt herself go cold. She thought she heard footsteps in the corridor, but she still inspected the rabbits. The harnesses were to keep their heads perfectly still, with little devices to hold their eyes open. So something could be sprayed into the eyes. That morning she had got soap in her eye, and the sting was terrible. But she could blink. She could dish cold water into it. The rabbits couldn't.

And where was Bingo, she wondered with growing terror, as the steps came closer. Carrie slowly raised the shotgun, stared at the rabbit whose eyes were so ravaged they looked like molten wax. The pain must have been unbearable. Her hands were shaking but she could still hold the butt to her shoulder as the steps came nearer. *Your Majesty* — she pretended to be addressing the Queen — *I think I'd call this the "termination condition."*

Carrie shot the rabbit.

From the doorway, a voice said, "Hold it right there, Carrie."

Pasco. *Constable Pasco.*

⚜

Jury switched the motor off far enough from the gate that he doubted anyone could have heard the car approaching.

"I don't believe it," said Melrose Plant. "I mean I *do*, but it's so —"

"It's so. And it was simple, really. Foolproof. A killer not even around when the victims die. Just scare the hell out of Una Quick, find out she's told Sally MacBride about that snapshot with the name 'Lister,' and Sally would probably have told Donaldson." Jury's smile was grim. " 'Probably.' Why the hell take chances? Una *did* muck about with the post." Jury hit the steering wheel. "Damn it! The post, the bloody post! It should have been so obvious."

"Hindsight always is. And as you said, anyone could have seen Carrie outside the Silver Vaults. And gone home with her. Or followed her home." He looked from the lab to Jury. *"Trompe l'oeil,* is that it?"

"That's it. You weren't at 'La Notre' that first day. Come on, let's get in there." They got out, walked across the squelchy ground. "God, you'd think Fleming would have floodlights on that place, wouldn't you?"

As they drew nearer, Jury saw the door on one end, the main door, and assumed there was probably one on the other end. "I'll take the door on one end, maybe you can go round to the other."

"I forgot my keys," said Melrose.

"Very funny. You don't know how to pick locks?"

They were in the process of hoisting themselves over the wall. "I can't *imagine,*" said Melrose, "invading the privacy of others in such a way."

In spite of everything, Jury smiled.

Thirty-one

*A*nd Constable Pasco knew how to use a handgun. He held it in both hands, crouching slightly. "Put it down!" he yelled.

"Where's Bingo?"

"I don't know about Bingo. Dammit, Carrie, I've had enough from you. I was driving from Selby. This place should have been lit up like Harrods at Christmas —"

The shot threw him twisting into the air. And then he fell, a dead weight in the corridor.

Carrie stared. *Constable Pasco.* She watched the blood slowly ooze through the back of his shirt and thought for one nightmare moment she must have fired.

Who was out there?

There were tiny steps that seemed to recede in the distance, running. Sweating, she reloaded the shotgun, switched off her torch, and did what she'd seen all the police do in those films she went to with the Baroness. Quickly, she stepped into the corridor and fired straight down it at a figure all in black — including a kind of ski-cap thing. The typical demonstrator.

Or someone pretending to be. It could have been anyone, and it disappeared into one of the rooms farther down the hall. Carrie ran into the next room, where dogs were barking.

But through the sound of the dogs she could hear breathing, fast breathing, and her name whispered.

There was no time to load up the shotgun, and she hoped the torch would blind whoever it was at least for a second or two when it fell on a figure in the corner. "Neahle!"

Neahle Meara was crouched down and crying, her hands fisted against her face.

Carrie went over to her. "Neahle, I might have killed you —" Neahle kept shaking and shaking her head, weeping soundlessly, quiet as the cats. Carrie knelt beside her and whispered, "How'd you get here? How'd you get in?"

"The door at the other end." She kept shaking her head until Carrie put her two hands on Neahle's own to make her stop. "Listen, we'll be still as mice. Okay? I'll sit here beside you." And she did, back flat against the cinder block. She whispered, "I've got this gun, Neahle. No one can do anything. Okay?"

Neahle had stopped the sobbing, was rubbing her eyes, and Carrie shut hers tightly, thinking only of the dead rabbit. And then shocked at herself for not thinking of Constable Pasco first. He was her friend, even if she pretended not. *God, please* — she stopped the thought; she did not believe in God.

Neahle was holding her hand. "I knew something bad was going to happen. I knew you were in trouble when —"

They both froze. The sound of other feet. But the feet stopped. And Carrie knew whoever was there had to look into each room. The gunfire hadn't given her away; it had confused the person coming down the corridor. Thank God it was a long one.

440

Carrie took out more ammunition, loaded the .412 again, and tightened her grip on Neahle's hand. "When what, Neahle?"

"The man from Scotland Yard. He had a picture of this place, but I was afraid they were looking for you. So I didn't tell them. I took the short-cut through the woods and ran all the way. I didn't tell." Neahle shook Carrie's arm. "Did I do wrong?"

She had steeled herself seven years ago against tears. Now the disappointment was overwhelming. If only Neahle *had* told him. "You did right."

Neahle put her head on Carrie's shoulder. Those footsteps were coming nearer. Neahle whispered, "We're going to get killed, aren't we, Carrie? And Bingo?"

"Anyone that walks through that door is going to get a hole blown in him a deer could jump through. You take the torch. When — I mean *if* the door opens, switch it on. It's a strong light, like hunters use."

Neahle merely nodded, looked down at the electric torch, back up at Carrie. "What if it's the wrong person that walks through?"

It was what Carrie needed. She started to giggle and clamped her hand over her mouth and so did Neahle, giggling too. *We're probably both going to die,* thought Carrie, *and we're laughing.*

"Neahle. Do you believe in God?"

"I guess." And then, disconsolately, "But, then, I'm Irish."

This made them clamp their hands to their mouths again and hang on to one another to keep from making any sound. They had to choke back the silliness. *Death,* thought Carrie, *is silly. It sure doesn't get you anywhere* — and she had to put her head down in spite of the steps coming closer to keep from laughing and it was Neahle who had to shake Carrie this time and tell her, *Listen!*

For there were other footsteps. Different.

441

Neahle was clearly frightened when Carrie stood up. Carrie heard her name spoken in a whisper.

It was a voice she would have known anywhere — Superintendent Jury's.

Who didn't know what he was walking into.

"Stay right there," said Carrie. "Quiet."

"Carrie?" said Neahle.

There was a small but mounting hysteria even in the one word. "You're all right, Neahle. *We're* all right."

"Carrie?" said Neahle.

Neahle didn't believe her. Carrie reached round her neck and undid the little clasp of the necklace. She dropped the necklace and amethyst ring into Neahle's hands. "Besides Bingo, this is what I like most. You know that. So hold on to it for me. Okay?" There was no logic in this, and Carrie knew it. But Neahle wouldn't. To her, it would be an icon, something to trust in.

The steps were muted but getting nearer. Carrie picked up the shotgun, simply held up the palm of her hand to Neahle's indrawn breath, and went toward the door.

She opened it a slot narrow as a penny. Superintendent Jury. No.

There was a sound from the other end of the corridor he was walking down.

No.

Carrie opened the door, butted the shotgun against her shoulder, and aimed at the figure halfway down the corridor.

"Carrie!" yelled Jury.

Carrie had lowered the gun because she couldn't understand why she was aiming at the figure in black, now without the mask. Gillian Kendall.

And Gillian's handgun was trained not on her, but at Superintendent Jury.

No, thought Carrie, leaping in front of him.

☓

The shot caught her as it had Pasco. She looked up at Jury. "Neahle," Carrie pointed behind her.

But Gillian brought the gun up again. He said to Carrie, "Neahle will be okay. So will Bingo." Then he looked down the corridor. Ruth Lister.

"I'm pretty easily taken in, Ruth. Aren't I?"

Carrie's eyes were closed, but the lids fluttered. "Ruthie? The zoo . . ." Her eyes closed again.

The zoo, Jury thought. "It was you who took Carrie. Of course, she would have gone with you."

Ruth Lister nodded, but her attention was wholly on the girl she thought she'd put paid to for the second time. Carrie was still breathing.

The gun moving slightly, she said to Carrie, "If you'll give me the necklace, love, I promise it'll all be over."

She was insane, thought Jury. How could it be over? How did she think she'd get away with this?

Torch the lab. Just another crazy demonstrator. Nothing but bones. And she'd have the little ring to prove that Carrie Fleet, Carolyn Lister, was dead. Whatever her story. She'd be capable of any story. A very plausible woman. Jury looked down at Carrie, whose eyes had opened again. She was smiling. There was only a bit of blood. . . . *For God's sake, Plant . . .*

"How'd you find Carrie, Ruth? I mean after you missed getting her from the Brindles? You wouldn't have taken the chance on presenting yourself to old Joe, surely, and asking her whereabouts?"

"Not as myself. But social services really *must* know where its charges are."

Jury kept Gillian talking. "You didn't simply end up in Ashdown by accident, did you?"

She laughed. "No. And I certainly wouldn't have pressed myself into service with the Baroness Regina. I was following Carrie. Did you know it was me, then? How?"

"Not until tonight. Not until I thought that the one person who had most to do with the post would be, of course, the secretary. You simply took the snapshot which the Brindles had sent with the letter out of the envelope."

"But Una had seen it first. And told Sally MacBride. Who *might* have told Donaldson. One has to cover all bases."

Jury felt blood oozing through his fingers. "How did you know Una Quick had told Sally MacBride?"

She smiled slightly, shaking her head. "Richard. You think things are so complicated. I merely asked her. Called her on the Monday night and threatened her. Actually, I hoped that would finish the job, but to make sure, I told her to be at that call box on Tuesday. Richard, this is fascinating, but I can't believe you came alone."

"Wiggins is trying to get ahold of Paul Fleming."

"Well. My little affair with Paul at least got me a key to the lab and the drug to give Grimsdale's hounds. It took some working out, you see. I knew that getting Carrie's dog here was the way to get *her* here."

From the shadows at the other end of the hall Jury at last saw the shape of Melrose Plant emerge. *Took you long enough.* It was the ragged breathing of Carrie Fleet that enraged him. More than this woman who had led him right up the garden.

"And the other animals —?"

The safety on the gun snicked back. "I suppose I owe you something. Another minute, perhaps."

Carrie Fleet groaned and raised her hand to ward off whatever devils were forming in her semiconscious state. "No."

Gillian said, "Red herrings, Richard. Easy enough to dose the cat up with aspirin — which is, incidentally, what I took tonight. Not a sedative."

"It was a convincing act. Hysteria, the works." He watched as Plant got closer, moving in total silence. "Do you

444

know how much you look like Carrie? The perfect profiles. The first day at 'La Notre,' I should have seen it. Like seeing double."

"Bingo," said Carrie.

"The damned dog's all right. He's in the last room down the corridor." She raised the gun up and brought it down. "About you, Richard, I'm truly sorry." She smiled.

Melrose was behind her. "Mind dropping that?"

Ruth Lister laughed. "Lord Ardry. *Not* Sergeant Wiggins." She paled, but kept the gun steady. "Knowing you, I doubt very much that's a gun at my back."

"It isn't."

Jury watched her expression turn from a ghastly smile to a blindfold look. She seemed to stand stock still for a long time. And then she dropped like a stone.

Melrose pulled the swordstick from her back and let it clatter to the floor.

Then he went into a room at his right and came out with the terrier, Bingo, which he put on the floor beside Carrie.

Jury called Neahle's name and she came running from her hiding place in a room down the corridor. He wanted to tell her that things were all right.

Things were not.

Jury was holding Carrie in his arms, his head against her silver hair, his hands sticky with blood.

There was blood everywhere. Pasco. Gillian. It snaked down the corridor.

Neahle was wild-eyed. Slowly, she bent down, then simply lay across Carrie, who said, "Got the ring?"

The dark brown head was close to the silvery-blond one. "I got the ring, Carrie."

Carrie Fleet held out her hand, now strangely transparent, for the necklace. Its reflection in the weird amber light turned her blood almost to gold.

☿

445

Melrose Plant remembered that shape coming out of the fog, passing from kennel to kennel.

She said to Neahle, "It might be worth something, this ring. Maybe the Baroness would help . . ."
Carrie's head fell on Jury's shoulder. "Sanctuary."

The Past is such a curious Creature
To look her in the Face
A Transport may reward us
Or a Disgrace —

Unarmed if any meet her
I charge him fly
Her rusty Ammunition
Might yet reply.

—Emily Dickinson

Help the Poor Struggler

To Leon Duke,
who leant a hand

And Mike Mattil,
who helped a poor struggler

Her mind lives tidily, apart
From cold and noise and pain,
And bolts the door against her heart,
Out wailing in the rain.

DOROTHY PARKER

O, man, dear, did ya never hear
Of pretty Molly Brannigan?
She's gone away and left me
And I'll never be a man again;
Not a spot on me hide
Will the summer sun e'er tan again,
Now that Molly's gone and left me
Here for to die.

IRISH FOLK SONG

Help the Poor

PROLOGUE

THE little girl stood in her flannel nightdress holding the telephone receiver. She carefully dialled the numbers her mother always did when she wanted the operator.

A silky-haired cat at her feet arched its back, yawned, and began washing its paw as the little girl waited through several *brr-brr's* for the operator to answer. Maybe they didn't wake up until late, the little girl thought. Her mum always said they were lazy. She looked out of the leaded-glass window almost lost under its thatch collar to see it just pearling over with early-morning light and the moorland beyond floating in morning mist. There was a spiderweb with beads of dew between the thatch and the window. The *brr-brr* went on. She counted ten of them and then hung up and picked up the phone again. The cat leapt to the table to sit and watch the spider painstakingly finish its web.

Bloody operators. That was what her mum always said, sitting here at the table, looking out like the cat, over the blank face of the moor that surrounded their hamlet. The phone kept *brr*-ing. The veil of grey light lifted like a delicate curtain drawn back showing the far horizon where a line of gold spun like the spiderweb.

448

There was a click, and someone answered. Her voice seemed to come from a great distance, as if she were calling across the moor out there.

The little girl held the black receiver with tight hands and tried to speak very clearly because if they didn't like you they'd just hang up. That's what her mother had always said. *The cheek of them. Think they're the bloody Queen, some of them.* Her mother spent a lot of time on the telephone and slammed it down a lot.

"My mum's dead," she said.

There was a silence and she was afraid the operator was going to hang up, like the Queen. But she didn't. The operator asked her to repeat what she'd just said.

"My mum's dead," the little girl said patiently, despite her fright. "She never died before."

Now the operator sounded much closer — not way off across the moor — and was asking her questions in a nice tone of voice. What was her name and where did she live?

"My name's Tess. We live on the moor." *This bloody moor,* her mother had always said. She'd hated where they lived. "My mum's in the kitchen. She's dead."

Last name?

"Mulvanney."

The cat's white fur gleamed in the newly risen sun. The spiderweb was spangled with diamond-dew, and as Tess tried to answer the operator's questions the web broke and the spider — it was a tiny brown spider — hung on a silver thread. The cat's tail twitched. The operator was saying they must live in a certain *place* on the moor. A village? And what was their telephone number?

"Clerihew Marsh," said Tess, looking down at the dial. She told the operator the number there. "She's in the kitchen and she won't get up. I thought she was playing. Are you going to call the hospital and will the ambulance come?"

The operator was very nice and said, Yes, of course. She told Tess maybe her mum wasn't dead at all, just sick, and

449

they'd get the doctor. The operator told her very clearly *not* to hang up, that she'd call someone and get back to Tess straightaway.

Silence again. The operator was being very nice, but the operator hadn't been in the kitchen and didn't understand. The cat wore a halo of light, and the spider was repairing its web with infinite patience.

When Tess heard the operator's voice again, she tried to explain: "I thought she was playing with my fingerpaints. We have paints at school. I thought she got the red pot." The operator asked her what she meant. "There's red all over the kitchen. She's cut. It's blood. It's on her dress and in her hair."

Quickly, the operator told her again not to hang up, that she had to call someone else. Soon she was back and talking to Tess in a soothing voice about things like school. Yes, said Tess, she went to school. They called it babies' school, but she wasn't a baby. She was five years old. She told the operator about her teacher, who looked like a toad. They talked a long time and Tess understood why the operators hardly ever answered. They were talking to people.

The cat yawned and jumped from the table, and Tess knew it wanted its breakfast and would wander into the kitchen. "I've got to hang up. I don't want Sandy — that's our cat — to go into the kitchen." Tess hung up.

Rose Mulvanney lay beneath the kitchen table, her legs jackknifed, her dress blood-soaked. Blood had splattered the kitchen floor, the white daub walls, and even the low, dark beam of the ceiling.

Teresa Mulvanney wondered how it had got up there. She shook and shook her head, forgetting everything as her mind drifted and filmed over. She closed her eyes and scratched her elbows. What must be happening was that she was having one of her "bad" nights; she was dreaming. It must all be paint, after all, or tomato ketchup. Her mother, Rose, had

450

said that in films they used that. Tess, with her eyes still closed, told her mother it was all right and she could get up now. It was a game and it was all a dream anyway. Even the *brr*-ing of the telephone and the far-off double note that made her think of ambulances came as dark figures in fog. She began to hum a song that Rose Mulvanney used to sing when Teresa was a baby.

She forgot to feed the cat.

When Detective Inspector Nicholson and Sergeant Brian Macalvie of the Devon-Cornwall constabulary got to the small cottage in Clerihew Marsh, Teresa Mulvanney was humming and writing her name on the white wall in her mother's blood.

Brian Macalvie had never seen anything like it and he never forgot it. At this time he was twenty-three years old and was generally thought to be the best CID man in the whole Devon-Cornwall constabulary. It was an opinion held by practically everyone, even Macalvie's enemies — also practically everyone. He was not fond of taking orders; he was always talking about his Scots-Irish-American ancestry and dying to get out of England; he was always getting promoted.

He worked on the murder of Rose Mulvanney even after the file had been officially closed. Three months after the Mulvanney murder, they'd arrested (according to Macalvie) the wrong man — a young medical student who lived in Clerihew Marsh and went to Bristol University. He'd been arrested on flimsy, circumstantial evidence — he'd had a heavy crush on Rose Mulvanney, fifteen years older, and, being a medical student, he knew how to use a knife. The motive was unrequited love; the evidence (said Macalvie), Nil.

During the same period, he moved in on six other cases that he felt the department was snailing along on and solved those, so that it was difficult for the divisional commander to tell him to get off the Mulvanney case. Macalvie was his own police force. When he walked into the lab, the pathologists and technicians clung to their microscopes. It was Macalvie's contention their fingerprint expert couldn't find a bootprint on a hospital sheet. If it came down to it, the whole department couldn't find a Rolls-Royce if it was parked in front of the Moorcombe headquarters on Christmas Day.

Thus when the divisional commander told him to get off the Mulvanney case, that the case was closed, Macalvie dropped his ID on the table and said, "Macalvie, six; Devon-Cornwall, Nil." He wasn't halfway across the room before his superior's tone changed. As long as Macalvie didn't let the Mulvanney business interfere with his other duties . . .

"Tell that to Sam Waterhouse," said Macalvie, and walked out.

Sam Waterhouse was the medical student who had been sent to Dartmoor prison. It was a life sentence with the possibility of parole, since there were no prior convictions and the murder of Rose Mulvanney was judged a *crime passionel.*

Macalvie had not hesitated to let the Devon-Cornwall constabulary feel the full weight of his personal displeasure. They had ruined the kid's life and, possibly, a brilliant career.

And if there was one person who knew about brilliant careers, it was Brian Macalvie.

The tiny hamlet of Clerihew Marsh was nothing more than a few fat cottages huddled on either side of a curving road, giving the distorted image of dwellings reflected in a pier glass or a fun-house mirror. After the first clump of houses, so stuck together they looked as if they shared the same thatched roof, the cottages straggled a little, like a sleeve unravelling. The Mulvanney cottage was the last in the fringe. It sat by itself, windows on every side, quite visible to anyone passing.

But apparently no one had been passing when Rose Mulvanney was being cut with a knife. No one had seen anyone go in or out. No one had seen any strangers about. No one had heard anything. No one who knew him believed Sam Waterhouse could do such a thing.

Macalvie followed every conceivable lead — there were few enough—down to the milkman, and had the little wren of a woman who ran the sub-post office chirping nearly daily about the way Rose bought her food. Macalvie had browbeaten the teacher of the Infant's School into delivering up her small quota of information about Teresa Mulvanney. Nor was he beyond using the same tactics with the odd school chum if he could collar one. The headmistress finally complained to the Devon-Cornwall police.

One of the most important persons in the case, one he had not questioned initially, was Rose's older daughter. She'd been away on a school trip when the little sister had made the awful discovery.

She'd come bursting into Macalvie's office, a lanky kid of fifteen with toothpick arms and no breasts and long hair. She'd stood there with fire in her eyes and yelled at him, spattering obscenities like blood on his office walls. Her baby sister, Teresa, had been taken to hospital. Teresa was catatonic. All she did was lie on her cot, curled up like a baby, sucking her thumb.

It was as though Macalvie had been sitting in a warm bath of his own infallibility (it never occurred to him he wouldn't come up with the answers), and this kid had come along and pulled the plug. She got so hysterical she slammed her arm across the stuff on his desk, sending papers, pens, and sour coffee cups all over the floor.

He never solved the case; he never forgave himself; he never saw the kid again.

Her name was Mary Mulvanney.

Twenty Years Later . . .

I

The Alley by the Five Alls

ONE

SIMON Riley never knew what hit him.

That was, at least, the opinion of the medical examiner called to the scene by the Dorset police. The wound in the boy's back had been administered very quickly and very efficiently by a knife honed to razor sharpness. The pathologist agreed and added that, given the angle of the downward thrust, the knife had been wielded by someone considerably taller than Simon. That didn't help the Dorset police greatly, since Simon had been a twelve-year-old schoolboy and was wearing, at the time of his death, the black jacket and tie which constituted the school uniform. That the killer was at least a foot taller would not be particularly helpful in establishing identity.

The boy lay face downward in the alley by the Five Alls pub, crumpled in a foetal position against the blind wall which was the pub's side facing the alley. Scattered around the body were a ten-pack of John Players Specials and a copy of *Playboy*. Simon had been indulging in every schoolboy's twin sins — smoking fags and looking at naked women — when the killer had come up behind him. This was the construction of Detective Inspector Neal of the Dorset police, and there was no reason to think it inaccurate.

It was the kitchen girl at the pub, opening the side door of the Five Alls to toss a bag in the dustbin, who had been unlucky enough to find him on that awful evening of February tenth. She had come in for some stiff questioning and had had to be sedated.

The Five Alls was a tucked-away place on a Dorchester side street. The squinty little alley where the boy had been found dead-ended on a blank wall. For Simon Riley's secretive pastimes, it was well located. Unfortunately for Simon, it was just as well located for murder.

TWO

RILEY's. Fine Meat and Game. Superintendent Richard Jury and Detective Sergeant Alfred Wiggins looked through the shop window at their own reflections superimposed over the hanging pheasants. The shop was (a sign announced) licensed to sell game. A young man and an older one were serving a queue of women who were armed with wicker baskets and string bags. From the description given Jury, he took the older man to be Albert Riley himself, the boy's father. It was two days after Simon's body had been found and one day before his funeral. Jury was a little surprised to see the boy's father working.

Apparently, best British beef was in strong demand and short supply, given the way the drill-sergeant eyes of the line of women followed Jury's and Wiggins's progress to the front of the queue. There were mutterings and one or two astringent voices telling these two interlopers where the end of the line was just in case they were blind.

When Jury produced his identification, the young man's face went as white as that part of his apron which was still unblotched. Then he turned to the master-butcher, who was defatting some pork chops with swift and measured strokes. It was an unpleasant reminder of the autopsy performed on his son. Riley's knife stopped in midair when his underling turned him toward the Scotland Yard policemen.

Riley handed over the pork chops to the youth as the women behind Jury and Wiggins passed the information along like buckets of water in a fire brigade. Scotland Yard. Jury realized that Riley's fine meat and game might be even more popular today; murder usually had that effect.

Simon's father wiped his hands on a cloth and removed his apron. His thick spectacles magnified his small eyes and made his round face rounder. He was soft-spoken and apologetic, clearly embarrassed at being caught working in such dreadful circumstances. The authority with which he'd used the knife was completely lost when he put it down.

"Shop was closed yesterday," he said. "But I thought I'd go mad, what with pacing up and down and the wife — that's Simon's stepmother — yelling her head off." While saying this, he was leading them to a door at the rear of the shop. "Suppose you think it's cold-blooded, me working —"

Wiggins, seldom given to irony, said, "Not our business to wonder whether it's hot or cold, sir. Just that it's blood."

Riley winced as he led them up a twisting staircase. "Scotland Yard. I told the wife to leave off with that Queen's Counsel person of hers. Told her Dorset police could handle —" Then, seeming to feel he'd made a blunder, he quickly added, "Expect they need all the help they can get. We keep this flat over the shop. Have another house, but this is handy. The wife'll make a cuppa. I could do with something stronger myself."

The "something stronger" was Jameson's and the wife was not at all inclined to make a cuppa. Although it was lunch-

461

time, she was more interested in whisky than in lunch or tea. Her own hand didn't shake as she downed her drop, but her husband's did, as if he had palsy. When Riley took off his glasses to pinch the bridge of his nose, Jury saw the eyes were red-rimmed — from tears, probably. Mrs. Riley's were red, too, but Jury supposed that was owing more to the bottle than to bereavement. Since she was not the natural mother, she might have thought that released her from weepy demonstrations.

Beth Riley was a big, brassy woman; her face would have done better with a simple hairstyle than with the florid waves, red-rinsed, that framed the head. She was better spoken than her husband, even given her lubricated voice. She had been at the Jameson's already.

"Beth insisted on getting that Q.C. in London to ring you people—"

"It's just as well *one* of us knows someone in high places." She turned to Jury. "Leonard Matching, Q.C. He's to stand for Parliament in Brixton." From the vague reports Jury had got of mealymouthed Matching, he doubted very much if Brixton would stand for him. The only reason Jury and Wiggins were here was that an assistant commissioner was a personal friend and had handed the request down the line to Chief Superintendent Racer, who had wasted no time in deploying Jury to the provinces. Too bad (Jury imagined Racer thinking) it was only a hundred and sixty–odd miles from London to the old market town of Dorchester rather than Belfast. Jury could just guess how much Inspector Neal enjoyed having his authority presumed upon, but Neal was too much of a gentleman to make Jury's life hell. Many would have.

". . . and not two decent relations to rub together," Beth Riley was saying in a shocking display of acrimony. The child was dead. What had family connections to do with it?

"All right, all right, love," said Riley, in some attempt to shush her. Though why the father should have to minister to the totally unfeeling stepmother, Jury couldn't say. Indeed, he couldn't see the two of them together at all, if it came to that. She lost no chance to remind him of her superior education, and Jury simply let her get it out of her system as his eye travelled the room. Over the fireplace were photographs that might bear out her claim, for all its coldness. There was even one of those mahogany coats-of-arms that tourists seemed forever gathering in the race for their roots; there were also framed documents, one with a seal.

"I'm sorry to intrude upon your grief," said Jury to Mrs. Riley. His tone was icy. "But there are a few questions."

Beth Riley sat back, said nothing, left the question-and-answer period up to her husband. Simon had been (she reminded Jury) *Albert's* son.

"Have you remembered anything at all since you talked to Inspector Neal, Mr. Riley? About your son's friends . . . or enemies?" Predictably, Riley disclaimed any enemies — how could a lad of twelve have enemies? It was true the Dorset police had established to their satisfaction that Simon Riley had neither. He was not popular with his schoolmates, but neither was he hated. Nor did anyone seriously believe a schoolboy would be carrying the sort of knife around Dorchester that had inflicted the wound.

Inspector Neal had looked almost unhappier than the father himself when Neal had said *psychopath.* What else could it be? *You know what that means, Superintendent? Child-killer. In Dorchester?*

I wouldn't like it much in London, either, Jury had thought.

". . . psychopath." Albert Riley echoed the word of Inspector Neal. He was wiping his eyes with a much-used handkerchief. Jury's feeling about Riley had changed when he realized that the man probably did have to work to keep from crumbling. Certainly, he was getting no support from his wife.

463

But with Neal's and Riley's verdict upon who killed Simon, Jury did not agree. The single wound in the boy's back was clean, neat, quick — not the multiple stab-wounds one might have expected from a person who was out for blood or boys. There had been no molesting of the body. This was all Jury had to go on, but he still thought the murder was probably premeditated and that it was Simon — not just any child — the killer had been tracking. According to Neal's report, Simon's mates — though not close ones — hadn't known he stopped in that alley to smoke fags and look at dirty pictures. Thinking of it that way, the wrong questions were perhaps being asked. Certainly, it was possible the boy had an "enemy." It was also possible that the Rileys themselves had.

He did not pose that question at the moment. All he said to Riley was that he wasn't convinced the boy's death was the work of a deranged mind.

Riley looked utterly astonished. "What other reason could there be? You sound like you think someone wanted to — murder *Simon.*"

"I could think of half a dozen, Mr. Riley. They could all be wrong, of course." Jury allowed Mrs. Riley to give him another shot of Jameson's, more to keep her in a comradely mood than because he wanted a drink. Beth seemed actually curious about other reasons. She perked up a bit. Jury found her curiosity and perkiness as depressing as the grey weight of the sky beyond the window. "One is that someone actually meant to kill your son — I'm sorry," he added, when Riley flinched at the suggestion. Jury took a sip of the whisky under the approving eye of Beth Riley. Approving what? That the Law drank on duty? Or that someone had meant to kill her stepson? "Another is that Simon might have known something that someone didn't want him to know. Seen something that someone hadn't wanted him to see. Simon could have had knowledge he didn't even *know* he had, too. The thing is that he was in an alley that none of his schoolmates seemed to know about. It's not on his way home from

464

school. And school had been out over an hour, if the medical examiner fixed the time correctly. Somewhere between five and perhaps eight o'clock. It might make one think that someone had been, possibly, following him —"

Riley was into his third whisky, drinking with blind eyes, the handkerchief wadded against his face. "He could have been dragged there —"

Jury was already shaking his head. "No. There'd be — signs, if that were the case." Bloodstains, marks — Jury didn't elaborate.

The Rileys exchanged glances, but shook their heads.

"Could he have been meeting someone?"

They looked blank.

"Kids get up to things —"

Riley was out of his chair like a shot. Wasn't it enough the boy was dead? Did the police have to go about ruining his character, too? Even Beth got in on this scene. She mightn't have missed Simon, but the family name was something else again.

Jury rose and apologized for intruding upon them, as he took another look at the pictures, the memorabilia over the fireplace. Beth as a young girl, Beth as a young woman. Nothing of Riley that he could see. Wiggins stood beside him, notebook clapped shut, pocketing his pen, taking out his lozenges.

February was hell this close to the sea. Dorchester was ten miles from it, but that was close enough for Wiggins.

They stopped outside and Jury lit a cigarette. "We wouldn't have got any more out of them. And the boy's funeral is tomorrow. Leave it for now."

The queue of shoppers had disappeared, but Jury saw in the faces of passersby more fear than curiosity. They walked on the edge of the pavement, as if coming nearer the scene of such a tragedy might contaminate them, might spread danger to their own children.

465

The Closed sign hung a little askew. Wiggins was studying a brace of pheasant, feet trussed up, heads dangling down. "No need to cause more suffering." Jury thought he was referring to the Rileys, until he added, "That's why I've been thinking of going vegetarian."

Jury tried to drag his mind from the man whose son was dead and the son himself, to say, "No more plaice and chips, Wiggins? Hard to imagine."

Wiggins considered. "I think I'd still eat fish. But not flesh, sir."

"No more missionaries, that it?"

"What?"

"Never mind." Jury smiled bleakly. "There's Judge Jeffries restaurant just down the road. You hungry? Nothing like eating under the eye of the Hanging Judge." Jury looked at the pheasant.

Man, beast, bird. Life is cheap.

II

And he knew just how cheap when they got back to Wynfield, where the Dorset police had its headquarters.

"There's been another one," said Inspector Neal, looking a little greyer than when Jury had last seen him. "In Wynchcoombe. Another boy: name, Davey White. Choirboy." Neal's voice broke and he did not look at all pleased that his theory was probably being proved correct. At the same time he looked slightly relieved, and guilty for the relief. "Not ours, though. This is the Devon-Cornwall constabulary's manor. Wynchcoombe's in Dartmoor." He was interrupted by the telephone — a call, apparently, from his superior, for he kept nodding. "Yes, yes, yes. We've got every man on it we can spare . . . yes, I *know* the town's in a panic . . ." After more from the other end, Neal hung up, shaking his head.

Jury said nothing except, "How far's Wynchcoombe, then?"

Neal looked a little surprised. "Forty miles, about."

A police constable — a pleasant-looking young man — showed Jury the map on the wall. "You'll want to go to headquarters first, I expect. That's just outside Exeter —"

"Why do I want to go there? What's the quickest way to Wynchcoombe?"

"Well, I was just thinking you'd want to check with headquarters. Sir," he added weakly.

"It'd only waste time."

Neal was making a fuss over some papers on his desk seemingly in desperate need of rearrangement. "That's Divisional Commander Macalvie's patch, Mr. Jury."

"I don't much care if it's Dirty Harry Callahan's. We've got a boy murdered in Dorchester and now another one in Wynchcoombe. So I'd like to get there as soon as possible. The divisional commander will understand."

The constable just looked at Jury. Then he said, "I worked with him once. Right cock-up I made of something and —" He pulled back the corners of his mouth. In a distorted voice he said, "I loss ma teeth. Crowns, these are".

Jury picked up the map the constable had marked the route on as Wiggins leaned closer and peered at his teeth. "I only wish I had your dentist."

II

The Church
on the Moor

THREE

T HE silver chalice lay on the floor of the choir vestry, staining it darker with the wine that had been mixed with water, now mixed with blood. Before the Scene of Crimes man had come, no one could touch it. After he had finished with it, no one wanted to. The lab staff of the Devon-Cornwall constabulary seemed to be avoiding it, superstitiously. As for the pictures, the police photographer had apologized to the curate for the little bursts of light in Wynchcoombe Church.

Police, both uniformed branch and CID, were all over the church, searching the chancel aisles, the nave, the main vestry. Wiggins and several others were outside going over the Green, on which the church fronted, and the deserted church walk, leading to the vestry doors on the other side.

Dr. Sanford, the local practitioner, had finished his examination and said the boy had probably been dead around ten hours. The curate couldn't believe that the boy could have been there all that time and no one had found him until three or four hours ago.

It had surprised Jury, too, who was standing by the altar with DC Coogan. He looked up at the altar, his mind a blank. Wynchcoombe had a beautiful church. Even with its high spire, it appeared smaller on the outside than inside. The chancel and nave together measured over a hundred feet.

He could think of nothing to say to Betty Coogan, who was crying. She couldn't help herself, she said; she'd known Davey and his granddad, the vicar of Wynchcoombe Church. "Whoever'd want to do this to Davey White?"

In any other circumstances, Policewoman Coogan would have been a gift with her red hair and good legs. But not now.

It was the expression on the clear face of Davey White that had struck Jury most—a look not of terror but more of impish surprise, the mouth slightly open, smiling even, as if he'd thought it had been rather a wizard trick, this being struck without warning. Now here he lay, ten years old, another schoolboy, dead two days after Simon Riley.

Betty Coogan was talking about the boy in Dorchester, blowing her nose with Jury's handkerchief, voicing the opinion of the Dorset police: they had a psychopathic killer on their hands. Jury was more inclined to agree than he had been before, but he still withheld judgement. The method was the same. Simple. A knife in the back.

The fingerprint man came up to Jury and Coogan. "Where in hell's Macalvie?"

She shook her head, another bout of tears threatening. "In Exeter, on that robbery case. I tried to get him. Well, they must have got him by now—"

The print expert mumbled. "Ought to be here—"

He was. Divisional Commander—or Detective Chief Superintendent—Brian Macalvie came through the heavy oak doors of Wynchcoombe Church like the icy Dartmoor wind he brought with him. And he didn't tiptoe down the aisle.

The look he gave his DC Betty Coogan did nothing at all to steady her. She seemed to sway a little, and Jury put his hand under her arm.

Chief Superintendent Macalvie looked briefly up at the altar and slightingly at them and said to Jury, "Who the hell are you?"

Jury took out his warrant card; Macalvie glanced at it and then at DC Coogan (having dismissed Jury and all the credentials that went with him), saying, "You knew where I was. Why the bloody hell didn't you get to me sooner?"

She simply lowered her head.

"Where're you hiding the body, Betts? Might I have a wee look?"

There was a Scot's burr, probably put on when he felt like it. Macalvie's accent seemed to have got stuck somewhere in the mid-Atlantic. But the Scottish ancestry reigned at the moment: accent, coppery hair, blue eyes like tiny blowtorches. Jury could understand why Betty Coogan didn't snap back.

Still with head lowered, she said, "He's in the choir vestry."

Macalvie stood in the vestry, still with hands jammed in trouser pockets, holding back his raincoat — which was the way he had come in. "By now, fifty per cent of anything I could use has washed down the Dart." It sounded as if he were privy to some invisible world of evidence from which mere, mortal cops (the Jurys of the world) were excluded. Macalvie had been standing and looking down at the body, looking round the vestry, looking out of the vestry door. He was standing now at the door, still with his hands in his pockets, just like anyone who might have been speculating on a sudden change of weather.

To his back, a CID sergeant named Kendall said, "Nothing's been touched, sir. Except for Dr. Sanford's examination of the body."

"That's like saying an archaeologist left the digs as neat as my gran's front parlour," said Macalvie to the mist and the vestry walk lost in it.

Jury saw Dr. Sanford look at Macalvie with a wild sort of anger—at the man standing there communing with the trees. The doctor opened his mouth, but shut it again.

Constable Coogan, cheeks burning, decided to fight fire. "You'd think anyone else just *looking* at the crime scene before you get there erases clues—"

Macalvie turned those blowtorch eyes on her. "It does."

He nodded at the chalice. "What's that doing in the choir vestry?" Macalvie was down on one knee now, looking at the body of Davey White.

Dr. Sanford was an avuncular man. His smile—his first mistake—was condescending: "I assure you, Chief Superintendent, that the boy *wasn't* brained with the chalice. He was stabbed."

Macalvie favoured Dr. Sanford with the same look he'd shot at DC Coogan. "I didn't say he *was* 'brained', did I? I'm a simple, literal man. I asked a simple, literal question." He turned back to the body.

No one answered his question, so Dr. Sanford filled in the silence. "He's been dead, I'd judge, since about six o'clock this morning. Of course—"

"It could have been earlier or later." Macalvie finished the comment for him. "Not even you can tell the exact time of death. Not even me."

Dr. Sanford controlled himself and went on: "There's rigor, but the lividity—"

"You think it's hypostasis."

"Of course." Sanford continued his discourse on the blood's having drained and the darker patches of skin showing where the body had been in contact with the floor.

Macalvie, still with his eyes on Davey White's body, held out his hand as if he weren't paying any more attention to Sanford than a pew or a hassock. "Give me your scalpel."

Dr. Sanford was clearly shocked; his tone was frosty: "And did you intend to perform the autopsy here and now? You *do*

473

have a pathologist—" He stopped and looked extremely uneasy. He might just as well not have been there at all, given the lack of response. Still, the doctor ploughed the furrow: "I really don't think—"

Macalvie's hand was still outstretched. Jury imagined that when Macalvie was thinking, he didn't want those thoughts lost in the crossfire of underlings—DCs, doctors, or even Scotland Yard.

Dr. Sanford reopened his bag and produced a scalpel.

Macalvie made a tiny incision in the centre of one of the purplish stains and a bit of blood oozed and trickled. He re-returned the scalpel, pulled down the boy's vest, and said nothing.

Again, as if it were necessary to fill up silences Macalvie left in his wake, Sergeant Kendall said, "The curate couldn't understand how the lad could have been lying here for all that time—"

"Because the kid *wasn't* lying here all that time. That's a bruise, not hypostasis." He ignored Sanford and addressed himself to Jury, figuring perhaps, since one nitwit had got it wrong, he wanted to hear if the other one would. It was the second time he'd spoken to Jury; Wiggins, he'd managed to neglect altogether. "What do you think?"

"I think you're right," said Jury. "He probably wasn't killed here and certainly hasn't been lying here for ten hours."

Macalvie continued to stare at Jury, but said nothing. Then he turned to his fingerprint man and indicated the silver chalice that had been carefully dusted and photographed. "You through with that?"

"Sir." He nearly clicked his heels and handed over the chalice.

In spite of its already having had a thorough going-over, Macalvie handled it with a handkerchief, holding it up to the light as if he were administering the sacraments.

Betty Coogan, completely unnerved by her divisional commander and (Jury supposed) sometime lover, asked, "You think he was killed somewhere else and brought here? But why? That doesn't make sense."

"Really?" said Macalvie in his loquacious way.

Jury shook his head. "That's taking a hell of a chance, unless the murderer was making a point. The chalice wouldn't be in the choir vestry except for someone's wanting to smear it in the boy's blood. An act of desecration."

Macalvie nearly forgot himself and smiled. "Okay, let's go and have a talk with his dad."

"Grandfather. Davey's own father is dead," said Wiggins, sliding a cough drop into his mouth.

"Okay, grandfather." Macalvie held out his hand as he had for the doctor's scalpel. "Mind giving me one of those? I'm trying to quit smoking."

"Good," said Wiggins, promptly letting a few Fisherman's Friends drop into Macalvie's palm. "You won't regret it."

II

Although the housekeeper was weeping when she opened the door, Reverend Lindley White's eyes were as dry as his voice.

Wiggins had been dispatched to get what he could out of the housekeeper (which, if nothing else, would be a cup of tea), and Jury and Macalvie were seated in two ladderback chairs on the other side of Mr. White's large desk. Even with one less policeman in the room, the vicar appeared to think the ratio of two to one was unfair, though God was supposedly his ally. He could tell them absolutely nothing that would throw light on this "sad affair"—a favourite summing up, apparently; he used it several times.

"Sure, you can throw some light on the matter," said Macalvie, pleasantly. "Such as why you didn't like him."

The vicar was vehement in his denial of this charge, especially coming, as it did, before he could find a persona to fit it. "David has been living here for just a little over a year. My son and his wife, Mary" — the *Mary* called up someone he'd sooner forget, apparently —"died in a motorcycle accident and shortly after that, her aunt simply dropped David — quite literally — on my doorstep. It was supposed to be for a few days. I've not laid eyes on the woman since. I don't know why I was surprised." Under a grey cliff of eyebrow, the vicar's eyes burned with un-Christian-like feeling.

Jury wondered if, in the vicar's fight against his feelings for Mary, he had won the battle but lost the war. The Reverend White could — as he went on to do — call Davey's mother "pig-track Irish," but Jury saw the tattered flag of emotion in all of this, and thought it probably sexual.

Macalvie said, "So you didn't like Mary. Either."

"Now listen, Superintendent —"

"Chief." It must have been almost unconscious. Macalvie wasn't even looking at White; his eyes were raking over the room as they had been doing ever since he sat down.

"*Chief* Superintendent. This has been one of the worst experiences of my life."

Macalvie looked at him then. "What was the other one?"

"What?"

"It must have been pretty bad if your grandson's murder is only one of them. I can't believe there were more than two. So what I gather is, since you hated the mother, you didn't much care for the sight of Davey around the house. Constant reminder, right?" He had just stuck a Fisherman's Friend in his mouth and was sucking at it.

Colour drained from the vicar's face until it matched the shade of the bisque statuette on his desk. "*Certainly* I was fond of David. What are you trying to say?"

476

"I never *try* to say anything. I just say it. So was his mother the only reason you didn't like Davey?"

The vicar was half out of his chair now. "You persist in this judgement—"

"Judgements I leave to God. Sit down. He was killed sometime early this morning. Five, six. Why would he have been out at that hour and in Wynchcoombe Wood?"

Mr. White was astonished. "But he was killed in the *church!*"

Macalvie shook his head. "He was *put* in the church. Probably at that hour there was nobody about. And barely light. But would no one have been in the church this morning? A cleaner? Anyone?"

The vicar shook his head. "Not necessarily. And no reason for anyone to go into the choir vestry."

"You don't keep a very sharp eye on your grandson, do you?"

Jury interrupted, much to Macalvie's displeasure. "Why would Davey have been out that early?"

Mr. White coloured, smarting still under the bite of Macalvie's comment, probably, Jury thought, because it was true.

"Davey was a bit odd—"

Macalvie's impatient sigh told him how much he believed that excuse.

"I *only* mean that he occasionally liked to get out of the house before breakfast, before school, and go to the woods to, as he said, just 'think about things.' He hadn't many school chums . . ." The vicar's voice trailed away under Macalvie's blue gaze.

Jury was himself thinking about Simon Riley. "Thinking about things" could have meant smoking the odd cigarette. Or just getting away. Another lonely boy, perhaps, in a cold house. But he didn't voice his opinion.

Macalvie did. "Must have had a great life, your Davey. Didn't you worry about him, out in the dark or the dawn,

477

alone in the wood?" He had got up to prowl the room and was now looking over the vicar's bookcases.

"Nothing's ever happened in Wynchcoombe Wood."

Macalvie raised his eyes from an old volume. "Something has now. And didn't you read about that kid in Dorchester, Mr. White?" he asked casually.

For the first time, the Reverend Lindley White looked frightened. "I did. You're not saying there's a psychopathic killer loose?"

Macalvie's answer was another question. "Can you think of anyone who hated your grandson?"

"No. Absolutely not," he snapped.

"How about someone who might hate you?"

This time, the vicar had to stop and think.

III

What Wiggins had learned from the housekeeper verified the information they had got from the vicar. Except the housekeeper did wonder why Davey hadn't come back for his breakfast and his schoolbooks. Wiggins read his notes, and they were, as usual, thorough. Jury told him to go along to Wynchcoombe Wood. Macalvie cadged a few Fisherman's Friends and told Wiggins he wanted Kendall and his men to comb that vestry walk inch-by-inch. Davey could have stumbled, fallen, been dragged. That might account for the bruises.

Wiggins put away his notebook. "Yes, sir. Are you having an incidents room set up, sir?"

His yes was grudging. "Tell Kendall to get a portable unit and stick it in the middle of the damned Green." He nodded toward the clutch of villagers standing in front of the George and the tea room. Even from this distance, they seemed to pull back a bit, as if from fear, or, perhaps, the divisional commander's eye. "No, Wiggins," said Macalvie wearily, as the sergeant wrote it down. "Put it in that car park—" Macalvie nodded off to the right and a large space, probably meant for the cars and caravans of summer tourists. "And tell Kendall to keep it staffed with the few men from headquarters who won't be stumbling all over their own feet. Much less mine."

The church had been cordoned off; now, perhaps to disengage themselves from the scene of the tragedy (or from Macalvie's stare), several of the villagers repaired to the pub, there to overhaul their former estimate of life in sleepy little Wynchcoombe.

"Pretty place," said Macalvie, qualifying it with, "if you like this sort of village."

It was indeed a pretty place, with its stone cottages huddled around the Green and the spire of Wynchcoombe Church rising above it. An enviable peal of bells told them it was six.

"I need a drink," said Macalvie.

"The George?" Its sign claimed it to be a fourteenth-century coaching inn.

He grunted. "You kidding? With all the regulars in there having a crack about what happened? There's a pub a couple miles away I go to when I feel especially masochistic. How Freddie — you'll love Freddie — gets any custom on that stretch of road beats me."

Macalvie looked away to a ground mist just beginning to rise. "It's not far from a village called Clerihew Marsh. I want to tell you a story, Jury."

FOUR

ELP the Poor Struggler was the pub's full name, a wretched box of a building on a desolate stretch of road, whose ochre paint had dulled to the colour of bracken from the smoke of its chimney pots. Its sign swung on an iron post over its door and the windows were so dirty they were opaque. The building listed from either dry rot or rising damp. Only the desolation of pub and traveller alike would tempt one to join the other.

There was no car park. What custom the pub got had to pull up by the side of the road. Two cars were there when Macalvie and Jury pulled in.

Brian Macalvie was now pursuing, with what Jury supposed was the customary Macalvie charm, a line of questioning directed at an arthritic, elderly woman who was swabbing down the bar. The "saloon" side was separated from the "public" side only by a gentleman's agreement. The public bar off to the left had most of the action: bar billiards, video game, Art Deco jukebox that was pummelling the customers with Elvis Presley's "Hound Dog."

• • •

"Where's Sam Waterhouse, Freddie?" Macalvie didn't so much ask for as demand an answer.

"I don't naw nort," said Freddie. "Y'm mazed as a brish stick, Mac. D'yuh niver quit?" She was wall-eyed, wattle-armed, and skinny, and with her stubby grey hair sitting in a lick on her head, she reminded Jury even more of a cockerell. He guessed her sexual identity had been scratching with the chickens long enough to get lost.

"I never quit, Freddie. You treated Sam like you were his auld mum, the dear Lord help him."

"Ha! Yu'm a gret vule, Mac, the divil hisself. Cider hisses when yu zwallers it."

"Hell, *this* cider'd hiss on a stone. You're thick as two boards and your right hand hasn't seen your left in forty years," said Macalvie, picking up his cider and moving to a table.

Freddie grinned at Jury. "What c'n I do ver 'ee, me anzum?"

Jury grinned back. "I'll try the cider. You're only young once."

"It was the stupidest arrest the Devon-Cornwall cops ever made." Macalvie was talking about the Rose Mulvanney case. "Here's this nineteen-year-old kid, Sam, who's living in Clerihew Marsh and indulging in fantasies, maybe about Cosy Rosie. Rose Mulvanney could start breathing heavy over anything in pants. In the U.S. she'd freak out in a corn-field over the scarecrows."

From what Macalvie had told Jury during their drive to the pub, it was certain the divisional commander's heart was in America — his mother was Irish-American — even if his body was in Devon. Obsessive as he was about police work, still he took his holiday every year and went to New York. His speech was littered with the old-fashioned, hard-boiled speech of a Bogart movie: *dames, broads*—that sort of thing.

"How do you know all this stuff about Rose Mulvanney?"

"Through extremely delicate questions put to the inhabitants of Clerihew Marsh," said Macalvie. "Like, did Rose screw around—"

"I'm sure that's the way you put it." Jury took a drink of cider and could believe in the sizzling throat of the devil.

"Be careful, Freddie makes it herself. My questions to the villagers were more disgustingly discreet. But what turned up when I collared the milkman and the old broad that runs the post office stores was that Rose Mulvanney, a couple of days before she died, started taking more milk and buying more bread. *This* even though her kid Mary was away on a school trip. The extra groceries went on for maybe five days. Now, she sure as hell wasn't doing that for Sammy Waterhouse. He lived right there in Clerihew Marsh."

"You're saying someone else was living with her?"

"Of course."

Jury tried not to smile. Macalvie was nothing if not certain of Macalvie. "I agree it's a possibility."

"Good. I can go on living." He popped another Fisherman's Friend into his mouth.

"So, assuming the Devon-Cornwall police picked on Waterhouse — why? Months went by before they arrested him, you said."

"It's expensive to mount a murder investigation; you know that. They wanted to get him a hell of a lot earlier, except I kept tossing spanners in the works, like trying to convince the effing Devon police that Sam Waterhouse couldn't have moved in with Rose."

"Aren't you making a lot out of extra bread and milk?"

"No. Rose wasn't buying bread for the church bazaar."

"There must have been evidence against Waterhouse. What was it?"

"That he was always mooning around Rose. He was *nineteen*, for God's sakes." Macalvie shoved the ashtray to the

482

end of the table. "And the dame next door said she'd heard them having a king-sized row a few nights before Rose died. She saw Sam coming out of the house in a right blaze."

"And Waterhouse — what did he say?"

"He didn't deny it. He was furious Rose had been 'leading him on' and he really thought she cared. Told him she had another boyfriend, stuff like that."

"What did forensics turn up?"

"Their hands. They just shrugged. Of *course* there were prints. All over. Sam had admitted to being in the house. But on the knife? No. He'd have wiped that clean, said my learned superior. So I said to him, Then why didn't he wipe everything *else* clean he'd touched? And after the elimination prints — the two daughters and a couple of friends in Cleri- hew — there were still two sets left over. Could have been anybody, and certainly could have been the guy who did the job, if he'd been living there for a few days."

"The girls? The daughters? Where were they?"

"The fifteen-year-old was off on a school trip. The little one must have been in the house, except for the odd night or two she was sent to play with a little chum from her school."

"But that means she must have seen the man at some point — assuming you're right."

Macalvie's look sliced up Jury as good as any knife. Could there be any doubt about a Macalvie theory? "That's true. All she had to do was say, 'No, it wasn't Sammy.' And believe me, she would have if she could; she was crazy about Sam. Both girls were. He was very nice to them. So she could have said it wasn't him and maybe identify who it *was*. Only Teresa never spoke another word." Macalvie turned to stare into the fireplace, as if he too might never speak another word, a rare silence for him, Jury thought.

In the public bar off to the left, Freddie had muscled an anti-Elvis fan away from the jukebox to feed in her own coins. "Jailhouse Rock" made way for "Are You Lonesome Tonight?"

Jury saw Macalvie glance toward the jukebox and thought perhaps he was going to answer the question put by Elvis — and, for that matter, by Freddie, who was singing along: "D'ya miss me tooo-night?" in her cups and out of key. Macalvie snatched up both of their pints, saying, "It wouldn't be so bloody bad if Freddie'd shut up." He walked over to the bar, had his brief quarrel with her — their standard means of communication, Jury imagined — and was back and picking up the story of the Mulvanney family. He chronicled their lives as if he'd been a relation. The details he'd picked up during the investigation.

"It still seems like pretty shabby evidence," said Jury.

Macalvie drank his cider. "Oh, of course the prosecution had their witness. No, not someone who saw it. Just a friend of Sammy's."

"Friend? Doesn't sound like much of one."

"Ah, but in the interests of Justice, we must all do our bit. He was a student at Exeter, too. Law. Claimed Sam Waterhouse had said several times he'd kill her. Good old George, standing right there in the box saying Sam came in that night with what looked like blood on his clothes. Liar."

"What was Waterhouse's answer?"

"That if he ever said it, it was only a manner of speaking. And the blood came from cutting himself in the lab. Terrific. The prosecution made mincemeat of Sam."

Whether from the after-effects of cider or the present effects of Elvis, Freddie was still singing along:

"Doon yer haaaart fill wit pain?
Should ay COME beck a-GAAAIIN?..."

wailed Freddie. Macalvie yelled at her to shut up. Freddie paid no attention.

"Christ, an Elvis song that doesn't bring down the walls and she's got to have a sing-along. The kid, Mary Mulvanney," Macalvie went on, "I saw her twice. Once at the inquest. She could hardly answer the questions."

He stopped, stared at the jukebox, then back at Jury.

"Unfortunately, I wasn't there. I wasn't in charge of the case. Bad luck for Devon. What I did, I did on my own. Didn't amount to much. A few questions here, a few bruises there." His blue eyes glinted with reflected firelight and he almost smiled. "That's supposed to be my style, you know. Threats, blackmail, bullets in knee-caps." He shrugged.

"I don't worry too much about style. When was the second time?"

Macalvie was staring into the fire again, shoving his foot against one of the huge logs sprawled on the hearth like an old dog. "For what?"

Jury knew Macalvie knew "for what." "The second time you saw Mary Mulvanney."

"Months later. After they tossed Sam Waterhouse in the nick. The kid storms in my office — fifteen, scrawny, and freckles — talk about scarecrows. But, man, did she let me have it. She knew some words even I didn't know; must have been some swell school she was going to. I never saw anyone so mad in my life."

"Why at you? You were the one person who kept the case open and did all the work."

"So to her that meant I was in charge, didn't it? She knew Waterhouse didn't do it. And she screamed at me, as she casually removed all the stuff from my desk with a delicate sweep of her skinny arm: *That's my mum got killed and my baby sister's in hospital and you'd fucking well better get who did it or I will!*' My God, could that kid get mad."

But Macalvie, who had seemed determined not to temper bad humour with good, was actually smiling. It was probably a relief to him to find somebody who wasn't afraid of him, even if she was only a skinny young kid.

"And then she stormed out. I never saw her again." The

485

look he gave Jury was woeful. "It was the only case I never solved."

He wanted Jury to think that was the source of the unhappy look. Jury didn't.

II

They had been sitting there for a couple of minutes, in a small pocket of silence not shared by the regulars who were being treated to the wonderful voice of Loretta Lynn. Unfortunately, the coalminer's daughter had to make way to the voice-over of Freddie, behind the bar wiping glasses and singing about how she too once had to go to the well to draw water.

Macalvie yelled at her, "The last time you ever drank anything but booze was when they tossed you in Cranmere Bog."

"What about the little one, Teresa?"

"What about her?"

"If you're right —"

Raised eyebrows. *If?*

"Then why in hell did the killer leave a witness behind?"

That this could be a hole in his theory did not seem to bother Macalvie at all. He could, apparently, plug it up like a finger in a dyke. "Say because the guy was sure Teresa couldn't tie him to her mother. Maybe Teresa *didn't* see him, or at least didn't know his name, or for a dozen reasons she simply wouldn't be able to point a finger at him. And if it were a crime of passion, it's possible that he couldn't see his way to killing a five-year-old, too."

"And the five-year-old? Could she have gone after her mum with a knife? Did you ever suspect her?"

The look Macalvie gave Jury could have carved him in pieces. "No, I always do thing by halves, Jury. I'm a sloppy cop. I didn't even notice the trail of blood she left all the way from the kitchen to the phone and all the blood over her

486

nightie and on the phone —" He waved a dismissive hand. "Don't be an asshole, will you? Of course, little kids can freak out. She didn't do it." He was silent for a while. Then he said, "I went to the hospital. It was obvious, at least in the mumbo-jumbo land of shrinkdom, that she didn't stand much chance of getting well. Her mind seemed to have split. Catatonic and curled up like a foetus. Anyway, they finally moved Teresa to Harbrick Hall. Ever heard of it? They call it 'Heartbreak Hall.' "

Jury had heard of it. It was one of those places he wished he hadn't. "I was there once."

"And you're almost cured?"

Jury ignored the sarcasm, thinking of Harbrick Hall. One of those cosy, innocent-sounding names that in no way reflected the huge, understaffed, overfull hospital. Endless corridors, bolted doors, grilles. The sickly, sour smell of urine and ammonia, and the grey-garbed cleaner with mop and pail in a corridor awash in hopelessness.

Macalvie went on: "The place is so big you could get lost just trying to find your way out. Anyway, Teresa Mulvanney supposedly had got a little better. No, she wasn't talking. She never talked. But at least she wasn't lying curled up like a baby. The Paki attendant 'very proud' of Teresa's 'progress.' Progress. You know what her progress was?"

From Macalvie's tone, Jury didn't think he wanted to know. Right now, he couldn't get the faces of Simon Riley and Davy White out of his mind. They seemed to merge and separate and break apart, like little faces behind mullioned and rained-on windowpanes.

"Fingerpainting," said Macalvie. "The Paki couldn't understand why 'she only like the red pot.' "

"Drop it." He blotted out the image of fingerpaints by trying to concentrate on the Irish singer someone had mercifully found on the jukebox. Jury was sure his display of weakness would earn him a surly answer.

But all Macalvie said was, "I did." He looked at his watch. "But Mary, the sister, couldn't, could she?" He turned to look at the jukebox from which came the lovely and mournful dirge:

> *I love you as I never loved before,*
> *Since first I met you on the village green . . .*

Macalvie was taking money out of his wallet and was out of his chair as quick as a cat. In one long movement, he tossed the money on the table of the man who'd slotted the 10p in the box and then he walked over and pulled the plug before the singer could finish *"as I loved you, when . . ."*

Freddie tossed down her bar-towel and started over; the man who'd played the song was bigger than Macalvie and getting out of his chair. Knowing that Macalvie — outsized, outweighed, or outnumbered — wouldn't hesitate to shove the man right back down again, Jury started to get up. Damned idiot. Couldn't he remember he was a policeman?

Apparently, he could. The jukebox was in the public bar and so were Macalvie and his newfound friends; Jury couldn't hear what he said, but Macalvie was shoving his wallet in the big one's face and smiling. Freddie was standing with her hands on her skinny hips. The party at the table got their coats together pretty quickly, and Macalvie turned to Freddie, who gave him a bar-towel in the face.

At least that pleased the regulars who were on their way out. Macalvie just shrugged and came back to sit down.

"Pulling rank? That could be dangerous down at headquarters," said Jury.

That earned him an uncomprehending stare. Dangerous for Macalvie? "I don't pull rank, buddy." His elbow on the table, he turned his watch so Jury could see it. "You never heard of the licensing laws? I just told them Freddie had to close early and asked if anyone was in a condition to drive, seeing all the cider they'd put down." He picked up his and

Jury's pints and strolled across the pub, which they now had to themselves."

Except, of course, for Freddie, who was filling the pints and Macalvie's ear with her opinion of him. It followed him across the room, silenced only by his turning and saying — Elvis done with, he didn't have to yell—"I'd have run you into Princetown years ago, Freddie, except I've got a certain respect for the murderers and psychos there."

He slammed down the pints, spilling the cider over the sides of the glasses as Freddie went to answer the telephone. "Christ, what a stupid old broad. That 'Freddie' doesn't stand for 'Frederika,' or any girl's name. Stands for 'Fred.' The mum and dad must've wanted a boy; they'd have settled for a girl; they got a mineral." He drank his cider.

"Telephone, me anzum," fluted Freddie.

"She must mean you, Jury. She'd never call me that."

It was Inspector Neal, who had tracked him down through Kendall. What he had to report about his end of the investigation was very little. But a Chief Superintendent Racer had called and asked — well, *demanded* was a better word — that Jury report to him. And how was he getting on with Divisional Commander Macalvie?

"Great," said Jury, "Friendly bloke."

"That's a first," said Neal, and hung up.

Jury went back to the table and started to collect his coat. "It's not that I don't enjoy sitting around with you, but we've got two murders on our hands."

"One's mine. Don't be greedy, Jury."

"One's yours. I'd never know it. You can sit here and drink the night away and yell at Freddie. I'm going back to Dorchester."

"Can you just sit down a minute and shut up. Do you think I'm relaxing in the Victorian splendour of this bug-ridden flashhouse because I want to? Why in hell do you think I've been talking about the Mulvanney murder?"

"Because you're obsessed with it, maybe?"

Macalvie didn't rise to the bait. "Because in my gut, I know there's a connection."

As Jury asked him what, the door of the Help the Poor Struggler opened and shut.

"I think it just walked in."

He sounded sad.

FIVE

Jury would have recognized the prison pallor anywhere; he'd seen it often enough. It wasn't the pale skin of a man who'd not seen enough of the sun. It was more as if one had put a paintbrush to an emotion — despair, desolation, whatever—and tinged it in that sickly whitish-grey. The pallor was accentuated by the black clothes: chinos, roll-neck sweater, parka. Accentuated too by the dark hair and eyes. He was tall, understandably thin, handsome, and maybe in mourning for nineteen lost years.

"Hullo, Sam," said Macalvie.

"I wondered who the car belonged to. I should've known."

Freddie came out from some inner room as if her antennae had at last picked up a welcome presence. "Sammy!" She flung herself against him so hard that Jury was surprised he didn't hear bones breaking. She stepped back and gave Macalvie an evil look. Then to Sam, she said, "How are yuh, me dear?"

"I'm fine, Freddie. Just waiting for the place to clear."

Macalvie, who always knew what everyone else was thinking, smiled. "I know. I cleared it. So sit down, Sammy." With his foot, he shoved out a chair. And, as if they were on the best of terms, he said, "Freddie, bring the man some cider and go and play Elvis. Just don't play 'Jailhouse Rock,' okay? Or I'll break your legs. Where've you been, Sam? You got out four days ago."

"You keeping track, Inspector? But it couldn't be inspector now. You must be chief constable."

"I will be. Right now it's commander. Or chief superintendent."

"Where'd you trip up?" asked Sam, as Freddie put down his pint. "Not over me, I hope." But his smile was hopeless.

"Who tripped up? You think I'm ambitious?"

Sam Waterhouse's laugh was so hearty that Freddie came out to see what was going on. She disappeared again.

"What've you been doing?"

"Seeing Dartmoor. Sleeping in an old tin-working or on the rocks. I like the moor. The way the mist comes up, the whole damned world disappears. Ever been up on Hound Tor? Nice. On a clear day you can see Exeter and police headquarters forever. Why don't you forget it, Macalvie?"

"Read any papers lately, Sam?"

Sam Waterhouse shifted uncomfortably in his chair and drank nearly half of his pint. "Sure. The newsboy was flogging the *Telegraph* all over Dartmoor."

"Meaning you have," said Macalvie. "Meet any other tourists?"

Jury both could and couldn't understand Sam Waterhouse's anger. If you'd been in a high-security lockup on a trumped-up charge. Except Macalvie was the one who'd always believed in Sam's innocence and who'd worked like hell to prove it.

"I saw the papers. A boy was killed in Dorchester. What's it to do with me?"

"And another kid was killed in Wynchcoombe. You

wouldn't have read about that yet. Look. I'm not asking you for alibis."

"What are you asking for then?"

Macalvie shook his head. "Not sure."

Jury was surprised Macalvie could say it.

Sam Waterhouse took one of Jury's cigarettes. He had the hoarse voice of a heavy smoker. Jury didn't imagine nineteen years in Princetown would make a voice mellifluous.

"You're still trying to solve that case." Sam shook his head.

"It's a blot on my career." Macalvie's smile did its quick little disappearing act. "Incidentally, you're sitting next to a CID man from Scotland Yard."

"Richard Jury," said Jury, embellishing upon Macalvie's gracious introduction. He shook hands with Sam Waterhouse.

"You can't be working our mutual friend Macalvie's manor? It's mined."

"Jury's working on the Dorchester case. It just happened to spill over into Devon."

"Too bad. But neither of them has sod-all to do with me."

"Has anyone accused you of anything?"

"Where would I get that idea? I walk into Freddie's, and who do I find but you, lying in wait." He leaned closer. "Macalvie, doesn't it occur to you that I want to *forget* about Rose Mulvanney?"

"It had crossed my mind. That 'other boyfriend' she had —"

"I don't want to talk about it."

"She never mentioned any names?"

Sam Waterhouse closed his eyes in pain. "Don't you think I'd have damned well *said* if I knew of anyone else? I looked at her diary; I went through her desk. All that got me was a shadowy snapshot of some man. I asked her who it was and she said her uncle." Sam shrugged.

"Well, we didn't find anything like that. Uncle must have taken diary, photos, and papers."

Sam's eyes glittered with anger. "Look, all of this has been said and said again." His face took on the look of the chronic loser. "For God's sakes, haven't you had any murders in Devon in the last nineteen years that you want to hook these up with the Mulvanney case?" Macalvie shook his head. "Then why here and why now?"

"Revenge, Sam. At least, that's what the papers —"

Sam Waterhouse shook his head. "I don't know what you're talking about. You've got a psychopath on your hands —"

"I don't think so. At least not in the sense you mean — that there's no connection between the kids' murders."

Freddie stomped in with a steaming plate of mutton, boiled potatoes and vegetables. She plonked it down in front of Sam and gave Macalvie an evil look as if he'd been the prison cook. Sam went at the food with a vengeance.

Macalvie went on: "You've been out walking the moor for four days? Why?"

"Because I've been in the nick for nineteen years and wanted to see a little open space. As soon as I'm finished with this meal, you can slap the cuffs on me. I'll go quietly, Commander."

"Well, arresting you's not what I had in mind. You staying here?"

"Probably. Freddie's been like a mother to me."

Macalvie feigned surprise. "A mother? She's not even female. What I was really waiting for was to talk to you. You could be helpful."

Waterhouse leaned back in his chair and laughed: it was a transforming laugh; Jury could see in his face the nineteen-year-old student of medicine. "Help the Devon-Cornwall constabulary? I think I'd go back to Princetown first." That incandescent look of youth fell away like a falling star. "Even if I *would* 'help,' I couldn't. I don't know any more now than I did then. And I didn't know anything then."

"How do you know?"

Sam looked up from his plate. "Meaning what?"

"You might know something that you didn't connect with Rose's murder, or you might know something you don't know —"

"I had nineteen years to think it over. Case closed."

"Let's say I just reopened it."

III

The Marine Parade

SIX

ANGELA Thorne had been told by her parents never to
stay out after dark, never to miss her tea, never to
walk along the Cobb, never to play along the shingle beach
when the tide was coming in. Angela Thorne was presently
engaged in doing them all, attended only by her dog, Mickey.

Dark had come by five o'clock, and she was still out in it
two hours later. Some of that time had been spent wandering
aimlessly in the well-tended gardens above the Marine
Parade. A further half-hour she'd spent going up and down
several little flights of steps along the Parade and moving
backward toward the stone wall to beat the running tide.

She was presently breaking another injunction by walking
along the dark arm of the Cobb that made a safe harbour for
the little fishing boats, creaking out there in the wind and the
water.

Mickey puffed along behind her. He was a terrier and too
fat because Angela kept feeding him scraps of food from her
plate, disgusting things like mashed swede or black pudding
or skate that always looked to her like the clipped wing of
some big bird. All Mickey was supposed to eat was dried dog

498

food. He was old, and her parents were afraid he'd have a heart attack.

She was tired of her parents and she hated her school. She hated nearly everything. Probably, it was because she wasn't pretty, and having to wear this long pigtail and hard shells of glasses. No one else at school had to wear thick glasses. Her classmates teased her constantly.

Angela stopped far out on the Cobb to look back at the lights of Lyme Regis along the Marine Parade. She had never seen Lyme at night from this distance. She liked that unearthly glow of the lamps. The little town seemed light-lifted above the black sea.

She wished it would fall in and drown. Angela didn't like Lyme, either.

The tattoo of Mickey's paws scraping stone continued as Angela walked on. Mickey loved the sea. When the tide was out, he'd tear away from her like a bit of white cloth in the wind and chase the ruffs of waves as if he'd never felt freedom before, as if he were having the time of his life.

II

She took off her cape and threw it over the little girl. Better to freeze than have to look at the blood-soaked dress of the body on the black rocks. The small dog was hysterical — running to nose at the cape, then back to Molly, going dog-crazy.

Standing on the high-piled rocks at the end of the Cobb, Molly Singer felt removed from the scene, a dream figure, looking down; a non-participant, the prying eye of some god.

In the seamless merging of sea and sky she could find no horizon. There was a chalky moon, and the sky was hammered with stars. And some distance off were the lights along the Parade.

Back and forth ran the dog. She would have to do something about the dog. Molly had a vision of the little girl and her dog, walking out along the Cobb, two dark silhouettes against the darker outline of the seawall.

She would have to get the dog back to shore. She was freezing, but at least she couldn't see the body now, which was the important thing.

Holding on to the dog, which struggled in her arms, she picked her way over the rocks and back to the seawall. On one of its nametags was the name of its cottage.

She found Cobble Cottage and left the dog there, inside the gate.

Molly stood on the deserted Marine Parade, her own rented cottage at her back, the cold forgotten as she leaned against the railing where seaweed was tied like scarves, thrown up by the tide. The wooden groynes along the shingle kept the sand from shifting. It would be nice if the mind could build itself such a protective wall.

She looked along the Cobb to the pile of rocks from which she had come.

All she could think of was the line from Jane Austen. *The young people were all wild to see Lyme.*

SEVEN

ELEVEN it might have been, but the manager of the White Lion didn't argue about the licensing laws any more than had Freddie's customers — though here it worked in reverse. The manager reopened the bar and smiled conspiratorially after Jury and Wiggins had booked rooms. "Residents only," he said.

Wiggins, probably in some attempt to stay the awful effects of sea air, went straight to bed. It was the weather that had forced Jury and Wiggins to stop on the way back from Wynchcoombe. Rain and sleet that finally turned to hail. Each time a rock-sized chunk hit the windscreen, Wiggins veered. Jury imagined he was taking it personally, the weather. Weather and seasons were judged only in reference to Wiggins's health: spring brought allergies; autumn, a bleak prognosis of pneumonia; winter (the killer season), colds and fevers and flu. Driving along the Dorchester Road, Jury knew what was going on in his sergeant's mind, though mind-reading wasn't necessary: Wiggins was always pleased to open his Pandora's box of physical complaints and enlighten Jury as to which one had just flown by.

Before that could happen, Jury pointed out the turn to Lyme Regis.

Wiggins wasn't any too happy about sea frets, either.

Jury got his pint, asked for the phone, and called headquarters in Wynchcoombe to let them know where he was. On his way back to the bar, he noticed a thin, elderly woman in a floppy hat watching a television as antiquated as she was.

Jury was slotting 10p pieces into a stupid video game when she passed behind him, saying, "You can put money in that thing all night and you won't get any back. It's rigged." She went up to the bar and knocked on it with her knuckles for service.

"Thanks for the advice," said Jury, smiling. "Buy you a drink?"

"I wouldn't mind."

The manager, coming from an inner room, didn't seem surprised to see her.

"You a resident, then?" asked Jury.

"Off and on." She was wearing spectacles with sunglasses attached on tiny hinges. Why she needed the sunglasses in the murky light of the saloon bar, Jury couldn't imagine. She flipped them up and squinted at Jury as if he were light that hurt her eyes. "What's your name?"

"Richard Jury."

She snapped the brown-tinted glasses down again. "Hazel Wing," she said. The manager had already set up a pint of Guinness for Hazel Wing. Jury bought a drink for the manager, too.

Hazel Wing raised her glass and said, "Here's to getting through another one."

"Another what?" asked Jury.

"Day." Up went the sunglasses again and she squinted. This time, probably, to see if he was a little on the stupid side.

"I'll drink to that, certainly."

"What do you do, if I may be so bold?"

"I'm a policeman."

This news did not seem to surprise her. She said, "Oh. I sort of thought so."

"Why? Do I look like one?"

"No. You're better looking. I just supposed it was about the little girl."

He felt himself go cold. "What do you mean?"

"That girl that's gone missing. Don't know her. Young. Got all of Lyme in a panic. You know. After that boy in Dorchester." Hazel Wing, who seemed the sort to chop off emotions as she did her sentences, still allowed herself a shudder. "Kids. Parents keeping them in. Dorchester's not far."

And neither was Wynchcoombe. "Excuse me." Jury put down his pint and made for the telephone again.

He stared in silence at the telephone in the lobby of the hotel. Constable Green, in the Lyme police station, had finally to ask if Jury had got the message. "Yes. Don't move her." He hung up while the constable was assuring him no one would touch her.

"Bad news," said Hazel Wing. It was a statement, not a question. News came only in one way to her.

"What's the quickest way to the Cobb Arms?"

"Walking or driving?"

"Whichever's faster."

Hazel Wing evaluated Jury's six-feet-two and decided, for him, walking. "Straight down the hill and right on the Marine Parade. That pub's at the other end. Ten minutes. If you're in a hurry."

"Thanks," he said.

"Good luck," she said, the words unconvincing. Luck, like news, was seldom good.

503

II

The little girl under the cape was lying as if she'd been stuffed like a small sack in the crevice of the rock.

"Hold the torch over here, will you?" Jury knelt down and picked the seaweed from her icy cheek. He knew he shouldn't have touched her at all before the doctor or Scene of Crimes expert got there, but he felt he had to get that stuff off her face. Bladder wrack. He remembered it from a seaside town he had gone to as a boy. It was the stuff that would pop if you squeezed it. A wave collapsed against the rocks, spewing foam in their faces. The wet rocks made standing difficult.

"Do you suppose she came out here," asked Constable Green on a hopeful note, "to get the dog and then was trapped by the waves...?"

"No," said Jury. "It was a knife."

III

When Jury and Green got back to the Lyme Regis police station, Chief Superintendent Macalvie had been there for a quarter of an hour and ticking off every minute of it like a bomb.

Throughout Green's explanation of the anonymous telephone call and his finding the body, Macalvie sat in a chair tilted against the wall, sucking on a sweet. "So where's the body?"

"Hospital," said Green. "We got the local doctor —"

"Did he see her before she was moved?"

Green retreated into monosyllables. "Yes."

"About this woman, Molly Singer —" Macalvie was waiting for Green to embroider upon his description. Green didn't, so Macalvie went on. "Correct me if I'm wrong: you know the cape belongs to the Singer woman, you have a suspicion it was this woman who left the mutt at the Thornes' cottage, and you also suspect she was the one who rang up, and yet with all of this, you haven't brought her in for questioning."

"We went to her cottage, sir." Green looked from Jury to Macalvie, uncertain as to who had jurisdiction here: Dorset, Devon, or Scotland Yard? "But you don't know Molly Singer, sir —"

"Obviously I don't know her, Green. She isn't here, is she?" Macalvie looked around the room. Then he said to Wiggins, who had been dragged from under his eiderdown quilt around two a.m., "Give me one of those Fisherman's things, will you?"

Wiggins did so. He was presently trying to fend off something terminal, in a chair drawn up to a single-bar electric fire, where his feet competed with a large ginger cat snugly curled there.

Macalvie went on. "Because if she *was* here, then maybe the three of us could have a nice chin-wag and figure out what the hell she was doing on the end of the Cobb tonight."

Constable Green kept his expression as flat as the side of a slag heap and answered: "The Singer woman has lived in that cottage facing the Parade for nearly a year. No one in Lyme really knows her. She doesn't chat up the neighbours. She isn't friendly. She doesn't go out, except I've seen her sometimes at night, walking my beat. You might say she's eccentric —"

Jury interrupted. "You might say she's phobic, from what you told me earlier. Doesn't go out to the shops; doesn't mix with people at all ..."

"I wouldn't know about that." Green turned to Jury with relief. "I've seen her a few times when I was making my rounds. I know that cape. Only, I couldn't make up an Identikit on her. That's how much she shows her face."

Macalvie's chair slammed down. "I don't believe it, Green. I just don't *believe* it — that a person you think could be a witness, could be even the chief suspect —"

"I never meant to say that." Green's voice rose in alarm. "It's just she won't talk to the police."

Macalvie looked at Green and shook his head. He leaned across the PC's desk and his blue eyes sparked like matches. "We're talking murder, and all you can say is the chief witness is incommunicado." Macalvie got up. "Come on," he said to Jury, heading for the door. He looked over his shoulder at Wiggins, who had now grown as sluggish as the orange cat that had oozed its body straight out, paws fore and aft, stomach to glowing bar. That it was lying across the feet of Scotland Yard did not impress it at all.

"Wiggins," said Macalvie. "You going to toast crumpets or move?"

"You think the three of us are going to the Singer woman's house?" asked Jury.

"Of course."

"Kick in the door? Is that it?" Jury was putting his coat on. Macalvie had never taken his off. "Try to browbeat someone who's agoraphobic and see how far you get, Macalvie. I'll go by myself, thanks. This is Dorset, remember? Not your patch; at the moment, it's mine."

Macalvie was still sucking on the Fisherman's Friend. "Pulling rank. Well. And would you mind if I went out on my own and had a word with the Thornes? The dad and mum? And as long as you're going on your own, can I borrow your sergeant?"

He didn't wait for permission. The door of the station slammed after Macalvie and Wiggins.

EIGHT

Jury's idea of eccentricity might have been Hazel Wing. It wasn't Molly Singer, in spite of her Oxfam clothes: a shapeless sweater, a long and equally shapeless skirt. Jury guessed she was in her thirties; he had expected someone much older.

The fire and a napping cat were the only things that gave the room a semblance of warmth. It was a typical holiday cottage, furnished with remnants that could have been washed up from a shipwreck—mismatched deckchairs, a small cabinet whose open shelf held several bottles of liquor, a lumpyish love seat now occupied by the cat. In front of the window was an all-purpose table. Nothing here but the bare essentials.

Probably she was following the drift of his thoughts. "In the summer, this place costs the earth. It's right on the Parade, has an ocean view, and the landlord cleans up."

"I can imagine," said Jury.

"I even had to buy the lamp—" She nodded toward a small, blue-shaped lamp, useless for reading or anything but giving off a watery light. "I hope you don't mind the dark. I'm used to it by now."

507

Jury looked down at some books of poetry on the table and wondered if there was a double meaning in the comment. Emily Dickinson. Robert Lowell.

"You like poetry? I've always liked those lines of Lowell: 'The light at the end of the tunnel / Is the light of an oncoming train.'" She seemed to be talking out of sheer nervousness. "You could say I rent the cat, too. It wanders in every day and takes the best seat." The cat could have been mistaken for a black pillow, it was so motionless. It opened its topaz eyes, looked at Jury warily, and went back to dozing. Molly Singer's black hair and amber eyes were like the cat's.

They still had not sat down, and she was turning the card he had slipped under the door round and round in her fingers. "You took a chance, didn't you, writing this message? 'What fresh hell can this be?'" Her smile was strained. "Who said it?"

"Dorothy Parker. Whenever she heard the bell to her flat."

"Sit down, won't you?"

The cat glared at Jury as Molly Singer picked it up and put it on one of the cold sling chairs.

She offered him a drink and, when he accepted, reached down into the cabinet by the couch and brought out another glass and a whisky bottle that was three-quarters empty. She gave him his and replenished her own glass.

Jury felt strange in this room that had housed so many guests, like a room full of ghosts. A log crumbled and the fire spurted up, one of the ghosts stirring the ashes.

"It's the cape, I guess."

Jury had been avoiding this sudden plunge into the death of Angela Thorne. He nodded. "Constable Green recognized it."

"Which puts me in the thick of it, doesn't it?"

"You must have known the cape would be traced to you. Why'd you do it?"

"You mean, kill her?" Her equanimity was more disturbing than a screaming denial would have been.

508

"I didn't say you killed Angela Thorne. It would be stupid to do that and leave that sort of evidence behind. What happened?"

"I was walking along the Cobb somewhere around ten or ten-thirty. I heard a dog barking. It sounded rather terrible, you know, panic-stricken. I followed the sound to the rocks and found her. I returned the dog; I couldn't return Angela," she said with some bitterness.

"Did you know her?"

Molly shook her head. "I think I saw her once or twice. I don't actually know anyone."

"How do you live?"

Her smile was no more happy than her laughter. "I bolt the door, Superintendent."

"You've lived here nearly a year. Why? Do you like the sea, then?"

"No. In a storm the waves crash over the walls; sometimes even drenching the cottages. Throwing up seaweed, rocks, whatever. It's all so elemental."

"So you found the body, covered her with your cape, took the dog to the Thorne cottage. Is that all?"

"Yes."

"But you rang up the police anonymously. Why?"

"I didn't want to get involved, I suppose."

"Then why did you leave your cape? You must have been freezing."

"I have another one," she said simply, as if that explained everything.

"Where did you live before?"

"London, different places. No fixed address. No job. I've got some money still. I used to be a photographer. My doctor advised me to find some nice little seaside town. I was taking pictures of Lyme."

Jury looked at two fine photos above the mantelpiece: the Lyme coast, the Marine Parade, with its lonely strollers.

She left the couch and walked over to those pictures. "Don't bother looking; I'm not much good anymore. The sea, the sea — it's so elemental." Her glass was empty, and she poured herself another double. "I drink too much, you've noticed." She shrugged and went back to the mantel. The light from the fire suffused her face, sparked the strange dark gold eyes and gave her an almost demonic look. He thought of the women of myths whom the ill-fated stranger — knight or country yokel — was constantly being warned to steer clear of.

"Have you been reading the papers?" Jury asked. She shook her head. "Where were you earlier today?"

"Here. I'm always here. Why?"

"There was a boy killed in Wynchcoombe. And two days ago, one killed in Dorchester. You didn't know about the Dorchester business?"

Her eyes had a drowned look. "My God, no. What are you saying — that there's a mass-murderer running round the countryside?"

"There could be. Look, there's no way you can avoid talking to the police. You don't want to go to the station. Then come along to the White Lion in the morning." He was silent, looking at her, all sorts of sham comfort trying to form itself into words: *it won't be bad; Macalvie is a nice chap; there'll only be the three of us.* All of it lies. It *would* be bad; Macalvie was *not* a nice chap. And "only three of them" might as well be the whole Dorset police and Devon-Cornwall constabulary together, as far as Molly Singer was concerned.

The silence waited on her. "Nine?" was all she said.

"All right."

Jury picked up his coat, once again dislodging the cat from its slumbers — and Molly went with him to the door.

She was still holding the card, folded and refolded, as if it were a message in a bottle that might give some report of land.

NINE

"GEORGE Thorne." In the dining room of the White Lion, Macalvie speared a sausage and shook his head. "One and the same. Witness for the prosecution."

"That doesn't make it look good for Sam Waterhouse, does it?"

"He didn't do it. Pass the butter, Wiggins."

Both Wiggins and Macalvie were having the full house. Jury, who couldn't stand looking at sausages and bacon and eggs, had ordered coffee and toast. "Who'd have a better motive?"

"Someone else," said Macalvie, with perfect assurance.

"But, sir —" Wiggins began and then stopped when Macalvie shot him a look.

"Both of you seem to have forgotten one salient detail. It wasn't Waterhouse that found the kid and tossed a cape over her. Oh, sure, Thorne was ranting on about Waterhouse out for revenge, et cetera. The guy looked like he'd just risen from the grave. Serves the bastard right. Big-deal solicitor." Macalvie was busy with bacon and a reappraisal of the waitress whose Edwardian looks — black hair rolled upward, slim

511

figure in ruffled white blouse and black skirt, and porcelain skin — he had already commented upon. "Yesterday, Angela Thorne was 'acting up' — her mum's words — and trying to plead off school by saying she was sick to her stomach and being a pill nobody wants to swallow. Her teacher said the kid had got into a fight because some other girls were making fun of her. They made up this song: 'Angela Thorne, Angela Thorne, don't you wish you'd never been born? Kids are so cute, aren't they?'"

"It was after one when you talked to the Thornes. When did you get a chance to talk to the teacher, for God's sakes?" Jury imagined Macalvie was one of those cops who never slept.

"Afterwards. Let me tell you, the Thornes don't go down a treat. The teacher I knocked up around three —" Macalvie's blue eyes glinted "— you know what that means in American? Anyway Miss Elgin — Julie — didn't especially enjoy having her door busted down by the Devon-Cornwall constabulary, not with her dressed only in a flimsy wrapper —"

"You make it sound like a gang rape, Macalvie. Maybe Wiggins could just read the notes."

Disinclined as he was to stop eating his boiled egg, Wiggins put down his spoon and took out his notebook.

"Put that away, dammit," said Macalvie. "*I* know who said what. So, the kids made up this silly song, mostly, I imagine, because *The Thornbirds* has been putting everybody to sleep for days now on the telly. You know; it's that mini-mind soap opera series. Julie —"

Macalvie could get on a first-name basis pretty quickly, Jury thought.

"— said Angela got a real going over with that pun on her name. None of the kids much liked Angela Thorne. Why?" Macalvie answered his own question. "Because she was sullen, bad-tempered, plain as pudding, wore thick glasses, and was so good at her lessons it even tired out the teachers. Julie

512

said the headmistress just wished Angela'd take her O levels and get the hell out. Pretty funny." Whatever Macalvie was remembering from the night before obviously delighted him.

"Not very funny for Angela. Wasn't this Julie Elgin a little cut up over Angela's murder?"

"Sure. Scared witless, like everybody else. News travels fast. At midnight parents were calling her to say their kids wouldn't be going to school. But the point is, nobody liked Angela, including her parents."

Jury put down his coffee cup. "Her teacher said that?"

"No. And she didn't have to, did she?" Again he answered his rhetorical question. "Mummy's eyes were red, but more from booze than from tears. George was more worried about his own neck than his kid's death, though of course, he put up a front—but it was all pretence, no pain—and the older sister, the one who got the looks, kept talking about being in shock, as if she'd like to go into it for my sake, but couldn't get the electrodes in place. In other words, it was all an act. I asked them for a picture of Angela. Mum and Dad kind of looked at one another as if they couldn't quite place their youngest, and finally Carla — the sister — had to go off and *look* for a picture. Funny. There were certainly pictures of the bosomy rose Carla all over the mantel. But not even so much as a snapshot of Angela."

"Then she must have been a lonely little girl. Let's get back to your theory of what happened."

"Well, it's the dog, isn't it?" Macalvie watched Jury lighting a cigarette as if it were a demonic act, meant to trap Macalvie into reaching for the packet.

"The dog? Macalvie, if you say anything more about the dog in the night, I'll do just what you want—leave." Jury smiled.

Macalvie's hopeful look vanished when Jury didn't actually get up. Then he shrugged: stay or leave, it was all one to Macalvie. "The person who killed the kid must have had some connection with her or Lyme Regis. How the hell did he or she know where to drop the dog?"

"Nametags, maybe."

Macalvie looked pained. "Oh, for Christ's sake, Jury. A perfect stranger wandering all over Lyme carrying a terrier looking for Cobble Cottage? No way. So it was either someone who befriended the Kid and the Poor Kid's dog," (Jury could just feel the sympathy welling up in Macalvie's breast) "someone not from Lyme, or someone who's been *living* in Lyme and knew the kid's habits."

"But Angela Thorne didn't habitually go against the rules, you led me to believe."

Impatiently, Macalvie stuffed a sweet in his mouth, sucked on it awhile as he hankered after Jury's cigarette, then tossed the sweet into the ashtray. "Wonder how Kojak stood it. ...Look at little Angela's feelings about Mum and Dad and school and so forth. Somebody could have befriended her and then hung around Lyme, waiting for a chance. What do you think?"

"I think no." Jury would have laughed had Macalvie not looked so serious. Disagree with Macalvie's theory?

"Why the hell *not?*"

"Aren't you overlooking the obvious?"

Macalvie gave Wiggins a *can-you-believe-this-guy?* look, got no reassurance from Jury's sergeant, and turned the sparking blue eyes back to Jury. "I never overlooked the *obvious* in my entire life, Jury."

"That's good. You do think Angela was killed by the same person that murdered the other two, don't you?"

"Probably," said Macalvie, cautiously, like a man being led into a trap.

"Then you'd have to assume that the murderer was friendly with *all* the victims. That's possible, but not very probable. I don't think the murders are indiscriminate or arbitrary, but at the same time, I don't think the killer took the chance of 'befriending' these children. Simply because it would have been a hell of a chance to take —"

"True. Especially for a man just out of prison."

And since Macalvie's theory left only one candidate for the string of murders, it was perhaps less than fortuitous for her that Molly Singer chose that moment to appear in the doorway of the White Lion's dining room.

II

It wasn't love at first sight when Molly Singer met Divisional Commander Macalvie.

The sparks between them made Jury think of an express train braking. She could sense Macalvie's hostility, even before he opened his mouth.

Jury offered her breakfast, and Macalvie offered her a grim-reaper smile, which was enough to kill anyone's appetite. Jury doubted she had one to begin with. She asked for coffee.

Today she looked different. Her eyes were less molten gold and more honey-coloured. That might have been because of the gold cape she wore. Her dark hair was pulled back, but the shorter ends clung to her face as if they were wet with seaspray or rain.

"I just wanted to have a little talk with you about last night," said Macalvie. "Your handling of the situation was kind of odd."

"Yes, I suppose it was. Though at the time I wasn't thinking too clearly —"

"Did you panic, or something?" His tone was almost friendly.

"Panic. Yes, I suppose you could say that."

"That's why you threw your cape over the girl?"

She nodded and looked away.

"Not because you wanted to hide the body." The tone was simply matter-of-fact.

Quickly, she looked at him again. "That's ridiculous. If I'd killed her, I certainly wouldn't leave my cape behind to lead police right to my door."

Macalvie shrugged. "You're not the only one in Lyme or hereabouts who owns a cape."

"You think I'd take a chance like that?"

"I don't know. Do you know the Thornes?"

She shook her head, looking down at the coffee brought by the patrician waitress, but not drinking it.

"How did you know where to take the dog?"

"The name of their place was on the tag."

"Very humanitarian. There's a pub in Dorchester called the Five Alls. Ever been there?"

"No. I don't go to pubs."

"Not a drinker?"

"On the contrary, I drink a lot. But alone."

Wiggins, who seemed to have taken a liking to Molly Singer as another victim of life's vicissitudes, looked sad. Jury was afraid he might take them all for a stroll down Gin Lane.

"As I'd guess," Molly went on, "you already know."

Macalvie's eyes grew round as a cat's. "How would I know that?"

She looked at Jury. "The superintendent might have told you. More likely you've already been at the dustbin men."

Macalvie laughed. "You're pretty smart." He made it sound like an indictment. "Where were you early yesterday morning? Around six, say?"

"In my cottage. Asleep. Why?"

"And where the afternoon of the tenth?"

"In my cottage. Or walking on the Cobb."

"Like last night?"

"Yes."

"Anyone see you?"

"Probably not."

"You don't go out much."

"No."

"You don't see people."

"No."

"Funny way to act."

"I think I'm agoraphobic." What there was of an embarrassed smile was quickly erased when Macalvie slammed his fist on the table.

"I don't care sod-all about some phobia. If you've been to psychiatrists, I'll subpoena their records if I have to. You don't go out, don't see people, and yet —" Macalvie pointed toward the street "— in that short-stay parking lot by the ocean you've got a great little Lamborghini that's clocked up over sixty thousand on an 'E' registration. You do a hell of a lot of travelling, don't you? In that car you could make it to Dorchester and back in a little more than an hour and to Wynchcoombe in two, I'll bet — provided a cop didn't get in your way. What's a little stay-at-home like you doing with a Lamborghini?"

Molly Singer got up slowly. "I think I've answered your questions."

"No, you haven't. Sit down."

"Wouldn't you rather finish your breakfast?" Before anyone could stop her, she tipped her side of the table, sending plates, food, cutlery crashing and rolling, and most of it into Macalvie's lap. Then she walked out.

"God! What a temper." Macalvie seemed perversely pleased, looking at his stained suit and the wreckage all around them: cups, kippers, broken glass.

It even broke the porcelain pose of the waitress in black and white.

III

Lyme Regis was one of many coastal villages whose beauty was reckoned in proximity to the sea. It had been two centuries ago so much the object of Jane Austen's affections that it now had, where the Marine Parade ended in a narrow street, a pretty boutique called Persuasion. Thought Jury, if Stratford-upon-Avon wants to put Shakespeare on sugar cubes . . . why not?

Macalvie came out of the newsagent's at the top of the street, at the triangle where Broad Street and Silver Street ran together down to the sea, taking tearooms, greengrocers, Boots, and banks with them. Wiggins had been left to see to the wreckage at the White Lion.

Just as Macalvie appeared, a Mini went speeding down the narrow street. He wrote the registration number in his notebook. Macalvie would do dog's duty just so long as it gave him the pleasure of collaring some miscreant.

He slapped the notebook shut and said, "Nothing there. She knew Angela because Angela would stand around reading *Whizzer and Chips* without paying. The old broad in there hated her. She chased her off yesterday evening somewhere around six. She was closing up late."

Macalvie was turning a carousel of postcards and removed one that showed the confluence of the streets they were on. He stuffed a stick of gum in his mouth, and said, "You're a minder, you know?"

Jury looked at Macalvie, who was frowning down at the postcard. "Meaning what?"

Macalvie shrugged. "A minder: kind of cop who watches over frail defenceless women."

Jury laughed. "You see too many American films, Macalvie."

Unoffended, Macalvie said, "No, I'm serious."

Indeed he did look it, staring from the picture-view of the street to the real thing. One would have thought he might be an artist, studying light and angles. "I'd like to know what she's doing in Lyme," he said, almost inconsequentially.

"Molly Singer?"

He shook his head. "Her name's not Molly Singer. It's Mary Mulvanney."

Macalvie slotted the card back in the rack and started up the street.

IV

The St. Valentine's Day Massacre

TEN

LADY Jessica Mary Allan-Aschroft looked from blank square to blank square on the calendar hanging in the kitchen and, with her black crayon, stood on tiptoe so she could reach FRIDAY: 14 FEBRUARY. She drew a giant X across that square, knowing she was cheating, since it was only tea-time and the awful day was not yet over. Another day as blank as the square. There were now five X's in a row. The picture above them showed some Dartmoor ponies doing what they always did — chewing grass. She looked at the picture for March. It showed the giant rock-formation of Vixen Tor and a few hardy pilgrims on their way up the rocks. Another pile of rocks they walked for miles to see.

Just last August she had been driving with Uncle Robert and had seen a lot of people with boots and back packs at one of those tourist centres, all kitted out to walk to one of the tors in the middle of Dartmoor. Jessie and her uncle were driving with the top down in his Zimmer, and she thought those people must be mad, walking when they could be driving. She told him this and he burst out laughing.

* * *

"Eat your tea, my love," said Mrs. Mulchop. Her husband, Mulchop, served as gardener and sometimes as butler and looked no more like one than he did the other. He sat now at the kitchen table eating a mess of something.

Mrs. Mulchop moved a pot in the huge inglenook fireplace, in the huge kitchen, in the huge house, in the huge grounds. . . .

Jessie's mind drifted like a veil of rain over all of this hugeness that was the Ashcroft house and grounds. "It's too big," she said, looking at the egg on toast on her plate. Its sickening yellow eye stared back at her.

"Your egg, lovey?"

"No. The house. I'm all alone." Jessie rested her chin in her hands.

Mrs. Mulchop raised her eyes heavenward and shook her head. She did not realize that beneath this surface melodrama, a true drama of heartsickness was playing itself out. "You're ten years old, not a baby. Wouldn't your uncle be annoyed to see you so sorry for yourself?"

Jessie's mind drifted like a veil of rain over all this huge- Uncle Robert would ever be "annoyed" by Jessie. "No! He'd understand." Now Jessie felt the threat of real tears. Real tears she could not contend with.

"Your uncle's only been gone a few days, lass. No need to get fidgety about it —"

"*Four* days! Four and a *half!* See —" Jessie scraped her chair back and marched to the calendar. "He didn't leave me a note. He didn't give me a Valentine, either." She went back to her chair as if she'd just proven all theories of a clockwork universe defunct in the face of this outrage against reason. But what she felt was more worry than outrage.

"He's probably only gone up to London to see to another governess for you." Mrs. Mulchop glanced at her husband, but his face was too near his bowl to return the look.

Jessie heard the slight sharpness in that *another.* She ran through governesses like a shark through a salmon-fall.

"And you're not all alone. There's me and Mulchop and Miss Gray and Drucilla."

The Dreadful Drucilla, Miss Plunkett, the present tutor-governess. Not a proper one, though. More of a minder Uncle Rob had settled for when he had discharged the Careless Carla, who was absolutely brilliant at maths, but a little absentminded about keys and spectacles. Out walking across the moor, she had lost Jessie one day, though there had been, in the confrontation with Robert Ashcroft, some doubt as to who had lost whom.

Battalions of governesses. How they sat so neatly and nicely when he was interviewing them. Uncle Rob questioned them closely about their former posts, their credentials, their ability to respond to emergencies; but now and then he would throw one in out of the blue, such as *And do you like rabbits?*

Jessie liked to see the corners of his mouth twitch and the bewildered look on the face of the prospective employee. *Well, yes. That is, I expect I've nothing against them. . . .* He had explained later to Jess that it was a matter of honesty, and Miss Whatever-her-name wasn't being honest. She was from Portland (where the Ashcroft stone had come from). *In Portland, one is never allowed to mention rabbits. They all hate them,* Uncle Rob had told her.

Thus that one had lost a very well-paying post, as did most of the prospective women who applied. They sat there saying, *Oh, yes, Mr. Ashcroft,* when they meant No; or *Oh, no, Mr. Ashcroft,* when they meant Yes. And a lot of them would try to snuggle up to Jessica until they realized she wasn't much good for a snuggle, and call her stupid things like "Poppit," and pet her dog Henry, to show how much they liked animals.

Robert Ashcroft could not go on forever relentlessly pursuing the perfect governess so, in the end, he left it up to Jessie, as she was the one who would have to put up with the woman. Uncle Rob often asked her why it was she avoided the nicer ones and chose the worst. There was the Hopeless Helen (who kept the key to the drinks cabinet in more or less constant motion); the Mad Margaret, who had trembled during the interview with a severe case of stage fright, but ended up roaring like a lion, acting being her field of expertise; the Prudent Prucilla, who left rather quickly one night, along with the Crown Derby. Of all of them, the Dubious Desiree had lasted the longest because she had done nothing absolutely wrong, short of hating her pupil, a fact that she kept very well hidden from everyone but Jess herself. Jess put up with the cold-blooded treatment because she knew Desiree was going to do herself in anyway, eventually. In the meantime, she did make Jess a little nervous because of her looks: she was dark and sleek and always winding herself on the couch like a cobra when he was around. But Uncle Rob was not easily fooled; the Dubious Desiree lasted a month.

It seemed a great puzzle to Uncle Rob — his niece's choices. Why Miss Simpson instead of Miss James? *Miss Simpson seemed a bit stiff to me. But Sally James was, well, rather smashing,* he said, before he had returned to the reading of his morning paper, the jamming of his morning toast.

Jessie was not about to have any Smashing Sallys around.

Thus Jessie had never complained about any of them because she knew, every time one of them got sacked, there might be another just waiting in the wings. The Amiable Amy.

Jessie was an omnivorous reader—largely owing to Mad Margaret, who stuffed books and plays into her like a sausage machine. Mad Margaret thought herself the heroine of all of them. Many was the rainy morning that found Jess curled up on the window seat in the library with Henry as a backrest, poring over *Jane Eyre* and *Rebecca*. Jessie knew just how sly some women could be: soft and kind and quiet-spoken and so sly (and amiable) they might even catch Jessie in their nets.

Her uncle had once been married — years and years ago — to a dazzling but false woman who had broken his heart, left him shattered with grief — or, at least, that was the way she put it to him at the breakfast table. "I know it must have left you shattered. You can never look at another woman, can you?"

He did not seem, as he slit open the morning post, terribly shattered. This was, unfortunately, confirmed when he said, "No — I mean to the 'shattered' part of your tale. As to the rest, I think I could bear to look at another woman again, yes. God knows I've looked at enough of them trying to find someone for you."

She had placed a consoling hand on his arm. "But she was beautiful, wasn't she?"

"Indeed she was. But she hated motorcars." He smiled.

"But she loved you madly."

"Not really." He went back to his paper.

All those governesses over the four years they'd been at Ashcroft. Look what they would get: wealth, position, the glories of Ashcroft itself — to say nothing of one of the most eligible bachelors in the British Isles. And nine motor cars.

The only thing that stood between them and Heaven was Lady Jessica Allan-Ashcroft.

II

The funeral had been held in a parish church, the body committed to the ground of a leaf-strewn cemetery in Chalfont St. Giles, where her father had been born and where Jessica's mother had died years ago. Her father had been the Earl of Curlew and Viscount Lindley, James Whyte Ashcroft; her mother, plain Barbara Allan, but plain in name only. And between them they had passed on their names to Jessica.

When her father died, Jessie was six years old, and mere days before this she had been chasing her dog, Henry, all over the grounds of the old home in Chalfont.

They had dressed her in mourning. An aunt with eager fingers had fixed the boater with its black ribbon to her head, placed the gloves in her hand. Jessie did not know the aunt, nor any of the cousins — a great ring of them around the grave — nor anyone except for a few of her father's old friends.

She was very silent, but Jessie wanted to scream when the vicar went on about Heaven and Rewards. She did not think her father would be tempted by Rewards. He would rather be back here with Jessie.

All around her stood those odd friends and relations, as stark and unmoving as pollarded trees. All in black and dreadful, some with heavy veils, or, hats in hands, expressions frozen, like skaters on a dark lake. One hand fell on her shoulder. She shook it off. The fingers felt like claws. When she looked all round the grave-site again, she saw red-rimmed eyes, not sorrow-laden, but the eyes of wolves.

Jessica Allan-Ashcroft was worth four million pounds to them. And that didn't even include the family seat of Ashcroft.

Just as the service ended, she noticed a stranger in a light-coloured Burberry. The mourners were going through the awful ritual of throwing a handful of earth on her father's grave. The stranger walked through the dark stalks of mourners, knelt down and brushed the blown strands of hair from her face. *"Cry,"* was all he said, but in such a tone that her mind split and the tears gushed out. In his own face, she saw something of her father's and even her own and she threw her arms around him and buried her face in his raincoat.

Solicitors were wandering everywhere, in and out of the house in Eaton Square, like dream figures. There were more relations to come, too, others whom Jessie didn't know, coming with long faces, bringing her things she didn't want and calling her "love" and "dear" and none of them meaning it, she knew.

The day after the funeral — to her it had seemed like months — she stood before the long window in the house in Eaton Square, wondering if the man in the raincoat would ever come back. The trees dripped rain and Henry looked up at her with red-rimmed eyes, a true mourner.

Everyone seemed to be keeping a vigil. The relations had gathered in the library with her father's solicitor, all of them coughing gently behind their hands.

When finally he did come, running across the road in the rain, Jessie ran to the door and listened. She heard voices in the hall, an exchange between the butler and the stranger, and then all was quiet again.

Until the will was read.

The solicitor, a plump man whose jowls reminded her of Henry, took her hands in his plump, perspiring ones and explained "the situation."

It was boring to Jessie, all this talk about money and property. The important thing was who her guardian was to be. As if on cue, a large woman and her smaller husband came through the door. The woman was the same one who had laid her hand in such a proprietary way on Jessie's shoulder. Her fingers flashed with rings and the poor fox-fur around her neck flashed its glass eyes. Jessie could tell, with one look, she wasn't an animal-lover. "What about Henry?" she asked.

Mr. Mack, the solicitor, found that very funny. "Now you do understand, Jessie. All your mother's property was left to you and your father. Now all of it goes to you. You must have someone to look after you."

The large, ring-studded cousin snorted, saying it should be her and Al to do the looking-after, and Mr. Mack asked her to leave. Her husband told her there was no use crying over spilt milk, and to come along.

Through the door came the man from the cemetery.

Mr. Mack told her that this was her Uncle Robert, her father's brother, Robert Ashcroft. Her father had appointed him trustee of the estate and Jessica's guardian.

"Henry's, too," said Robert Ashcroft, winking.

Thus amongst the raised voices that seemed to be calling for Robert Ashcroft's blood, or at least his bona fides, after his ten-year absence in Australia, Jessie felt as if, on the verge of drowning, she had broken the water's surface, dazzled by sunlight. His hair was dark gold and his eyes were light brown. As the thunder of the others' voices receded, Jessie felt the sun falling in shafts across the room and that all those vaults were really full of gold.

ELEVEN

T HE "letters" — they were what prevented the relations, some inarticulate, some artful — from breaking the will. Her father had been clever enough to leave tiny bequests to those relations whom he disliked (which meant most of them), acknowledging that they were "family," but sorry they were his. It was a little like leaving a small tip for poor service.

It was a very large family, but not a close one. "When I left for Australia over ten years ago, I was thirty" her uncle had told her. "In all those thirty years before, I can't remember seeing any of these relations who've now descended like vultures."

The vultures had flown after months of talking about "undue influence" and "unsound mind," and Jessie and Uncle Robert were sitting in the drawing room in Eaton Square, its furnishings flooded with April sunlight. "Undue influence." He laughed. "It would have been hard to have influenced your father in any case. So how was I supposed to have done it all the way from Australia? Ten years of letters." Robert had stopped and looked at his niece intently. "Jimmy — your father — in any event, how was I supposed to have done it all the way from Australia? Ten years of letters ..." He had stopped and then said, "It doesn't make you sad, I hope, talking about your father?"

"No. I want to hear about him. And Mother, too." Henry was lying between them, being used as an armrest. "Go on."

"There must have been, over the course of ten years, hundreds of letters. Jimmy was having a hard time of it after your mother died." He paused, thinking back. "And before that, even. He was depressed ... I don't know if it was because he felt some sort of prescience about Barbara's death, or what. I felt guilty leaving. But I had to."

"Why?"

He was quiet. "I just had to. Anyway, those letters showed we'd kept in touch. You know, when I was at a perfectly awful public school, when I was ten and Jimmy was twenty and my life was hell, he wrote to me three or four times a week. He knew how miserable I was. That's really something for a chap of twenty to do for a boy of ten."

Jessie had managed to circumvent the baggage of Henry to lean across and put her head on her uncle's shoulder. "You were friends. I bet when you were six he got into fights because the boys teased you and threw things at your dog and made fun of you and called you names. Didn't he?" Her tone was hopeful.

"Absolutely."

"Tell me about Mother," she commanded.

"She was beautiful. Dark hair and eyes. You look just like her."

So that her uncle wouldn't see her blush, she busied herself in trying to tie Henry's ears together. A difficult job, since they were hard to find.

"Talk about getting teased over your name! 'Barbara Allan' is an old folk song," said Robert.

"What about?" Henry awoke and shook at his ears.

531

Robert didn't answer at first, and Jess poked him. She refused to let any important question — meaning any of hers — go unanswered.

"About Sweet William's dying because he loved her."

It was the way he said it. Jessie didn't like his silence. "I've got a picture!" She bounced up, unsettling the cushions and comfort, much to Henry's displeasure. "I keep it locked up."

"Locked up? But why?"

Because she had always had a secret fear that if too many eyes saw her mother's picture, her mother would grow less clear, less distinct, the outlines blurring into the background until the beautiful face of Barbara Allan disappeared altogether. The worst was that Jessie was one of them. If she looked too long, the face in the picture would go away, as her mother had done. But she couldn't tell *him* such a stupid, silly thing. Jess went over to the ebony desk and took a key from a vase and turned it in the bottom drawer. It was only a snapshot. The woman there was kneeling in long grass, gathering wild flowers. Peering through the long grass was a funny-looking puppy.

"That's Henry," she said with feigned disgust. "I wish he hadn't followed her around like that. He made her trip once — I saw it — and she fell down. It could've *killed* her. He was a bad dog." She looked quickly at Henry to see if he might contradict her. "But Henry's okay, now." It was with a growing horror that she saw the weight she'd been carrying for years. She was afraid she'd done something to her mother. Killed her by being born, maybe.

And Robert knew. He put his hands on her shoulders and said, harshly, "Listen to me! You didn't do anything to hurt your mother, Jess. She looked healthy and was much younger than your father. But she was still a sick woman."

Jessie looked down at her mother's picture, the awful weight lifted from her shoulders. She rubbed the glass carefully, delicately, with the hem of her skirt. Then she set the picture atop the desk. Her mother wouldn't disappear just because Jessie looked at her too long.

But she was still embarrassed that her uncle had understood all this about her when she'd only just found it out herself. "I think it's time for Henry's walk," she said, smoothly. *Henry's walk* would have been only an annual event, had exercising him been left to Jess.

"Mind if I come?"

"Oh, I suppose not. But Henry will only listen to *me*. So it's no use you trying to make him catch sticks, or anything. He won't unless I command him."

It was no use *anyone's* trying to make Henry catch sticks, as Jess perfectly well knew.

II

Thus here she was, four years later, four years of picnics and open motor cars; and trains to London and Brighton; and Careless Clara and all the rest of the benighted ladies. Here she was musing over the past, while Mrs. Mulchop kept to the present, wrist-deep in dough.

Jessie leaned a cold cheek against her fist and punched the spoon down into the equally cold porridge with which Mrs. Mulchop had replaced the egg. And Jess let it sit there like the egg. It had hardened to such a thickness, the spoon stuck straight up. "He never goes off without leaving me a note or something." It was the tenth time she'd imparted the same information in different ways.

"Well, lovey, he just forgot this time —"

Forgot? Was Mrs. Mulchop stupid?

"— and he has to have his bit of fun, now doesn't he? Do you begrudge the man that, my lady? Think of him, not yourself: a man in his forties always in company of a ten-year-old —" The look in My Lady's eye changed her tune quickly. "— not that you're not fun. But your uncle should have a nice wife to look after —"

533

"He doesn't *want* one. He already *had* one." Jess had left the kitchen table and was taking down an overall from a peg by the back door. "It left him a broken man." She stuffed her legs into the overall.

" 'Broken man'? *Your* uncle? He's about as broke as Mulchop here."

Mulchop looked up from his huge bowl. He was bull-necked and stout-armed and had a spatulate face, flat as the spades he used on the flowers and shrubs. He seldom spoke and appeared to resent it if others engaged in conversation. Words were wasted on Mulchop.

"Where's the spanner?" Jessica levelled her eyes at his thick brows.

The spoon, which had but an inch to travel from bowl to mouth, stopped. "You not be foolin' with them cars, Miss!" Mulchop also took care of the cars; he and Jessie spent what little time they spent together haggling over Uncle Robert's cars.

While Mrs. Mulchop went prattling on about Mr. Robert's sad marital status, Jessie took the spanner from Mulchop's tool box and stuck her tongue out at both their backs.

". . . a nice wife, that's what he needs."

Not if the Lady Jessica Mary Allan-Ashcroft had anything to do with it.

She lay with the spanner and some old rags on a mechanic's creeper underneath the Zimmer Golden Spirit. It was a good car for thinking under; some of the others, like the Lotus and the Ferrari were a little too close to the ground for her to get comfortable unless she jacked them up, and Mulchop would always come out and raise a fuss. The Zimmer was one of her favourites, an astonishingly long white convertible, for which Uncle Robert had paid over thirty thousand pounds. Or Jess had paid. It took a platoon of solicitors to keep account of her money. Not that it made any difference to her if Uncle Robert used up all of it on his cars.

534

Jessie saw a bolt that looked loose and she tried to tighten it. That's what happened when someone went away.... Everything just fell apart. Her eyes widened. Forgetting where she was she sat up and bumped her forehead on the exhaust pipe. The cars.

"Well, *I* don't know, do I?" the Dreadful Dru was saying, as Jess stood there in the drawing room in her oil-stained overall. "You been muckin' about with those cars?"

"They're all *there!*" Jessie shouted. In a sort of ritual chant, she ticked off each one of the nine on her fingers.

Drucilla Plunkett tossed aside the fashion magazine she'd been reading and stuffed another chocolate in her mouth. Drucilla knew her days were numbered, so she wasn't being at all careful about what she did with them. The box of chocolates — a huge heart — Drucilla had said she'd got from an "admirer" down the pub. Most of her spare time was spent with one or another mystery man "down the pub," as she put it. "What do I know about those old cars?" Her bowlike mouth bit into a chocolate truffle.

"If he went to London, how did he go?"

"Say it once again and I'll *scream!*"

Jessie said she could scream the house down. All she wanted to know was where Uncle Rob was. "He's missing." Jessie turned and leaned her forehead against the cold glass, saw the ghost of her face in the slanting rain.

The Dreadful Dru screamed. Not long and loud, but a shriek nonetheless. Having exhausted her eyes with the latest fashions, Drucilla was now exhausting her mind with a newspaper. "God!" She sat up straight. "Look here, there's a prisoner let out of Princetown several days ago. The Axe-murderer — that's what they call him."

Drucilla's little scream might have come from the ghost out in the rain, trying to get in.

* * *

Nobody cared, that was clear.

Victoria Gray was a cousin educated well beyond the means of the jobs that might have come her way. Thus Jess's father had employed her in the ambiguous role of "housekeeper," and Victoria did perform what duties she could find. With Mrs. Mulchop, Mulchop, and Billy (the stable-lad), the household was top-heavy with servants. Victoria's servitude was minimal, the line between housekeeper and long-standing guest somewhat blurred.

"Wonder how old she is?" Uncle Robert had said one morning before they had moved from Eaton Square to Ashcroft. He was slitting open the morning post, letter after letter from banks and solicitors. "I believe we've inherited Victoria along with the heirlooms. Still, she's all right." He stopped in the act of opening a letter and said, reflectively, "Actually, she's quite attractive."

Because Victoria Gray had been around ever since Jessie could remember, she hadn't expected trouble from that quarter. "Fifty," she said, beheading her boiled egg smartly with a spoon.

Robert frowned. "Fifty? Surely not. She doesn't look forty to me. Did she tell you, then?"

Jessie had looked at him with cool eyes. "Would *you* tell if you were that old?" With her uncle looking at her that way, now she would have to come up with an explanation as to how she knew Victoria's age. Inspired by the letters lying on the table, she said, "It was a birthday card. She left it on a table. There was a great, big fifty —" Here Jess drew a 5 and 0 in the air, huge numbers, in case her uncle thought fifty wasn't all that much. Satisfied, she dipped a soldier in her egg.

Uncle Robert was looking at her with his head slightly cocked. And then came that bemused smile that bothered her. "If that's so, she must take wonderful care of herself."

Jessie concentrated on dabbing tiny bits of plum preserve on her toast. "She does. Victoria has lots of those little pots of colours and jars of cream and stuff. Before she goes to bed she wears the cream and a hair net."

Instead of being put off by this odious picture, he was fascinated and completely forgot about his mail. "Well, she certainly has beautiful skin. It must all pay off."

"That's from the mud."

"Mud?"

"Sometimes ladies put it on their faces when they're old to make their skin tight." Here, Jess pressed her fingers to the sides of her own flawless face, pulling the skin back.

Uncle Rob shook his head. "Poor Victoria. Paint, cream, mud."

Quickly, *The Times* came up in front of his face, but Jessie thought she might have seen just the beginning of a smile, snatched away.

She studied the beads of jam on her toast and wondered if she should have left out the mud.

That evening of the fourteenth, Victoria Gray broke into Jess's reflections on the weather, the fog, the condition of the roads. Night had descended on the moor like a black-gloved hand. But he hadn't take a car — that was the trouble.

"You're being childish, Jess. Better you go to bed and stop all this morbid worrying."

"I *am* a child, aren't I?" A fact she denied most of the time, using it only when it suited her. She watched Victoria collect the balled-up wrappers that the Dreadful Dru had aimed at Henry, now napping on a chair by the fire. He was always napping. She supposed she loved Henry, but he was getting boring.

Victoria was going on about the Dreadful Dru: ". . . glad to see *that* one leave. The only thing she's good at is penmanship. Probably a forger in her youth."

537

None of them seemed to understand the monumental importance of what had happened. "Did you see him leave?"

Victoria sighed. "*No,* for the tenth time. No. He obviously left early in the morning — he's done it before — when we were all asleep. You know your uncle is impulsive."

But that didn't explain the absence of a Valentine, the lack of a note.

"Jessie, dear." Victoria stood directly behind her now, doubling the reflection in the window. "Go to bed and stop worrying. Can't you allow your uncle to forget just *once —* ?"

"*No!* Come on, Henry!" Jessie ordered the dog before she ran from the room. Henry, looking tired and sad, had to obey this injunction, as it was usually the only one he ever got from his mistress.

But she didn't go to bed directly. First, she took down her yellow oil skin from the peg beside the overall and jammed her arms in it before she opened the heavy door leading out to what used to be all horse-boxes.

The stable now provided room for garaging nine cars. There were two horses boxed on the other side. Victoria loved to ride; Jessica hated it. She'd told her uncle there were so many ponies on the moor, just looking at a pony made her want to throw up. And she certainly wasn't going to some stupid riding school, only to go round and round in a ring.

"I want a car," she had said, as his collection grew.

"A *car?* Jess, you're seven years old."

She sighed. How many times had she heard that? "In a month I'll be eight. I want a Mini Cooper. You know. The one Austin Rover made." She was rather proud of having come upon this minuscule bit of information.

"Police don't look kindly on eight-year-olds driving."

* * *

538

The Mini Cooper was there. Henry slogged behind her, stopping when she stopped. He yawned, unused to this nocturnal inspection of cars in the dark and the rain. Rain blew the hood of her oil skin as Jessica walked round the old stables, beaming her torch on each one, touching the bonnet — almost *patting* the car, as if each were indeed a favourite horse.

TWELVE

JESSIE lay in bed in the pre-dawn hours, with Henry like a heavy duvet at her feet. She stared up at the tracery of light that the blowing branches etched on the ceiling. Then she turned on her side. Instead of counting sheep (which was horribly dull), she started counting off the rooms at Ashcroft. Her thoughts lingered on the long, dark corridor beyond her bedroom door, and on Uncle Rob's room, two doors down, full of leather and chairs and books and a high mahogany chest where he kept the pictures of her father and mother.

But she couldn't think of that room and sleep. Her mind travelled on to Dreadful Dru's—the room on the other side of hers. Dru was living the life of Laura Ashley (which didn't fit her a bit) — tiny flowers on wallpaper, tiny sprigs on curtains that made Jessie think of thorny hedges. Whenever she went into the Dreadful Dru's room, she felt trapped by stinging nettles. Next to Dru was Victoria Gray, whose room matched her perfectly. It was rather mysterious, with its silky velvet drapes that lay in heavy folds upon the floor.

None of this was helping her sleep. She counted the rooms in the servants' wing where Mr. and Mrs. Mulchop and Billy had their rooms. The other six rooms in that wing were empty.

Like a potential buyer viewing a property, her mind was led down the dark hall outside her room and down the sweeping Adam staircase to what was now a well of darkness: the big hall that on sunny days was bright, its floor of Spanish tiles, its circular table in the centre pungent with the smells of roses or jasmine.

She opened her eyes and saw that the black panes had lightened to purple. The sash windows rattled with the rain. Jessie turned on her other side and took her mind through the tiled hall, into the morning room where, at the dreary age of twenty or so, she would most likely have to talk to people like the local vicar or Major Smythe. . . .

"I don't want to grow up," she had told Uncle Robert a year ago. "To get old like sixteen and have to go to some boring boarding school like All Hallows."

It was a misty September morning. They had taken the Zimmer and a basket of lunch to Haytor.

Jess had held her breath, waiting for him to say something like *But you must grow up,* or *You'll love school.* Only, he couldn't say that, could he? Not after his own awful school-days.

What he did say was, "I don't see why you have to do anything before you feel like it."

She looked up at the sky that had changed from a sluggish grey to clear pearl. "But I *have* to."

"Go away? When you're ready. Otherwise, it just makes misery."

Now she felt adult and indignant at his lack of knowledge of the Real World. "Don't you know people are *always* having to do things they don't like to? Lucy Manners — she had to go to All Hallows whether she liked it or not."

"She's got spots, hasn't she?"

541

Jessica was trying to be serious. "What's that got to do with it?"

Uncle Rob was lying on the rock, an arm thrown over his face. "Don't they all have spots, the boarding school ones? Either spots or teeth that stick out? I don't think you should go because you're much too pretty. I'd hate to see you with spots and stuck-out teeth."

And she began to think of school in more kindly terms. "Lucy Manners would have spots *anywhere*," she said reasonably.

II

Jessie lay on her back and watched the shadows of the branches comb the ceiling in the gathering light. She was still debating what to do. She got out of bed.

Although Henry had no desire to move himself from the foot of the warm bed and follow, follow he did. *Come on, Henry,* were the three worst words in the language.

She could not reach the telephone in the kitchen because it was high up on the wall. Jess pulled over the cricket stool that Mulchop liked to sit on and smell the soup cooking.

The operator took forever to answer. Jess hung up twice, each time being careful to dial 100. Finally, she got one of them, frosty, far-off in her wired-up ice castle. Jess cleared her throat. "My name's Jessica Ashcroft and I live at Ashcroft. That's fifteen miles outside Exeter. My uncle's missing. I want the police."

The operator talked to her in that sort of slow, loud way that people used with deaf people and silly children. When Jessie explained that her uncle had been missing five days, the operator asked her why she thought he was "missing."

"Because he isn't *here!*" Jessie hung up. It was hopeless. How could she ever make the operator understand that he'd

542

never go anywhere without leaving a note — and, especially, a Valentine. Today — well, just yesterday, was St. Valentine's Day. Uncle Rob always remembered every holiday. And how could she make the operator understand about the cars? Jessie leaned against the black telephone and came close to crying. She gulped to stop the tears. Henry shook himself out of his lethargy and pawed at her leg and whined in sympathy. But his eyes closed like shutters and he dozed off again.

While she was sitting on the cricket stool, an image came back to Jessie. It was the Dreadful Dru on the couch, stuffing herself with chocs and trying to read the paper.

Jessie took down the receiver and dialled Emergency—999. A crisp, no-nonsense voice asked her what she wanted. Ambulance? Hospital? Police?

Jessie lowered her voice a notch, rounded her vowels, and enunciated clearly, in just the way Mad Margaret had taught her. "I am Lady Jessica Allan-Ashcroft." Dramatic pause. "I want Scotland Yard." The telephone nearly slipped from her hand because her palm was so sweaty. Her heart pounded. "That axe-murderer that was released from Dartmoor prison has been to this house and he's killed —" she looked down — "the Honourable Henry Allan-Ashcroft."

Nose on paws, Henry raised beleaguered eyes, unaware that his blood — according to Lady Jessica — was everywhere. Almost total dismemberment. Then he returned to his light doze, equally unaware that he had just been ennobled.

All the operator's questions she had answered coolly, almost indignantly, as if surprised that Lady Jessica Allan-Ashcroft should be questioned by such a menial. Directions were given. Times were given. Names were given. And she hung up, after being told to stay calm.

Calm? With blood running all over the kitchen floor? Was the woman *mad*?

She had begun to believe in her own fantasy until she looked at Henry, lying healthily by the hearth, and wondered how she was going to explain to the police how he was so un-bloody. And unbowed.

"Come on, Henry. We've got to think."

Henry showed as little inclination for thinking as for fol-lowing. In the pantry, Jessie found a tin of Chum, struggled with the tin opener, and put some in a bowl. This she placed on the pantry floor and had no trouble getting Henry in there for his unexpected tea at dawn. She shut the door.

As she walked through the dining room into the drawing room, where morning light lay in splinters on oriental carpets and velvet couches, it occurred to Jessie that the Devonshire police didn't know Henry. And Henry certainly wouldn't talk.

But she, Jessie, would have to. How would she explain the lack of blood? Blood was not easy to come by, and she had no intention of sacrificing any of hers. She sat on the same sofa as had the Dreadful Dru, trying to be calm, trying to think. Jessie looked out of the window and saw the cold, scabrous dawn slither up the grass like a snake and considered tomato sauce.

But where was the slaughtered body? Cold in only her nightdress, she still sat there, constructing and reconstructing her story. In the attic was a dressmaker's dummy. If she put it in a dark corner of the kitchen and tossed the tomato sauce all over, she could say she saw it and just had a fit.. . .

Yet, wouldn't that open up more questions? *Who* had put the dummy there and spilt the sauce all round?

At the same time as she heard barking from the pantry, she heard the double-note of sirens coming up the gravel drive. The revolving lights, the noise, caused a lot of thumping from the rooms upstairs.

Footsteps coming down the stairs, footsteps coming up the

gravel. She felt sorry for Henry, shut up in the pantry, and sorrier for herself. She was going to have a lot to answer for.

III

The Dreadful Dru came in holding a candlestick, like a leftover from the Mad Margaret's repertoire of characters. But the Dreadful Dru looked more like a horse fly than she did Lady Macbeth, heavy with sleep in her black peignoir.

Mrs. Mulchop was dressed in her mobcap and brown felt slippers. Victoria Gray in a velvet dressing gown.

Police were everywhere, some in uniform and some in plain clothes; there were also men in white coats, and a doctor with his black bag.

Jessica was surrounded.

There was a torrent of questions and a few shocked answers from Mrs. Mulchop and Victoria Gray. No, they knew nothing. The questions were orchestrated by the insistent barking of Henry. Mrs. Mulchop went to the pantry to investigate.

Jessica scratched at her ear and looked up through squinty eyes as if she couldn't imagine what had brought all this crowd together. The salvo of questions seemed to confuse her awfully, and the man in charge — an Inspector Browne — waited while she gazed all over the ivory and damask splendour of the Ashcroft drawing room. Finally, she asked, "Where am I?"

Drucilla Plunkett was wringing her hands as if to keep them away from Jessica's throat. "Where *are* you? Whatever are you going on about, you silly thing?"

Jessie rubbed her eyes and turned her troubled face to Inspector Browne. "I must've been walking in my sleep again."

Drucilla was yelling now: "You *never* walk in your sleep!"

Jessie considered for a moment. "Yes, I do. You just weren't around."

The logic of this escaped Drucilla, who, having put down the candlestick, raised it now as if she meant to bring it down on her little charge's head. Inspector Browne came between them. The house and grounds were swarming with police.

Nothing, was the report passed back along the line of the inspector's entourage. *Nil.* No body, no blood, no sign of forced entry or anything else. They all looked to Jessie.

"It was a nightmare," said Jessie. "I was having this awful dream about my Uncle Robert. He's been missing —" (and here she looked out of the window to calculate another dawn into the whole of it) "— six days."

Once again Drucilla raised the candlestick. Victoria Gray turned away, looking pained. And the playlet was interrupted by the return of Mrs. Mulchop, marching in with Henry. "And why was Henry shut up in my pantry, I'd like to know, Miss?"

One of Browne's men flipped through a small notebook. "Report was that a Henry Ashcroft had been the victim. The Honourable Henry Allan-Ashcroft."

Before Dru or Victoria or Mrs. Mulchop could react fully to this announcement, Jessie had jumped up from the couch. "*Henry!* You're all *right!*" She flung her arms about the massed wrinkles that were Henry.

They all looked down in wonder. A child and her dog.

THIRTEEN

BRIAN Macalvie seemed at first to be merely irritated by the telephone's ringing at four a.m. in the Lyme Regis station. He cradled the receiver like a bawling baby against his ear. Macalvie might, indeed, have been a new father, thought Jury; he didn't seem to need sleep. They had been all day in Dorchester and Exeter.

As he listened to the voice on the other end, Macalvie stopped sucking the Fisherman's Friend. Wiggins had left the packet before going back to the White Lion for some sleep. In slow motion, Macalvie's feet left the desk that had been supporting them; the chair creaked with his weight as he sat up. He nodded and said, "Yeah, I've got it." He hung up.

Then he put his head in his hands.

"What the hell is it?" asked Jury, surprised by Macalvie's look of remorse.

"Dartmoor. Bloody Dartmoor. It sounds like it's happening all over again."

II

"Dartmoor." Wiggins said it with a shudder as they drove off the A35 toward Ashburton.

"You'll love it, Wiggins," said Macalvie, "it's got a prison and ponies and it rains sideways."

He was right about the rain. Wiggins was huddled down in his coat in the back seat. "You should slow down a bit, sir. This road's sign-posted as not being appropriate for caravans."

"So who's driving a caravan?" said Macalvie, taking what looked like a single-lane road between hedges stout as stone walls at a good fifty miles per hour. God help them or anyone coming from the opposite direction.

It was seven in the morning but it looked like dusk — the rain, the ground mist, the dark rock formations rising against the sky. When they got beyond the hedged-in road, Jury saw acres of heather the colour of port, crippled trees, the occasional huddled house.

Ashcroft was visible from a turning a half-mile away, standing on its hill, a large and perfectly proportioned house. As they turned into its long, sweeping gravel drive, Jury saw the grounds were partly formal — well-groomed hedges, flower beds — and partly wild, as if the gardener had dropped spade and hoe in the middle of the job.

In front were two police cars.

"Nice little place," said Macalvie, braking hard enough to spit up gravel.

"What the hell do you mean, a *ruse?*"

Detective Inspector Browne looked as if he'd like to be anywhere but where he was now. "Sorry, sir. The little girl, Jessica Ashcroft — or Lady Jessica, I should say, I expect —"

"I don't care what you call her, Browne. Just tell me what's going on."

548

Eyes averted from Macalvie's, Browne explained. "And by the time we found out, you'd already left Lyme Regis. . . ."

Jessica looked up at the three new ones. She was still in her nightdress, as were the other members of the household. She sat on the couch, ankles crossed, patiently waiting for whatever scolding the new ones had to dish out. There should be enough brains among all of them to find her uncle, she thought. She did not particularly like the look of the copper-haired one who stood with his hands in his trouser pockets and had eyes like torches. The other, taller one had grey eyes and looked, somehow, comfortable. . . .

Macalvie looked over the lot of them. Victoria Gray was sitting patiently enough on the couch facing the girl. The older one was the cook and she wrung her hands. Then there was the rich pastry of a piece named Plunkett. Their backdrop, the drawing room itself, was heavy velvet and brocade, portraits and gilt. No one was short of money.

"This," said DI Browne, "is Lady Jessica Mary Allan-Ashcroft."

On facing sofas, Chief Superintendent Macalvie and Jessica Allan-Ashcroft squared off. Jury sat on a heavy brocade chair and Wiggins on a straight one by the fire.

"You can call me Jessica," she said, with extreme largesse.

"Thanks." Macalvie glared at her, took out a pack of gum, and stuffed a stick in his mouth.

"Can I have some?"

Jury was glad to see Macalvie managed to keep from throwing it at her.

They both sat there, taking each other's measure, chewing away.

"Start talking," said Macalvie.

"My uncle's missing."

That statement seemed to bring housekeeper, cook, and governess to the edge of hysteria. Victoria Gray, the most controlled, stepped back from it and said to Macalvie, "Robert Ashcroft. Her uncle. He left several days ago, probably for London, but she's convinced he's missing. It's ridiculous; Mr. Ashcroft goes to London now and again."

Macalvie's eyes snapped from Victoria back to Jessica. He chewed and stared. "You know, there's kind of a difference between an uncle going missing and a friendly call from an axe-murderer. That occur to you?"

Jury broke in. "What makes you think he's missing, Jessica?"

"Because he didn't leave a note and he didn't leave a Valentine present."

"For a box of chocolates," said Macalvie, "you got half the Devon-Cornwall constabulary running across this godforsaken, bloody moor with some cock-and-bull story about a murderer. You know that, don't you?"

To that deadly voice, Jessie sighed and said, "I'm sorry."

"You're sorry."

She smoothed the skirt of her nightdress, folded her hands, and said gravely, "Yes. I'm sorry you're so disappointed that there wasn't a lot of blood and torn-up bodies and we weren't all murdered, including Henry." She took out her gum, inspected the pink wad, and put it back in her mouth.

Macalvie's eyes were like lasers. He opened his mouth but was interrupted.

"Don't forget about that man that got out of Dartmoor." As if police weren't keeping abreast of the news, she handed Macalvie a neatly folded paper. It contained the clipping that Drucilla had read earlier.

Macalvie tossed the paper aside, angrily. "That *man* was *released* on good behaviour. Your behaviour I'm not so sure I could say the same about. Not only the Devon-Cornwall police, but the person sitting over there"—and he nodded in

Jury's direction — "just happens to be a Scotland Yard CID superintendent."

"Then why isn't he asking the questions?" Jessica directed her attention to Jury. "My uncle disappeared five days ago, six, counting today." She was pleased the thin one was making notes of what she said. At least *someone* was taking her seriously. "He never forgets any holiday and he always lets me know if he has to go somewhere. Besides that, all his cars are out there." She pointed in the direction of the stable-yard.

"What do you mean, 'all,' Miss?" asked Wiggins.

"All nine. The Zimmer, the Porsche, the Lotus Elite, the Mini Cooper — that's really mine — the Ferrari, the Jaguar XJ-S that goes from zero to sixty in under seven seconds, the 1967 Maserati, and the Aston Martin." She sat back.

Wiggins cleared his throat. "That's only eight, Miss." He counted with his lips again.

Jury thought Macalvie was going to hit one of them; he wasn't sure which.

Jessica looked for a thoughtful moment at the ceiling. "Did I say the Benz? I don't like it that much."

Wiggins wrote it down. "Your uncle's a collector, is that it?" He wet the tip of his pencil.

"Yes. He's five-feet-eleven with gold hair and light brown eyes." She looked back at Jury. "He's handsome. He took me in when my father died four years ago."

There was a slight laugh from Victoria Gray: "Wasn't it more like your taking *him* in?"

Jury looked more closely at her: good-looking, eyes heavy-lidded, as if she preferred not to have her thoughts read in her eyes. She seemed embarrassed now, having given voice to one of those thoughts. "Excuse me, but I'd like to get dressed." She drew the velvet dressing gown more closely around her.

"Go ahead," said Macalvie. "Except for missing uncles there's no reason for us to be here."

Jessie looked around the room. "You're not even going to look for him, are you?"

Jury was impressed with the little girl's conviction that something was really wrong. Her uncle must be a very dependable person. "We will."

Macalvie was standing now, hands in pockets, turning the blowtorch look on Jury. "Isn't there enough on your platter already?"

"I just thought I'd ask Lady Jessica a few questions."

"Hell, ask away. I'm going down to Freddie's. Browne can drop me off and you can bring the car along whenever you're finished fooling around here. Come on, Wiggins. One drink of Freddie's cider and you'll never be sick a day in your life. You'll be paralytic."

Wiggins looked at Jury; Jury nodded. It amused him that Wiggins — or the pharmacy Wiggins carried with him — had become indispensable to Macalvie.

III

There in the drawing room, Jury listened patiently to the fabrication of faithless loves and deaths from broken hearts attributed to her mother. Jessica had gone to a table on which stood some framed pictures and brought back the one of Barbara Allan-Ashcroft. The woman in the picture, even squinting and half-blinded by the sun, Jury could see was, herself, blindingly beautiful. She might indeed have broken many of the hearts Jessica claimed she had.

The second picture was of her father: he was an older and more wasted version of the man in the portrait above the fireplace; a grave illness would explain it.

"She's pretty, isn't she?"

"She's more than pretty. She's quite beautiful. You look like her, you know." The woman was probably in her twenties, at any rate she was a good twenty years younger than her husband. Jury could almost believe the tale of woe and

552

heartbreak Jessica had spun. Unfortunately, though, Jessica suffered from the Scheherazade syndrome. Whenever there came a pause in her tale of gloom and doom and Jury tried to get up, Jessie would spin out an even richer thread. Scheherazade or Hephaestus — Jury wasn't sure which. He would start to rise and *plunk*, the golden net would fall and toss him back once more onto the couch. Her contriving the axe-murderer's visit was small potatoes, compared with the tragedy of Barbara Allan. If as many suitors had died for love of Jessica's mother as Jessica would have him believe, the population of London W1, Devon and Chalfont St. Giles would have been considerably diminished. Jessie was careful to assure Jury, however, that her mother would never have deliberately hurt whatever Sweet William happened to be in love with her at a given moment.

Barbara Ashcroft had died a few months after Jessie was born. When her Uncle Robert had gone off to Australia, Jessie had not yet been born. Victoria Gray (according to Jessie) had come to her mother's funeral and, being a cousin, had been urged to stay on by her father. There was an old cook who was especially fond of Barbara Ashcroft and who had preferred to leave once she was dead. Thus, Mrs. Mulchop had come on the job afterwards. And so had the string of governesses.

No one in the present household had known Robert Ashcroft before he came back from Australia.

Jessie went on about her father, her uncle, her other relatives (all of whom were very distant). "After the will was read, they kept coming and calling, until Uncle Rob got rid of them."

"Do you know who your family solicitor is, Jessie?" asked Jury. They were out in the stableyard now, behind the house, a handsomely converted stableyard.

"It's Mr. Mack. Or, at least, he's one of them. We have —"

She seemed uncertain as to how much they had. "— trunks full of money. Do you like cars?"

"How long has he been with the family?"

She frowned. "Who?"

"Your solicitor, Mr. Mack."

"Forever. Do you like *cars?*"

He felt an odd presentiment. Wynchcoombe, Clerihew Marsh, Lyme Regis, Dorchester. Only the last was outside a forty-mile radius. But the Ashcroft place was certainly within it. And she was ten years old.

"Yes. I like cars," said Jury.

They had come to the last of the nine—one of Jessie's favourites—the Lotus elite. "Nineteen fifty-seven," she solemnly pronounced. Then she went on to interweave fact and fiction, using expressions like "stroke dimension" and "wishbone front" with all the assurance of an expert.

It was during this recital that there came a rush of footsteps and raised voices and a man striding across the courtyard toward the old horse-boxes. "Jess! What the devil's going on?"

The look on her face made it clear to Jury that Uncle Robert was no longer missing.

FOURTEEN

HE would have needed no introduction. The way Jessie hurled herself like a discus into his arms would have told Jury that this was Robert Ashcroft.

"But I *did* leave a note," he was saying as Jury walked up. "I slipped it under your door. Who's our visitor?" He looked from Jessie to Jury.

"Scotland Yard." Jury handed Ashcroft his card, smiling to show his was a friendly visit. "It seems Lady Jessica got a little worried and told the police you'd gone missing. The Devon police have been and gone."

Ashcroft looked down at his niece, astonished. "Good God, Jess. You called in the police—" He looked at Jury and down at Jury's card. "Scotland Yard? I can't believe it."

"Well, I happened to be working on another case and came along with the divisional commander —"

Again, amazement was stamped on Ashcroft's face. "A superintendent and a divisional commander, Jess? Where's the Prime Minister? You left her out? How in the name of heaven did Jess manage to drag you all out here on a missing person case?"

Jessica was studying an interesting cloud formation and saying maybe they should go in as it looked like rain. Inspired by another means of changing the subject, she called for Henry. "Where's Henry? He came out with us. *Henry!*"

The sad face of Henry appeared slowly, rising behind the windscreen of the Ferrari.

"He likes to go for rides," said Jessie, as she pulled away from her uncle and made Henry clamber down from the car.

Out of sight, out of mind, thought Jury, smiling. "Sorry about the police intrusion, Mr. Ashcroft. All a mare's nest. I've been working on a case in Dorchester —"

"I read about it. Terrible."

"What's more terrible is there've been two others since then."

Ashcroft looked at his niece and went a little white. "Children?"

Jury nodded.

Jessica was back with Henry in tow. "One got killed with a knife and the other one got his head bashed in, or something." She made a dreadful sound, apparently her version of bashing.

"It's nothing to be making light of, Jess," said her uncle, sharply.

"I wasn't. I was just showing you — it happened in the church, too."

Ashcroft looked puzzled. "What church?"

"Over in Wynchcoombe."

Her proximity to murder did not seem to upset her, but Ashcroft looked worried enough as he studied Jury's face for some reassurance. Jury doubted that he wanted to go further into details in front of his niece, and said nothing.

Jessie, however, had garnered plenty of details: "It's Drucilla who told me. She likes to read me the worst part of the papers. An axe-murderer got out of the prison in Prince-town —"

556

Jury laughed. "Hold it a minute. The man was *released,* Jessie. There was even some question whether he'd ever done that—business. And he certainly wasn't an 'axe-murderer'; the papers like blood and thunder."

Ashcroft was angry, though not at Jury. "Drucilla's days are numbered. She shouldn't have been reading you that sort of stuff. And didn't you get the chocolates I paid that stupid bloke she runs about with to deliver?"

"Drucilla said the chocolates *were for her!* She's been stuffing them in till she's sick."

"I'll see to her. At any rate, I've found you a new governess. This one I think will finally do."

Jury could almost hear the *Oh, no* directed toward her uncle. Beseeching eyes. Down-turned mouth. "But you always let me choose before!"

"I'm sorry, Jess. But they've all turned out to be such a bad lot — well, anyway, this time I advertised in the London papers. That's why I went up to London. You'll like Sara. I'm sure of it. And if you don't—" Ashcroft shrugged "—she goes. Alright? In the meantime, I think you might want to meet her. She's in the drawing room."

Jessie didn't answer. Her eyes were on the ground

"If there are no further questions, Superintendent — ?"

Jury was fascinated by Jessie's little act. She might have been going to a hanging. "Questions? No, Mr. Ashcroft. No questions." He looked back toward the boxes that housed not horses but cars. "I was wondering, though, if I could have another look at your collection —"

"Certainly. Help yourself."

Jessie held him back, saying, "That's another thing. Why didn't you take one of the cars? Why didn't you drive?"

Ashcroft smoothed back her dark hair. "Because there was an advert in the paper about a Rolls; I was sure I'd buy it and drive it back. But it wasn't what I wanted. And as it turned out, Miss Millar — that's Sara — had her own car. So we drove back."

557

Looking at Jessie's face, Jury thought the news couldn't have been worse. He only hoped, for the niece's sake, Miss Millar's car was a beaten-up Volkswagen.

Jessie and Ashcroft walked off, hand in hand. Jury doubted that it would take much time for Jessie to sort out the new tutor.

He walked along the courtyard, looking at each of the expensive cars in turn: the Ferrari, the Porsche, the Aston Martin, the incredible Zimmer Golden Spirit (he whistled under his breath), the Mercedes-Benz (that probably didn't get much use), the Jag—there was a fortune here.

His skin prickled. Jury took out his notebook and wrote down the name of the solicitor, Mack. Robert Ashcroft's explanation had been plausible enough: note slipped under the door (Jury bet that had been mistakenly toosed out by a maid); chocolates meant to be delivered by surprise—and clearly were, since Miss Plunkett had been eating them . . ..

Yet there was that same reluctance to leave as there was when Jessica had been spinning her stories. He wished he had some legitimate reason for coming back—

He could suggest to Ashcroft that, with a killer loose nearby, his niece might need police protection. But Robert Aschroft would hire a personal bodyguard and get a matched set of Alsatians if he thought his niece was a target for a killer.

Jury was standing in front of Jessie's car, the Mini Cooper. It might as well have been a police-issue Escort for all that Jury knew about cars.

But then he smiled and ground his cigarette out on the stone and left.

V

The Jack and Hammer

FIFTEEN

An air of somnolence hung over the Jack and Hammer's saloon bar, an air not altogether caused by the fly droning around the black beams overhead, nor to Mrs. Withersby's dozing by the fire, nor to the report of the latest takeover bid of another shipyard, which was what Melrose Plant was reading about in *The Times*. Indeed, the only thing moving—and possibly responsible for the general heaviness—was Lady Ardry's mouth.

"*Gout!* That is ridiculous, Melrose." She addressed the newspaper, behind which was the face of her nephew. "It most certainly is *not* gout!" Now she addressed the painful foot, elastic-bound and supported by the cricket stool that Mrs. Withersby ordinarily claimed for herself. On this occasion, the usual Withersby enterprise had exchanged it for a double gin, compliments of Melrose Plant, the nephew Lady Ardry was now upbraiding. "And if it *is* gout, *you'd* have it, not I!"

He lowered the paper. "I'd have *your* gout, Agatha? That would be a first in the annals of medicine."

"Please do not try to be witty with *me*, my dear Plant."

"That would be difficult." Melrose turned to the book reviews, having exhausted global conflict.

"What I meant was, as you perfectly well know, that it's *you* who drinks the port, not *I*." She raised her glass of sweet sherry, toasting her own powers of deduction.

Melrose lowered his *Times* once again and turned his eyes to the beams above, wondering if the fly would fall like a bullet in the vacuum of their conversation. "Gout has many causes, Agatha. Perhaps you have fairy-cake-gout. Who knows but that if you eschew those rich pastries, your foot might become less inflamed, as the condition is not irreversible." He wondered if life were, though, when talking to his aunt. He continued. "Gout comes from the Latin *gutta*. It means 'clot' or 'drop.' Surely, you don't believe that every old pukka sahib drinking port beneath the palms wound up with gout? Gout is caused by uric acid. Sort of thing you get with too many sardines or whitebait or offal. You haven't been at the offal again, have you?"

"This is just what I would have expected of you, Plant. No sympathy whatever."

"Then why did you come clumping into the Jack and Hammer on your cane, if you already knew?" Trying to change the subject from gout to books and thinking that Agatha might be interested (by some weird crossover of the stars) in American writers, as she herself was American, Melrose said, "Now, just look at this —"

Look at this might better have been said of the man coming through the Jack and Hammer's door — Long Piddleton's antiques dealer, Marshall Trueblood. Trueblood always managed to appear on any scene like a voyager on the deck of a departing ocean liner, all confetti and coloured streamers. Nothing so much resembled one as the purple crepe scarf loosely knotted at his neck and trembling in the same wind that stirred the cape of his cashmere inverness.

Dick Scroggs, the publican, looked up from his paper, spread out on the bar, and with that welcome reserved for regulars said, "Close the bleedin' door, mate." He then returned to his paper.

"My *dear* Scroggs. How can you be so churlish when trade is this good? There are at least three — well two and a half" (he corrected himself, looking at Mrs. Withersby) "— customers. Plant, Agatha." He unwhirled his handsome coat and took a seat as close to Lady Ardry's lame foot as would allow for a little bit of pain.

She said *ouch* and glared at Trueblood, whom she loathed only slightly less than Mrs. Withersby. Trueblood, after all, had money. Not as much as her nephew, but money nonetheless.

Trueblood called to the publican for drinks all around, and included Mrs. Withersby with a helping of gin-and-it. He offered his Balkan Sobranies, lit up a lavender one (in tune with his scarf), and brushed a mite of cigarette ash from his seagreen shirt. Trueblood was the jewel in the crown of Long Piddleton, a dazzling little collection of cottages and shops in the hills of Northamptonshire. Scroggs brought the drinks and Trueblood asked Plant what he was so deep into reading about.

"Book reviews."

"How lovely. Anything useful?"

Trueblood, though certainly no miser, couldn't help but think of everything in terms of usury.

"I was going to read this review to Agatha, since she's American —"

"I *do* wish you would stop referring to me in that way, Plant." Tenderly she touched the bandage like a newborn baby's cheek. "You always seem to forget that I married your uncle, and that —"

She was always shaking relatives from his family tree, as if Melrose couldn't remember them on his own. He ignored

564

her. "Listen. 'This tone of easy superiority can sometimes be grating, primarily because it is symptomatic of a culture in its imperial phase —' "

"Who are they reviewing?" asked Trueblood. "Gunga Din?"

"No. It's this collection of essays by John Updike. But what in hell does it mean? Even leaving off the 'imperial phase' stuff—I mean the U.S. And just what is Updike's 'easy superiority'?"

"It's probably what Withers has." Trueblood called over to Cinders-by-the-ashes. "Withers, old trout! Another gin-and-it?"

Mrs. Withersby spat in the fire at the same time as she hobbled over to the bar for a refill.

Trueblood went on. "No, I'd say easy superiority is what Franco Giopinno has. Vivien's slippery Italian."

Vivien Rivington, a long-standing and (in some minds) beautiful friend, was off in Italy visiting her "slippery Italian."

"Ah, yes. That's it precisely," continued Trueblood, marvelling yet once again at himself. "Do you suppose she's gone to Venice to break it off or put it on — oh, sorry, old trout —" He turned to Agatha with innocent eyes. "That did sound a bit off-colour."

"You needn't apologize to *me*, Mr. Trueblood! I'm sure I can put it on with the best of them."

Trueblood and Melrose exchanged glances.

"But if she thinks herself a woman of such superiority —"

"Uh-uh. *Easy* superiority," Trueblood said. "It's like easy virtue. What do you think, Melrose? I know how fond you are of Viv-viv."

It was deliberate. It always was with Trueblood when Lady Ardry was around. Melrose knew she would gladly have given Trueblood a crack with her cane, had it not been more important to divert Plant's attention away from Vivien into other and less attractive quarters.

"*I* find the review extremely un-American."

"Well, it's certainly anti-Updike," said Melrose. "'An American confidence which can treat the whole world as a suitable province for its judgements.'" He could only shake his head. "For the British to talk about imperialism . . . Cheap shot."

The only cheap shot Agatha was concerned about was where her next sweet sherry was coming from.

"And here's another American writer being gunned down. She's described as writing a book 'ladylike in an American way.' That only makes me want to meet American ladies, to find out in what way they're so differently ladylike." Melrose looked at Trueblood, but doubted that he would have much to offer on that point.

"As far as I am concerned," said Agatha, "I mean to stay right here in dear old England." She patted her upraised ankle. "You will never get *me* back to the United States."

That was a good reason for a mass exodus, thought Melrose. But, then, why *should* she go back to the States? She had everything here she could ever want. Unfortunately for her, all of it was up at Ardry End — the crystal, the Queen Anne furniture, the servants, grounds and jewels. . . . Well, perhaps not *all* the jewels, for Melrose noticed that riding on her bosom this afternoon was a delicately chased silver brooch he had last seen in his mother's possession. The Countess of Caverness had been dead for a number of years; his aunt seemed set on slipping into her shoes, even though Agatha was not, properly speaking, a Lady in any sense of the term. She had been married to Melrose's uncle — the Honourable Robert Ardry. Agatha had decided to let the dead bury the dead, but not the title, and had long since wedded herself instead to the cake stand and the sweet sherry.

"I cannot imagine," said Melrose, "one's giving up America to come and live in a country of amateurs."

Trueblood raised an eyebrow at that. "And do you include

566

purveyors of furniture in that category?" His description of himself and his antiques was hardly accurate.

Agatha sighed loudly. "I don't know what you're talking about, Plant."

She seldom did. It inspired Melrose to dip into further shallows of conversation, even if it was like wasting a good fly on a dead fish. "I am referring to amateur shopkeepers, amateur publicans, amateur politicians, amateur butchers —"

Lady Ardry sat up a bit too sharply and winced with pain. It was all right for Melrose to toy with prime ministers, but certainly not with the source of her daily chop. "Amateur butchers! You'd insult Mr. Greeley — after that magnificent joint we had yesterday evening—?"

"I'm not insulting Mr. Greeley's joints. But he's back there with hatchets and cleavers and saws, for all I know." Perhaps it was this reference in the paper to the release of a prisoner from Dartmoor who had been dubbed the "axe-murderer" that had allowed him to see Mr. Greeley in that light.

"Melrose! You're putting me off my sherry."

Melrose continued reading. It was possible to talk to Agatha and read simultaneously. "What I'm talking about is this: I bet you don't find American butchers greeting their customers while wearing blood-smeared aprons with knives in their hands. Every time I see your Mr. Greeley I'm reminded of the *Texas Chain Saw Murders* or whatever that execrable film was we saw on ITV. And there's another category, too — amateur criminals. You've got — meaning America has, or had — Al Capone and Scarface and the Godfather and Richard Nixon. All we've got is Brixton and the IRA."

"I must say, old bean," said Marshall Trueblood, "that's hardly a compliment to the U.S.A."

"Not meant to be. I'm merely saying that when the Americans do something — at least the professional criminals, it's a bang-up job. Not slapdash, like most of ours."

"You're mad as a hatter, Melrose. Right round the twist.

567

I'd like another drink, if you would be so kind." Agatha was not in the habit of inspecting her bread closely to see on which side it was buttered.

Melrose continued with his thesis. "Don't you remember John McVicar, who escaped from Durham? That's a high-security lockup, just like Dartmoor. No one had done it before —"

"Which merely disproves your point, old chap." Trueblood rose to get the drinks, and Mrs. Withersby snapped to attention.

"No, it doesn't. Two of them got out. One broke his ankle going over the wall or something and the plan for the pickup had to be dished. Well, there goes John into the Wear or the Tyne — whichever river — and he swims for it. But now he's got the problem of making contact with his friends on the outside. Guess how he does it?"

Agatha sighed even more loudly because Melrose was keeping Trueblood away from the bar. "Can't imagine," said Trueblood.

"Goes into a public phone box. I mean, for God's sakes, can you imagine Capone or Scarface in a phone box searching for a 10p piece—?"

Scroggs interrupted by calling from the bar, "Phone for you, M'lord." Dick Scroggs had never been able to work his mind round to Melrose Plant's having given up his title.

"A call?" said Agatha. "Here? Who would be calling you at the Jack and Hammer? I find that odd . . ." She kept on casting about for reasons all the time Melrose was making his way to the phone on the other side of the bar.

It was Ruthven, his butler. Melrose was so mystified by the message that Ruthven had to convince him that, Yes, those were Superintendent Jury's directions. He would very much appreciate Lord Ardry's driving to Dartmoor in his Silver Ghost — "He was very specific on that point, My Lord." Superintendent Jury had left clear instructions as to what he would like Lord Ardry to do.

"Yes, all right," said Melrose. "Yes, yes, yes, Ruthven. Thank you." Melrose hung up.

His friend Jury might have asked for some odd things over the years of their acquaintance, but why would he want an earl with a Silver Ghost?

VI

The End of
the Tunnel

SIXTEEN

JESSICA stood in the doorway of the drawing room that morning, refusing to put her foot inside, as if she hoped that might spirit away the person to whom she was being introduced. She wouldn't look up and she wouldn't come forward despite her uncle's growing impatience. It was because she knew what she'd see.

The Amiable Amy.

In that wonderful catchall tone that Uncle Rob could use when he was cross with her, yet understood her dilemma (a common occurrence in the household), he said, "Miss Millar will think you are determined always to address her from the other side of the room, Jess."

With daggers in her eyes, she looked at her uncle, and then quickly down again lest the eyes might meet Miss Millar's.

Now it was Miss Millar's voice — amiable as could be — saying, "I can remember once having to meet a new teacher. I can remember being very shy of her."

Shy? *Shy?* Jessica Mary Allan-Ashcroft? Never in her life — or, at least, in the life she had led after Uncle Robert had come along — had Jessie been called "shy." Her face coloured with rage, which only made her more furious because now it would be taken as proof of her being shy.

"Come on, Jess," said her uncle. Seldom could she remember him sounding as if Jessie's behaviour were an embarrassment to him. Now, that's just how he sounded.

Henry, hearing the *Come on*, drifted out of his light doze, even though he was on his feet.

"Not you," she murmured, giving him a little kick.

The amiable voice continued: "Well, then, perhaps we can talk at luncheon. Or dinner." Now there was amusement in the voice. "Breakfast? Though I might not last that long. . . ."

That was clever of the new governess. It was as if she were trying to make light of what even Jessie knew to be perfectly odious behaviour on her own part. Of course, the Amiable Amy would have to have a sense of humour. Because Uncle Rob had a smashing sense of humour, and Jessie knew humour would make up for all other sorts of defects. Except, perhaps, absolute ugliness If Amy looked like an ogre or gnome ... Jessie hazarded a quick glance upward. The case was hopeless. The Amiable Amy was almost *pretty*. Hopeless. She also had patience. Patience on a monument, she was. Jessie knew a lot of Shakespeare because the Mad Margaret had shovelled it — play after play of it — down her throat, Margaret acting out scenes and bawling soliloquies. Margaret had always wanted to be an actress. She was good at Lady Macbeth.

"Jess." There was Uncle Rob again, being beastly. "What *are* you doing, standing there like a statue and wringing your hands?"

Eyes closed, Jessie said, "Not *wringing*. I'm *washing* them. I must wash my hands. Nothing will make them come clean. They're incar——" She couldn't remember that word. It was something like carburettor.

Uncle Robert was actually beginning to sound concerned. "Jessie. Are you ill? What's the matter?" He laughed uncertainly. "You seem to have gone a little mad."

Quite. She smiled to herself and turned and ran from the room.

Since the exit included no *Come on, Henry,* Henry continued to doze in the doorway.

SEVENTEEN

"So here's what happened," said Macalvie. They were sitting in the mobile unit in Wynchcoombe, Macalvie having cleared the place of the sergeant manning the telecom system, three constables going in and out, and DC Coogan. The only person (besides Jury and Wiggins) who had held his ground was Detective Inspector Neal, calmly observing Macalvie over the rim of his coffee cup.

"You've solved it, Macalvie?" Neal's tone was wry. "I sure as hell hope so. Because I don't seem to be getting anywhere. Our chief constable is a little upset. He keeps getting these calls from frightened parents."

Macalvie leaned back in his chair, hands laced behind his head. He gave Neal his laser-look. "That's too bad. Give Dorset my blessing and ask your chief if he'll grant me another twenty-four hours."

Neal smiled and dumped the rest of his coffee in the sink. "I'll do it straightaway. In the meantime, I better go back and look for the Riley boy's killer. Don't you think?"

Solemnly, Macalvie nodded. "It'd be a great kindness to the Dorset police."

Neal left, shaking his head.

Macalvie started talking as if it hadn't been Neal, but Neal's wraith that had just floated out of the door, part of a spirit-world sent to drive him mad, since the forces of the real world couldn't dent him.

"Take the name of the pub where this string of killings started, the Five Alls: the sign is usually divided so you see these five figures representing authority. 'I pray for all' — that'd be a priest or other symbol of the church; 'I plead for all' — barrister or solicitor; 'I fight for all' — military, right? 'I rule all' — a lot of positions fit that; and 'I take all.' Interesting, that figure. Sometimes the Five Alls sign says, 'I pay for all,' meaning king, queen, and country. Other times the fifth figure is John Bull, who 'pays for all.' But in our Dorchester Five Alls, the fifth figure is the Devil, who 'takes all.' Like lives. Now, we've got George-bloody-Thorne, solicitor; we've got Davey White's granddad, vicar —"

Wiggins interrupted. "But you're forgetting Simon Riley's father is only a butcher."

Macalvie smiled slightly. "True, but his wife's got some family connection with a Q.C. who's running for Parliament — 'I rule for all,' in other words. That's two figures left: the soldier and the Devil. The Devil's the killer. So that leaves one more murder." He looked at Jury. "Your expression tells me you don't like my theory. Disaster." Macalvie held out his hand to Wiggins, who rolled a lozenge into it.

"I'm sure you noticed the portrait of Jessica Ashcroft's father."

"Of course. He was a Grenadier. Military." Macalvie opened the top drawer of a desk and took out a pint of whisky and a smudged glass. "I'm going to quit this lousy job, I swear to God. Go to America. The booze is cheaper." He looked up at the ceiling as if the geography of the United States were etched there, uncapped the bottle, took a drink, and handed the glass to Wiggins.

576

"We might have come to the same conclusion by different routes," said Jury. "That is, if you're thinking of Jessica Ashcroft."

"Yeah. I'm also thinking of Sam Waterhouse. He sat in a cell for nearly nineteen years, knowing he was railroaded." Macalvie shook his head. "I still say he's not the type. He wasn't once and he *still* isn't. Are you reading your fortune in the bottom of that glass, Wiggins, or are you going to pass it along?"

"Waterhouse would be a dead cert, given *your* reasoning. Hatred of authority. And he got out just before these murders were committed."

Macalvie lapped his hands round the glass and studied the ceiling. "I still don't think it's Sam."

"What about Robert Ashcroft?"

Macalvie stopped looking at the ceiling and took his feet off his desk. "Meaning?"

"Four million pounds. And being gone throughout the time of the murders. No one in the present Ashcroft household had ever seen him before he returned from Australia. I'm going up to London to talk to the Ashcroft solicitor. But even if Ashcroft *is* the real brother, there's still —"

Macalvie interrupted. "The Campbell Soup Kid's money. Right?"

Jury nodded.

"Then why the other killings? A blind?"

Jury nodded again.

Macalvie shook his head as if he were trying to clear it, poured some more whisky in the glass and handed it to Jury. "What's his story about taking British Rail to London?"

"That he thought he'd be buying a Roller advertised in *The Times.*"

"I'll have somebody checking the paper on that one, to see if there *was* a car. And check to see if Ashcroft really went to see it. But let's assume — just for the sake of the argument —"

"I'm not trying to argue, Macalvie." Jury handed the whisky glass to Wiggins, knowing he wouldn't drink from the same ditch. "I just think Jessica Ashcroft's in trouble."

Macalvie went on as if Jury hadn't interrupted. "— that Ashcroft's guilty. Ask again — why didn't he drive up to London? He stayed at the Ritz. The doorman would have noticed any of those cars of Ashcroft coming in and out. He couldn't have used his own cars. They'd attract too much attention. It's got to be either train, bus, rented car. No, renting's too risky. Probably train. Early morning train from Exeter to London on the tenth, and he has a talk with the stationmaster to make sure he's remembered *leaving* the area. He checks into the Ritz. Train back to Dorchester — it's only a three-hour trip—six hours coming and going. Or he could even have got off in Dorchester, killed the Riley boy, then gone on to London. On the twelfth, to Waterloo Station, late night train to Exeter — no, not Exeter. The stationmaster might remember him. Axminster. What about Axminster?"

Wiggins shook his head. "Why would he go to all that trouble? Going back and forth? If he wants to put us on the trail of a psychopath — ?"

"Because he's got to be *out* of the area the killings are done in," said Macalvie.

"Then what does he do," said Jury, "after he gets off your Axminster train? He can't *walk* to Wynchcoombe. How does he get there? And how does he get to Lyme Regis?"

"Not the train, then. So he doesn't rent a car. He *buys* one in London. Something fast and pricey that's already M.O.T.'d. Buys it from one of the sleazy grafters all over London. They don't give a damn what name you tell them. That gives Ashcroft the thirteenth to do his interviewing of tutors and allows her to pack up and they go back to Ashcroft on the fifteenth." He looked at Jury. "So what do you think?"

"Do you care?"

"Not particularly. We'll circulate pictures round the used-car lots. Pictures. But I don't want to breath on Ashcroft hard enough to make him suspicious." Jury's theory had now become his. "I can't send a police photographer."

"We've got a photographer," said Jury.

Macalvie frowned. "Like who?"

"Molly Singer."

Macalvie smiled. "You mean Mary Mulvanney." He sat back and put his feet on his desk.

"Okay, just for the sake of argument, I'll go along with you. Let's say she *is* Mary Mulvanney. Given Sam Waterhouse, given Angela Thorne's father, that certainly adds up to a lot of coincidences. Too many. There's a connection between the murders. The old one and these new ones. The same theory that applies to Waterhouse might apply to her. Revenge. Though the killing of the Riley boy and Davey White isn't clear. Anyway, we get Molly into Ashcroft as a photographer for some classy magazine about cars or the country gentleman. We can certainly work up some bona fides."

Macalvie took his feet off the desk and frowned. "Jury, you're saying you want to put your chief suspect in the *same house* with Jessica Ashcroft?"

"Who says she's my 'chief suspect'? And what about Waterhouse? Anyway, Jessica's living there right now with another suspect. Her uncle. If Molly Singer were guilty, she'd hardly try anything in the house on a photography assignment."

"Mary Mulvanney." From his wallet, Macalvie drew a snapshot. It was a smiling trio of a woman, a little girl, and an older girl with pale skin and dark hair who was the smiling centre of the three.

Jury shook his head. "I don't see any more resemblance to Molly Singer than to any other dark-haired girl."

Macalvie returned the picture to his wallet.

That's what got Jury. He'd been carrying it around for twenty years. "You'll never get over that fifteen-year-old kid walking into your office and telling you the law's scum, police are scum, and especially *you're* scum. She really got to you, didn't she?"

Macalvie didn't answer for a moment. "No, Jury. She really got to *you*. Let's go talk to her, if that's the only way to convince you who she is."

"A little browbeating?"

"Who, *me?*"

"Just let me handle the photography business, will you? After a chat with you she might not feel like cooperating with the police."

II

Macalvie had made himself at home in the chair by the fire, having picked up the black cat and dumped it on the floor. The cat sat like lead at his feet, its tail twitching.

They had appeared unannounced, Macalvie overriding Jury's objections. It had taken enough persuasion on Jury's part to keep the chief superintendent from dragging Molly Singer into the Lyme Regis station.

"I don't know what you're talking about," said Molly, looking from Macalvie to Jury.

"The hell you don't," Macalvie said, working the old Macalvie magic. "Twenty years ago your mother, Rose, was murdered in a little place called Clerihew Marsh —"

"I've never heard of it," said Molly.

"In Dartmoor, maybe forty miles from here."

Her face was a mask, unreadable; her body rigid, untouchable. But the emotion she was holding back seemed forcibly to spread through the room. Jury felt simultaneously drawn to her and held off.

What interested him was that Macalvie seemed totally unaffected. It wasn't that he was an unfeeling man; he just didn't seem bothered by the electricity in the air.

"Would you like to see my birth certificate to prove who I am?"

"Love to." He popped a hard sweet in his mouth and leaned toward her. "Papers don't mean sod-all. You could bring in the priest who officiated at your baptism and all the rest you've made your weekly confession to — you *are* a Catholic, I suppose — and it wouldn't matter. You're still Mary Mulvanney. What the hell are you doing in Lyme?"

"Must I get a solicitor?"

Macalvie smiled slightly. "Of course *Singer* could be your married name. Is it?"

"No."

"Why don't you finish telling us just what happened in Clerihew?"

The question surprised Jury. It clearly surprised Molly Singer. And as he asked the question, he had taken the snapshot from his wallet and handed it to her.

She wouldn't take it, so he dropped it in her lap.

"I don't know what you're talking about."

"You really overwork that line, you know?"

Molly looked at Jury almost hopefully, as if he might untangle the web Macalvie was weaving. Jury said nothing, even though, strictly speaking, he had precedence. This was Dorset, not Devon. But there was a chemistry in the room, a delicate balance that he might upset if he intervened.

"Sam Waterhouse is out — but I expect you read about that."

"I've never heard of him." Her voice was flat; her expression bland.

Macalvie had played two aces in a row right off the bottom of the deck — showing her that picture and then suddenly bringing up Sam Waterhouse. Macalvie, for all his surprises, didn't use cheap ones. He grew serious. Unless that too was a trick. Maybe Macalvie's pack didn't have a bottom. "Let's go over that story of what happened on the Cobb again."

581

Molly Singer merely shook her head. Still she hadn't touched the picture. "Why? You wouldn't believe it."

He slid down in the chair, crossed one leg over the other, and said, "You'd be surprised." He sounded almost friendly.

She told him. It was the same story she'd told Jury. And she had no explanation. Impulse, she said. To Jury, her story had the form of a dream . . . this woman out on those rocks, finding a dead child, carrying back the dog . . .

He saw Macalvie look at him, reading the expression. His smile was taut and his message clear: *Minder.*

Molly was talking again: "It's the truth, what I told you. I know you don't have sympathy for what might loosely be called 'neurosis' —"

"Try me."

He sounded perfectly sincere. But what did that mean? "When you walked into the hotel dining room, you recognized me, didn't you?"

"I never saw you before that day," she said.

"Well, I sure as hell knew you: the kid who walked into my office twenty years ago and took the place to pieces. You've got to watch that temper, Mary — excuse me, *Molly*—or someday you'll wind up killing somebody."

She stared at him. "So now I'm the chief suspect." She looked down at the picture and shook her head. "It's a poor picture. How could anyone say this girl and I are the same person?"

"I'm not going by the picture and you damned well know it." He reached out his hand for the snapshot.

"What motive would I ever have for killing Angela Thorne?"

"I'm no psychiatrist —"

Bitterly, she said, "That's obvious."

"—but I imagine it'd be very hard to think of your baby sister writing on the wall in her mother's blood. Hard going to that nut-house and seeing her catatonic. And what you screamed at me twenty years ago was that no matter how

582

long it took you'd get your revenge — against police, judges, God — anything responsible for not finding the real killer. Sam Waterhouse was a friend of yours. And you wouldn't look kindly on anyone who helped put him away. George Thorne. The kid's father."

Her face was blank. "I don't know her father *or* what he does or did. You're just determined to make a case up out of nothing—"

"The cloth's already cut to fit you, Mary."

She glared at him.

"Circumstantial evidence alone —" said Macalvie.

"It would have been pretty stupid of me, then, to leave my cape and bring the dog back."

"True. I haven't worked that out yet." There seemed to be no doubt in his mind that he would. "Like I say, I'm no psychiatrist."

Molly Singer got up. "And I'm not Mary Mulvanney."

As Macalvie rose, the black cat's tail twitched again, the inverted triangles of its pupils glaring up at him as if to ask, *What fresh hell can this be?*

EIGHTEEN

"EAT your soldiers, Jess."

Robert Ashcroft spoke absently from behind his newspaper. At the breakfast table now sat three where two had been perfectly comfortable before.

"I don't like my toast cut in strips," said Jessie, fingering a page of one of the books she had brought to the table.

Uncle Rob looked up from his paper. "Since when?"

"I don't like my egg topped, either. I like to peel it." Casually, she turned a page of *Rebecca*.

Sara Millar, the third of their party, cocked her head. She was sitting with her back to the window, and the morning light made her pale hair glow.

(*Bleached,* thought Jessie.)

"I'm sorry, Jessica. I guess I just assumed . . ." The quiet voice trailed off. The Selfless Sara had undertaken the job of getting Jessie's breakfast, thereby relieving the underworked Mrs. Mulchop of yet another chore.

"You're still angry with me, aren't you?" Robert Ashcroft looked unhappy.

Jess was sorry for the hurt look on his face and pained be-

cause she was its cause. But this was going to be a battle of
wits, make no mistake. Thus she must harden her heart. She
simply shrugged her indifference.

Of course, that worried her uncle more. "You're acting
awfully —"

Sara Millar interrupted, thereby cleverly deflecting the
thrust of Robert's words. "What are you reading, Jessie?"

She was clearly determined to be nice as ninepence. "*Rebecca* and *Jane Eyre.*" Jess looked Sara straight in the eye.
Sara had nice eyes, widely spaced and the same bluish-gray of
the suit she had worn yesterday. The eyes were set in just the
face that Jessie would have expected: clear-skinned and, if
not absolutely *pretty*, it was far from plain, framed as it was
by that ash-blond hair. Round her hair was a dusty-rose band
that matched her jumper. All her clothes (Jessie bet) would
have that dusty, subdued look—colours muted, makeup un-
derstated, just that bare hint of lipstick. The metamorphosis
would come later, after she got her claws into Uncle Robert.
Then would come trailing the plummy gowns, waterfalls of
jewels (Barbara Allan's emeralds, maybe?), the blond hair
coiled but with little tendrils struggling free as Sultry Sara
swept down Ashcroft's magnificent staircase.

But, for now, Sara Millar was perfectly content to let her
beauty lie skin deep.

She had been talking about the books during Jess's rumina-
tions over her transformation: ". . . two of my favourites," said
the Selfless Sara.

Jess looked up from the book she was only pretending to
read. Uncle Robert had once told her it was rude to read in
others' company, but she had merely taken him to task about
his morning paper. Jessie was not disposed to bring books to
the table, anyway, before now.

"Two of my favourites." Sara would have said that if Jess
had brought *Beano* and *Whizzer and Chips* along.

Sara quoted, " 'Last night I dreamed I was at Manderley

again . . . ,' " and she had the nerve to look around the dining room as if Ashcroft might give Manderley a run for its money. "Isn't that a smashing line? I only wish I could write one a quarter as well."

Robert Ashcroft looked at her, seeming pleased. "Do you write, then?"

Sara Miller laughed. "Nothing you'd want to read, I'm sure."

Jessie glared. If she was dreaming of Manderley, why didn't she go back to it? She gave a little kick under the table.

Sara lurched slightly. "What's that?"

Uncle Rob pulled up the tablecloth. "What's Henry doing there? Get him out, Jess."

"It's all right," said Sara, recovering quickly from the paw that had hit her silk-stockinged leg. "I was just surprised. Hullo, Henry."

Jessie watched the traitor Henry burrowing out and accepting a stroke, all uncaring of the knives grinding in his mistress's mind. "May I be excused?" she asked in a determinedly polite manner.

"To go where?" asked Uncle Rob. "You have to begin lessons."

A look passed between Sara and Uncle Rob. Jessie could barely control her rage. But the Mad Margaret had taught her a lot about control. *"No, no, no, my dahling, No! You don't scream the line out — 'Not all the perfumes of Arabia can ever make this little hand clean.'"*

"I'm going to sit on the wall."

"The wall?" Sara looked puzzled.

"Around the *grounds*," Jess answered, in a tone that suggested Sara must be a bit dim if she didn't know grounds had walls. "I like to sit and look at the prison. Where the axemurderer escaped from."

"Jess, for the umpteenth time, no one *escaped*."

She shrugged as if that made no difference. "Anyway, what

586

about the murders?" This question was directed to Sara Millar. Jess hoped it might take the place of Rochester's crazy wife.

"Jessie, you oughtn't to be afraid —" Jessie's look stopped Sara.

Afraid? Jess wasn't afraid of anything except her uncle's getting married. With her two books clutched to her chest — and wishing Mrs. Mulchop would wear black and give Sara Millar evil looks, just as Mrs. Danvers did the mouse that married de Winter, she started toward the door.

Victoria Gray was coming in, dressed for riding.

The good-mornings were spoken. Victoria was welcome to share the table, but she stood instead at the sideboard, helping herself to coffee from the silver pot. Since Sara had turned back to her own coffee, she didn't see that dagger-like look that Victoria Gray planted in her back. Jess glanced from the one woman to the other. Although Victoria was better-looking, she was old. At least, nearly as old as Uncle Rob. Selfless Sara was young and dewy, maybe just the age of de Winter's mousy wife.

"Well, I'm off," said Victoria. "Do you ride?" she asked Sara, without enthusiasm.

"A little," Sara said, smiling.

Like she wrote. Probably she was the Brontë sisters and Dick Francis all rolled into one.

II

Don't talk to strangers, Jess, Uncle Robert had cautioned her. As if whole platoons of strangers were walking by the wall trying to engage her in conversation.

She was sitting on the part of the wall that abutted onto one of the end posts that formed Ashcroft's entrance to its long, tree-lined driveway, like a double-barricade against the drive's low, stone wall. On the post was a simple bronze plaque, saying ASHCROFT. Jess often sat here, hoping she'd see something interesting on the road, but she never saw anything except the occasional car or a farmer with a bunch of sheep.

It was too high for Henry to clamber up, and she wasn't going to help him because he was doing penance for that stroking he'd allowed Sara to give him. Henry didn't seem aware he was doing penance; his position was, as usual, prone.

The full horror of her situation was beginning to wash over Jess. Sara Millar had been sitting at breakfast as if she belonged there just as much as the egg cups and the teapot and the toast. A familiar fixture. Yet, there had been no hint at all of her having "taken over." She was merely — at ease.

Jess hit at the stone with her spanner and crumbled a bit of it that drifted dust down onto Henry. He didn't care. No one . . . What was that?

Down the road to her right a car was coming, coming very slowly. Probably tourists limping along, taking their time. Then her eyes opened wide. *What* a car! It was long, elegant — a classic. And it seemed to be in some sort of trouble.

The car drew abreast of her and stopped. The driver rolled down the window. "I beg your pardon. You wouldn't know of a garage around here?"

Jessie hopped from the wall and strolled over to the white car with its glistening finish. A dozen coats of paint, she bet. Red leather interior. And the winged bonnet ornament of a Rolls-Royce. She sighed. "No, there's nothing for miles and miles. What do you want one for?"

He smiled. If he was the axe-murderer, he was certainly a good-looking one. Green eyes and sort of straw-coloured hair. "Something's wrong. It keeps cutting off —" On cue, the chariot of fire cut off.

"Let's have a look under the bonnet."

He laughed. "I'm not much of a mechanic." He got out.

Jessie squinted up at him. Rich. Good-looking and rich. She took the spanner from her pocket. "I am." She gestured with the spanner, a plan forming in her mind. Where Jessica's thoughts darted, lightning often followed.

Removing his driving gloves, he looked hopefully toward the long tunnel of trees. "Perhaps up there, at the house —"

"Open the bonnet."

III

The moment he saw her sitting on the wall, Melrose Plant swore. If there was one thing he didn't need at this juncture, it was this child. He knew about her; he knew about each member of the household, since Jury had given him details over the telephone. He just hadn't expected her to turn up in dirty overalls with a spanner in her hand.

The plan to get the Silver Ghost just far enough up the drive looked about to be scotched by Jessica Ashcroft. It had been Melrose's intention to let the Rolls rest peacefully on the Ashcroft drive so that he could walk to the house and summon Robert Ashcroft to the rescue. That *was* the plan.

And now here was this ten- or eleven-year-old with black, fringed hair and big brown eyes, with a damned spanner in her hand and a threat in her voice. She stood there, solid as the wall, obviously not about to make a spritely run to summon her elders and betters. He'd have to humour her.

Bonnet up, the two of them peered inside. She did a little clinking about with the spanner and, for one ghastly moment, Melrose was afraid that here might be some mechanical wizard, some garage-prodigy who'd *fix* the damned car. Ah, but she couldn't. Not unless she had a fan belt (which he had removed a quarter of a mile back) to a Rolls in her pocket.

"Look, I wish you wouldn't go banging that thing about. I mean, the old Roller can't take too much of a beating."

She got her head out from under the bonnet and heaved a

sigh. "Probably the carburettor. Only I can't see why—not on a Rolls-Royce."

"Nothing's perfect."

Her eyes widened. "*That* is." She pointed the spanner at the car.

"Do you think the people in that house up there would just let me pull into the drive and use the telephone? I think I can get it started again."

Her smile absolutely transformed the sullen little face that had glared from the wall. "I'm *sure* they would. It's *our* house. And my uncle knows lots about cars. He has nine, but not a Rolls-Royce."

"Nine! Imagine that!"

"I don't have to," she said, squinting up at him as if he might be a bit dim. But the tune changed again after she'd run behind the wall and come back with the strangest-looking animal Melrose had ever seen — a dog, he supposed. Though he wouldn't swear to it. "Do you mind if Henry sits with me? You won't get anything dirty, will you, Henry?" she fluted to the odd assortment of laps of skin. It sat on the seat like a wrinkled stump.

She got in; Melrose got in and turned the key. "That's an incredible dog you've got. Isn't it a Shar-pei?"

"Oh, it's only a stray. It might be Chinese." She glanced at Melrose. "It's got green eyes."

The engine turned over and Melrose said, "I can't see its eyes."

She sighed. "No one can."

Melrose got the Silver Ghost halfway up the drive before it stopped.

"Don't worry," said Jessica. "My uncle can mend it. Unless he has to send to Exeter for parts. Come on, Henry!" The dog clambered down. "If he does, it'll take a couple of days, I expect." The expectation made her smile.

The house was magnificent — Palladian, made of Portland stone. Must be spare rooms all over. "Look, now. I don't want to put your uncle to any trouble."

Her answer rang with sincerity. "You won't! Really! My name's Jessie Ashcroft. What's yours?" And then she was skipping backwards like any ordinary ten-year-old. Happy, carefree.

"My name's Plant. The family name, that is." This was the part Melrose abhorred.

She stopped dead. "You mean you've got a title?"

Jessica Ashcroft would know about titles, given that her father had had one.

"Well, yes. Yes, as a matter of.fact. Earl of Caverness."

Her eyes widened. "My *father* was an earl." And then her glance was a little wary. "I suppose because you're expected home you're going to have to ring up the countess?"

"No. There is no Countess of Caverness. I'm not married, you see."

She saw. Her smile beamed at him again. As they ascended the broad steps of Ashcroft, she told him about her uncle and Mrs. Mulchop and Victoria Gray and her new governess, Miss Millar.

And she continued to paint the canvas of Sara Millar in the most astonishing colours. She was beautiful, beneficent, agreeable . . .

Melrose noticed Henry was not with them.

"Oh, him?" Jessie said to his question. "He likes to sleep in cars; he's probably climbed back in. Never mind him." And she put the last dab of colour to the portrait of Miss Millar by saying, "Honestly, she's almost saintly."

IV

"Wonderful," said Robert Ashcroft, his head half-buried under the bonnet of the Rolls-Royce. "Absolutely terrific. Just look at the way . . ."

591

Thus had Mr. Ashcroft gone on, while Melrose shifted from one foot to another, bored to tears with the lesson he was getting in auto-mechanics.

"It's only the fan belt. Can't imagine one simply slipping off. But we can get one from London."

Jessie beamed up at Melrose.

"So please," said Ashcroft, "be my guest, won't you?"

"Oh. But I couldn't *possibly* impose . . ."

No one seemed to notice Plant was a few steps ahead of them as they started toward the house again.

NINETEEN

WHY Sara Millar had been presented by Jessica Ashcroft as the well-wrought urn round which played all the lively virtues, Melrose could not imagine.

Sara Millar was not overly smooth, often clever in her conversation, and very nearly pretty. She seemed to just miss being all or any of those things completely. She wasn't so much the urn, but a very mixed bouquet done up quickly for the occasion. Melrose thought she might be somewhat too much of a soft touch for the likes of Lady Jessica. But then he thought he detected in Miss Millar's velvet glove something of an iron hand. He doubted that Jessica would welcome anyone's telling her what to do.

Other, that is, than her uncle, whom she clearly adored. The feeling seemed to be mutual: Robert Ashcroft thought the world of his niece.

But, then, if one is sitting next to four million pounds, one might not find it difficult to give it a loving pat on the head. Cynical of him. Yet, he had been sent here to be cynical — or, at least, objective. Who was it in the household Jury suspected if not Ashcroft himself? It was too bad that the man was so likeable. He was unpretentious and hospitable, not particularly impressed by Melrose's titles. Yet Jury told him to trot out the whole batch of them. Agatha was missing a rare treat in not hearing all that Earl of Caverness; Viscount Ardry, Nitherwold, Ross and Cromarty; Baron Mountardry stuff dragged out.

The introductions were handed round in the drawing room during a pleasant hour set aside for cocktails. There was Victoria Gray, who did not fit at all the role of housekeeper-secretary. In her background were culture and breeding, more so than in Sara Millar's. Victoria Gray was also better-looking, although a trifle witchlike. She was dressed in black, with a long-sleeved jacket of some sequined material. Her hair was black, turned under slightly—perhaps it was all this that gave Melrose his impression. Perhaps his mind was tired, what with the drive itself, the trumped-up mechanical trouble, and Dartmoor. As they had walked up to the house earlier, even though scarcely noon, their feet were buried in mist, which rose until the trees were gloved in fog.

"I like your dress, Victoria," said Jessica, who was herself quite dressed up in a blue frock.

Victoria Gray looked at Jessica with a frown. (It seemed compliments from Jessica were rare enough to be suspect.) "You do? Thank you."

"It's beautiful. All spangly. It makes you look ever so much younger."

Robert Ashcroft looked at his niece sharply and then laughed it off. His instinct was probably right. Calling attention to Jessica's rudeness might only have made the matter worse, though Victoria seemed to take it in her stride.

"That's why I wore it," she said. "Takes at least a hundred years off my age. What about you, Jessica? It's the first time I've seen you out of your mechanic's outfit in ages. And what have you done to Henry? It looks like a ribbon in his collar."

Since it was difficult to see Henry's collar, buried as it was in his furled skin, the bow peeked out as a tiny ruff of green. "I dressed him up for company. It matches his eyes."

Ashcroft was surprised. "Henry's eyes? Didn't know he had any."

"You *know* he has green eyes," Jess said, looking innocently into their guest's own.

However unprepared Mulchop was to be butler, Mrs. Mulchop certainly wasn't to be cook. Smoked salmon, double consommé and roast duckling with a stuffing unlike anything Melrose had tasted before. He would like to have the recipe to give to his own cook, he said.

It was Sara Millar who told him: "Herbs and such, and mushrooms, anchovies and poached sweetbreads. Delicious, isn't it?"

Jessie, who had just taken a bite of this delicacy, stared at her plate. "Yuck! Why didn't somebody *tell* me?" She pushed the offending stuffing onto her small side plate and set it on the floor. "There, Henry," she said sweetly.

"No feeding Henry *at the table*, Jess," said Ashcroft.

Melrose had until then been unaware that Henry made one of their party. It also surprised him that, rather than Jessica's insisting she sit next to the fascinating stranger, she had allowed Sara that honour.

"You must forgive Jessie," said Victoria.

No one looked in less need of forgiveness.

"Poor Henry." Jessie sighed, as if the world were against him, and reached down to pat him in a lightning gesture that rid her plate of a particularly uninteresting turnip that had been lolling there. Then she set about eagerly eating her potatoes and making conversation before someone noticed the gap. "Lord Ardry . . ."

"Lady Jessica?"

"Oh, don't call me *that!*"

"All right, if you don't call me 'lord.' The family name is Plant. It's really horribly complicated, isn't it?"

595

"Yes. My father's name was Ashcroft. But he was also the Earl of Clerihew."

Ashcroft said, "You mean Curlew. Eat your dinner, Jess." Robert Ashcroft seemed disturbed by all this talk of lineage.

"I can't eat, not after you told me about the *brains.*" She readdressed herself to Melrose. "My mother's name was Barbara Allan." Pointing her fork at the wall opposite, she said, "That's her portrait. Wasn't she beautiful?"

The picture hung behind Robert Ashcroft, who, Melrose saw, had put down his fork. He also seemed to have lost his appetite.

The Countess of Curlew was indeed beautiful—slender, tall, dark and wearing a smile that implied having one's picture painted was silly.

"She was also very nice," said Victoria Gray. "So was James, her husband."

Undercurrents, thought Melrose. Or an actual undertow.

Jessica, however, was not going to let her mother's reputation hang by this slender thread of "goodness." "She had a very tragic life —"

Her uncle said, "Leave it alone, Jessie. *Mulchop* — stop lolling there and bring us some more wine!"

Melrose suspected that Ashcroft merely wanted to get their attention away from the Countess of Curlew.

It was no deterrent to Jessica. "Grandmother Ashcroft was mad because my mother was only a commoner and her family was in trade. My father always thought that was a good joke. 'In trade.' You can make a lot of money 'in trade,' he kept saying. Like being shopkeepers, if you have a lot of shops."

Robert interrupted. "I don't think our guest is interested in the family tree, Jess."

But Jessica continued to wash the dirty linen. "There was one of them that ran a pub. . . ." As she continued the Barbara Allan saga, it was clear that not only did the Allans have the

596

money, but that hearts had shattered to smithereens wherever the woman walked.

Victoria told her to stop exaggerating and stubbed out her cigarette violently.

"I'm *not!* It's just like the song — isn't it, Uncle Rob. You told me."

Ashcroft smiled and clipped the end of a cigar. "I'm not sure who told who at this point. There seem to be a few frills and furbelows that I don't remember."

In her gossipy way, Jessica went on: "She was lots younger than my father. . . . Though there's nothing wrong with that. I think it's all awfully romantic. But Gran thought it was just to get the title and was furious about it —"

Sara Millar broke in: "I don't think this should be trotted out in front of well, *two* relative strangers, Jessica." Her voice was soft and pleasant.

Melrose wanted to laugh. In Jessica Ashcroft he had an unexpected ally. She would make sure he stayed and *stayed,* as long as he took Miss Millar when he left. Romantic things like that happened in Jessica's mind, he was sure. In this case, the romance would also be most fortuitous.

The subject of the recent murders came up — was brought up by Jessica, that is — when they were seated in the drawing room with coffee and cigars and cigarettes.

Robert Ashcroft and Sara Millar were seated side by side on the small sofa. Melrose regarded it as a marvel of logistics, the way Jessica worked herself round to sit between them. She was merely leaning against the arm of the sofa when she said, "The vicar's son. It was really grisly —"

While Jessica enjoyed the grisliness, Melrose studied the portrait of James Ashcroft, which hung above the marble fireplace. He only half-heard the conversation while he thought about James Ashcroft. Clerihew. Curlew. An easy enough error to make . . .

When Melrose turned his attention back to the conversation, he heard Jessica talking about the boy in Dorchester —

Magically, she was now sitting between the two grown-ups.

"Bed, Jessie," said Ashcroft.

"Very well." She sighed. "I only wish I could go for a ride tomorrow."

"That," said Victoria, "is one of the few positive things I think I've heard from you. It's about time I put you up on that horse —"

"*Horse?* Who said *horse?* I mean a motorcar. Sara and Mr. Plant haven't had any rides at all in your cars. Couldn't Mr. Plant drive your Aston?" She looked at Melrose. "It goes from zero to sixty in five-point-two seconds."

"It might, but I doubt if *I* could go from zero to one in under an hour. Must be the Dartmoor air." He yawned.

"*You* want to ride around Dartmoor, Jess?" Ashcroft said. "You're always telling me how boring it is."

"That's only because we *live* here. It's always boring where you live. But they'd like it —" She looked from Sara to Melrose. "Just as long as we stay away from Wistman's Wood and the Hairy Hands. *Come on,* Henry."

And she and the dog walked slowly off to bed.

II

Victoria Gray was arranging flowers in a shallow cut-glass bowl for the circular table when Melrose came down for breakfast. She was dressed in riding togs.

"Good morning, Lord Ardry." She cut the stem of one last chrysanthemum, stuck it in the centre of her arrangement, and stepped back to look at it with a critical eye much like a painter evaluating his canvas. "Will it do?"

Melrose smiled. "Very nicely, I'd say. Am I the last one down?"

"Except for Jessie. She said she had a sick-headache, and asked to be excused from your excursion into the wilds of Dartmoor."

"I see. But she was to be our tour-guide."

Victoria smiled. "She told me to give you this map. As far as I can see, it's to be a grim tour. Wynchcoombe, Clerihew Marsh, Princetown. I'll have coffee with you, if you don't mind. All the food's still warm, though Mulchop did his best to wrestle it off the sideboard."

"Mind? Indeed not. One gets tired of breakfasting by one-self." Just as one, thought Melrose, gets tired of talking like a peer of the realm. Melrose was having difficulty with his earldom, a difficulty he had never had before he gave up his title. He was perfectly happy talking like a commoner *then*. He felt like someone Jury had dragged out of a ditch, dusted off, and said, "Okay. You'll do."

On the sideboard was a lavish display, all kept cosily warm in their silver dishes. He spooned up some kidney, took a portion of buttered eggs, layered on a couple of rashers of bacon, and helped himself to toast and butter. Then he frowned at his plate and wondered if a peer would gorge himself in this fashion.

Victoria Gray helped herself to toast and coffee. When she had settled at the table across from him, Melrose said, "If you don't mind my saying it — you don't fit the stereotype of 'housekeeper.'"

She laughed. "If you mean changing the linen and towels and wearing keys at my waist — no, I don't. This position is a sinecure. I do take care of the horses pretty much — Billy's a bit lazy — type the odd letter or two for Robert, and arrange flowers." She smiled. "Barbara—Lady Curlew—and I were first cousins, though she was born in Waterford. County Waterford. A typical Irish colleen, she was. We were also very good friends. Barbara made an excellent marriage — well, she deserved it, didn't she . . . ?"

599

She seemed to be talking to herself. Or in the manner of one who is addressing an intimate acquaintance.

"The late Lady Curlew was Irish? You mean her daughter's tale of gloom and doom is true?"

"Of course not. Barbara didn't leave a trail of fallen hearts behind her like petals in the dust." She paused. "At least not knowingly."

He wondered what she meant by that. Barbara Ashcroft's face looked down at him from the far wall. The smile was inscrutable, a Mona Lisa smile. "If that portrait doesn't flatter her —"

"Flatter —?" Victoria Gray turned to look. "Oh, not at all. If anything it diminishes her beauty. Jessica will be that beautiful too, one day. You can see it when she isn't dressed in that oily overall she loves to wear and carrying tools around."

"She's quite the mechanic."

"Jessie? She doesn't know a battery from a silencer. I'll bet she told you it was your carburettor."

"Right."

"Her favourite word."

Melrose laughed. "Well, she needs some sort of occupational therapy, wouldn't you say?"

"Believe me, she's got an occupation — though I don't know how therapeutic it is. Keeping her beloved uncle from marrying." She picked up a piece of toast and munched it; then she said, "It's fortunate for Jess that Dartmoor isn't peopled with eligible women."

Seeing the faraway look on her face, Melrose wondered if the fortune weren't divided.

"Why do you think she's been through such a string of governesses?"

"Didn't know she had been." He accepted another cup of coffee from Victoria's hand. "Tell me: why did the Ashcrofts not make the obvious choice and have *you* take care of Jessica? You say your job is a sinecure: seems to me it'd simplify things all around."

Victoria laughed. "Precisely because I *would* take care of her. Did you ever see a child so indulged? I wondered when Robert would get wise and choose a tutor himself, like Sara Millar."

But she did not look at all as if she felt the choice had been wise. She looked, indeed, inexpressibly sad. Melrose could read it in her face: if only Robert Ashcroft's feelings were as certain as this sinecure of a post she held.

III

He had asked Victoria if there was some writing-paper about, and was now sitting in the drawing room, looking up again at the portrait of the rather formidable Earl of Curlew. He then wrote no more than a couple of sentences on the rich, cream-laid Ashcroft stationery, took another sheet and wrote the same sentences. Then, he addressed both to Jury — one to his flat in Islington; the other to him at the Devon-Cornwall headquarters. If he posted them today, Jury would be bound to get one tomorrow, whether in London or Devon.

Melrose stood beneath the portrait, holding out a finger length-wise, and squinted, in this way ridding James Ashcroft of his full moustache. There was a strong resemblance between the brothers. As Curlew resembled Clerihew.

TWENTY

AT least, thank God, it was a closed car. The mist looked as if it meant to hang about all morning, making distances deceptive, bringing the giant tors closer than they actually were. The moorland ponies were huddled against the leeward wall with that instinct they had for an approaching storm.

And, thank God, she was not one to feel sorry for herself. It was only owing to Melrose's judicious questioning that Sara was telling him the story of her life, a life she had herself described as placid, at best; at worst, dull. To Melrose, however, it sounded like neither — more a Dickensian tale of abandonment and woe. There was the boardinghouse through whose portal she had been shepherded by the aunt into whose care she had been given when Sara's mother died. It was run by an iniquitous woman, Mrs. Strange, the embodiment of her name, said Sara.

"Fiery red hair she had that looked like a tent right after she'd washed it. I suppose, though, I ought to be grateful to her. Since she was lazy and I was older than the others, and hadn't much to say in the matter, the care of them often fell to me. So did my own education. I had to read a lot, as she kept me out of school. To take care of the children."

"Good Lord, why should you feel 'grateful'? You might have gone on to do something more suited to your intelligence than acting as overseer to other people's children."

"Thanks. I had only the one good reference, really. But as it came from a countess, Mr. Ashcroft seemed suitably impressed. I'm fond of children."

"I'm fond of ducks. It doesn't mean I want them running round under my feet all day."

Sara laughed. "With Jessica, it's not being underfoot that I'm in danger of; it's more in being undermined. She doesn't care for me too much."

"On the contrary," said Melrose, slowing to peer through the fog at a signpost, "as we were walking up to the house, she was singing your praises."

"That in itself's suspect, since I'd only just arrived the day before. I wonder how long I'll last? Mr. Ashcroft said his niece was running through tutors at the speed of, well, this car. There were three of us to be interviewed in London. I suppose he winnowed out the rest by mail. Given the salary he offered, he must have been deluged. It's a post anyone would give her eyeteeth for." She paused for a moment, and then went on. "It's rather odd, though . . ."

"Odd, how?"

"To do the interviews that way. It was rather like being cast for a role." She paused. "I only wish I knew the script." She sounded uneasy about her new post.

"Ashcroft strikes me as an amiable, informal chap. Unlikely he's reading from a script."

"'Amiable'? He certainly is. And goes to no end of trouble for Jessica. I only meant I wonder why he held those interviews in London rather than at Ashcroft?"

"Perhaps because Lady Jessica wasn't having too much luck herself in choosing the proper person." He slowed the car again to look at another signpost, trying to bury his question — "When was this unnerving interview? Sounds a bit Jamesian to me. Think I'll turn here" — in a comment about their direction.

"What do you mean by Jamesian?"

"*The Turn of the Screw.* The governess goes up to London and finds a handsome, prospective —" Melrose didn't go on. Probably, he was embarrassing her.

"When was the interview? Just a few days ago. The thirteenth. Why?"

"No reason. Will this mist never rise?"

As Melrose negotiated a sharp turn on the narrow road, she said, "Isn't this signposted for Wynchcoombe? And isn't that where the little boy was murdered?"

"Don't you want to go there?"

"Frankly, no." She shivered.

"Oh, come on. Be a sport. Can't we be just a couple of bloodthirsty thrill-seekers?"

Sara laughed. "Do you hang around accident sites?"

"Of course."

II

The vestry of Wynchcoombe Church was still sealed off. A constable stood on the walk outside as stiffly relentless as a guard at Buckingham Palace. The rest of the church, though, was open to worshippers and visitors.

"I don't know that I want to go in," said Sara, "now we're here."

"Superstitious?"

"No, afraid," she said quite simply.

Melrose would have made a burnt offering of his Silver Ghost to have a look in the choir vestry, but the presence of another policeman told him there'd be no joy there. The constable, however, seemed to be finding a bit of joy from a *Playboy* magazine, turning it sideways and upside down to get the full effect of a centrefold who must have managed an extremely acrobatic position for the photographer.

Nothing ventured, nothing gained, thought Melrose. At least this policeman looked a bit more human, lacking in the granite calm of the constable outside.

Thus, while Sara walked down the nave, Melrose moved to the vestry door, taking out his visiting-card case. He handed the P.C. his card. "Don't suppose there's a chance of getting in there . . . ?"

"About as much as getting into Buckingham Palace," said the P.C., pleased he had precedence over a peer.

Melrose went to join Sara Millar. She was studying a small picture of the sacrifice of Isaac.

"The God of the Old Testament didn't pull his punches, did he?" said Melrose. "Job, Abraham, voices from whirlwinds." He saw her fingering the silver cross she seemed always to wear. Filtered light from the stained-glass windows made a coloured tracery over her pale rose jumper and paler skin. She looked delicate, almost otherworldly, and innocent, as if her youth were still unspent. So engrossed was she with the painting, he thought she hadn't heard him. But she answered, "It's beyond belief. I mean, outside conventional belief. It doesn't count for anything, I think."

Melrose was somewhat astonished at this interpretation of a father's being asked to murder his innocent son. " 'Doesn't count' . . . ? I'm sure Isaac would have felt you to be cold comfort." His smile, when she turned on him, was a little fixed.

She had looked angry; now she looked sad. A woman much like the Dartmoor weather, he thought. Forever changing. Interesting, though.

"I only meant," she said, "that the whole notion of God and Abraham must transcend human understanding."

605

As they walked over to the other wall, Melrose said, "Then what's the point? What's the point of a moral lesson that requires transcendent vision?" She was reading an account in a glassed-over case about the Devil honouring the church with a visit. "It seems someone who owed him his soul fell asleep in church and Satan simply took the roof off and collected him." Sara shook her head. Melrose was wondering if the vicar would ever appear, or whether this was simply not his day. He looked at his watch. Eleven. The pubs would be open. He was afraid if he didn't divert this discussion, she'd have them stopping here all day talking transcendentalism. "The only way I can justify God's way to man is by malt, as Housman said."

She smiled slightly. "I take it you noticed the George."

Sara was, in spite of her transcendent streak, quick enough and a good sport. He looked around as the heavy door to the church opened and shut behind an elderly man, who then made his way down the aisle with a proprietary air. Melrose wondered if this might be the Reverend White. Certainly, the man paid no attention at all to the Devon-Cornwall constabulary, so Melrose assumed he was not just another pilgrim. This was borne out by the Devon-Cornwall constabulary's quickly closing his magazine and shoving it under the cushion of his chair.

Melrose told Sara he'd be back in a moment and walked down the aisle in the wake of this white-haired man, making up his excuse as he went.

"Terribly sorry to intrude upon your grief." This comfortless cliché embarrassed Melrose. "You *are* Mr. White?"

The vicar said he was, and appeared to be less griefstricken than a grandfather might have been. Less than Abraham, certainly, and Abraham was only following orders. The vicar's eyes were stony-cold.

"What was it you wanted?"

Melrose removed a card from the gold case that had been his mother's (before Agatha had appropriated it); the cards had been his father's, the seventh Earl of Caverness, and Melrose, the eighth, simply thought what was one earl, more or less?

The vicar read it and handed it back. There was something about one's own card being given back to one that was extremely discouraging.

"Sorry, but should I know you? You're not local. I'm not aware of the family."

Melrose almost wished Agatha had been there to hear *that* judgement passed. He felt a lack of locality stamped on his face, much like the coat-of-arms stamped on the card. "No. My home is in Northamptonshire. The account of your grandson's death in the paper gave the mother's name as Mary O'Brian." Melrose looked up at the intricately painted roof-bosses, each one of them apparently different, and wondered what sum of money would entice the vicar to look at life in a more worldly fashion. "You see, years ago we had a Mary O'Brian employed at our home — Ardry End — as upstairs maid."

"Yes? But it's a common name."

Melrose realized he had stirred something in the vicar's breast, for the man's face coloured somewhat and he added, "But, then, Mary was a common woman."

Even Melrose, no stickler for men of the cloth being more than human, was a little surprised by this. Apparently the Reverend White was not worried about the roof caving in. "It's been some years since she was there. I've had a bit of a time tracking her down —"

"That doesn't surprise me — given Mary."

Melrose would have been happy to wander through the dark wood of the vicar's feelings about his daughter-in-law had the vicar shown any sign of wanting to lead him. But the remark simply fell and lay there like a tree across their path.

Mr. White reminded Melrose of someone he couldn't quite place.

"This has to do with a small bequest in my father's will."

"Oh?"

"My father found her to be an especially dependable servant; she went to a great deal of trouble nursing my mother through a long illness —"

"Mary? It's the last thing I'd have expected. At any rate, Mary's dead. Didn't the account mention that?"

Melrose, having seen no obituary, could only say: "Yes, it did." He thought perhaps he shouldn't elaborate on what the "account" *did* tell the world.

"Both of them died in a motorcycle accident. Mary liked fast living. David was in divinity school before he met her. He would perhaps have followed in my footsteps. Then he met Mary." The vicar closed his eyes as if he were hearing the painful news for the first time. "Whatever gift your father wished to bestow upon her . . ." He shrugged.

They had been standing all this time in the aisle. Melrose wished they could sit down, but a church pew seemed an unlikely place for such a conversation.

"Perhaps then you would accept it for the church? In memory of your grandson?"

"David?" One would think he had to be reacquainted with the name.

"I realize five hundred pounds is not all that much —"

The Reverend White looked Melrose up and down. Melrose felt conscious of the suit from his bespoke tailor, the handmade shoes, the silk shirt, the handsome overcoat.

"Well, Lord Caverness, if you consider five hundred pounds meagre, you must be wealthy indeed." He managed to make inherited wealth sound like plunder.

"I am," said Melrose simply. "I'll see the bequest is sent to the church, if that's suitable."

"Thank you."

With what struck Melrose as a rather summary dismissal in the circumstances, Mr. White started to turn and leave. "Just one more thing, sir. I was wondering about the Ashcroft family."

With five hundred pounds in the balance, the vicar must have felt something was due to this Nosey Parker of an earl. "Wondering what?"

"Well, I've rather made a hobby of heraldry and that sort of thing. How long have the Ashcrofts been feudal overlords of Wynchcoombe and Clerihew Marsh?" The question, of course, would annoy the vicar.

"Feudalism is dead, Lord Caverness. At least the last I heard—"

Melrose smiled fatuously. "Dying, perhaps. But I sometimes wonder if the liberties the feudal barons took were not still being taken . . .?"

"Sir, I have a very busy schedule."

He seemed willing to look a five-hundred-pound gift-horse in the mouth after all. "I'm sorry. It's just that the Ashcroft family appears to be much the most important family about. James Ashcroft was the Earl of Curlew, wasn't he?"

The vicar frowned. "Yes."

' I just wondered if perhaps 'Curlew' weren't some deviant spelling of 'Clerihew.' Or it would have been the other way round, I mean? 'Clerihew Marsh' ought really to be 'Curlew Marsh.' The curlew being a bird and the crest on the Ashcroft coat-of-arms."

"That is correct." Again he turned to go.

"And your first name, vicar. 'Lindley.' James Ashcroft was the Viscount Lindley and one of his other names was 'Whyte.' Spelled differently, of course."

"If you're wondering whether I'm a relation of the Ashcrofts, yes, I am. But certainly a very distant one. His bequest to the church was even more surprising than yours. But he was generous, I'll say that for him."

Melrose wondered what the vicar *wouldn't* say for James Ashcroft.

The vicar continued: "I was certainly surprised at his leaving fifty thousand pounds."

So was Melrose.

Sara had been patiently hovering in the shadows all this time, reading the account of the storm that precipitated a visit from the Devil who knocked the spire off the church.

"Sorry," said, Melrose.

"Oh, that's all right. Was that the vicar?"

"Yes, I'm thirsty. How about you?"

"I could do with a cup of tea. But I expect you prefer the pub?"

She was certainly agreeable. And attractive. And—well, quite the sort of young woman that a de Winter or a Rochester *might* marry.

No wonder Lady Jessica was trying to hand her over to Melrose.

After they left the church, they stood looking for some moments at the moss- and lichen-veiled headstones.

"Now I remember who the Reverend White reminds me of. Hester's Chillingworth"

Sara was puzzled. "Chillingworth?"

"You know. *The Scarlet Letter*. I wonder if he looked upon Davey as a benighted little Pearl.

"Whatever were you talking about all that time? You hadn't heard of him before, had you?"

Melrose paused to consider the question and decided two lies were no worse than one. "No. You don't see a post office about, do you? I need to post these letters."

They walked off in search of one. Melrose took the quiet walk as an opportunity to reflect.

TWENTY-ONE

THE cat Cyril sat on Fiona Clingmore's typewriter watching the noonday ritual of the rejuvenation of Fiona's face. Powder, mascara, lipstick, eyeliner. When Jury walked in, Cyril appeared to have entered into some symbiotic relationship with Fiona, in his stately posture on the typewriter, drawing his paw across his face, the student testing the lesson of the master.

There had been a great deal of speculation about the cat's appearance in the halls of New Scotland Yard. It was generally thought that Cyril had discovered the tunnel, originally meant for theatregoers, to a theatre that never materialized and where the headquarters of the Metropolitan Police now sat, owing to some misadventure over cash flow or architectural fault or need. In any event, the cat Cyril had been seen prowling the halls as if his antennae were searching out (like some medium's familiar) the office of Chief Superintendent Racer. With Racer, Cyril enjoyed a slightly different symbiotic relationship from the one with Fiona; and in Racer's case, it was doubtful that the relationship was of benefit to both. But it certainly seemed to go down a treat with Cyril, who could outwit and outmanoeuvre Chief Superintendent Racer any day.

It was testimony to Cyril's staying power that he had been hanging around Racer's office for upwards of a year (maybe even two), which was more than could be said of any member of the Met—uniformed, CID, or civilian. Except for Superintendent Jury, whose staying power (and, Jury suspected, slight masochistic streak) matched Cyril's. Fiona, of course, was made of such steely stuff that she could have walked under falling ladders or falling bombs and still remained upright. Only such a woman could have stood it as Racer's secretary. She was constantly being told to get the mangy rat-catcher *out* from under Racer's eyes and feet or he'd fire her and kill Cyril. Fiona paid far more attention to refurbishing her eye makeup than she did to the exhortations of her boss. Racer himself had often tossed Cyril out in the hall. But Cyril always returned, like Melville's Bartleby, to sit on a convenient sill and stare from a window at the blind brick wall of another part of the Yard.

Thus both Fiona and Cyril were engaged in their prelunch ablutions when Jury walked into Racer's outer office. "Hullo, Fiona. Hullo, Cyril," said Jury.

Fiona returned the greeting while running her little finger around the corners of her mouth; Cyril's tail twitched. He always appeared happy to see Jury, perhaps out of admiration for a soul-brother, one who could stick it.

"You're early, for once," said Fiona, snapping her mirrored compact shut with a little click. Jury often wondered where she came by these pre–Second World War memorabilia: he hadn't seen a woman with one of those Art Deco compacts since he was a kid. Fiona herself was like an artifact: she had been and still was, in her way, pretty. Pretty like the old photos of movie starlets with cupid-bow mouths and upswept blond hairdos used to be. Jury suspected that Fiona's own yellow curls came from the bottle, neat. That there were some silver threads amongst the gold Fiona had attributed to a good job of frosting at her salon. "He's still at his club," she added.

Jury yawned and scrunched down in his chair. "White's? Boodles? The Turf?"

Fiona laughed and rested her newly primed face on her overlapped hands. "You think one of them would let him in?" She checked a gold circlet of a watch — also from prehistoric digs — and said, "Been gone two hours, so he ought to be popping in any minute."

"Thanks, I'll wait in his office — give him a fright, maybe." He winked at Fiona, who then asked him if he'd eaten yet. It was as much a ritual when Jury was there as the revamping of her face. Jury made his excuses. A policeman's life is full of grief, he told her. It was Racer's cautionary phrase that covered everything from being first on the rota to finding a mass-murderer in your closet.

He noticed as he stood up that she was taking out her bottle of nail varnish—a Dracula-like deep purple, almost black. Fiona favoured black. All her outfits—sheer summer frocks, winter wools—were black. Maybe she wanted to be sure she was ready for Racer's funeral.

The cat Cyril, seeing his chance, followed Jury into Racer's *sanctum sanctorum* and plumped himself on the chief's swivel chair. Jury sat on the chair directly across from Cyril and the broad expanse of Racer's empty desk. If there was one thing the chief superintendent believed in, it was delegating authority. Seldom did Jury see folders, notepads, papers—the usual junk — defiling his chief's desk. Jury looked at Cyril, whose head alone could be seen over the top of the desk, and said, "What was it, sir, you wished to see me about? Oh? Yes . . . well, sorry. A policeman's life —"

He hadn't got the end of the old Racer shibboleth out before his chief's spongy step came up behind him. "Talking to yourself again, Jury?" Racer hung his Savile Row overcoat on a coatrack and walked around to his swivel chair. Cyril had slipped like syrup from Racer's chair and was now under the desk to study (Jury was sure) the best avenue of attack.

Racer went on: "Well, it certainly can't be from over*work*, lad. Obviously, you haven't been doing much on the Dorchester case or you'd have *reported in*, now wouldn't you? Not to say anything of the two others murdered! I do not like the Commissioner breathing down my neck, Jury. So what have you got to report. Meaning: what progress have you made?"

Jury told him as much as he felt was necessary for Racer to get the Commissioner off his back. It was, as always, too little for Racer. He would only have been satisfied with Jury's actually producing the murderer right there, in his office.

"That's *all*, Jury?"

"Afraid so."

"As far as I'm concerned — what the hell's *that?*" Racer was looking under his desk. He punched the intercom and demanded Fiona's presence to get the beast out from under his desk. "This ball of mange has used up eight of its nine lives, Miss Clingmore! Swear to God," he muttered, levelling a glance at Jury that suggested Jury might have used up nine-out-of-nine.

Fiona swayed into the office and collected Cyril. Fiona was certainly in no danger of using up *her* lives. The black-patent-leather belt she wore to nip in her waist sent the flesh undulating up and undulating down. Racer's eyes always seemed undecided on which direction to take.

"So go on," said Racer, when Fiona had left.

"Nothing much to be going on with. Sir." Jury always hesitated a little before the *sir*.

And Racer always noticed it. Thus Jury was in for the "ever-since-you-made-superintendent" lecture, one that Racer must have practised in his sleep, so refined had it become, so ornamental — like intaglio figurines around a priceless vase. There was always something new to comment on, regarding the skill of the artisan.

Jury yawned.

"Where the hell's Wiggins? What's he been up to, except contaminating the Dorset police?"

Jury made no comment other than to say Sergeant Wiggins was in Devon.

"You do realize, don't you, how this psycho has hit the press? Three kids dead, Jury, *three*." He held up his fingers in case Jury didn't understand the word itself. "And you can't nail one of these suspects?"

"Not on the evidence we have now, no. I want to see the Ashcroft solicitor."

"Then get the hell out and go and see him. I've got enough work to do as it is." The pristine condition of his desk did not attest to this.

II

"Robert Ashcroft? But I've known him as long as I've known — knew — his brother James." He got up from his chair to pace several yards of cushioned carpet.

Mr. Mack, Jury decided, was solicitor to more than one moneyed family, given his surroundings: thick carpet, good prints on the walls, mahogany furniture, including the desk that shimmered like a small dark lake beneath its coats of beeswax. Its principal ornament was an elegant bronze cat, probably some pricey Egyptian artifact.

What interested Jury was that Mack did not simply reject the idea of imposture out of hand. Perhaps he was simply a very cautious fellow who would see all the facets of an argument, no matter how prismatic.

His pacing was interrupted by the entrance of his secretary bearing a number of documents. His glance strayed up to Jury occasionally, as if he were turning the idea over as he turned the pages before him, signing each with a flourish.

The young lady who was Mack's secretary was the antithesis of Fiona Clingmore. One could tell her dress was expensive, not by its showiness but by the cut of the cloth. She was herself — hair, skin, nails — as polished as the desk itself.

But she lacked that certain something — that nice seamy presence which was the Fiona *brio*. Indeed, Jury wondered, as he watched the solicitor signing papers, if, in his realm of Ideas, Plato wouldn't have plumped for Racer, Fiona and Cyril, instead of Mack, Miss Chivers and the bronze cat.

Mr. Mack recapped his pen and Miss Chivers gathered up the papers and slid softly out, hazarding another look at Jury as she left. He smiled. She blushed.

Mack returned to the question of the Ashcroft identity. "No, it's improbable, Mr. Jury, that this Robert Ashcroft is not the real one. As you say, there was no one in the household who had known him, and the relations were all distant ones — but, no. When the will was probated, we certainly asked for Robert's bona fides — indeed, we did that of everyone. Victoria Gray, for example."

"I wasn't aware she came into a part of the Ashcroft fortune."

"She certainly did. Not much as an outright legacy, but a very substantial legatee were something to happen to Jessica. Very substantial. And insofar as Robert himself is concerned, I'm quite satisfied." He had resumed his seat and rested his chin on the tips of his fingers, prayerfully.

"What about other bequests? Any other substantial ones?"

"Yes. There was one to a church. And also to his wife's former nurse, Elizabeth. She was a cousin of Lady Curlew's." He ran a finger over the bronze cat. "Not a very pleasant person, as I recall." A heave of shoulders here. After all, solicitors can't be choosers. "But the thing is, you see, none of these were outright bequests. I didn't care for it, but there it was. All of the money went to Jessica."

"You mean, that as long as Jessica Ashcroft is alive, no one gets anything?"

Mr. Mack shook his head. "James Ashcroft wanted everything to go to Jessie. She can, of course, when she comes of age, honour those bequests immediately. Until that time, Robert is executor of the will and receives a fair allowance—"

"What's 'fair'?"

"I believe in the neighbourhood of five thousand pounds a year."

Jury shook his head. "That'd be a slum for Ashcroft. It certainly wouldn't do much by way of supporting his habit. No, no, Mr. Mack—" The solicitor's eyes had widened. "— not drugs. Motorcars. Vintage, classic, antique."

"Ah, yes. Well, Robert has access to Jessica's money, you see. All he need do is apply to me. If I think the expense suitable, I let him have it. You're quite right, those cars of his are pricey. But a drop in the bucket when we're talking millions of pounds. James and Robert were extremely close. Even when Robert went to Australia, they wrote to one another regularly. Those letters, you see, were paramount in establishing authenticity. Why are you suspicious of Robert Ashcroft, may I ask?"

"No reason, except for the convenient arrangement of the household. Even the relations who came to the funeral hadn't seen him in a long time, if at all."

"Yes, that's true. When that much money and property's at stake, odd lots of relations come crawling out of the woodwork, some of them hoping to break a will unfair to them. Claiming what they consider their 'fair share,' or claiming the one who gets the lion's share isn't really the lion." Mr. Mack allowed himself a little purse-lipped smile.

"So the brother James more or less allowed Robert *carte blanche?*"

Mack frowned. "Yes. And I frankly don't approve of open-ended arrangements like that. Messy." He squared a cigarette box and adjusted the alignment of the bronze cat. "But James had the devil's own trust in Robert." There was another fussy

617

little smile. "Not the best way of putting it, perhaps. But the other relations, by blood or by marriage, were rather a sorry lot. So far as I could see, they had absolutely no claim on the money, not to say upon James's affections. But he was—I advised him to do so—smart enough to leave small sums to the ones whom he felt would be the troublemakers."

"I'd like to see a copy of that will, Mr. Mack."

Mr. Mack rocked back in his chair. "Is that really necessary?"

Jury smiled. "I'd like to see it, necessary or not. The will's been probated. Public property now."

"Hmm. Very well. Miss Chivers can make you up a copy." He punched his intercom and gave his secretary directions.

"And I'd also like to see those letters."

"The ones from James? Well, Robert has them, of course." Mr. Mack frowned. "Are you suggesting an analysis of the handwriting?"

"Something like that, yes." Jury thought, really, that the Ashcroft solicitors would have done it themselves. He rose to go. "Thanks for your help, Mr. Mack."

On the way out he collected the copy of the Ashcroft will and another appraising glance from Miss Chivers.

Mr. Mack's office was in The City. Jury made his way to Aldgate tube, wondering what was bothering him. Something he'd seen? Something he'd heard? James Ashcroft's will was thick. There was a great deal of property. The will had been signed by Ashcroft, witnessed by Mack and two other solicitors. One of the names was George Thorne.

George Thorne. Again.

Jury changed at Baker Street to get the Bakerloo line and, as he waited for his train, looked over the tiled wall of the platform, where the profile of Sherlock Holmes had been wonderfully contrived during the station's renovation. It was a hard act to follow.

III

"So sad it is," said Mrs. Wasserman, who lived alone in the basement flat of the building in Islington. Jury's own flat was on the second floor, but he had stopped off to see how she was doing. To admit him, she had had to throw two bolts, release a chain, and turn the deadlock. There were grilles over her windows, too. Mrs. Wasserman could have slept with ease in the middle of the Brixton riots. But Mrs. Wasserman was never at ease, except when the superintendent was around who mercifully (for her) lived upstairs.

They were eating her homemade strudel and drinking coffee and she was talking about the case Jury was on. "I know you don't discuss," she said, "but it frightens me to death to see these children —" Unable to bring it out, she stopped, shook her head, drank her coffee. "I know you don't say, of course you can't, but this person, he must be crazy." And she made a tiny circle round her ear to demonstrate craziness.

"I expect so, Mrs. Wasserman. We don't know the motive."

"Motive? Who says motive? Crazies don't *have* them, Mr. Jury." Her smile was slight and forgiving, as if she couldn't expect this novice policeman to know everything, could she?

Indeed she was right on that count. "Psychotics do have motives, even if the motives are irrational and obscure. Or displaced."

"What is that, *displaced?*" She was suspicious of psychoanalytic jargon.

"Just that the killer's actual object isn't the person he kills."

She thought this over, chewing her strudel. "What a hideous waste of time." Mournfully, she glanced up at him. "The papers, Mr. Jury, are full of it."

Jury knew about the papers. And he also knew he had described, without consciously meaning to, Mrs. Wasserman's own phobia. How old had she been during the Second World War? Fifteen, sixteen perhaps. Whatever horrors she had suffered then had gone underground, submerged in her mind, but bonded to that scrap of memory she could allow—the Stranger who followed her, whose step behind her she could pick out of a hundred footsteps, whose description Jury had taken down in his notebook time and time again, knowing there was no such person. And it was Jury who had helped her with the locks, the chains, the bolts. Mrs. Wasserman could have written the book on agoraphobia.

Jury looked at her windows, grilles and shutters. He looked at her door, locked and bolted. "You bolt the door —" He really hadn't meant to say it aloud.

"What?" Of course I bolt the door." Her large breasts shook with laughter. "*You*, of all people! You helped me with the bolts." Then she grew concerned. "It's sleep you need, Mr. Jury. You never get enough. Sometimes it is not until two or three in the morning you get in."

Jury only half-heard her. His eye was still fixed on that impregnable door. "But what, exactly, does it keep out?"

She seemed puzzled, suspicious even — in the way one is suspicious that a dear friend might be going off the rails. "Why, Him, of course. As you know."

And she went back calmly to eating her strudel.

TWENTY-TWO

I T was five miles on the other side of Dorchester, in Winterbourne Abbas, that it hit him — what had seemed insignificant at the time. Jury pulled into a petrol station, asked for a phone and was told there was one in the Little Chef next door.

The restaurant was almost antiseptically clean, right down to the starched uniforms of the waitresses. Jury asked for a coffee, said he'd be back in a moment. He put in a call to the Devon-Cornwall headquarters and was told that the divisional commander was in Wynchcoombe.

It was DC Coogan in the mobile unit there who told Jury (testily, he thought) that Macalvie had taken Sergeant Wiggins and gone to the Poor Struggler to make "inquiries." Jury smiled. Although Betty Coogan didn't believe it, Macalvie probably was doing just that. She gave him the number.

Jury could hear Elvis Presley in the background singing "Hound Dog" after someone answered the telephone at the Poor Struggler. Not Freddie, probably the regular who happened to be nearest the phone.

"Don't know him, mate. Mac-who?"

Jury could almost hear the phone being wrenched from the other's hand, along with a brief exchange that had Macalvie working the old Macalvie charm, complete with expletives. "Macalvie here." And he turned away to shout to Freddie to turn the damned music down or he'd have her license. "Macalvie," he said again.

"What are you doing there, Macalvie?"

"Oh, it's you." There was the usual lack of enthusiasm for New Scotland Yard. "Talking to your friend. The one passing himself off as a bloody earl. Seems okay, though."

Macalvie always seemed to like the very people Jury was sure he'd hate. He cut across the latest Macalvie theory by telling him what he'd learned from Mr. Mack.

"*Thorne?* He was one of the Ashcroft bunch? When? I mean for how long?"

"I don't know. Get one of your men to give him a call. Wiggins there?"

"Yeah, sure." Macalvie seemed to be carrying Wiggins around in his pocket. "For God's sakes, I should have known about Thorne."

"Why? You're not a mind reader."

There was a small pause, as if Macalvie were debating this point. "Yeah. What do you want to tell Wiggins?"

"Just let me talk to him."

"It's a secret between you two?"

"No. I want to check something. Stop pouting and put him on."

"Sir!" Wiggins was probably standing at attention.

Jury sighed. "As you were, Sergeant. Listen: when we were in the Rileys' flat, or as we were leaving, that is, you noticed a framed document above the mantel —"

"That's right. Mrs. Riley was a nurse. Had been, I mean."

"What name was on it?" Wiggins was not always spot-on when it came to sifting facts down to a solution, but he could usually be counted on to remember the facts themselves. A master of minutiae.

There was a silence on the other end of the telephone. Wiggins was thinking; Jury let him. Jury also thought he heard paper crackle. Opening another packet of Fisherman's Friends, probably. "Elizabeth Allan, sir."

"That's what I thought, Wiggins. Thanks. And thank Plant for his letter. I got it this morning." Jury hung up. He paid for his coffee but didn't bother drinking it.

II

"What's me being a nurse got to do with it?" asked Beth Riley. "What's it to do with Simon?"

"Maybe nothing, maybe a lot," said Jury, replenishing her glass with the bottle of Jameson's he'd the foresight to bring along. The glass in her hand welcomed the bottle in Jury's. She sat in the same cabbage-rose chair she had the first time Jury had visited their lodgings. The husband wasn't here today, and she seemed to be trying to make up her mind whether she was flattered or a little frightened that it was she whom the superintendent wanted to see. "So given you were nurse to Lady Ashcroft before she died, and also her cousin, you knew Jessica and Robert Ashcroft."

Her answer was surly. "Yes. Not all that well. Jessica was only a baby, and the brother — I'd seen him at the Eaton Square house in London off and on. That was before Barbara got so sick she needed someone all the time."

"Is he much changed?"

"Changed? That's an odd question. Though I guess ten years in Australia's enough to change anyone."

"I mean, did he appear as you remembered him?"

Again, she frowned. "Well, yes — wait a tic." She leaned toward Jury, the flashy rhinestone brooch winking in the light of the lamp. "Are you telling me that's *not* Robert Ashcroft?" Obviously, no news could have pleased her more. Mrs. Riley had been the most adamant of the relatives who questioned James Ashcroft's will.

"No," said Jury, watching her hope dissipate along with the John Jameson's. He calculated that somewhere during the third drink she'd reach the confessional stage. "No, I'm stumbling in the dark, hoping I'll fall over the right answer." He smiled.

Beth Riley, cushioned by cabbage-rose pillows and Jameson's, gave him a once-over that strongly suggested she wouldn't mind being what he fell over. Once again, she held out her glass. Self-pity would take over pretty soon, he knew. He was happy to help it along. He poured her a third drink and looked at the display over the mantelpiece: the nursing degree with its gold seal, the family photographs, the mahogany-backed coat-of-arms. The same coat-of-arms, emblazoned here, that Jury had seen on the writing-paper, the note that Plant had sent him. It was the crest, the curlew embellished as carefully as some monk's Biblical illumination.

"We're none of us perfect," said Beth. "I made a mess of things, marrying as I did. Oh, not that Al's not a good *provider* . . ."

Jury wanted to steer clear of Riley's good points, which were certain to end with the bad. He was interested in facts, not in her soul-searching, the whys and wherefores of her marriage. "What was — or is — your relation to the Ashcroft family, Mrs. Riley?"

"You can call me Beth." Over the rim of her glass she looked at him coyly.

Jury assumed he'd damned well *better* call her Beth if he wanted information. He smiled a warm, insincere smile. "Beth. Your relationship with the Ashcrofts?"

"To hear *him* talk — that Robert — I'd no more to do with them than the horses in the stableyard."

(Jury thought that Robert was probably right.)

"I was cousin to Barbara. *First* cousin." She made sure he understood that it was no fly-by-night relationship. "We were both born in County Waterford. I came to England when I was small, long before Barbara." She said it as if this gave her some proprietorial right over the country which Barbara lacked. "But I hardly ever saw them until she got sick. Just trust that kind of people to want your help, and then not to remember how much help you gave."

"But Ashcroft certainly did remember, Beth. You'd come into a sizeable sum." He paused. "If anything happened to Jessica Ashcroft."

"What's likely to happen to *her?*" The whisky hadn't softened her up enough, apparently. Nor did she respond to the implication of what Jury had said. "That's no way to leave an inheritance — you have to wait until somebody *dies*. It's Riley, that's what it is! Robert Ashcroft is too much of a snob to have us round. But then they always were the worst kind of snobs."

Jury was sympathetic as he topped off her glass. "That does seem a bit unfair."

She hooted. "Unfair? *I'll* say it's unfair. Listen: we were perfectly willing to take the girl in, to be mum and dad to her —"

(Like you were mum to Simon, Jury thought.)

"— but, no. She was handed over bag and baggage to him. As if he'd ever done a thing in his life for the child." She turned on Jury one of the most vindictive smiles he'd ever seen. "Though I wouldn't deny he might have done a good deal for the mother. Barbara."

The implication was clear. But Jury didn't want to give her the satisfaction, at the moment, of indulging her fantasies.

They were interrupted by her husband's coming into the sitting room, dazzled to see Jury there, as if he'd stepped into white light from the darkness of a theatre. He blinked. "Superintendent?"

625

Jury rose. "Mr. Riley." They shook hands. "I was just asking your wife a few questions that I thought might be relevant to Simon's death. I've got to be going now."

Riley led him to the top of the stairs. He looked back over his shoulder, then whispered to Jury. "She gets a bit tearful after a drink. Not much of a drinker, is Beth. What about Simon?"

"Nothing new, I'm afraid. I was just trying to sort out the family connections. You see, I didn't know your wife was related to the Ashcroft family."

He was not so far gone in sorrow that he couldn't laugh at this. "You must be the only one in Dorchester who doesn't know it, then. What a row she made after the funeral." He sighed. "Water under the bridge, why quarrel? Are you anywhere nearer finding out who did this?"

Jury debated his answer. "Yes, I think so, Mr. Riley."

"Dear God, I hope so. After reading about the other two — it's a dreadful thing to say, Mr. Jury,"— another confession —"but I'm glad Simon wasn't in it alone." He gave Jury a furtive look, as if there stood the messenger of God who would condemn him to the everlasting fire for such a thought. "I can't help it."

"I know. I only wish I could."

And Jury went down the stairs and out of Riley's: Fine Meat and Game.

TWENTY-THREE

T HE black cat, tail twitching, sat on the stone balustrade tracking the progress of two seagulls on their unwary way toward half a discarded sandwich. When Jury's appearance disturbed this tableau — the oafish stranger walking between the tourist's camera and its vision of scenic wonders — the cat turned its yellow eyes on Jury as if any sacrificial victim were better than none. Then it jumped down and walked over to sit on the stone step and stare the door out of countenance. There was food in there somewhere.

Jury was surprised to see the curtains undrawn. And she must have been watching from a window, because the door opened as he raised his hand to knock. The cat marched straight in.

Molly looked down and up and smiled. "He'll make straight for the kitchen and glare until I give him something. Come on in."

He felt an odd reluctance to put his foot over the doorstep. The sensation might have been something akin to what a medium feels when suddenly, across an entrance, there's a cold spot. It only lasted a second or two, his hesitation, but she noticed it.

Her smile now seemed almost left over, and she glanced at the windows as if she'd like to close the curtains, in the way she had just, in a flash, drawn one across her smile.

He had let her down, the last thing he wanted to do. But with Molly Singer he supposed it would be very difficult not to; it was not that she expected too much of the world, but that she expected too little.

She took his coat and went to feed the cat. From the kitchen she asked him if he'd like sóme coffee and, in an attempt at banter, told him he'd better take her up on the offer; it didn't come round often. He could not see her, only hear her. Her voice was strained as it hadn't been when he'd come to the door.

"Then you'd better bring it quick," he called back.

She must have had it ready, for she brought it in straight-away, after he'd heard dry food rattle into a bowl.

They went through the business of how much sugar and cream, and she had some toasted teacakes, which she cut with a knife that might have done them more service in cutting the tension. Finally, she said, "It was nice of you to send the message you were coming." She was studying her tea-cake. "I don't think Superintendent Macalvie would have."

Certainly, *that* couldn't have been truer. "You know the police." He nodded toward the kitchen door where the black cat was washing its kingly self. "We're worse than *him*. Hell on wheels, beat down doors, storm right in." Jury mustered the best smile he could.

It was, apparently, good enough, for the invisible curtain opened and she said, "You didn't. You're not very frightening for a policeman, Mr. Jury."

"Richard. For God's sakes, don't tell Macalvie I don't scare people. He'll send me back to London."

"I doubt one just sends Scotland Yard 'back to London.'"

Jury laughed, and she sat back with her coffee and relaxed a little. Today, she had relinquished her Oxfam-special for what looked more like Jaeger — a wool dress in such a warm shade of gold she should have been able to cut through the cold spot, send the ghosts packing, tame the demons. She couldn't. Could anyone? "Macalvie —" He hadn't meant to say it aloud. He added quickly, laughing again. "You don't know Macalvie. . . ."

Although he hadn't meant to bring it up that way, or to make light of her dilemma, he knew it was as good a way as any. So he didn't retract when he saw the look on her face, a look of disappointment replaced quickly with a getting-down-to-business smile. He thought of that scene in the hotel. Molly could rise to an occasion. With a vengeance. That worried him.

"I didn't imagine," she said, "you'd come on a social call."

But one could always hope. Jury said nothing.

"Superintendent Macalvie will twist things into whatever shape suits his purposes."

"No. Macalvie's too good a cop; he doesn't twist things."

As the black cat positioned itself on the twin of Jury's chair and gave him a fiery-gold look, so did Molly Singer. "Well, he might not 'twist' them into shape, but he doesn't seem to mind battering them." She reached down to the bottom shelf of the table by the little couch and brought out a bottle of whisky. She raised it slightly. "Want some in your coffee?"

Jury shook his head, watching her as she held the bottle on her knee. It was a fresh bottle, and she broke the seal. But she didn't uncap it; she stared at it as if the bottle were an old friend turned stranger. He did not think she really wanted a drink; he thought she wanted something to do for distraction. Her need for something no one was able to give her was so intense, it drained him to think that any comfort he could offer would be pretty cold comfort coming from a policeman.

That's a great rationalization, Jury, he said to himself. He could have given it. The truth was, there was something about Molly Singer that made him feel afraid of being drawn in.

629

"Why is Chief Superintendent Macalvie so certain I'm this Mary Mulvanney?"

"She was hard to forget." He smiled. "So would you be."

"Because we throw things?"

"No. You're afraid that Mary Mulvanney would be even more of a suspect?"

"She would be."

"Why?"

"Because Chief Superintendent Macalvie thinks so."

Jury smiled. "He could be wrong."

"Oh? Why don't you try telling him that? Because you value your life." She made a poor attempt at a smile, and then said, not looking at him, "Do you remember what it's like to be in love when you're sixteen?"

"Same thing as when you're forty, I guess." He looked at her long enough to force her to turn her eyes back to his. "Why?"

She sat forward on the couch, slowly, as if she were very tired and, even, very old. "Oh, Superintendent . . ."

You understand nothing. She didn't say it, but from her expression, she might as well have.

Mary Mulvanney would certainly have a reason to hate the world. Indeed, Mary Mulvanney might have become obsessive. Like Molly Singer . . .

"You're thinking the same thing he is."

Jury looked up, surprised. She had been studying his face — carefully, he was sure — for hints of increased suspicions, and found them.

He tried to pass it off with a smile. "You read minds."

Leaning her head against her hand, she returned the smile. And her face had a tinge of the glow it had when he'd first come.

That she thought Jury had a particularly nice one was pretty clear, and he looked away, toward the cricket stool where he imagined the house-ghost stirring the ashes. At least her reply brought him to the point: "You'd be pretty good at that, being a photographer." He looked back at her. "We'd like you to do us a favour."

Her head came up from her hand, and her body tensed. Even before he'd asked, she saw the red light of danger. "Me? I can't imagine what."

"There's a place in Dartmoor more or less equidistant from Princetown, Wynchcoombe and Clerihew Marsh." Her expression didn't change. "It's called Ashcroft. Quite a large house—"

"Go on." It was as if the suspense that clung to that word *favour*—which could only mean action of some sort—was pulling her from the couch. She was leaning forward, hands clasped so tightly the knuckles were white.

Jury simply brought it out. "We need a photographer —"

"No." She shook her head slowly, her eyes shut. "No."

"Say No, if you want, but let me finish. There's a little girl in that house; she's ten years old. She's the sole heir to the Ashcroft millions. Her father was a peer. There've already been three children murdered, Molly. We're not looking forward to a fourth."

Molly looked up then, astonishment stamped on her face. "Whatever it is you want from *me* — dear God, *why?* I'm your main *suspect!*"

"A suspect. Okay, I won't deny it, though I doubt you had anything to do with these killings." Doubt was not certainty; but the doubt was strong.

Astonishment gave way to something like hope and a half-smile. "You're outvoted."

"Macalvie?" Jury smiled. "Then it's one against one. Not outvoted."

"If Chief Superintendent Macalvie has the other vote, believe me, you're outvoted. But go on. I'll just say no at the end, but go on."

"We want pictures — photographs — of, well, everything.

Your bona fides are all arranged. There's an expensive, sleek new magazine that specializes in classic and antique cars. You're their top photographer: and you know what a professional does because you've done it." He smiled. "Piece of cake."

"Dipped in cyanide. Are you mad?" Her voice was going up a ladder of tension. "Richard—"

As she leaned toward him, he felt his name in her mouth as something strange, saltwater on the tongue. "Molly." Again he smiled.

Quickly she looked away, and for something to do, tried petting the black cat taking its ease beside her in this tension-filled room. It merely looked around and glared at her. "I don't even go out of the house here. And you think I'd have the nerve to gather up my Leica and go and do an *impersonation* in the house of a millionaire? God. I'd almost rather talk to the gracious Chief Superintendent Macalvie— don't tell me *he* expects me to do this?"

Jury nodded and offered her a cigarette, which she took, saying, "Thanks, it's an excuse for a drink. I don't suppose you'd care for one?"

"Try me."

Having poured the drinks into mismatched water tumblers, she sat back, raised her glass in a salute. "To your crazy idea. First of all, if you want a photographer, the Dorset police, the Devon constabulary — and Scotland Yard — must have darkrooms full of them. Why me?"

"Because they wouldn't be suspicious of you, Molly."

"I don't see why they would of a clever cop — you are trained in the lively art of worming your way into people's confidence."

It wasn't anger but pain he heard in that remark. "The people at Ashcroft would sniff out a cop all the way across Dartmoor. At least one of them would, I'm sure."

In spite of herself she was curious. "Who?"

"Better you don't know, or you'd be falling all over your tripod every time the person said Boo."

The whisky was relaxing her. "I'd be falling all over it *anyway,* you idiot." Her raised voice disturbed the black cat. It moved, recurled itself, and gave them both a squinty gold look. "And if I don't agree to this incredible scheme — I suppose you'll blackmail me into doing it: 'Go along with us, baby, and maybe we'll go easy on you —' "

Jury laughed. It was a perfect mimicry of Macalvie's hard-boiled-detective tone.

"Thinks he's Sam Spade." She took a drink. Two. "Photos of what? What are you looking for?"

"Given the mag and Ashcroft's collection, you'd be concentrating on the cars. And the people at Ashcroft. We need some photos for identification purposes —"

"You're *police.* Just go in and take the bloody things."

"We don't have any reason to: we don't have a bit of evidence that would get us in, and it would only put everybody on guard. You wouldn't, see."

"I know I wouldn't because I won't be there. But — out of curiosity — why?"

"Because you're running scared and that timidity is going to make Ashcroft — the girl's guardian — even more courtly, and the rest will be trying to put you at your ease."

"Thanks!" she snapped, downing some more whisky. "That sort of person hardly sounds like one a high-powered magazine would be sending out on jobs."

"They would if she had your talent.'

She lowered her head. There was no sarcasm in her voice, only defeat. "I can't do it. And I don't see any reason why I should."

"I do."

"Oh, I know that old crap. 'Do it for yourself, Molly, it's what you need to —' " He could hear the tears beginning.

"No. Do it for me."

There was no sound but a log splitting and the waves beyond the window. She did not look up and did not move, but sat on the couch, feet drawn up, curled much like the cat, and just as silent.

Jury waited.

Looking not at him but at the glass she turned round and round in her hands, she said dully, "I'll need some film. I suppose this magazine wants colour. Extracolour Professional or Extrachrome X." She smiled coldly. "Oh, I forgot. None of this is real, so I'll just use what I have."

"No. Treat it as if it were the real thing. Take along equipment you'd take if it *were* real."

She looked up at Jury then, still with that cold little smile, shook her head. "Do you know the difference?" Her face turned toward the fire. "Then get me a haze filter."

He wrote it down, feeling rotten as he did.

Jury got up and went over to the couch. He leaned down, pushed back the black hair that had fallen across her face, and kissed her cheek. "Thanks, Molly."

It happened the way it had in the hotel. At one moment she was statue-still with her glass on her knee. At the next she was up and flinging it against the grate. She turned her back on him.

Jury made a move to get the glass out of the way. The cottage reeked not of whisky, but of desolation.

"Don't bother trying to pick up the pieces."

TWENTY-FOUR

EVEN before Jess saw the passenger, she felt slightly ill just seeing the car. It was a Lamborghini. Apart from the Ferrari, it was the best sports car there was. Uncle Robert had been trying to find one for years.

It was sleek, smooth, and silver. Almost the same thing could have been said about the woman who was getting out of the car, hiking an aluminium case over her shoulder. She looked so — *London,* Jessie thought. Annoyed enough about the car, must the person driving it be good-looking, too? Under the grey cape, which got in the way of the aluminium box, she wore a pearl-grey blouse and skirt and grey leather boots. It was almost as if she were choosing her clothes to match the car.

Her uncle and the rest were out. The photographer was supposed to get there at two o'clock and it was only a little past one. She was early. Jessie watched the woman come up the broad stairs and ring. Mrs. Mulchop and Jessie collided as both of them went for the door. "Now behave, for once," said Mrs. Mulchop, hand on door. "Don't be getting up to anything."

Jessie smiled benignly. The only thing she was considering

635

getting up to was getting the photographer in and out as quickly as she could. It shouldn't take long to take pictures of a few cars.

"Hello. I'm Molly Singer," the woman said.

Mrs. Mulchop said she was sorry that Mr. Ashcroft wasn't there at the moment. He hadn't expected her until two o'clock. Would she like a cup of tea?

"If she works for a magazine," said Jessie, "she's probably got a lot of things to do. She probably doesn't have time — "

"Be quiet, child." Mrs. Mulchop gave Jess a kiss-of-death glance and repeated her offer of tea. "Or coffee, perhaps?"

"That's very kind of you. But I suppose — if you don't think Mr. Ashcroft would mind — I could get to work straightaway."

"Oh, *he* wouldn't mind at all," said Jessie. "I'll just show you where the cars are. They're outside."

Mrs. Mulchop grumbled. "I don't expect Miss Singer thought they were in the drawing room."

Molly laughed. Besides having a nice, low voice, she had a nice laugh. Nicer than Sara's. And Sara only had that old Morris Minor. . . . Jess was beginning to feel sick again. "Come on, then."

"What's your name?" asked Molly as they walked through the expanse of marble hall, through morning room, dining room, butler's pantry (where Mulchop was topping up his glass of sherry), and kitchen.

"Jessica Allan-Ashcroft. My mother's picture is in the dining room. She led a tragic life."

"Oh, dear. How sad."

"It was, really." Jessie had stopped and taken her overall from the peg. "I always wear this when I work on the cars." She looked this new woman up and down. "You wouldn't be able to get under them, not the way you're dressed."

"Well, I hadn't planned to, actually," said Molly as they went through a dark little hallway and out to the courtyard beyond.

636

"It won't take you long. I'll tell you what's what and you can snap your pictures and go. My uncle has always wanted a Lamborghini. Stable at one hundred and eighty mph," she added, casually.

"You certainly do know a lot about cars." Molly had taken her thirty-five-millimeter camera from the case.

"Yes. What you could do is just get them all together if you stand back far enough and you wouldn't be wasting film."

"Not to worry. I have plenty."

Jess was afraid of that.

"Let me look them over first —"

"That one's a Ferrari; that's a Jaguar XJ-S — silent as a Rolls and does zero to sixty in under seven seconds. That one's an Aston Martin — you know, the James Bond car; there's the Porsche; this is the Lotus; this is my Mini Cooper —"

"Yours? You mean you drive it?"

"No." Jess hurried on with her description, curtailing questions. "That one's a Mercedes two-eighty-SL, a convertible. That's a —"

Molly laughed. "Hold on, there! You're going much too fast for me to remember them all."

Jess kept going. "That's a Silver Ghost, and that one's —"

"My word, a Silver Ghost. That must have cost your uncle a mint."

Jess wished she'd stop commenting so she could get on with it. "It doesn't belong to him. It's our visitor's." And then she thought of bringing in the rear-guard action. "You'd *love* him. He's an earl, like my father was. Only, of course, not that *old*. He's handsome and rich. And very nice."

"Umm."

Jessie thought her description rated more than an *umm*. But some people just couldn't be pleased. "You don't really have to know the *names* of the cars, do you, if you're only taking pictures?"

Molly adjusted the lens of the camera. "Yes, I'm afraid I

do. It wouldn't do the readers of the magazine much good to have the cars but not know what they were, would it?"

Frustrated, Jessie crossed her arms and scratched at both her elbows while she watched the photographer go about her business. She was being so careful with all her equipment, at this rate they could be staying here all afternoon. "What time is it?"

Molly looked at her watch. "One-thirty. If you have something you want to do, go ahead."

"No, that's all right. What about your husband? Does he take pictures too?"

"Haven't got one."

Glumly, Jessie looked her up and down again. No doubt about it, she was the best-looking one yet — all that glowing black hair and strange yellowish eyes with little flecks of brown. "Too bad."

"Not being married? You think being married's the best way to live?" Molly smiled.

"What? *No!* I think it's pretty silly. Except for my mother and father—that was all right."

Molly fixed the camera to the unipod. "You sound like Hamlet. He said there should be no more marriages."

"I know." Mad Margaret had made an awfully fat Ophelia.

"You *do?* You must be going to a very good school if you already know Shakespeare."

"It's not school. There isn't one in spitting distance. I have tutors. They don't last long. What's that? I thought it was a cane."

Molly laughed. "I'm not quite *that* old. It's a unipod. You use it to hold the camera steady." Going through the routine might help to steady *her.* She was beginning to feel the disorientation that triggered a panic-attack out here in this unfamiliar place.

"What's that thing?" asked Jessie. She sounded worried.

"Just a spot meter. So I don't have to unthread the camera to judge the lighting or if I want a close-up."

"It sounds complicated. It sounds like it's going to take a long time. I have a camera. All I have to do is point it."

"Do you want to take some pictures?"

"No, no," said Jessie, hurriedly. "It would waste your time."

Molly was beginning to feel beads of water on her forehead. With the hand that held the spot sensor, she wiped them away. Maybe she's right. *Just take the damned pictures and get the hell out,* she told herself. *Let them worry about Identikits.* She stiffened when something moved in the rear seat of the Ferrari. "What's *that?*"

"What's what? Oh, *Henry!* Don't worry, it's just Henry. He likes sleeping in cars. You look kind of pale. But Henry's safe, really. He never bit anything in his whole life. He doesn't even bite bones now, he's so old."

"I've never seen a dog like that in my entire life." Molly laughed, feeling the pressure in her mind ease up a little.

"It's just a stray we found." Jessie would never give Henry credit for his blue-blooded lineage. "He's funny-looking, isn't he?" She reached down into the Ferrari and heaved Henry out.

Molly looked up at the cirrus cloud scudding across the grey vault of endless sky and felt a wave of nausea. It always started like this, the panic-attacks. She found some tissues in her pocket and wiped the perspiration from her face.

"There's not going to be much light in a little bit. Maybe you'd rather leave and come back later. Anyway, you look kind of pale. You're not sick, are you?"

Molly had to smile over the little girl's attempt to get rid of her, though she didn't know what prompted it. The smile faded quickly, though, and she had to turn her face to the camera to keep it from cracking like a mirror. She had the unipod far enough back that she could see all ten cars together, each slotted into its box, like race-horses in their starting boxes. Irrational as it was — which made these attacks worse — she had the ugly feeling the headlamps would

639

switch on and come racing toward her. She felt she'd been dropped into one of those silly films in which a car takes on the human potential to kill. They looked diabolical.

In this open court there was no safe place to stand. No walls, ceilings—nothing. She felt, as she always did, a prescience of something awful.

"You *do* look sick."

"I'll be — all right. Just a moment . . ." Molly laid her head down on the arm supported by the unipod, and rested the other on Jessica's shoulder. The little girl put her hand over Molly's.

Even though she was out here in what seemed like an endless waste of sky and ground, Molly had the feeling of being shoved, stuffed into a dark closet where she would fall into a deep well. If only she could get back into her car —

And then she heard voices, people coming around the side of the house, laughter. People. The last thing she wanted. She was perilously near to blacking out.

Then she raised her head and saw the two men and the two women. One of the men started walking toward her, smiling. She looked at him, looked at the others, the man and the two women. Her eyes widened. She stared at this tableau vivant for a second before she felt the unipod slip beneath her weight. And she heard from what seemed a great distance, "It was Henry's fault. He scared her."

Molly Singer wanted to laugh. *Oh, the dog. The poor dog.*

When she came round, she was sitting in the Ashcroft library, being ministered to by Mrs. Mulchop with a cup of tea, Sara Millar with a cold towel, Robert Ashcroft and the other man looking concerned, and Jessica looking very guilty. It was as if her wish for release from the threat that Molly Singer represented had caused Molly's "bad spell."

Which was what Jessica was calling it as she patted her silk-sleeved arm.

"Sorry," said Molly. She put her head in her hand and tried

640

to laugh. "It certainly wasn't Henry's fault." She smiled at Jessica.

The man standing by Jessica's uncle was introduced as Lord Ardry. "I nearly fainted myself when I saw the Ashcroft collection." He was offering her a snifter of brandy, which she took with far more gratitude than she had the cup of tea. "Thanks. Yes. It's quite a stunning display, but —" She had been about to say it would be better if she came back another day, and watched with a sinking heart as they seemed to be settling into chairs for a relaxing chat. Again, gratefully, she took a cigarette offered by Lord Ardry, who seemed to be observing her with more acuity than she would have liked.

"What's your magazine, Miss Singer?" asked Ashcroft. "I've forgotten."

With mounting horror, Molly knew she'd forgotten too.

"*Executive Cars,* wasn't it?" said the Earl of Caverness.

Their eyes met. He smiled. It was almost conspiratorial. What on earth did this perfect stranger know?

"Yes, that's right." She leaned back, crossed her legs, tried her best to imitate herself — the old, fairly confident Molly Singer, photographer. And very good one, too. "It's a bimonthly. You've probably seen it."

"As a matter of fact, I haven't. I didn't think it would have much to do with the old ones. More modern-day stuff."

"No. It's got a misleading title. I keep telling them to change either the title or the image." She tried on a little laugh. It worked. Especially since the peer had given her a bit more cognac. "Let's try again, shall we. I shall try to remain upright this time."

"If you're sure — ?" Ashcroft stubbed out his cigarette. "You want me in the picture?"

He asked the question shyly.

She smiled. "Of course. *And* you, young lady."

Jessica returned the smile. The scared look had vanished.

Apparently, she was willing to let Miss Singer hang around as long as she wanted, now.

Indeed, Jess went all out: *"She* has a Lamborghini."

Robert Ashcroft laughed as they trailed out of the library. "Believe me, I noticed."

Maybe, thought Molly, just maybe she'd get through it.

TWENTY-FIVE

THE din from the jukebox would have paralyzed any but the worst of addicts, Jury thought, when he walked into the Poor Struggler that evening. Macalvie, Wiggins, and Melrose Plant were sitting at a table in the corner.

"You've been long enough," Macalvie said to Jury.

"For what?"

"For anything," said Macalvie. "The three of us have been sitting here putting two and two together and coming up with five. Well, four-and-a-half, maybe. I bet we did better than you, Jury."

"I didn't know we were running a marathon."

"Wiggins, get the guy a drink; he looks like he could use one." Macalvie held out his hand for the holy dispensation of another Fisherman's Friend. Wiggins slid one from the packet.

Plant shook his head. "Why do you suck on those things if you think they're so vile?"

Macalvie smiled. "I tell myself every time I take one that cigarettes taste even worse." He was waving away the fragrant smoke of Plant's hand-rolled Cuban cigar. "Plant took the new governess up at Ashcroft for a ride yesterday. They went to Wynchcoombe." He turned to Melrose. "Go on. Tell him." It didn't surprise Jury that Plant had dispensed with his earldom after a few hours with Macalvie. At any rate, London had very quickly sent the fan belt (Melrose told him), and he was on the road again.

"I already have. Some of it."

Jury took out Plant's letter, and read, " 'The Earl of Curlew was also Viscount Lindley, James Whyte Ashcroft. The vicar of Wynchcoombe is named Lindley White. And "Clerihew" might have been "Curlew." Any connection?' It sounds like it. What did you find out?"

"He said, yes, he was some distant relation of the Ashcroft family. James Ashcroft had left the church a generous bequest. The Reverend White was surprised."

Macalvie broke in. "Someone has it in for the Ashcrofts, then? But why kill the kids? The worst possible revenge? Let me see that will."

Jury handed it over to Macalvie. "I had a talk with Simon Riley's stepmother. Maiden name — Wiggins reminded me — Elizabeth Allan. Born in County Waterford, but not much Irish blood flows through her veins or her voice."

Macalvie was silent for a moment, combing through James Ashcroft's will. Then he turned to shout over the jukebox din that if Freddie liked "Jailhouse Rock" that much, he could arrange for her to hear it from the inside. "I told you these cases were related. And I told you about Mary Mulvanney, except you still don't believe it." He grinned. "Scotland Yard, two; Macalvie, two." He looked Plant up and down. "You, one."

"Thanks," said Melrose Plant, offering Macalvie a cigar, which (to Wiggins's fright) Macalvie took.

"Robert Ashcroft, Molly Singer —"

"Mary Mulvanney," Macalvie corrected Jury automati-

644

cally, eyes closed so that he could enjoy the inhalation of smoke to the maximum.

"God, Macalvie," said Jury. "You're so damned *right* all the time."

Macalvie opened his eyes. "I know."

"Sam Waterhouse. Just assume for the moment he was guilty of Rose Mulvanney's murder —"

Macalvie shook his head.

"Where is he?"

Macalvie shrugged.

Jury almost laughed. "You're the only person I know who can lie with a shrug. You're worse than Freddie. No wonder you hang around here. Why the hell don't you stop trying to protect Sam Waterhouse?"

Macalvie studied the lit end of his cigar. "Okay. He was in here."

Jury looked at Melrose Plant. "You met him?"

Plant nodded. "It does sound as if the police were looking for a scapegoat. The evidence against him was pretty circumstantial. You think so, too, don't you?"

"I don't know. But I certainly think the evidence against Molly Singer is circumstantial."

"Mary Mulvanney." Macalvie's kneejerk response.

"How'd she do at Ashcroft?" Jury asked Melrose.

"Miss Singer? Incredibly well —"

"She's no more phobic than I am," said Macalvie generously.

Melrose Plant smiled. "I'd be careful with comparisons if I were you, Mr. Macalvie."

"So we've got the pictures, so what have we got? Yeah, there *was* an advert. Robert Ashcroft went to see a Roller in Hampstead Heath." Macalvie stuffed a couple of Plant's cigars in his pocket before he got up. "The hell with it. It's time we had a little talk with Robert Ashcroft."

On his way out, Macalvie kicked the jukebox and "Don't Be Cruel."

II

"Mr. Ashcroft," said Macalvie, "you usually interview potential tutors or governesses or whatever you call them at home, don't you?"

There was a decanter of whisky at his elbow, and Macalvie had no hesitation in helping himself. It went down well with Plant's cigars.

"That's right." Robert Ashcroft looked from Macalvie to Jury to Wiggins taking notes. He frowned. "I'm sorry. I don't —"

Macalvie made a sign with his hand that Ashcroft didn't have to understand a damned thing. Yet. "But this time you went to London to interview the applicants."

Ashcroft smiled. It was an easy smile. "I decided it might be better. I believe I'd misjudged my niece's ability to make the final choice."

"The lady Jessica not being such a hot judge of character?"

Ashcroft's smile was even more disarming. "On the contrary, a wonderful judge. She always chose the one least suitable."

Macalvie frowned. "As a governess?"

"No. As a wife. Jess is afraid I'm going to be snagged by Jane Eyre."

"With you as Rochester," said Macalvie. "So you're not in danger of marriage, then?"

"I never thought of marriage as 'dangerous.' Are you suggesting some sexual leaning? That every couple of months I go up to London to indulge my perverse tastes?"

Macalvie turned the cigar round and round in his mouth. "We weren't thinking particularly of you down in your lab drinking something that would turn you into Hyde, no."

"Superintendent —"

"Chief." Macalvie smiled.

"I beg your pardon. Are you still upset about that idiot ruse of Jess's that brought you all out here?"

"Hell, no. Kids will be kids, won't they?" His smile flickered less like the flame than the moth. "You stayed at the Ritz, right? On the tenth to the fifteenth?"

"Yes. What's that — ?"

"You interviewed several applicants for this post." Robert Ashcroft nodded, frowning.

"What else did you do?"

"Nothing much. Went to see a Rolls-Royce in Hampstead But it wasn't what I wanted."

"And — ?"

Ashcroft had risen from the sofa and gone to toss his cigarette into the fireplace. The picture of his brother hung over him. Jury wondered how heavily. "I went to the theatre and the Tate. Walked round Regent's Park and Piccadilly. What's this all about?"

"What'd you see?"

Ashcroft's bewilderment turned to anger. "Pigeons."

"Funny. The play, I mean."

"*The Aspern Papers*. Vanessa Redgrave."

"Good?"

"No. I walked out."

Macalvie put on his surprised and innocent look. "You walked out on Vanessa Redgrave?"

"I didn't exactly throw her over for another woman."

"I don't imagine many people walked out."

"I wasn't checking. Except my coat," Ashcroft said, acidly.

"So since probably *no one* would walk out on Vanessa, I bet the cloakroom attendant would remember you."

Ashcroft was furious, "What the hell is this about, Chief Superintendent Macalvie?"

"What was at the Tate?"

"Pictures."

It wasn't as easy to unnerve Ashcroft as Jury thought.

"Mr. Ashcroft, would you try not playing this for laughs? What was at the Tate?"

"The Pre-Raphaelities."

Macalvie was silent, turning the cigar.

"Ever heard of them?"

"Rossetti and that bunch. I've heard. Why didn't you drive to London with all those cars sitting around out there?"

"For the obvious reason. I thought I'd be buying a car — the Rolls."

Jury sat there, smoking, saying nothing.

Robert Ashcroft had an answer for everything. And Macalvie knew it.

TWENTY-SIX

"**T**HAT's it for tonight, then." Sara slapped the book shut. Jessie, whose bed they were lying on, since she refused her nightly story in the Laura Ashley room, had been getting so drowsy her head had nearly drifted onto Sara's arm. Quickly, she snapped out of it. To have Sara think she was actually cosying up to her would be dreadful. "You've left off at the best part. Where Heathcliff is carrying Cathy's dead body around."

"You do put things in the most morbid way."

"*I* didn't write it, did I?" said Jess, reasonably. She felt as if Sara had reprimanded her, no matter how mildly. Jess gave Henry (who was lying at the bottom of the bed) a little kick. If *she* was being scolded, then Henry would have to come in for his share of it. What was really bothering her was that, against her will — and *that* would require a strong force indeed — she was afraid she might begin to *like* Sara. The Selfless Sara. Jessie sighed. But she didn't think she liked her as much as that lady photographer. Maybe it was because the one named Molly had fears, just as Jess had, only she wouldn't admit it.

649

It was an awful dilemma, liking someone you wanted to hate, the worst dilemma since the axe-murderer call to the police. All that blood in her mind had become so vivid it might have been really running down the walls. She shuddered.

"What's the matter?" asked Sara.

"Nothing." Jessie picked up the glossy magazine Molly Singer had given her. *Executive Cars.*

Sara was saying something about Heathcliff. "I thought you thought he was so romantic."

Romance? How disgusting. Better to imagine murderers stalking her (and Henry) across the moor. Green, green bogs with liverwort and moss, like Cranmere Pool, and peat, and rush ground where you could be sucked down, your head just dangling, as if guillotined, your little hand (and Henry's paw), the last thing to disappear from the sight of all those gathered round, throwing ropes, calling to you. . . .

"Romance is stupid."

Sara hit her lightly over the head with the book. "You're the one who asked me to read it." Sara sat up suddenly, her back rigid. "What was that?"

"What was what?" Jessie was looking at a picture of a Lamborghini, newer than Molly's. Twenty thousand pounds. Maybe Mr. Mack —

"It sounded like a car. Down the drive."

Jessie yawned, her eyes getting heavy. "Maybe it's Uncle Rob and Victoria coming back." She thought her uncle had been awfully moody at dinner. Victoria got him to go out for a drive and a drink at a new pub several miles away. Maybe Victoria would worm out of him what was wrong. Her eyes snapped open.

Victoria, Jessie realized suddenly, was rather good at getting her uncle in a better frame of mind. She frowned and thought about that.

"It's too early for them to be back," said Sara.

Now Sara looked moody and worried What was the *matter*

with everyone? "I want hot chocolate and toast. Come on, Henry."

Moody himself, Henry clambered down off the bed.

II

Jess sat at the kitchen table, turning the pages of *Executive Cars*, while the kettle for tea and the pan of milk for chocolate heated on the hob. Sara got out the granary loaf to cut and toast. "I wish the Mulchops were here," she said.

The Mulchops had gone to Okehampton to visit some relative or other. "Them? Whatever for?"

Sara shrugged. "I just feel — edgy."

Jess slapped over another page, annoyed. "Well, *they* wouldn't be any help. I mean if some ghost was walking around or something."

"Stop talking like that."

Jess shrugged. Sara was spoiling one of Jess's favourite times. The kitchen chilly around the edges, but nice and warm right here by the fire, without Mrs. Mulchop bustling and kneading dough and Mulchop slopping down soup and giving Jessie evil looks. He didn't like her, she knew, because she got under the cars.

Probably because she was "edgy," Sara started humming to herself, and then singing while she sliced the bread. She must have thought ghosts and vampires and werewolves ran away when they heard old Irish tunes. Jess glanced up when she heard ". . . *when she was dead, and laid in grave . . .*"

"That's 'Barbara Allan.' "

Sara looked stricken. "Oh, I'm sorry. Really. I suppose it's because I hear so much about your mother —" She stopped, staring toward the kitchen door, the one that led out to the courtyard. "There *is* a noise out there."

This time Jess heard it too. A sort of scraping sound. But the wind was getting higher, and one of the stable doors

651

banged; the sound could have been anything. "It's just the horses." She really wished Sara weren't such a mouse about things. It was just like the wife in *Rebecca*. She thrust that thought from her mind.

Sara went back to cutting the bread, and just as suddenly stopped. "It sounds like footsteps." She listened intently, shook her head, went back to the bread.

Well, it *had* sounded like footsteps, but Jess refused to give in. "It's just Henry; sometimes he scrapes his paw in his sleep." Henry never moved *anything* in his sleep, as Jess knew perfectly well.

She went on looking at the cars. Daimlers, Rollers, Ferraris ... next page, another Daimler and some cheaper cars, but still collector's items. Beside the black Daimler was a little Morris Minor, vintage.

The Daimler ... she kept her eyes averted because they were filling with tears. Her father James had been taken to the cemetery in a Daimler. And once again the graveyard scene sprang up, as if it were yesterday, and she saw herself standing beside the grave. The mourners — thick-veiled women, black-suited men. Her uncle had been the only spot of light in that dark-shrouded world.

That Daimler had had a *Y* registration. Jess blushed from remembering having noticed, even in her grief, the registration on the funereal Daimler. And then her skin went cold.

She turned back to the page before. Morris Minor. Black. *R* registration. Jess's thoughts stopped suddenly, braking. It must be what an animal feels, maybe even Henry. The thoughts stop. Senses take over. You see, you hear, you feel fright. . . .

What she heard, and Sara, too, given the knife had stopped slicing bread, was the creaking in the kitchen entry. Sara's face was pale, looking toward the door that, when Jess had nerved herself to look around, was opening.

Molly Singer stood there in her silvery cape, white-faced,

black-haired. In her fright, Jess almost thought she *was* seeing a ghost.

Except that this ghost was holding a gun in her black-gloved hand.

Despite all this, the only thing that Jess could see in her mind's eye was a black Daimler and a Morris Minor. *R* registration. Not vintage.

She stared at Molly Singer and then back at the kitchen table, where an entire loaf of bread lay sliced, and wondered, what had Sara Millar's car been doing at her father's funeral?

II

Five miles away in the Help the Poor Struggler, Macalvie was still arguing that Ashcroft had gone about the whole interviewing business in a damned peculiar way.

Melrose Plant was drinking Old Peculiar and smoking. And wondering about Robert Ashcroft's "interviews."

"He could have left that play *deliberately* so he'd establish that he'd been in London. How many people walk out on Vanessa?" asked Macalvie.

Wiggins said, "The cloakroom attendant recognized the picture immediately. No luck yet though with the car parks. But we've only had a few hours." He made a bit of a production of unzipping a box of lozenges to call the divisional commander's attention to the fact that Macalvie was smoking. Again.

"And why didn't he call home? Gone for five days and not a word back to his beloved niece," Macalvie went on, looking from Plant to Jury, irritated that he seemed to be arguing without an opponent.

"It was coincidence that the note to Jessica went under the rug. A coincidence with wretched consequences, unfortunately. Wasn't it the same thing Angel Clare did?" asked Jury.

"Who the hell's Angel Clare?" asked Macalvie.

Melrose Plant looked at him. "Commander, if you were hiring a tutor, you'd damned well make sure he or she was extremely well read, wouldn't you?"

Macalvie gave him an especially magical Macalvie-smile. "If you need a tutor, Plant, I'm sorry I don't come up to your standards."

"Ah, but you do. Superintendent Jury told me the pre-Raphaelites held for you no horrors. Nor did *Jane Eyre*. What about Hester and Chillingworth?"

Macalvie cadged a cigar and looked at Plant as if he'd gone mad. "What the hell is this? A literary quiz?"

"In a way."

"*The Scarlet Letter*. So what?"

Plant shrugged. "I'd just think any tutor would —"

"*Tess of the D'Urbervilles*," said Jury, absently. He looked very pale and was getting out of his chair. "My God, all of this time and we forgot —"

He made for the telephone in the middle of the heartrending voice of Elvis singing "Heartbreak Hotel."

It was one of the last songs Elvis Presley had sung.

III

At first, when Molly Singer said the name, Jess thought she was talking to her. But then she said it again.

"Let her go, Tess."

Jessie knew what real fear was as the arm tightened around her shoulders and the knife nearly bit into her throat. Sara — but was that her real name? — whispered, "Get out! *Who are you?*"

"Mary."

The arm moved up, nearly cutting Jessica's throat. She wanted to cry but she couldn't. Where, where, was everybody? She heard Henry whine. Henry knew she was in trouble.

The flat, now unfamiliar voice of the young woman choking her was saying, "I don't know you. I don't know you."

"But I know you, Tess." Molly's voice wavered, but the gun-hand didn't. "I took some pictures. Of the Marine Parade. I had one of them blown up because there was something familiar about the girl in the picture. It might be years since I've seen you, but I'd know you anywhere, anywhere. You always looked like Mum, even when you were little."

It was as though Sara didn't hear her. "Put down the gun or I'll cut her up right now, right here. I was waiting for him to come back, damn him and all the Ashcrofts. It has to be here in the kitchen. I'll write him a message in her blood. . . . *He killed Mum, don't you realize that?* They were there in the house together. And then I came down in the morning . . ."

This was coming out in gasps, and Jess felt tears on the top of her head, on her hair. But the knife was still there, sharply honed, edge now against her chest. "So you've got to put down the gun, Mary."

Jess could see the gun shake in the hand of Molly Singer. *Don't let her have it, please, please.* She would have cried it out, but the arm was like a steel band around her shoulders. And then, in despair, she watched Molly drop the gun. The sound when it hit the floor flooded Jess with terror.

Teresa was shoving Jess toward the kitchen table, whispering to her, or to Molly, that it was just the sacrifice, you see, of Isaac. It had to be done. Like the others. "Only I didn't have to cut the others up."

"And you're not going to do it to Jessica, either."

It was another voice, a man's.

Jess felt the knife move away from her, the obstructing arm torn from her shoulders and the voice saying, *Run, Jess.*

She ran toward the little hall.

But then she remembered Henry. Jess ran back, bunched

655

him in her arms, and flew out of the door into the shielding darkness of the night.

The rage of Teresa Mulvanney made her faster than either of them. She was out of his grasp and sliding across the floor to grab at the gun before Molly's hand could get to it.

Tess Mulvanney whipped the gun around, and from where she lay on the floor she shot Sam Waterhouse.

Molly opened her mouth to scream. But she didn't. Instead, she tried to inch her way to the table where lay the knife and the load of cut-up bread. She tried to talk to her sister, while tears slid down her face. "Tess. That's Sammy. Don't you remember? You loved him —"

Teresa's eyes widened. "It's not." As she closed her eyes, as if in an effort of remembrance, Molly took another step nearer the table. "They put him away. I read about the trial a year ago. When I got out of hospital. Everybody lied — *don't touch that!*"

Molly had almost had her hand on the knife when her sister grabbed it up. She raised the gun and slowly lowered it again. The look of rage turned to emotions confused and more gentle. "Mary." Tears ran down her face. "Don't you understand that I should've saved her? I should've saved Mum. If only I'd been brave enough to stab him, but I didn't know what —" She looked at the knife in her hand and let it fall on the floor. Tess ran the hand holding the gun across her wet forehead, but when Molly edged toward her, she steadied the hand again and shook her head violently. "Good-bye, Mary."

And she was out of the door, the same one Jess had run through carrying Henry.

Molly knelt by Sam. The bullet had caught him in the side. His eyes were closed and she was terrified. But then he came round. Blood was seeping through his fingers. "I'm okay. But for God's sakes, get Teresa. Or she'll be back —" Sam passed out.

Molly could see, through the kitchen window, a path of light cut by a torch. Then she heard a car door slam.

Teresa couldn't afford to stop to look for Jessie out there in the dark; Robert Ashcroft could come driving up at any moment —

And then she remembered the Lamborghini.

Molly ran through the house, out of the front door, down the drive toward her car. She heard, way off behind her, the distant sound of another car starting up.

There was only one way out of Ashcroft.

IV

"Heartbreak Hall," said Jury. "That's what you called it." Jury had his coat on.

Macalvie stared at him and got up. So did Plant and Wiggins.

It was the first time Divisional Commander Macalvie had looked ashen and unsure of himself. Or was at a loss for words. But he finally found them as the four men headed for the door. "God, Jury. Not *Teresa Mulvanney*. I forgot to check out Tess —"

"*We* forgot, Brian. The forgotten little girl. You told me about Mary Mulvanney coming into your office. She said she couldn't stand to go back there again. According to Harbrick Hall, Teresa Mulvanney appeared to be coming out of it, like someone coming out of a fugue state. That was six years ago. Over the next year her improvement was miraculous. They gave her jobs to do. She did them well. She was articulate, well-behaved, calm. And it was a Lady Pembroke, charitable old dame, who told them she'd take over the care of Teresa Mulvanney."

"Let's get the hell out of here." Macalvie turned to Melrose. "You mind if we use your car, pal? Mine won't go from zero to ten in under an hour."

There was an apprehensive glance from Wiggins when

657

Melrose handed the keys over. "This one will go a little faster."

That was an understatement, or so Macalvie proved it to be. Wiggins was hunched down as far as possible in the back seat. The narrow road, the occasional thick hedges, the night, the murderous moor-mist, all contrived to make driving nearly impossible.

Macalvie didn't seem to notice as he careened the Rolls around a turn. "How did she know? How on earth could she hand-pick her victims like that?"

"Pitifully simple. As I said to Mr. Mack, a will that's been probated is in the public domain. Sara Millar–Teresa Mulvanney simply looked at the heirs to the Ashcroft fortune. As far as George Thorne was concerned, well, she might have thought of him as — who knows, a conspirator. And there was also the simple matter of geography. The final object was Jessica. The others she killed . . . on the way." Jury felt sick.

Macalvie scraped the left-hand bumper cutting the curve of a stone wall too sharply. "Sorry, friend."

Melrose, smoking calmly in the back seat, said, "I can always get parts."

He hit the steering wheel again and again with the heel of his hand. "But goddamnit, Jury! They were kids! Why the hell didn't she just go after Ashcroft if he's the one who murdered Rose Mulvanney?"

"She couldn't."

Macalvie took his eyes off the road for a crucial second and the bumper got it again. "What the hell do you mean?"

"He was already dead."

V

It was a long driveway, a drive like a tunnel, and Molly could hear the car, which must have been coming round the side of the house. She didn't yet see the headlamps.

She started to switch on the Lamborghini's lights, and paused. Tess could easily think it was Robert Ashcroft returning and head right into him. Molly found she had at least a little interest in living, which surprised her. There might be a way to stop Teresa without actually killing herself. Something to take her by surprise, make her veer off into the thick trees, maybe an accident, but not a fatal one. The camera equipment. Flashbulbs? Not enough bulbs, not enough time. And now when she looked up she saw, at the end of the tunnel, far off, the headlamps of Tess's car.

The light at the end of the tunnel / Is the light of an oncoming train.... The lines of Lowell suddenly came back to her. She snatched the unipod from the rear seat, smashed out the right-hand headlamp, tossed the lamp in the back and got in. Was there anything more disconcerting to a driver than to see only one light coming toward him rather than two? What was it? Car? Motorbike? And the moment of confusion —

The other car was halfway down the drive, its lights hazy in the middle distance. Molly started the engine and headed up the drive. *Hell. You only die once.*

They weren't more than a dozen yards apart, when the wheels of the Morris screeched and the car swerved and rammed into the wall. Then it went into a spin and rammed the front of the Lamborghini.

The Rolls was only a minute away from the Ashcroft drive when they heard the sound of tearing metal.

Macalvie jammed on the brakes at the entrance. The four of them piled out.

The Morris burst into flames as they ran.

Molly's car was a disaster, but it wasn't burning. It was a distance from the flaming Morris, and it was tougher.

And for the seconds it took Macalvie to pull her out of the wreckage, so was Molly Singer.

Blood trickled from her ear, and a tiny line of blood ran

from the corner of her mouth. But she did not look bruised or broken. She looked up at Macalvie, who was holding her in his arms. She smiled. "Damnit. Why do you *always* have to be right, Mac——?" She didn't get out the last of it. The long fingers that clutched his shoulder slid down his coat as slowly as a hand playing a harp.

Macalvie started shaking her and shouting: *"Mary!"* He shouted the name until Jury pulled him away.

Melrose Plant took off his coat and put it under her head.

Jury took off his own coat and covered her with it.

A trickle of petrol from the Morris reached the Lamborghini. All Jury could think of was the log falling and sparking in Molly Singer's cottage.

TWENTY-SEVEN

Jury found her on the mechanic's creeper under the Zimmer. She was holding tight to Henry.

Jessica did not want to come out.

"Please, Jessie. It's all over. It's okay now."

Okay. It would never be okay, not for Divisional Commander Macalvie. He had disappeared into the trees and the fog.

"It's better here," said Jess. There was a silence. "I don't want to get hurt. And I don't want Henry to, either."

Jury sat down, there on the cold stone of the courtyard, cold as hell himself without his coat. She was silent. "Was Sara the axe-murderer?"

"No. there was never an axe-murderer, Jess. Sara—" He didn't know whether to tell her or not, then decided he might as well come clean. "Sara was sick, very sick. She was the one who killed the children."

"But why me? Was she their governess too?"

"No. No, she wasn't. Why you? Because she was confused. A long time ago, much longer than before you were born, someone hurt her and she wanted revenge. Someone killed her mother. You can see how terrible that would be."

"But *we* didn't do it — I mean me and Davey and that other boy and girl! Stop it, Henry! Henry doesn't like it under here, but I'm afraid something will happen to him."

She was crying, Jury could hear. "Nothing can possibly happen."

"Well, he'd rather be *in* the car than under it. So you put him up in the seat. But don't let him *go* anywhere." She said it pretty fiercely, as if she wanted to be sure, now Jury was there, that he stayed.

"Come on, Henry," said Jury. He lugged the dog out and put him in the front seat of the Zimmer. Henry shook himself and seemed to open his eyes. A new world. Strange, but new.

And strange and new for Jessica Ashcroft too. "Well?"

"Sorry. Well, what?"

"You didn't answer my question. We didn't kill her mother."

"I know."

"*Well?*"

Jury thought she must be getting better. She was certainly testier. "Let me tell you something that's very — difficult to understand, Jess. I think what was wrong with Sara was she felt guilty. She was only five when her mother died. And she *saw* it." Jury stopped for a moment. He remembered his conversation with Mrs. Wasserman, how he'd asked, without thinking, what the bolted door kept out. Him. To Mrs. Wasserman all the fears were focused on Him. Displacement, whatever a psychiatrist might have called it. "I think Sara felt, well, horribly guilty —"

From under the sanctuary of the dark car, Jessica said. "I know. She thought it was her fault. She thought she did it. And maybe she thought she was killing her own self when she killed Davey and that girl. And almost me."

He could hardly believe his ears. Until he heard her crying

again, and then realized how much guilt she must have felt about the death of the most beautiful, the kindest woman Jessica had ever imagined, yet never known. And how she could easily have felt responsible. Barbara Allan had died so soon after her daughter was born.

Jury could think of nothing to say.

"How is that man who saved me?"

"He's fine; the ambulance just got here to take him to hospital."

She rolled out. She got off the creeper. Her nightdress, her face, her hair were smudged with oil and grease. "Come on, Henry," she said, her tone its usual testy self.

Henry clambered out of the car and followed them as they walked slowly across the courtyard. Jessie was holding Jury's hand.

"I'll tell you something," she said grumpily.

"Yes? What?"

"I hope I never meet Jane Eyre."

II

When Robert Ashcroft and Victoria Gray were driving, a few minutes later, toward home, they heard the sirens, saw the whirring lights, saw the fire in the driveway.

"Oh, God, oh, God," whispered Victoria.

Robert Ashcroft pushed the Ferrari up to seventy.

He jumped out of the car, threaded his way through the police and ambulance crew, and ran into the house calling for his niece.

Jury had never seen a man look so terrified, with one exception, and then so relieved. No exception there.

Jessica stood, hands on hips, grease-smudged face and oil-bedewed hair, glaring up at her uncle. "I don't want any more governesses. Until I go away to school, I want a bodyguard. I want that man that saved my life."

Ashcroft merely nodded. He had tears in his eyes.

"Come on, Henry." They climbed the stairs slowly. But halfway up she turned to deliver her parting shot.

"You're always away when the axe-murderers come." Then she and Henry continued their weary ascent.

VII

Pretty
Molly Brannigan

TWENTY-EIGHT

THE old cleaner was singing in Wynchcoombe church and wringing her mop in a pail. Out of deference either to Jury or the vicar's lad who'd been buried only yesterday, she stopped singing and kept on swabbing the floor.

Death did not stop the stone from getting dirty or flowers from wilting, and the ones on the altar looked in need of changing. He watched her running the grubby mop over the stone floor and wondered how something that made such an enormous difference to so many—all those deaths— could make little more than a dent in the daily round of cleaning.

The old woman with the mop and pail paid no attention to him, one of the many who came to see this little marvel of a church that towered cathedral-like over its valley in the moor.

Jury dropped some money in the collection box, listening to the cleaner, who couldn't resist her bit of music, change to humming. He thought of Molly Singer and imagined that somewhere in Waterford or Clare or Donegal, a clear-voiced Irish girl might be doing her washing-up, maybe humming from the boredom of it.

Damn it, why are you always right, Mac?

Jury looked at the painting of Abraham and Isaac, the knife near the terrified boy's face. His father ready for the sacrifice. All God had to do was say *Go.*

To Macalvie, who had been right all along about her, she was Mary Mulvanney.

To Jury, she would always be Molly Singer.

He felt the old cleaner watching him as he walked out of the church.

II

When he got to the Help the Poor Struggler, it was almost a relief to hear Divisional Commander Macalvie shouting over the noise of the jukebox that he'd tie Freddie to a tree in Wistman's Wood if she didn't stop singing along with Elvis. It was the version of "Are You Lonesome Tonight?" where Elvis forgot the words and was laughing at himself and the audience was joining in. What rapport, thought Jury, Elvis Presley had had with his audience. It was a song he must have sung a hundred times, yet he'd forgotten — probably because of his failing powers — the words. But his fans hadn't. They never would. There were some things people never forgot. Like his last concert.

"Y'r a rate trate, no mistake. He be dead, man. Hain't yuh got no respect fer the dead?"

Macalvie was silent for a moment. Then he shouted back, "If I did, Freddie, I'd have some respect for *you*. Hullo," he added grudgingly to Jury. Melrose Plant was sitting with Macalvie. It was a drunk Brian Macalvie. "How about one of your fancy cigars, friend?" he said to Plant. And to Wiggins, who had opened his mouth, Macalvie said, "Shut up."

Freddie, who must have heard something and was being halfway human to Macalvie, set his pint on the table and said to Wiggins — or all of them — "No use to argie-fy with Macalvie."

"How's Sam?" asked Jury.

"Fine. He's fine. Be out of hospital in a couple of weeks." Macalvie smoked and stared at his pint.

"How'd he know, Brian? That Jessica might be in danger?"

Turning his glass round and round, Macalvie said, "The bloody coat-of-arms. The letter Plant wrote to you. That and the picture. You remember, he went through her desk. The unidentified man. Sammy saw Robert Ashcroft at the George in Wynchcoombe. James and Robert looked a lot alike. At first he thought Robert was simply a man who looked a hell of a lot like the one in Rose's snap. It was seeing the coat-of-arms that he'd seen on a piece of notepaper in the desk that finally did it. Anyway, he thought he should keep an eye on Ashcroft."

"You were right. There *was* something he knew that hadn't surfaced. James Ashcroft was indiscreet, writing to Rose Mulvanney."

"To say the least. He let Sammy waste his life in prison. Bastard."

Plant said, "I think Robert Ashcroft will try and make up for that in some way."

Macalvie glared at him. "Buy him a car, maybe. Sam told me he watched that house from a spot on the moor where he set up camp. He figured something would happen." Another silence. "It happened."

A big, beefy man was plugging money into the jukebox. "Play a few Golden Oldies, or something, will you?" yelled Macalvie.

The perfect stranger looked around, and not in a friendly way. "Play what I like, mate." He rippled muscles as best he could under the leather jacket. "Who the hell you be, anyway?"

Macalvie started to get up.

670

Jury pulled him down. "Forget it, Brian."

Having to yell at someone, Macalvie turned again to Freddie. "Bring us four more and try and keep the tapwater out of it this time."

"A course, me 'anzum," said Freddie, over the double-din of the music and the casuals off the road. Considering the usual lack of custom, the pub was almost jumping. Even the dartboard was getting a workout.

And then an Irish voice from the jukebox, thin and silvery, was singing. Apparently, leather-jacket was a sentimentalist.

> *"O, man, dear, did ya never hear*
> *Of pretty Molly Brannigan —"*

The cigar stopped halfway to Macalvie's mouth. His expression was blank.

> *"She's gone away and left me,*
> *And I'll never be a man again —"*

Macalvie had taken out his wallet and checked the contents. "Being an earl," he said to Melrose, "and probably owning a big hunk of England, I don't suppose you'd be good for a loan of, say, eighty quid, would you?"

Without any questions, Melrose took out his wallet, peeled off four twenties, and handed them over.

> *". . . Now that Molly's gone and left me*
> *Here for to die."*

Macalvie walked over to the bar where Freddie was singing along and spread a hundred and thirty pounds in front of her.

> *"Oh, the left side of me heart*
> *Is as weak as watered gruel, man;*
> *Won't ye come to me wake*
> *when I make that great meander, man. . . ?"*

671

Freddie, watching him, shouted, " 'Ere, Mac, wot be yu on upon?"

Macalvie had already positioned himself, taken aim, and shoved his size ten straight into the jukebox.

The song splintered like a broken windscreen, flying into pieces, shivers of metal and glass. It caught the entire room in a freeze-frame. No one moved.

Except Macalvie, who walked back to his chair and snatched up his coat. He looked around the table and said, "Macalvie, nil. Mulvanney, nil."

Then he turned with his coat slung over his shoulder and walked out into the dark where, not far away, the prison rose through the mists of Dartmoor and hung over Princetown like a huge raven.